FATAL FUGUE

Books by BV Lawson

Scott Drayco Series

Novels

Played to Death
Requiem for Innocence
Dies Irae
Elegy in Scarlet
The Suicide Sonata
Deadly Dance
Melody of Murder
Fatal Fugue

Short Story Collections

False Shadows
Hear No Evil
Vengeance is Blind

Adam Dutton & Beverly Laborde Series

Steal Away
Hide Away
Burn Away

Fatal Fugue

A Scott Drayco Mystery

BV Lawson

Crimetime Press

Published in the United States of America.

For information, contact:

Crimetime Press
6312 Seven Corners Center, Box 257
Falls Church, VA 22044

Trade Paperback ISBN 978-1-951752-16-3
Hardcover ISBN 978-1-951752-17-0
eBook ISBN 978-1-951752-15-6

Memories with the Dusk Return

The yellow dusk winds round the city wall;
The crows are drawn to nest,
Silently down the west
They hasten home, and from the branches call.
A woman sits and weaves with fingers deft
Her story of the flower-lit stream,
Threading the jasper gauze in dream,
Till like faint smoke it dies; and she, bereft,
Recalls the parting words that died
Under the casement some far eventide,
And stays the disappointed loom,
While from the little lonely room
Into the lonely night she peers,
And, like the rain, unheeded fall her tears.

poem by Li-Tai-Po (trans. L. A. Cranmer-Byng 1909), music by Granville Bantock

1

Sunday, January 9

Sheriff Ernie Baylor frowned as he stood over the body, which was lying in a pool of crimson liquid. He reached down to pick up a knife and handed it to Deputy Nellie Skyler, who thrust the weapon into her pocket. Baylor then knelt to touch a black smudge on the victim's face and declared, "It's obvious this wasn't a suicide. We're talking cold-blooded murder."

Deputy Skyler put her hands on her hips. "Are you sure?"

"Dead sure," Baylor replied, tipping up the brim of his olive-colored hat.

In a back corner of the room, Scott Drayco leaned toward his companion to whisper, "This is ludicrous. They're doing it all wrong."

Reece Wable whispered back, "That's showbiz for you."

"Cut! No, no, no." The expression on director Rada Bluestone's face was as dark as her all-black pantsuit, and even the necklace she wore featuring a mysterious symbol seemed to tremble in annoyance. Her voice shot garish Pepto-pink spikes into Drayco's brain, sending his synesthesia into overdrive. It was almost painful.

He tensed, worried he'd blown it via his whispered exchange with Reece despite the camera not being turned on for the scene rehearsal. But when the director started ranting about the lighting being a mess, Drayco began to relax.

Bluestone pointed at a crew member who looked ready to cry and said, "Reset this, and then we'll go live with the scene from the top." As a low droning sound cranked up outside, she growled, "And that awful engine noise is back. Can somebody kill that?"

While another crew member scrambled out of the building, Reece asked Drayco in a more normal voice, "Okay, so what was wrong with what the actors did?"

"Not checking to see if the victim is even dead. The 'sheriff' not wearing nitrile gloves, and the 'deputy' with only a single pair, meaning her prints or other evidence could transfer to the knife. The deputy putting the weapon in her pocket, not an evidence bag. The sheriff kneeling down and getting blood on his clothes and contaminating the crime scene with fabric threads or other trace evidence. Making an instant and unfounded declaration it's not suicide."

Drayco took a deep breath and tried not to do any growling of his own. "Do you want more?"

"I get the point." Reece removed his monocle briefly to clean it. "But you seem a little cranky today."

Drayco replayed his behavior that morning in a mental stream which made him wince. Okay, *maybe* he was a bit short with Maida Jepson at the Lazy Crab B&B where he was staying. And *possibly* he drove too fast down Route 13, and *perhaps* he'd switched from Bach to Black Sabbath on his car's stereo.

He ran his hand through his hair. "Sorry, Reece. Guess I've been stuck in a dark-mood rut."

"Any particular reason?"

"I suppose it started at the end of my last case."

"You have a lot of difficult ones. What was so rough about that?"

"Everything."

"Getting kidnapped not to your liking?"

"That was the easy part. The outcome of the case was the real punch to the gut. Plus, if there's anything I hate, it's wasted potential. Feels like that's the theme of most of my cases lately."

Reece studied Drayco through his non-glass eye. "Then I give you permission to go on being cranky."

Eager to change the subject, Drayco took advantage of the lull in action to study the cast and crew. The actor playing the sheriff had deep-set eyes set off by a trendy chin stubble. The woman playing the deputy was likewise attractive and reminded him of a real deputy in the county, Nelia Tyler, down to the blonde hair fashioned into a braid—though Drayco was fairly certain he'd never seen Tyler wear high heels on the job.

He asked Reece, "The title of this movie is *Fatal Fugue*? Whatever for? I don't see any music involved."

"Oh, it's the psychological term."

"Someone in a dream-like state not remembering their actions afterward?"

"That's the one."

"I think I need to get a copy of the script so this can make more sense."

While the lighting drama continued to play out, Drayco studied the pristine Victorian house. The wood ceilings were architecturally interesting, with tray insets matching the paneling, and a nearby door sported jewel-colored ruby, amethyst, and emerald stained glass. He said, "They're doing all the filming in this house, Reece?"

"Mostly. It's one of those claustrophobic plots. There's a wrap party following a play, a murder happens, and nobody can leave the premises. Creative, huh?"

"Then why use the Eastern Shore at all? Why not a Hollywood set?"

"The crew *is* filming in other places around these parts. I suppose they thought this area was a bargain. Cheap water views and cheap charm."

Drayco couldn't argue with that. He had a pretty good idea of the giant chasm between housing costs—even rentals—in Hollywood versus Cape Unity. Easily an order of magnitude greater.

Reece added, "You should see all the local businesses vying for their moment of fame."

"I'll bet. Did the crew ask to shoot any footage at the Historical Society?"

"Sadly, no, but they borrowed a few items from our files. As my consolation prize, I get to observe the action."

"I hope they're also paying you actual money for your assistance."

"A pittance. We could have used extra moolah for the coffers."

As the temporary break continued, various personnel milled around touching up makeup, rearranging props, and double-checking the unfortunate actor playing the victim who couldn't move yet, thanks to the "blood." Drayco spied crew members Reece had identified to him earlier, including the First Assistant Director, Chrystina Valentine, and her brother, Hoyt, the Production Designer, sporting an unlit cigar dangling out of one corner of his mouth. The remaining actors Drayco had caught in action in previous takes, with most looking to be under forty.

He counted the heads on the set. Other than the director, the Valentine brother-sister duo, and the lighting guy, he saw one other technical crew member plus six or so actors. He noted, "A small number of people. I expected more…well…everything."

"Oh, this film is an indie. I think they call it a 'contained' project." Reece used his fingers for air quotes. "Small budget. Rada, the director and a control freak, is doubling as cinematographer. Guess it's easy for her since that's her background. Plus, they have all these handheld cameras now. Phone videos, even."

"I did notice some of that."

Reece nodded. "Everybody's doubling up. Chrystina is 1st AD and also production coordinator. One actress, Jaxine Gordon, is also serving as makeup guru, although I don't see her right now. Sachio Spafford, the poor fellow dressed down by the director, is both gaffer and grip. And get this—most of the actors are playing at least two roles. Including our corpse over there."

"Ah. *Very* low budget."

"The sole person with one and only one job is Isaac Batey," Reece pointed at a man wearing headphones and adjusting a shotgun microphone. "The sound engineer."

"If the budget is that micro, any townspeople expecting riches will be disappointed."

"Money is money. They'll take what they can get."

The director continued to yell commands at the lighting guy— otherwise known as gaffer-grip, Sachio Spafford—about tweaking the console settings and booms. It was unclear how long such a process was supposed to take or even what the director was unhappy about. To Drayco's eye, the changes she demanded made little difference.

Just then, a low creaking grew louder as a lighting boom began swaying back and forth. Like a scene more out of a dark comedy than a crime drama, the boom toppled into another, taking both down and crashing into a nearby wall. A cloud of dust and plaster spread through the air, and people started to cough and sneeze.

Drayco caught a whiff of a slight acrid smell he could almost taste. Sulfur? Maybe bacteria or mold? Or perhaps the old plaster had tinges of Victorian-era "distemper," made from boiled horses' hooves.

Rada Bluestone cursed, and Sachio Spafford's eyes were wide with horror for good reason—a gaping hole now lay in the center of the wall, exposing wood beams. But something else caught Drayco's attention. In the open cavity, he saw a yellowish-white heap of what looked like bones.

Chrystina Valentine slapped her forehead. "This wasn't in the script. All right, who planted the fake skeleton? Funny, haha."

Drayco maneuvered around the fallen lighting gear to take a closer look. The remains included a human-sized skull wedged into the opening, along with bits of a faded dress still clinging to the bone pile. Definitely not an animal. Traces of a white powder also littered the floor underneath the bones.

Drayco turned to Chrystina. "I don't believe this is fake."

She and the director both stared at him, dumbfounded. Chrystina said, "How would you possibly know that?"

Reece pointed at Drayco. "Former FBI agent."

One of the supporting actors moaned and sank into a chair. Frazier Prentiss, the actor playing the sheriff, uttered words that would ordinarily make Drayco laugh. "Should…should I do something?"

Drayco whipped out his cellphone to call a familiar number as he replied, "Why don't we leave that to an actual sheriff."

A voice in the background muttered, "Oh my god, this production really is cursed."

After Drayco made the call to Sheriff Sailor and waited for the forensics team to arrive, he mused about that "cursed" comment. What did the person mean? Were there other literal skeletons hiding in literal closets here?

But more importantly, what was a skeleton doing entombed in the wall of a century-old house? And when and why was it placed there? Murderous life imitating murderous art, it seemed. But this was one body that wouldn't hop up and go home at the end of the day.

Drayco's mood got even darker as he conjured up possible motives behind the skeleton's entombment. He wasn't about to jump to conclusions like the actor-sheriff. But it was hard to imagine a scenario where a person intentionally crawled into a wall and waited patiently while being sealed up and left to die. One thing was sure—Sheriff Sailor's forensic team wouldn't make the same unprofessional mistakes the actors' characters did, not by a long shot.

Since he didn't see any official law types nearby, not even one lone security guard, Drayco parked himself in front of the hole in the wall and made sure everyone stayed back. Then he settled in for what was likely to be one marathon of a day.

2

It took fifteen minutes for the genuine Sheriff Ernest Sailor—as well as Deputy Nelia Tyler, and a few other deputies and members of the Prince of Wales County forensics team—to make their entrance. They might not be the best-funded outfit in the state of Virginia, but they were among the finest, in Drayco's experience.

As Sailor supervised, Tyler and her colleagues went about photographing, measuring, and cataloging the skeleton and its wall tomb, while an ambulance waited outside to whisk the skeletal remains away to the medical examiner in Norfolk. The actors playing Sheriff Baylor and Deputy Skyler watched closely, as if fascinated.

Drayco said to them, "That's how you do it."

In a voice that wasn't as deep and raspy as when saying his lines, "Sheriff" Frazier Prentiss said, "Would make terrible action on the screen. Too tedious. I mean, do they have to do all of that? Is some of it for show?"

Drayco had a pretty good idea of what the real-life Deputy Nelia Tyler would do to Frazier if she overheard that remark. Drayco replied calmly, "If they gave out Academy Awards for forensics, Sheriff Sailor's team would be in the running."

Frazier just yawned and called out to Chrystina, who was off to one side, "We're out of sparkling water, Chrys. You know I can't drink plain water." She made a face, and he wandered off, presumably in search of something carbonated.

The other cast and crew had drifted off to take vaping breaks or to raid the refrigerator in the kitchen. But one man, with wavy dark hair and a ready smile, strolled over to Drayco and joined him in watching the sheriff's team as they went through their tasks. This was the actor playing the "corpse," and he still had traces of red movie-blood on his white sweater.

He asked Drayco. "This is totally rad, isn't it? Howdja know it was a real skeleton? Are you really ex-FBI, or was that a joke?"

"I'm a private consultant now. And I've seen skeletons before, both real and fake."

A beam of light through a window reflected off a gold dolphin pin the man wore on his collar, making Drayco turn away to avoid being blinded. Part of the actor's costume, no doubt, seeing as how the setting was near the shore.

Drayco said, "I haven't caught a scene you're in yet. That is, where you're not playing a corpse."

"I only have a few lines. That's why they call us 'extras.' It's okay, though. If you have even a single word to say, you get a pay bump. Better than rhubarb."

"Rhubarb?"

"Gibberish dialog, which an AD can ask for. So they don't have to pay actors. Like they would for scripted dialogue."

"Ah, I see."

"So, a skeleton, huh? How long ya think it's been there?" The man blinked his eyes several times like a flashing caution light.

"Hard to say. But judging by the clothing and desiccation, it could be years. Maybe decades. This house is a century old."

"Once the body goes off to the examiner, does it take days or months before you get answers?" More eye blinking.

"Again, hard to say. If this isn't a recent case, contemporary victims move to the head of the line. Plus, it's tricky to extract evidence from old bones. The latest technologies are good, but it depends upon how degraded the materials are."

"That's too bad. It's a much more interesting mystery than this lame movie plot."

Drayco smiled at him. "Why are you so interested?"

The other man hesitated before replying. "I've got family members in law enforcement. Can't wait to tell them about this." He blinked several more times before adding, "You really think the skeleton is that old? As old as this house?"

"It sure looks that way."

The "extra" stuck out his hand. "Oh, the name's Mark William Smith. But folks call me Ellery."

"Ellery? Are you a mystery fan, à la Ellery Queen?"

"More a history buff. But Mark's an ordinary name. In Hollywood, you need a spicier handle, right? Kinda rad? Besides, SAG-AFTRA doesn't let working actors use identical screen names. Mark Smith was taken."

Ashleigh Salinger, the "deputy," marched up and linked arms with Drayco. "You're monopolizing the gentleman's time, Ellery. I just learned this man is a real detective. Mr. Drayco, you simply must give me tips." Ashleigh's voice wasn't at all like Nelia's coppery shimmer but more a fog of lavender polka dots, the equivalent of a synesthesia watercolor.

Ellery shrugged and wandered back to the kitchen, pausing to take quick cellphone photos of the hole in the wall. As Ashleigh pulled Drayco off to the side, he had to remind himself this wasn't Nelia Tyler, even though she *was* a little taller—maybe her high heels made her a few inches shorter than his six-four? When he turned to face her, he caught a glimpse out of the corner of his eye of the real Nelia watching them.

Ashleigh said, "You must tell me where the best eateries are around here. I've exhausted the obvious ones." She looked him up and down and added, "I mean, it's so hard to find good meat locally."

Drayco cleared his throat. "I, um, I'm sure I could give you a few tips."

A woman Drayco hadn't seen before, with short blonde hair topped with a yellow headband, stormed past them as she headed toward the director for a heated discussion. Ashleigh explained to Drayco, "Genna Ransford. She's afraid the production will be shut down. It's her house. They're paying her a pretty hefty sum to use it."

Drayco asked, "Aren't you worried it will be shut down?"

"You tell me. You know these police types. I mean, isn't that what they do?"

"It all depends."

Frazier Prentiss called out to Ashleigh, and she gritted her teeth. "That man takes this sheriff-deputy relationship way too far. It's like I'm his underling in real life." She released Drayco's arm. "Don't forget those restaurant recommendations. And I was serious about wanting to pick your brain about police procedure stuff."

As she headed toward Frazier, Drayco spotted the still-fuming homeowner, Genna Ransford. She was by herself this time, slouched down on a chair that matched her hair and gold sweater dress, making her all but disappear into a golden cloak of invisibility.

He approached her and introduced himself. "How are you doing, Ms. Ransford?"

"Like I need a bucket of cawfee with a vodka chaser. It's not only because this production could be clipped." Her voice had an Eastern Shore drawl but also hints of a New York accent, an odd combination. "I mean, that's bad enough. But they'll think I had something to do with that thing over there," she pointed toward the skeleton. "It being my house and all."

"Not if the bones are as old as I suspect."

The woman's tone changed. "Old? How old?"

"We won't know for sure until the M.E. investigates further. But possibly decades."

She got quiet, which made him curious. He said, "I would imagine you'd be happy. This could prove you weren't involved."

Genna's eyes glistened with tears. "I don't want to discuss it any further right now." When she excused herself and vanished into the rear of the house, he stood there staring after her. First, she's angry she might be blamed, and then she's in tears when she realizes she won't?

Drayco didn't have a chance to mull it over because Chrystina Valentine, the 1st AD, approached him. He almost laughed at his sudden "popularity." Chrystina asked point-blank, "I saw you chatting with Genna Ransford. And I can't get one word out of Rada. Tell it to me straight—are we getting shut down or not?"

"I wish I had an answer."

Chrystina tapped her foot on the floor. "Don't know whether to start looking for another gig. I can't afford the downtime." She kept glancing down at a cellphone in her hand, which she checked every couple of minutes.

He said, "When the sheriff's crew finishes their work, you'll find out then. But I have a question for you, too. Earlier, someone said the production was cursed. What did they mean?"

She winced. "Superstitious Hollywood bunk. More of those woo-woo crystals and psychics and all. Just because some weird crap happens, they think there's a curse."

"What kind of 'weird crap'?"

"An actor breaking his leg before production starts and having to replace him with Frazier Prentiss at the last minute. Things like that." She put her cellphone in her pocket and pulled out a tube of gloss with scents of vanilla and oranges that she applied to her lips. Drayco had a sudden craving for a Creamsicle soda.

He said, "Makes it even more curious there aren't security guards around. If people believe the production is cursed."

Chrystina stopped her lip-glazing to laugh. "This production isn't just on a shoestring budget. Hairstring, maybe? We're paying one guy to drive by at night and keep an eye on the place."

"Isn't that taking a risk?"

"We were told this was a safe area."

The man Reece had identified as Chrystina's brother, Hoyt, sidled up to them, still chewing on an unlit cigar. "You find out if we've got jobs or not, Chrys?"

"Not a word." She thrust the lip gloss back into her pocket and turned pleading eyes to Drayco. "Could you ask the sheriff? It's really important to us."

Drayco looked over at the deputies. "I'll see what I can learn."

He crept closer to Nelia and the forensic team, careful to stay out of their way, and watched them work. Nelia removed an item from the pocket of the dress on the body, and it appeared to be a paper, yellowed and faded. She looked up and locked eyes with his, her gaze saying volumes without having to spell it out. The find could be a huge discovery. With luck, even ID the victim and offer a time frame for the death.

There were times Drayco missed his FBI days when he had official—and often first—access to such finds. Still, he was close enough to see the paper in Nelia's hand and a few words on the outside fold. He couldn't quite make them out, but it looked like Spanish.

He also got an even better peek into the wall-tomb and glimpsed more of the white powder. Lime? Or it could be calcium carbonate, building material, degraded lead, or just products of decomposition.

Not wanting to hinder the deputies' progress, he didn't press Nelia about the movie being shut down and left her to her work. He shrugged apologetically toward Chrystina and Hoyt. Sure, it would be difficult for the cast and crew if the production shuttered permanently, and he wasn't unsympathetic. But that was real life, not Hollywood life.

He retreated to a corner where he could observe everything. Ellery Smith, the extra so interested in the skeleton, chatted with a fellow bit player he referred to as "Trent," who was munching on a chocolate bar. Drayco looked around for Reece, but the historian had disappeared, likely outside to get fresher air. The dust from the wall left a fine layer over much of the furniture and wouldn't help Reece's on-again, off-again asthma.

Genna Ransford also hadn't reappeared after her tearful exit. Through a window, Drayco saw Frazier Prentiss and Ashleigh Salinger out on the lawn in a heated discussion. But when Ashleigh looked up and spied him watching, her expression brightened as she smiled and waved. Nice that someone seemed happy to see him.

Feeling at loose ends, Drayco chatted with the crew he hadn't met. Isaac Batey, the sound engineer, and Sachio Spafford, the gaffer-grip, filled him in more on that indie budget Reece mentioned. They both lived in Virginia Beach and commuted the two-hour round trip daily, saving the production some money for housing.

The men looked like polar opposites. Sachio stood around five-eight with short hair, wearing a purple scarf and sporting a purple fedora with a red feather. Isaac was tall and thin with long hair under his backwards baseball cap and a wad of chewing tobacco in his cheek. But they both agreed on one thing—even if the project survived the unforeseen wrinkle of a skeleton found in the wall, it would fall behind schedule. And being behind schedule meant going over budget.

Sachio sighed, adding, "We'll cross that bridge when we get to it," prompting Isaac to retort, "Man, you need to dump the clichés. I'm gonna buy you a shock collar that goes off whenever you use one."

Sachio said, "What, not a shot in the arm?" In reply, Isaac punched him in the shoulder.

As the two men drifted outside, the EMTs and forensic team transferred the newly uncovered bones to a body bag with care. Considering Eastern Shore history predated the seventeenth century, it was hardly surprising there'd be interesting archaeological finds. But it seemed Drayco had been handed more than his fair share—his Opera House bequest, the pirate skeleton from a previous case, and now this. Some might say the movie wasn't cursed, it was Drayco. Or a predestined fate of his.

A lot of philosophers had a lot of ideas about fate. But the way Drayco saw it, it wasn't predetermination or bad luck but rather how you choose to put yourself out in the world. *Faber est suae quisque fortunae.* Every man is the crafter of his own fortune. Or, as with sadder endings like this, a crafter of their own misfortune.

An old skeleton entombed in a wall, a dress, a yellowed paper, and a few Spanish words—not much to go on. It made him uneasy, but not due to any curse. Maybe the thought of being buried in a wall had kicked his claustrophobia into high gear. He didn't think so, but he had absolutely no idea what else it might be.

3

As Drayco suspected, the movie-set investigation took all day, which is why he trudged into the Lazy Crab well after six. A couple of other guests were staying at the B&B, and Drayco waited until they'd finished their supper before he joined the inn's proprietors, Maida and Major Jepson, at the kitchen table for one of Maida's famously "potent" toddies.

When she handed Drayco a tall glass mug, he held it up in the air. "It's very…red. And what are those starry things floating around?"

"Star anise. The red is cranberry. Matches my hair, don't you think?" She grinned. "There are a few other goodies in there, too."

"Definitely festive." Drayco took a sip and coughed. "Bourbon?"

"And cranberry liqueur. Too much?"

He took another sip, and this time let the warm tingling from the drink attack his dark mood, forcing him to relax whether he wanted to or not. "I like it."

"The liqueur is left over from Christmas. Why should cranberry only be for holidays?"

Drayco leaned back in the lighthouse-shaped chair. "Did you have more traffic during the holiday season?"

"Quite a few guests. Cape Unity has a big Christmas shindig now. A parade, fireworks, flying drone displays, and lighted boats on the water. I was hoping you could join us."

"Things got too busy, alas." He took another sip of the toddy, taking pains to avoid chewing on the star anise—were they even edible? He added, "I saw public works staffers removing decorations on Main Street."

"Kind of sad to see them go. I liked the lighted wreaths the town purchased."

"I also noticed brand-new light fixtures. And they finally filled in that giant pothole in front of Tallent's Antiques."

"Movie money."

"Movie money?"

"The production company got tax breaks, but they've bought supplies locally. Plus, there's catering and hotel room rentals and the like."

That was a little perplexing, but "small budget" by Hollywood standards could mean "big budget" to Cape Unity. He replied, "I'm surprised no staff are staying here."

"We don't give out house keys to all guests willy-nilly. Just trusted ones like you. Plus, the movie people tend to stay out late partying."

"And they needed a place where they can come and go at will."

"Exactly. We had a couple of location scouts bunk here. A few months ago."

"Is Lucy Harston still doing catering? It's not like she has to now, does she, with the inheritance?"

"She enjoys having something creative to do. You'll see her on set again with her famous pastries. If the production doesn't close up shop, that is."

Drayco gave the odds of that around fifty-fifty. "If the show goes on, I don't suppose your lovely B&B is going to have a cameo?"

"If they'd asked, I would have said no. Too many legal problems. And notoriety. Honestly, I was afraid they'd trash the place."

Drayco appreciated her principles, but bits of the inn's interior paint and furniture still looked faded. At least the B&B had fixed the Lazy Crab sign, with the "R" returned to its rightful slot. No more "Lazy C ab." He'd hoped to pass along leftover funds after fixing up the Opera House, but he was already battling cost overruns.

He stopped himself from groaning aloud. Always a touchy subject, his inherited Opera House. But he didn't want to negate the good mood from Maida's drink, so he pushed aside thoughts of his Opera Albatross and drained his glass of Cranberry Comfort.

Maida got up to get Drayco a refill. "Did you see Virginia Harston or Barry Farland on the set? They drop by now and then."

"No, thankfully. They're both mature young people, but I'm very grateful they didn't witness the skeleton surprise." He took a sip of the refill, even heavier on the alcohol than before. "Is there a special reason they've been hanging around the production?"

"Barry is friends with one of the temp crew hired from Cape Unity. And Lucy thought it would be a great homeschool project for Virginia. Reece arranged it."

"I guess it has educational value. Skeletons notwithstanding."

"I'd say it's a textbook study of human psychology. Everybody's going nuts. Some are starry-eyed and want to be in the movie, while others are grumbling about crime, traffic, uppity actors, and so forth."

Drayco grunted. "Like the old days when the circus came to town."

Maida nodded. "Folks may grumble, but I think secretly everyone wants to be an actor."

"Not everyone."

"Not you, you mean?" She grinned.

"It's not high on my list, no. Although you could say everyone's an actor, adapting their behavior to suit any occasion. Social chameleons."

"Making it hard to know who people really are. Which is why detectives like you exist."

Drayco lifted his glass in salute.

Maida slid into a chair. "A skeleton? For real?"

"Yes, but how did you hear about it?"

"Gretta at my hair salon."

"News travels fast, as usual."

"Nowadays, it's all texting instead of the old-fashioned phone call of my day."

Drayco eyed a container of peanut butter fudge on the counter and fought the urge to grab it. He was surprisingly ravenous. "I suspect the skeleton will turn out to be an old case."

"Because of where it was found? In the wall?"

"That, and a paper with the body, yellowed and faded. Plus clothing that looked mid-century."

Maida tilted her head. "Paper?"

"Nelia Tyler will have to conduct a forensic analysis to see what it is. The paper was folded up, and she'll need to be careful lest it disintegrate, but I noted a few words on the outside of the fold. In Spanish."

Major Jepson, who'd been half-dozing, sat up straight, stroking his braided beard. "Spanish, eh? You mean Spain or the Americas?"

"Nelia's analysis should be able to pin that down."

"Well, now, we've had seasonal workers from the Americas. Mexican folk mostly, who help out with the fishermen during crabbing season. But that's a newer thing. Don't recall hearing about such workers long ago." Major let out a belch. "This makes two skeletons found on your watch. You're a skeleton magnet."

Drayco sighed. "I'm sure Sheriff Sailor will blame me for this somehow. He wasn't all that happy getting a call-out to a crime scene on a Sunday." Drayco had learned the movie crew was on a seven-day schedule, but the sheriff's office *tried* to take a day off.

Maida tapped her foot on the floor. "It's new fodder for him to chew on, unlike drug arrests. We've had issues with that, but it's ramped up lately."

"Since the movie production came to town?"

Maida hesitated. "I hate to point fingers."

"That's why I respect you so much, Maida. You think things through logically and never jump to conclusions."

He got a whiff of something fishy and fried. The reason became apparent as she hopped up to grab a plate of blue crab fritters she set in front of him, explaining, "So the alcohol won't give you heartburn. They may look odd, but they'll get the job done."

He immediately wolfed a few down. Yep, ravenous. Recalling his "odd" encounter with the movie-house homeowner, Drayco asked, "Do either of you know Genna Ransford, who owns the house where they're filming? I met her briefly."

"Only that she inherited the place from her father." Maida put a dish of garlicky sauce in front of Drayco. "We never saw much of him or Genna. Before that, it belonged to her grandfather."

Major added, "I remember her grandfather. Duff Ransford. A decent man, but a prankster. Fun to talk to. He liked swapping stories about his father's days in the Army during WWII. And my father's stint in the RAF. I didn't know his son so well."

Drayco mulled that over. "So Duff Ransford was the original owner of the house?" If that was indeed the case, and the skeletal victim died decades ago, then it would have happened while Major's friend owned it. Drayco didn't like the ethical drop-off where that train of thought seemed headed.

"Original owner?" Major replied. "I'm not sure. It's possible."

"Since we're on the subject of old buildings," Maida took a quick nibble of a fritter. "How are the Opera House renovations coming along?"

Drayco sucked air through his teeth. He couldn't avoid the topic, it seemed. "Probably looking at an opening date in late spring."

"And you'll be the headliner, naturally."

"I'm not sure anyone would pay to hear me play these days. My piano career was so long ago."

Maida looked disappointed. "You *must* be part of it. You're the reason the Opera House was saved from the wrecking ball."

"We'll see. But I can't make any promises."

Maida patted him on the shoulder. "You haven't touched our Chickering piano yet, and I had it tuned just for you. I won't let you leave until you do."

Drayco gave a small smile and a nod. A recital for one devoted fan—he could do that.

She added, "And I want to hear some of your own pieces. I understand you're a composer now."

"It's nothing. A stress reliever." He had a good idea of who told the Jepsons about that—Nelia. So, she had no problems discussing him behind his back, just not to his face? The ever-astute Maida got the hint, so she didn't press further.

Not a fan of indulging in self-flagellation, Drayco focused on the image of the skeletal remains from the movie-set house. Not much was left of the poor unnamed victim. Once real, once alive, likely with her own hopes and dreams. That is, he guessed the victim was female, considering the dress.

He hated naming such victims with the customary "Jane Doe," so in his mind, he was calling her "Elise," after Beethoven's famous piano bagatelle. He'd done that with his first anonymous-victim cold case in his FBI academy courses, dubbing her Alma Perdida, or "lost soul" in Spanish. Even after all these years, he kept a copy of a facial reconstruction sketch from the young woman's skull as a reminder. *Never forget.*

Drayco picked at the fritters, trying not to dwell on all the lost souls never identified, if found at all. Yet, it was as if some force in the universe wanted this skeleton to be discovered. If the movie production hadn't chosen that house for filming, and if the lighting hadn't crashed through that particular wall, the skeletal remains could have remained hidden for decades more.

But did it ultimately matter? As he'd told Ellery Smith, cold cases often sat on the back burner. And as busy as the sheriff's department was, "Elise" could easily stay anonymous forever.

4

Monday, January 10

Drayco once asked a psychologist about hypnopompic hallucinations upon waking and was told ten percent of people experienced them. The psychologist admitted Drayco's chronic experience was rare and wondered if the synesthesia tied into it all.

Months had passed since Drayco's last bout, and he'd forgotten how disturbing the hallucinations were. Whispering voices and shadowy faces hovered over him, with the sense of something crawling on his skin. Often, he was trapped in a fire he couldn't escape.

He lay in bed for a few minutes, staring at the ceiling. It took a while to shake off the bizarre images and sensations, and he felt as drained as Sheriff Sailor looked when Drayco made it into Sailor's office an hour later. If Sailor had any hair left to pull out, it would not have been surprising if he'd done so right then and there.

Since Drayco had occupied his favorite swivel chair in Sheriff Sailor's office so often, he told Sailor they should put Drayco's name on it. The sheriff was not amused by that idea. In fact, Sailor wasn't amused whatsoever with anything Drayco wanted to talk about.

Drayco motioned toward the coffee maker in the corner and asked if a shot of Sailor's infamous java that smelled like burned popcorn would help. But the lawman didn't crack a smile.

Drayco did learn the sheriff's team believed they'd extracted everything they could get from the crime scene, so they were going ahead and releasing the house to the movie production company. But Sailor also admitted he did so reluctantly.

Sailor's dour mood matched Drayco's own, and he soon learned the reason when the sheriff grumbled, "The county board is putting pressure on me to sweep any trouble under the rug. They don't want to make the town look bad. Tourist dollars are at stake, they say. Same old, same old."

"Is it as complicated as all that?"

"You kidding? I have to toe a fine line here. There's the board on the one hand. And complaints from the movie folks about locals jacking up prices on the other. Which I can't deny. Even the Fairmont Hotel, where a few movie crew are staying, doubled its rates."

"Cape Unity denizens gouging the Hollywood royalty? I'm shocked, just shocked, I say."

Sailor scowled. "Joke all you want, but I'm the one in the middle who has to try to keep a lid on it."

"But how? Free enterprise and all."

"Using language in the town's charter, that's how. Which isn't making me the most popular person around these parts."

Drayco shook his head. The hard-working sheriff deserved better. "Did the movie pay you or Tyler for using you as their inspiration? Sheriff Ernie Baylor? Deputy Nellie Skylar? Come on."

Sailor scowled. "What do you think?"

"I'll take that as a 'no.' Why didn't they hire you as a consultant?"

"Again, money. Guess they thought it was an honor for the characters to be loosely based on us. And I do mean *loosely*." Sailor glared at the mounted flounder with the piranha-like teeth still hanging on his wall. It glared back at him.

"Please tell me you didn't contribute anything to that wretched script."

"A rep from the film crew interviewed me. After I consulted with the town council and city attorney. CYA. They asked about my job, procedures, my work. But the sheriff they came up with is nothing like me."

"He's not even like Andy Griffith."

"Andy was fine for 1960s television, but too boring for movies now. No, instead Hollywood comes up with either a clownish buffoon or a hard-assed bumpkin. A *corrupt* hard-assed bumpkin."

"Reminds me of that film featuring nearby Onancock years ago. Despite the fact it's on the Chesapeake Bay, they wrote it as a mountain-lake town."

Sailor snorted. "And mispronounced it, too."

Drayco took a spin around in the swivel chair. Might as well give Sailor some amusement. He drew up his legs up to avoid hitting anything, but he still came within an inch of knocking into a file cabinet. And that reminded him of what a cast member had said.

Drayco stopped swiveling. "I overheard a movie staffer talking about a curse on the production. An actor broke his leg prior to shooting, and his role had to be recast."

"Gives a whole new meaning to that break-a-leg motto."

"Yes, but the skeleton find feeds right into that curse talk."

Sailor finally got up to pour some coffee and handed Drayco a cup. "My department's certainly feeling pretty cursed."

"I'll buy you a four-leaf clover. Did Tyler discover anything on that paper she found with the remains?"

"She's working on it. Still doing a job-share with Regina Reymann. She does what she can, when she can."

"She'll have to return to law school soon, right?"

"In a couple of weeks." Sailor drew in a breath. "I'm proud of her. But selfishly, I want to keep her here."

Right on cue, Nelia Tyler popped her head through the open door. "Got more from the paper we found with our skeleton."

Sailor looked at Drayco as if to say, *Speak of the devil*, and then replied to Nelia, "I'm all ears. But please tell me it's a very old, very cold case."

"The watermark is from a paper company in Europe that no longer exists. They were bought out in the 1960s, so this was before that."

"Were you able to make sense of it?"

"With a VSC we had on loan for another case, yes. Bits of it."

Drayco interrupted, "VSC, as in Video Spectral Comparator?"

"Yup. For the rest, we'll need a forensic document examiner." Nelia held up a logbook and read from her notes. "The name on the paper was Madalena Delfin Zamora, aged nineteen. There's a date, January 15, 1947, and the word *L'Escala*, a town in Spain. Plus a string of numbers, but it was cut off."

Drayco said, "Sounds like immigration papers."

"I found similar documents online from that era, and this looks like the real deal."

Sailor groaned. "Great. All I need is the Spanish embassy getting involved, if it's one of their citizens." He pointed his finger at Drayco. "This is all your fault. Every time you pop up, there's a skeleton."

"In all fairness, I wasn't the one who found either skeleton. And neither find was part of my investigations. So you could say the Eastern Shore is a hotbed for old skeleton finds. Or it's even *your* aura, Sheriff."

That made Nelia laugh, which Drayco was glad to see. When she caught her breath, she added, "And I did a preliminary analysis of that white powdery substance found with the body. Quicklime, calcium oxide. Combined with fluids, it would have formed calcium hydroxide."

Drayco said, "Slaked lime."

"Corrosive, likely damaged the corpse, but it could have killed off some of the putrefying bacteria and dehydrated the body."

"So, less odor."

"A murderer's best friend, if it works."

Drayco asked, "When will the M.E. be able to pinpoint anything about the victim or cause of death? Or timing?"

Sailor piped up, "They aren't in a hurry to tackle ancient history. Besides, this may not be a crime at all."

"What do you mean?"

"Maybe this young woman crawled into that space during a game of hide-and-seek. Or maybe it was a joke. Stories abound of skeletons found in walls or chimneys. Like that Arkansas woman who fell into an attic crawlspace. Wasn't discovered until years later."

"But several of the victims in those stories were criminals doing something illegal, like breaking and entering."

Sailor nodded. "There you go. More fodder for the hypothesis she wasn't murdered. A tragic accident based on a poor decision."

"How else do you explain the quicklime? I doubt our victim doused herself with it, crawled in there, and waited to be sealed up."

"Until the M.E. says otherwise, I'm not worrying over it. The homeowner at the time is long deceased. Perhaps justice will have to take place in the hereafter."

When Drayco opened his mouth to argue, Sailor cut him off, adding, "Look, we've got 'now' crimes to solve. Like thefts, assaults, other various forms of attempted murder. And like an increase in drug offenses since the movie crew arrived. I've developed a respect for your hatred of coincidences."

"Nice to know I've rubbed off on you."

Sailor picked up a pen and tapped it on his desk. "How long are you in town for?"

"A few days. Enough to take care of some business at the Opera House."

"It's ready for prime time?"

"Getting closer." Drayco took the subtle hint he'd overstayed his welcome, so he hopped up to leave.

Nelia stayed behind in the office. Maybe to discuss the case, or maybe she still wanted to avoid him. Was this the way it was going to be now?

Seeing her at the crime scene, just like when he first met her, had taken him back to a happier time. He missed the less-fraught relationship they had then. Sure, she'd make a fine attorney one day and likely find a perfect post-divorce soul mate. And good for her. So why did it feel like he'd personally lost something?

As he made his way out of the office toward his Starfire in the lot, he mused on Sailor's talk of skeletons and the possible age of the victim. Only nineteen, if the immigration papers were correct. When Drayco's sister Casey passed away, she was a few years younger, but Casey had family with her at the end. This girl likely died alone—if she was still alive when she entered that opening in the wall.

He voiced the name aloud, "Madalena Delfin Zamora." Not Elise, but nicer, real. He hoped she was in a better place now, if you believed in that kind of thing, and not alone or afraid anymore.

Possibly Sailor was right, and her death was a tragic accident. Or perhaps it was darker than that. Intentional, premeditated, coordinated. He'd have to research serial killers of that era to see if that was a factor. Okay, it wasn't Drayco's case, and he wasn't in the business of investigating serial killers, but it helped to keep his skills sharp.

He toyed with offering his services for free to the sheriff on this one. And he might, if he hadn't received a call hours ago from a potential client in D.C. Not just any client, but a power player with deep pockets. Such money could help stretch the Opera House renovation dollars and allow him to slip extra funds to the Lazy Crab and Reece's Historical Society. It was just too bad the highest-paying gigs were often the least appealing, and this case was a type he hated most, insurance fraud.

His dark mood returned, but the best solution for that was always work, staying busy. And returning to a crime scene—even if it was simply more research to "keep his skills sharp"—counted as work, did it not?

5

Director Rada Bluestone wasted no time. Drayco wasn't shocked to learn the movie shoot was back on after what Sheriff Sailor had said about releasing the crime scene. The show must go on, more so if you were on the hook to lose a bunch of money.

But he was surprised Lucy Harston was the one who requested Drayco return to the set. She was there to drop off baked goods, but he doubted that's why she wanted him along. She hinted that her daughter, Virginia, would be present for her homeschool project and Lucy would feel better if Drayco stopped by, considering the skeleton incident.

But as Drayco walked into the movie-set house, he saw Lucy holding hands with Reece Wable in a corner. Reece hadn't mentioned it, but his relationship with Lucy must be going pretty well. Drayco was more perplexed when he also saw Virginia's friend and fellow artist, Barry Farland.

Three bodyguards were plenty enough. But four? Lucy was over-protective, but this seemed a bit much. Of course, Barry, twelve years older than Virginia, thought of her as his younger sister, so perhaps he was the protective one?

The hole in the wall where the skeleton was found still gaped open, a yawning portal into oblivion. Yellow-and-black crime scene tape now covered it, and the movie crew had repositioned cameras to avoid having the wall in any shots.

Someone must have waved a magic vacuum-cleaner-wand because no traces of the powdery plaster dust remained. The Victorian silk moiré settee, tassel pillows, and ivory lace curtains all looked pristine.

Yet, slight hints of the sulfuric distemper odor still lingered in the air. It was a good thing this movie didn't have Smell-O-Vision.

"The show must go on" mantra must be deeply ingrained with these folks, as no one appeared upset about yesterday's events. Drayco overheard the actress-makeup guru, Jaxine Gordon, even referring to the skeleton as "their mascot" and they should ask for it back. Drayco didn't find that amusing whatsoever.

But Sailor was right regarding the financial angle. The crew needed the money from their jobs, the actors and director needed money from box office receipts, and the townspeople also had their hands out. What was the discovery of a skeleton to stand in the way of all that? Even if it was potentially a poor teenager far from home who died horrifically.

Virginia and Barry huddled in a corner chatting with a young woman wearing glasses who Drayco noticed the other day but hadn't met. She sported the same pink hoop earrings she wore then and a purple scrunchie to hold back her long, curly hair. He headed toward them, and Virginia greeted him with a hug as she introduced the young woman as Nancy Farmery, a local girl from Onancock.

Nancy smiled at him. "Virginia tells me you're a real-life detective. Color me impressed. Kinda nice to meet the actual deal. Instead of these imitations," she gestured at Ashleigh Salinger, who slouched in a corner checking her phone.

"You're not acting in the movie, Nancy?"

She fiddled with her earrings. "As an extra. No lines. Otherwise, I'm a lowly production assistant. I make coffee, copy scripts, provide transportation, and help with catering. Like Lucy Harston's to-die-for pastries." Nancy uttered an embarrassed giggle. "Was that in poor taste? Yuck, even more puns. I'll stop talking now."

Drayco asked Virginia, "Do you also help your mom with the catering?"

"Some." The teenager pointed down at her new leg prosthetics. "I'm still learning how to use these."

"How do you like them?"

She walked back and forth in front of him. "Better than a wheelchair."

"As you once told me, it'll make walking on stage to accept your Hugo Boss prize easier."

She beamed at him. "You remember that?"

He nodded, but then her smile turned to a frown. "They discontinued it, you know."

"Actually, I didn't. But there are other awards. You'll win them all." His words caused her frown to vanish, and he asked, "So what's your homeschool project about?"

"Movie production, duh. I'd stay all day if I could, but they chase me off for most of the filming stuff."

"Are you thinking of changing careers from art to movies?"

"I never thought about a movie career before all this. But Nancy pointed out that if I tried acting, it could inspire other disabled actors."

"Hollywood can be hard and unforgiving. Perhaps you should start with local theater productions."

Barry chimed in, "Besides, your artistic talents shouldn't go to waste, Ginnie. You could be a set designer. They also give out Academy Awards for that."

Drayco agreed. "That they do. Whatever you decide, I'm thrilled you're adjusting to your new prosthetics." He really was, too. In fact, seeing Virginia getting around so well cheered him up more than anything else had in a long while.

The director, Rada Bluestone, had issued an edict that only essential cast members and crew were to be present indoors during live scene shots. Fortunately, Drayco timed his appearance well since filming hadn't resumed.

Bluestone also wasn't allowing anyone to go near the hole in the wall, which made Virginia cross. She grumbled, "I want to see inside."

A man's voice behind Drayco's back startled him, saying, "Me, too. Why would it matter if we took a peek?"

Drayco turned to find Ellery Smith, the same movie extra from yesterday who was deeply interested in the skeletal discovery. Like a broken record, Ellery asked in his nasal tenor with red spikes, "So, Mr. Drayco, have they identified the skeleton? The sheriff isn't telling us squat. Surely, there's family who'll want to know what happened?"

"I'm not sure there will be much family left who remember her."

"Her?" Ellery's eyes lit up. "It was a woman?"

"The medical examiner will need to verify that." Drayco stared at the fellow. Why was he so interested when all the other cast and crew had moved on? Having law enforcement members in your family didn't feel like a strong enough reason. Maybe he was addicted to true-crime podcasts.

Drayco asked him, "Do you live around here? Must be a fun opportunity to be involved in a production like this."

Ellery started his caution-light blinking again. "Not so much from around here. But not too far away. Doubt you've heard of it. Unionville. A small town in the western part of the state."

"I've flown over it before. It's close to Charlottesville."

"Flown over it?"

"I'm a private pilot. I fly now and then for fun or business."

"For real? That's pretty rad."

"I suppose it is. So, how did you hear of this production?"

"Did some theater work. Got bitten by the bug. I checked the notices and saw an ad in a trade mag. Looked like it'd be a blast. Like you and flying." He laughed awkwardly. "Never know when that lucky break will come your way."

"You must have Hollywood aspirations, then."

"Who doesn't?"

Hadn't Maida said the same thing? Drayco asked, "And what have you learned about this strange business?"

"Hollywood types are like everybody else. They just have a higher profile job. One that can be brutal on mind, body, and soul. Even if you get that big break."

Drayco motioned toward the camera and lights. "What did you do for a living before all of this?"

"Other than those theater gigs, odd jobs here and there. Guess I never found my true calling."

Virginia, who never missed a beat, said, "Gobs of people don't find what they want to do right away. You don't have to keep working a boring job your whole life anymore. You're lucky."

"Lucky. Yeah, I suppose so." Ellery waved and headed off with the excuse of seeking out Lucy's fabulous blueberry crumble muffins.

So that's what Drayco was smelling. Freshly baked muffins. With lots of cinnamon.

After Ellery disappeared into another area of the house, Virginia asked, "Was it something I said?"

Drayco replied, "I don't think so. That man is 'off.' I'm uncertain how or why, but maybe you should keep your distance."

Barry put a hand on Virginia's shoulder. "Duly noted. I'll make sure she does." He peered out the front windows of the house. "Speaking of dangerous things, did I see bullet holes in your Starfire?"

"Uh, that would be affirmative."

"Oh, man. For real? I could fix those for you."

"Still working at Hafferty's Body Shop?"

"Yeppers. I'm being let out of the cage today 'cause I finished a big project. A reconditioned engine on a Land Rover. You should let me work on those bullet holes, you know. I've got all the materials for your Starfire. Even done it before to another car."

Drayco did a double-take. "You've had another car with bullet holes?"

Barry grinned. "You're not the only one who leads an interesting life."

"If getting your car shot up means 'interesting,' I could handle dull for a change." Drayco glanced around. "By the way, I don't see Genna Ransford."

"Haven't seen her today. Nancy, here, said she looked real shook up after they found that skeleton in her wall."

Drayco had witnessed Genna's reaction first-hand and still didn't know what to make of it. Was she superstitious and worried about "ghosts" haunting her house? Or else she was afraid the appraised value would plummet, and it would be harder to sell. But whatever the reason, her reaction was strange.

He took a step back, which happened to be on a loud, squeaky floorboard that echoed throughout the space and sent sepia cactus needles straight into Drayco's brain. Rada Bluestone glared in his direction and yelled to no one in particular, "Can we kill that squeak? Put putty in the joint or whatever." She threw her hands in the air and stalked out of the room.

Sachio Spafford, still wearing his purple scarf and fedora, rushed over with a small jar of wood putty and a trowel as Drayco retreated to a less squeaky spot. The poor gaffer had an ironic expression of beatific suffering, like a man acting as a martyr who hopes to be canonized for his trouble one day.

Since Drayco was invited to the set to help keep an eye on Virginia, keep an eye on Virginia, he did. However, she appeared to be having more fun than anyone else—when she wasn't casting longing gazes at the yellow caution tape covering the hole in the wall.

Drayco knew how she felt. He hadn't had the chance to study the opening himself and wouldn't anytime soon. He swallowed his disappointment, but he had no right to be there in the first place, let alone get involved with a cold case nobody seemed to care much about.

Sachio finished his repair job and grimaced at sound engineer Isaac Batey, summing it up— a director on edge, a production on the brink, and jobs on the line made for one unhappy bunch. Who said Tinseltown was all starry walks and golden statuettes?

6

When Virginia, Barry, Lucy, and Reece left the movie set—or after Chrystina Valentine kicked them off for an intense scene called a "goofie"—Drayco declined their offer to join them for lunch at Lucy's house. He wasn't sure why, but something gnawed at him about the skeleton find. It would be oddly soothing if Sheriff Sailor could have joined him for one of their infrequent confabs at places like the Seafood Hut. Sadly, the Hut's post-fire renovations weren't complete yet.

He opted for the Island View Restaurant, which still had the lighthouse-style tower on top and large plate glass windows where he could look out toward the barrier islands. The chilly air kept him from sitting outside on the deck, but he still had some views of the greenish-blue water and a few boats in the distance.

He'd barely had time to grab a menu when a blonde woman, carrying a drink and a plate filled with a crab sandwich, pulled out a chair across from him, sat down, and put her food on the table. He looked over at Ashleigh Salinger. "Slumming with the locals?"

She grinned. "You're not exactly a local. Plus, I'm tired of other actors. And I can't think of many people I'd rather slum with right now than you."

"Because of my real detective-y charm?"

"I still can't believe you actually are one. You almost look more like an actor playing the role yourself. I mean, those eyes. Yikes."

"Too something?"

"No, a very much something. Deep blue, popular in Hollywood. Paul Newman, Elizabeth Taylor, Daniel Craig." She leaned in, "A little purple, too, in a certain light. Ever done any acting?"

"That would be a hard no. At least, not outside my law enforcement career."

"I've never met a real FBI agent before."

"And you haven't now. Not an active one."

She grinned at him. "I don't have any FBI jokes, but I've got a cop joke. What do you call a police officer who takes up gardening?"

Drayco gaped at her. "Um..."

"A copse."

He shook his head but couldn't stop a small smile from forming before he tossed the menu onto the table and ordered a duplicate of what Ashleigh was having.

She munched on the sandwich with a blissful expression, and he said, "Must be good."

"Mmmm." She washed the bite down with ginger-peach tea and eyed him closely. "How tall are you, six-three?"

"Four."

"You wouldn't need a manmaker, then."

Drayco tilted his head. "Um…manmaker?"

"Think shoe lifts. Or a box. Whatever will make a man a few inches taller during filming. Which someone in this cast knows all about, I might add. But you didn't hear it from me."

Drayco took a sip of a something-with-pineapple-juice drink. "How did you get into acting, Ashleigh?"

"By accident. Went with a friend to a casting call. For emotional support. They hired me, not her."

"Ouch. Still friends?"

"Believe it or not, yes. She does a bunch of work in the theatre. Even off-Broadway shows."

"Where are you from originally?"

"San Francisco, and forgive me for dissing your stomping grounds, but I much prefer the West Coast to the East."

"On account of the earthquakes?"

She grinned. "Earthquakes, landslides, wildfires, floods, and possible tsunamis. What's not to love?"

He let her eat more of the sandwich as he studied her. Finally, he said, "You don't talk like I expected."

"What did you expect? Valley Girl?"

"Or vocal fry or uptalk. Or...I don't know."

"You haven't met enough actresses."

That made him smile. "You are correct."

"But I can do it if you want. I mean, gag me with a SPOOOOON." Her voice trailed off with a glottal creak, and then she added, "I mean, totally, fer shur," and her voice rose at the end.

"I'm impressed. Vocal fry and uptalk simultaneously."

Ashleigh grinned, but her face grew even more animated when her eyes darted to the front of the restaurant. She waved at someone behind Drayco, and he turned around to see none other than Deputy Nelia Tyler heading toward them.

Ashleigh said, "Nelia, you must join us. I have more grilling for you."

Nelia looked at Drayco with question-mark eyebrows. He nodded. "By all means."

Ashleigh said, "I was wrong about this town. It's not as sleepy as I imagined. Unless you're *not* always finding real skeletons in closets."

Nelia grabbed a chair across from Drayco and sat down. "Just a couple."

"Okay, so question number one. I noticed you photographed the skeleton and used these little numbers and a ruler-like doodad. What are they for?"

Nelia waited to place a quick salad order before she answered. "The scale provides a point of reference for sizes and dimensions. The markers denote items of interest and specific locations in photos. And the relationship or orientation of items of evidence to one another."

"And what about that white powder? You collected some and put it in a bag."

"Standard procedure when you find any unusual material. It's taken back to the lab for analysis later."

Ashleigh thought for a moment. "I overheard you say the skeleton was old. Can you still get evidence from remains like that?"

"A lot, most of the time."

"Like what? Oh wait...." She dug into her purse, pulled out her cellphone, and clicked on a video icon to start recording.

Nelia had a gleam in her eye as she rattled off, "Forensic anthropologists and osteologists can apply radiographic techniques like X-rays, computer tomography, and MRI. Or even sonography. Osteometric boards help measure human stature from the femur, tibia, and ulna, while spreading calipers measure head length and breadth."

"And what about DNA?"

"Trace amounts of DNA are sometimes found in dense bone and teeth. Scientists have even recovered small amounts of DNA from bones thousands of years old."

"That's fascinating. You didn't see any bullets or anything, did you?"

Nelia frowned. "Everything is still preliminary at this point. I shouldn't discuss specific details of the case."

Ashleigh turned off the recording. "I also wanted to ask if you'll give me more gun tips. I mean, I don't want law enforcement types in the audience catching me doing anything too stupid. Lots of people in the cast got firearms training. But it's pretty basic."

Nelia rubbed her temples. "I can check with Sheriff Sailor."

"You should show Frazier, too. I don't think he's into the role. If it were up to me, I would have hired someone else." Ashleigh polished off her sandwich and said to Drayco, "Since you were in the FBI, you know how to handle a gun, right?"

"When needed, yes."

Nelia muttered, "Expert marksman in the Bureau's quarter-inch club doesn't qualify you to know how to use a gun?"

Ashleigh looked from Nelia to Drayco. "Quarter-inch club?"

Drayco shot Nelia a sharp look. What game was Nelia trying to play bringing that up? He replied, "Agents who can place three shots within a circle no more than a quarter inch in diameter at two hundred yards."

"Wow. Then you *must* show me all your tricks." She took another swig of her drink and said, "I've got to visit the powder room. Talk amongst yourselves."

When she was gone, Nelia told Drayco, "You know she's really a brunette, right?"

"I wondered. When I looked her up online, she had brown hair in her photos."

"I think she dyed her hair to imitate me."

"She also has the same style you do."

"See what I mean?" Nelia flinched. "Ouch. *She's* the one who says 'I mean' all the time, so now I'm copying her. Anyway, she's way too sexy to be a deputy. And she works in high heels. As if."

"I noticed that. Made me laugh."

"As well it should." Nelia leaned forward with her arms planted on the table. "Why were you looking up Ashleigh?"

Drayco fought the urge to rub his own temples. First, Nelia treated him like he had the plague, and the next thing he knew, she acted almost jealous. Almost. He'd never seen her in that state, so he wasn't sure. But he was not in the mood for any more arguments about their raw, often bleeding relationship, so he kept it light. "I researched background info on all the actors and crew."

"Before or after the skeleton find?"

"After. Seemed prudent."

She skewered a cherry tomato on her fork and waved it in the air between them. "You're going to get involved in this, aren't you?"

"Nope. I'm only here on Opera House business."

"Hmm." She put the tomato in her mouth and chewed on it slowly as Drayco chose to look out the window toward the marshes beyond. She was trying to kill him. That must be it. Some sort of revenge.

He added, "With any luck, you and Sheriff Sailor should be rid of me in a couple of days. I suspect there will be much rejoicing in the land."

Ashleigh returned from the bathroom and overheard his comment. She said, "You're not going to be here long? That's a pity."

Nelia choked on her salad and grabbed some tea to wash it down. Drayco kept an eye on her to ensure she was okay, then replied to Ashleigh, "The movie production's not going to be in town much longer, either, as I understand it."

"That depends. The skeleton delay set us back. The gig was supposed to last a few weeks, a month tops." Then Ashleigh surprised him by adding, "That poor soul. I mean, I've heard people say they'd rather go out in a blaze of glory than a slow decline in a nursing home. But that lost soul, whoever it was, deserved the chance to decide for themselves."

So, not all the movie crew were lacking in compassion. The only other person expressing sorrow was Genna Ransford, the homeowner—if her tears were real. For that matter, why was Drayco himself feeling so affected by the discovery of this victim? Here he was with morbid thoughts even while in the company of two beautiful and lively women.

His face must have registered his musings because both Nelia and Ashleigh stopped talking and stared at him. He offered up a weak smile and said, "Dessert, anyone?"

7

Drayco stopped by the Opera House on his way back to the Lazy Crab. He couldn't wrap his head around the fact he wouldn't even own the thing if not for the bequest of one grateful client. And if it weren't for the generosity of *another* grateful client, he'd never have enough funds to restore it.

He knew crunch time neared to choose an official title other than "Cape Unity Opera House," but he'd struggled with this one aspect the most. He would prefer to name it after his mother, but everyone expected him to christen it after one or both of those clients. Or some other important person with historical ties to the area. That decision would just have to wait another day. Maybe he'd put it to a vote and wait for something like Opry McOperaHouse to win.

The building was still an architectural Frankenstein, but Drayco had grown to prefer it that way. Patterned shingles were now patched, and the weathered copper rosettes flanking the gables shone. The recently sandblasted orange brick walls and white stone highlights gleamed. New windows also replaced the dingy, cracked ones, and the front entry had a fresh coat of paint.

The aging Christmas wreaths, hung by contractor Troy Mehaffey, sported brown spots and falling needles. He'd have to contact Troy to take them down. It was Troy who came up with the perfect tagline for the building, but one Drayco couldn't use in any publicity materials: "The fading movie star who stumbles on the fountain of youth."

Drayco didn't want to spend much time there without Troy, so after checking on the latest lighting and sound gear installations, he headed to the Lazy Crab and discovered the other guests had departed. Once again, he was the sole customer and secretly glad. Social chit-chat and bland pleasantries weren't his favorite pastime—especially now, for some reason he didn't feel like psychoanalyzing into submission.

He'd no sooner ensconced himself in his peaceful oasis-of-a-bedroom when someone knocked on his door. When he got up to open it, Maida apologized. "Sorry to bother you, Scott, but there's someone downstairs to see you. It's Genna Ransford."

Despite wanting nothing more than to settle into bed and read a biography on composer Lili Boulanger he'd brought to Cape Unity, his curiosity got the better of him. He made his way down to the study, where Maida had left Genna. Maida's choice of room mystified Drayco until he remembered the more guest-worthy den had freshly shampooed rugs. He didn't mind, since the study was one of his favorite rooms with the largest fireplace, flanked by two imposing cast-iron lions.

Genna, dressed in yellow again, was standing when Drayco entered. He asked if she'd like to sit, but she declined and parked next to the lion on the left, fingering the sculpted mane. Without fanfare, she blurted out, "I want to hire you."

He perched on the edge of a leather club chair. "For what purpose?"

"To solve the puzzle behind that skeleton they found in the wall." With her combo New York-Eastern Shore accent, she drew the word out as wah-yull.

"The sheriff's office is amazingly capable, and they're looking into it—"

"I spoke with Sheriff Sailor. He told me they don't have the resources to follow up immediately. I got the feeling they were writing it off."

"I doubt that. But I'm curious—last time I chatted with you, you were worried about being a suspect. Since it now appears the victim died decades ago, why are you still interested?"

She paced in front of the fireplace and finally flopped onto the overstuffed sofa across from him. "I inherited the house from my late father. And my father inherited it from his father. So I'm pretty sure

Gramps was the homeowner when that skeleton was placed in the wall."

"Meaning your grandfather could have murdered the victim, depending upon the dating of the skeleton?"

Genna nodded vigorously, which made her headband slide forward. "I'm hoping the timeline doesn't work out. But if it does…"

She paused to push up the headband, and then clasped her hands together. "I can't bear thinking of Gramps as a killer. He wasn't a saint, but he was a good man. In fact, he was a former state senator and had powerful friends. Other lawyers, politicians, even a state Supreme Court justice."

Drayco didn't point out there were plenty of unethical politicians. Perhaps her grandfather was indeed a good man, or maybe his granddaughter saw him through rose-colored glasses. "We shouldn't get ahead of ourselves until we hear an official report from the medical examiner."

When she looked disappointed, he added, "But just in case, did your grandfather ever mention a young woman staying or working at his house? From Europe, possibly Spain?"

"Not that I recall. He loved to tell stories. So I think he would have mentioned such a person."

"And he didn't discuss it with your father, that you know?"

Genna shook her head.

She kept licking her lips, so Drayco asked if she needed anything to eat or drink, adding, "Maida's pies are legendary."

Genna's eyes lit up. "I love a good pecan pie and coffee." Her mix of pee-can and cawfee again marked her hybrid-state upbringing—South and North, all in one sentence. "But I'll take a rain check."

Drayco smiled. "When did your grandfather buy the house?"

"In his early twenties. It was right before World War II."

"Had he spent time overseas in the war? And if so, how did he have the money to purchase this house in the first place?"

"His father up and died from a heart attack and left him an inheritance. So he bought it with that. He was in college studying and hadn't been called up yet. If the war had waged on longer, he would have. And I might not be here today."

"Ah, I see." Thus was the roll-of-war dice. Drayco's father was born between wars and never the right age to serve. And even for those who did, it was a matter of which spot you occupied in a trench when a bomb hit that determined whether you came home alive or in a body bag.

He asked, "Are you certain there aren't hidden scandals in your grandfather's past? And if another person found out, could it be worth killing over?"

"No way. If I didn't have faith in him, I wouldn't be hiring you now." She fished in her purse, hopped up, and handed him a twenty-dollar bill before sitting down again. "Consider this a deposit. If it turns out the skeleton dates from before my grandfather bought the house, it'll be easy to refund that," and she pointed at the bill.

He laid the money on the side table next to his chair. "My rates aren't the highest, but neither are they inexpensive."

She chewed on her lip. "I realize that."

When she paused, he half-expected her to take the bill back after changing her mind. But she just pushed her headband up again. "I'm trying to turn things around with the movie-people money. We worked out a good contract. It should cover your fee."

"Turn things around?"

"I've had a bad go of it." She sank deeper into the sofa, which welcomed her into its chenille embrace. She had a habit of disappearing into furniture. "My father was an alcoholic and got chopped all the time. Abusive toward my mother, though he was hardly ever around, off gambling and drinking with his buddies. You could say we were estranged. Which is why I was stunned to find out he'd left the house to me."

"What about your mother?"

"My parents divorced fifteen years ago, and she moved to Alaska. Has a B&B, kind of like this one. Cold weather drives me plum crazy, and it's so far away and expensive to travel up there. I don't see her often."

"You don't have any siblings?"

"My brother Jim. Lives in Florida. My mother calls him a ne'er-do-well, but I thought he and Dad were real close. That's the impression I got from Jim."

Ah, the suck-ups of life who curried favor with a relative in hopes of an inheritance, only to be left out in the cold. Clan karma. One thing was certain; both Genna and her brother were too young to be involved in the skeleton's entombment. The grandfather, however…that depended upon the all-important timing.

He gently asked Genna, "Did your grandfather ever mention an odd odor in the house? It's hard to believe no one smelled the body decomposing." He didn't add, "Even with quicklime."

She frowned. "I vaguely recall my father saying how strange it was that Gramps liked to have flowers around. He said it was for my grandmother. But it was really Gramps's choice, not hers. She had allergies."

That wasn't damning, and Drayco didn't want to upset Genna unnecessarily. But it could be a sign her grandfather tried to cover up lingering aromatic evidence from the crime. Still, if Genna's father had remembered the flowers, he couldn't have been an infant, more likely of elementary school age. Any odor would be long gone by then.

Genna studied him and said, "I know what you're thinking. And I'm telling you, there is no way my grandfather was involved in this." She chewed on her lip as the seconds ticked by without her continuing.

He prompted her, "There's something else, isn't there?"

She replied with a half-apologetic expression, "Guess you'd find out. Gramps helped so many people, including this one fellow student during law school. The guy went on to be wildly successful. Told me he felt he owed his career to my grandfather. So much so, he wants to give a pile of money to the school to name a new building after Gramps."

"And if there's even a hint your grandfather was involved in a crime—"

"There goes the money. But it's more than that. Gramps is innocent. I know it in my soul." She pointed to the twenty. "And the minute you get any word about the timing, you call me."

"Will do. I'm eager to hear the results from the medical examiner myself."

Standing up, she added, "I have papers and effects handed down from Gramps. Would you want to see them?"

"If I take you on officially as a client, they might be helpful. But again, I must stress I can't guarantee a happy ending."

Genna smiled for the first time. "I understand, but I feel better already. I'll be able to let Gramps rest in peace. And he'll be immortalized as he deserves."

Drayco walked her to the door, and she waved as she headed to her car, which looked to be new. It must be electric from the lack of any noise it made as she drove off. A new electric car of that model wasn't cheap. Genna's motives for wanting to hire him sounded genuine, but she was also on track to receive money from that grateful friend of her grandfather—money that would dry up if her grandfather was outed as a murderer.

Not wanting to return to his room right away, Drayco craved one of Maida's potent nightcaps. The woman must have ESP, because he found her in the kitchen, where she added ice and a sprig of mint to a drink with a frightening color of blue and handed it to him.

"Maida, I need to hire you to be my personal bartender."

"You know what they say about bartenders. The best shoulders to cry on and the best ears to hear your troubles."

"Troubles? Can't say I'm having an excess of those."

"Oh? Couldn't tell by the look on your face."

"What look?"

"I've known you long enough to see when you're chewing on something bitter. And I don't mean the drink."

He peered out the window toward the garden, straining to see the pepperbush and other signs of Major Jepson's handiwork, illuminated by white fairy lights strung between a couple of trees. "Genna Ransford wants to hire me to prove her grandfather didn't kill our skeleton girl."

"That doesn't sound so bad."

"Successful cold case resolutions are rare."

"Surely she understands that."

Maida put a plate of homemade sesame crackers on the table, and he sat down and grabbed one. "I told her as much. And if I agree to take her on, I might have to investigate between my other cases."

"Unless you can solve it quickly." She studied his face. "That's not what's bothering you, though, is it?"

Drayco nibbled on a cracker until he choked on it and took a swig of the drink. Blue Curaçao, if he wasn't mistaken. More like Blue Courage. "There was this other cold case. At the start of my FBI career."

"I didn't know the FBI got involved with cold cases." Maida flopped onto a chair across from him and sipped from her own sapphire cocktail.

"They mostly consult with other law enforcement units. But the Bureau did create the Cold Case Initiative to investigate racially motivated cold cases. And there's the relatively new use of FGG."

At Maida's puzzled expression, he explained, "Forensic genetic genealogical DNA analysis and searching. But the case I'm referring to was used in our training. Another young woman, this one unidentified, had a similar story to Madalena's. She was found not in a wall but in the basement floor of an old house being torn down."

"Did anyone identify her? And did they know who killed her?"

"DNA on her body was uploaded to a database and eventually traced to a man arrested for a second murder who died in prison. But as far as identifying the victim, not to this day, no. Forensic techniques have improved in the fifteen-plus years since I was at the academy. But despite artist sketches and renderings, that Jane Doe is still a mystery."

"How many unsolved cold cases are there?"

"Hard to say. Lots of victims who go missing are unreported and never heard from again. But last I checked, hundreds of thousands of known cases existed in the U.S. alone. Globally, even more."

"I had no idea. You never hear that on the news." She put her drink down on the table and tsk'ed. "All those forgotten people."

He gazed out the window again to the garden. The fairy lights were like stars in a mini-cosmos. "I'm not sure why this FBI Jane Doe made such an impression. But she's haunted me, then and now." It hadn't helped that his hated former instructor of that Academy course mocked Drayco about wisdom-and-patience "bullshit," in his words. Focus on the action, not the emotional side that could affect your ability to do your job.

The instructor never talked to anyone like the mother Drayco vividly remembered, whose child had gone missing. That woman told Drayco she got herself hooked on narcotics and considered taking her own life. But she clung to the hope her daughter would one day return, and she wanted to be there for her. She'd pleaded with Drayco to help, but the case didn't fall under the Bureau's jurisdiction.

That case and that class changed Drayco's mind about becoming an agent. Until then, he wasn't sure he and the Bureau were a good fit, ready to call it off and pursue another career. But that Jane Doe and all the other victims in cases they studied called out to him. Maybe because his early life focused on giving a voice to composers long gone—to play the songs of the dead and keep them alive.

Maida hopped up to get a refill for his drink, and after placing it on the table, she put a hand on his shoulder. "You've got what my grandmother called a 'stirred soul.'"

"I've not heard that before. Is that good or bad?"

"Both. Stirred as in troubled. But also stirred as in the opposite of indifference."

"Sounds like an interesting woman, your grandmother."

Maida grinned and held up her drink glass. "Where do you think I learned to make these? My parents were both teetotalers."

"Then I'd definitely like to meet her."

"She died years ago. But I do have this image of her making cocktails for the Almighty and a host of angels."

Drayco lifted his glass. "A toast to your grandmother, then." And the image Drayco suddenly had of a choir of tipsy angels singing off-key gave him a good hard laugh for the first time in quite a while.

8

Tuesday, January 11

Despite Maida's attempts to cheer him up with alcohol and her characteristic humor, the next day dawned with Drayco feeling out of sorts. Again. He had two almost-clients, one in D.C. and one on the Eastern Shore, which meant he was between cases. Plus, his opera house contractor got called away on a family emergency, so Drayco was in limbo.

On the other hand, although the forensic analysis from the skeletal remains wasn't yet available, Drayco had the twenty-dollar bill Genna gave him as a retainer. It wouldn't hurt to check with his sympathetic contact at the National Archives, would it? Better than trying to cut through the bureaucracy he'd find at an embassy.

He called his contact first thing, hoping to get him early in the day before he got too involved with other projects. Working from the name and date from the paper found with the skeleton, the contact verified that a nineteen-year-old woman named Madalena Delfin Zamora emigrated to New York from Spain via a Compañía Transatlántica Española steamer in 1947. But no records for her beyond that.

Drayco then headed for another of his favorite sources, the locally infamous Cape Unity Historical Society, headquartered in a Victorian house even more immaculate than Genna Ransford's. A vintage painted-iron pedestal mailbox and new wicker rocking chairs on the porch joined newel posts and a pristine teal door with stained glass insets. More movie money?

Drayco entered, and right on cue, the bell above the door jangled, followed by cries of "Drayco sorry, Drayco sorry," and a loud squawk. Society Director Reece Wable, clad in golfer's plaid knickers and matching vest, squinted at the African gray parrot in its cage and wagged his finger.

Drayco pointed at the bird. "Andrew Jackson here needs new lines."

"I'm trying. He keeps picking up words of the four-letter variety. And I don't mean b-a-b-y."

As Drayco filled Reece in on what his National Archives contact passed along, he noted Reece stood in front of a WWII poster of a woman in uniform with the caption, "Are you a girl with a Star-Spangled Heart? Join the WAC now!" Somehow, that seemed appropriate for Madalena.

When Drayco finished sharing his news, Reece asked, "Was she Jewish and trying to escape from the Nazis?"

"Unknown. But since Spain played both sides during the war, leading to civil unrest, it's not hard to imagine someone wanting a respite from that. It also appears she was orphaned."

"Meaning few family members to wonder what happened to her."

"At least two fewer, her parents. It's unclear how she ended up on the Eastern Shore."

Reece opened a cabinet to get bird chow to put into a little bowl for the parrot. "Lots of rich vacationers had second homes. Did you know the train still made regular trips here during the war? Sent goods and services—and workers—all up and down the East Coast."

"She may have been lured here by an ad. Or by an agency hiring domestic help."

"I have files here with details on the railroad's history. Four trains a day traveled from New York to Cape Charles, can you imagine? But 1946 was the year of the big railroad strike across the country. Your Spanish girl arrived after that?"

"In early 1947."

"She got lucky with her timing. You said she emigrated from L'Escala, Spain, right?"

"Correct."

Reece whipped out his cellphone and tapped away for a minute. "Says here L'Escala was a smallish town back then. Has a festival dedicated to its famous anchovies." Reece made a face. "The Big Apple must have been frightening for a girl that age all alone. Perhaps she headed down with the rail lines until she got to a place more like home. Both towns are small, both on the coast, and both have fish. Well, maybe not the anchovies."

"Makes as much sense as anything else so far."

Reece motioned for Drayco to follow him to the reading room, where he had file folders on the table. Drayco smiled. "Not digitized yet, Reece?"

"Slowly, very slowly. But not these records." He picked up one of the folders.

"Which are?"

"The results of my research into your client's personal story from town archives. Prophett Properties built the house in 1930, and Genna's grandfather, Duff Ransford, bought it from the original owner in 1945. Duff was the one who arranged for the renovations, or so say the records."

"Which means it's likely Madalena was entombed in the wall after he bought the house. That's not good news for my client." Drayco leaned against a cabinet, taking pains to avoid the small HVAC diffuser pumping out air that smelled like almond biscotti.

"Didn't think you'd be turning somersaults."

"I assume the original 1930 owner is deceased?"

"Unless he's found Ponce de León's Fountain of Youth. Which, by the way, some folks say is on the Eastern Shore. If the guy were still alive, he'd be over a hundred." Reece went to a computer database on a nearby table and wagged his finger at Drayco. "See? Digital hocus pocus." After a few taps, he added, "Nope, no fountain of youth. That homeowner passed away three decades ago."

Another cold case dead end, not unexpected given the time frame. Drayco asked, "And Genna Ransford's grandfather, who bought the house from him, died of natural causes, I take it?"

"At age eighty-nine. So perhaps there is something to that fountain of youth legend. Anyhoo, the other parts of Genna's story check out. Duff Ransford's son, Bradley, inherited the house. The senior Ransford's wife was deceased by this point. And then Bradley Ransford died two years after inheriting the property and bequeathed it to your client."

"Genna told me her grandfather was a former Virginia state senator. I looked him up—no hints of inappropriate behavior toward young women. No bribery scandals. No scandals of any kind that were known."

"Ha-ha, I looked him up, too. Bit of a rogue in his youth, but the usual sorts of things. Grew up to move in powerful circles. Was friends with a man who's now a retired state Supreme Court justice."

"Genna mentioned that."

"It's known as the Supreme Court of Virginia now. But earlier, it was the Supreme Court of Appeals. One of the oldest active judicial bodies in the U.S., established in 1779."

"The state of Virginia was an original colony, so not surprising."

"I thought you'd be more impressed."

"Oh, I am." Drayco smiled briefly. "You mentioned Genna's grandfather and his powerful friends, but what about his son, Bradley? Genna said her father was abusive and hung out with people who weren't exactly Supreme Court justice types."

"I found nothing in newspapers—"

"Nor did I find anything via rap sheets. For him or any other members of Genna's family."

Reece tapped on the computer. "You didn't let me finish. The mainstream newspapers were no help, but I discovered an old regional gossip rag. Bradley Ransford was a wild young man. Worse than his father's youthful hijinks, too. What we used to call 'preacher's kid syndrome.'"

"You mean, where the children of preachers—or, in this case, respected political figures—are often hell-raisers?"

"I knew several as a lad. Though I take exception to the term hell-raiser. I found them fascinating."

Andrew Jackson squawked, "Hell. Damn."

Drayco grinned. "Yep, new lines, Reece."

Reece just glared at him.

"I'm guessing few members of Duff Ransford's circle of friends and colleagues are still alive? When you die at eighty-nine, you tend to outlive most people."

"*Au contraire*, my detective friend. There's at least one, that retired state Supreme Court justice, Talbott Josiah Clayburgh. Now that's a name for you."

"How old is he?"

"Ninety-two. Still going strong. In fact, I *might* have made an appointment to see him today. I don't suppose you'd want to tag along?"

"An appointment? As part of the case? That you arranged without asking me beforehand?" Drayco folded his arms across his chest.

"Nope. For my book. Well, books, to be exact."

"First of all, what book? Secondly, you said books, plural. More than one?"

Reece rubbed the back of his neck. "I've been planning a series of books on the history of the Eastern Shore of Virginia. Maryland and Delaware, too. I need to get original source material interviews before these older folks pass on. You up for a road trip?"

"Where does this Talbott Josiah Clayburgh live now?"

"Down in Cape Charles. Has a big house at the Chesapeake Resort & Golf Club. Likes to go golfing every single day." So that explained Reece's getup.

"At ninety-two?"

"Oh, he's allegedly in great shape. Ran marathons until recently."

"I'd love to meet him for that alone. But, on the off chance he has information on my client's grandfather and his house, I'm in."

"That's the spirit. And if you brought your classic Starfire, you're driving, my friend."

"It still has the bullet holes."

"Don't care. It's historic, I'm an historian. Saddle up."

9

Cape Charles lay at the southern end of the Delmarva, once the site of a train-ferry connection across the Chesapeake between the peninsula and the Tidewater area. Drayco never had the chance to see that unusual ferry in action before its decommissioning, and he regretted that.

The town of Cape Charles itself had grown up in recent years, now dotted with country club property and vacation homes. Just like Reece had said, they found the home of the former Virginia Supreme Court justice not far from the Chesapeake Resort and Golf Club, amid "Starter Castles," going up around the development.

Drayco noted the construction company name on a signboard and pointed to it. Reece said, "You thinking of buying a house here? The commute from D.C. can be a nightmare."

"I'd have to sell my townhome. I've grown attached to my little slice of Washington heaven."

"Only because there's so much crime up there to keep you employed."

Drayco ignored that crack. "Look at the name on that sign— Prophett Properties. The same company built the Ransford house where the skeleton was found."

Reece craned his neck to read it. "They must be successful if they've been around this long."

"Apparently." But it wasn't the company's continued success that interested Drayco. It was the fact they could be behind the renovations when Madalena was entombed. That said nothing about a motive, but construction workers would have had ample opportunity.

Talbott Clayburgh's mansion was not too far from the golf course, and true to the resort's name, the views showcased the bay and a tiny strip of beach. The breeze had a refreshing tang, probably because no self-respecting "privileged" beach would ever put up with any of that dead-fish smell. Here, it seemed like a plastic ocean air freshener straight from the store.

Around the side of the house, Drayco caught a glimpse of the backyard, which had a good-sized pool and a tennis court. The building itself was plantation-style with coral-colored fiber cement siding, three stories, and two wings. He and Reece parked in front and made their way along the brick entryway to the veranda.

Talbott Clayburgh himself opened the door and showed them into an airy living room with a fireplace bigger than the one in the Lazy Crab's study. No lions graced this fireplace, but hunting rifles hung above it, framing two large taxidermied heads of antlered bucks.

The man had a piercing stare, which Drayco figured he'd put to good use in his judicial days. Reece's briefing was on the money about how fit the ninety-two-year-old man was, appearing twenty years younger with a full head of hair and no hint of a halting gait. After they were seated, Drayco complimented him on his fitness.

Clayburgh replied, "My late wife made me eat vegan. But the secret is to never stop moving or your muscles congeal."

"You run marathons?"

"Until a year ago, when I broke my foot. Stupid accident. Tripped over a rake."

"You're in good company as a nonagenarian marathoner. Are you familiar with Harriette Thompson?" When Clayburgh shook his head, Drayco explained, "A concert pianist. But when she retired from that, she started running. And became the oldest female marathon runner at ninety-four."

Clayburgh chuckled. "Both of you look so astonished by that. And yet, I knew a man who ran marathons at age one hundred. His time wouldn't win the Boston or New York races, but he made it across the finish line."

Reece piped up, "You should be the one writing a book, Mr. Clayburgh. A 'how-to' about staying active into your nineties and beyond. A bona fide bestseller."

"Who knows? Maybe I will. I enjoy helping other people. Even if only in some small way."

"I doubt anyone would dub your career 'small.'" Reece pulled out a mini digital recorder. "Is it all right with you if I record our talk?"

Clayburgh pursed his lips. "I'm not certain. Call it my vanity. Or because of all those videos that wind up in strange places. I've been reading about that artificial intelligence stuff and fake videos using real people. Glad we didn't have that to deal with in my jurist days."

"I'll be happy to sign any legal documents you wish."

"And this other fellow?" Clayburgh looked at Drayco.

Reece maintained a deadpan expression as he replied, "My assistant on this project. He'll have to abide by those same legal documents."

"I had my own assistant look you up, Mr. Wable. You're a highly regarded historian and above reproach, near as we could tell. And I doubt you'd want to be the target of an expensive lawsuit. Go ahead with that audio device, if you must."

Reece pulled out his recorder and started by having the man recount his favorite cases. Clayburgh mentioned a few from his days as an attorney but was more hesitant when it came to the Supreme Court years. He was also quick to parrot what Reece had told Drayco about that body being one of the oldest continuously active judiciaries in the United States. "I was honored to be a member."

Reece said, "Your father was a powerful attorney before you. Was he your inspiration?"

Drayco looked around the room and noticed one framed painting of a stern figure on the wall. Clayburgh saw Drayco looking in that direction and said, "Yes, that's him there. A strict disciplinarian, the type that didn't think twice before pulling out a switch. Same with the Catholic nuns where I went to school. But his ways worked because I ended up on the right side of the legal divide."

Reece asked if Clayburgh's own children were following in his footsteps, and for the first time, Clayburgh had Reece turn off the recorder. When he was sure Reece had complied, he said, "My son and I are estranged and don't always see eye-to-eye. He suffered a wild youth."

Reece exchanged a quick glance with Drayco, who knew what he was thinking. The "preacher's kid syndrome" again.

Clayburgh continued, "He did turn his life around. I should reach out one day soon."

Reece said, "He was your only child?"

"Yes, that's right. His son, my grandson, is a chip off the old grandfatherly block. Has political aspirations of his own. Although I think he must fancy himself a Ronald Reagan type because of some acting gigs. He has one now in Cape Unity, as a matter of fact."

Drayco spoke up, "The *Fatal Fugue* movie?"

Clayburgh nodded. "I believe that's what he called it. An odd name."

"They're shooting it at the house of a former friend of yours, I understand. Duff Ransford."

"Is that so? Duffy Ransford, now that takes me back. We were great friends, Duffy and I. Thought he might make it to the state Supreme Court, too, but alas, it wasn't in the cards. He swore he didn't hold any hard feelings. But he still enjoyed beating me at golf. We also ran races together, and he also relished beating my times." Clayburgh uttered a hearty laugh.

Drayco asked, "How long had you been friends, sir?"

"Oh, quite a ways. We were law school chums."

"Do you remember when he bought that house in Cape Unity?"

"Yes, I do. Wasn't sure why he'd buy one there, but he liked the proximity to the Chesapeake and the Atlantic. Very much an outdoorsman, Duffy. Fishing, boating, and golfing, of course."

Drayco asked, "Did he ever mention hiring a young woman from Spain as a domestic worker?"

Clayburgh frowned. "What?"

"The movie crew shooting at his house accidentally opened a hole in a wall and discovered a skeleton entombed there. From papers found with the body, the sheriff's office determined she was nineteen and emigrated from Spain. Would have been a year after your friend bought the place, perhaps during the renovation."

Clayburgh was silent for a moment, deep in thought. Finally, he replied, "I had no idea. This is most disturbing news."

Drayco tried a different tack. "Can you recall anything suspicious concerning the house or Ransford's friends at the time?"

"That's an odd question to ask." Clayburgh stared at Drayco, who hastened to add, "Just looking at the historical angle here."

"Well, it was late in the war. I imagine there was PTSD and trauma from returning troops. Not that I want to cast aspersions on our heroic soldiers who helped save the world from a madman, but PTSD can do strange things to you. I was called up right as the war was ending, so I never saw active combat. But I knew men who did. They were never the same."

Clayburgh's face darkened, the veins on his neck standing out. "If you're thinking of accusing Duff Ransford of having something to do with a violent crime against that young woman and covering it up, you are sorely mistaken. He could be a hard-ass when he had to be, but he was also one of the most honorable men I've ever known. And I'd swear to that in a court of law." He gripped the armrests of his chair, and his hands were shaking. "I trust that's enough for your research, gentlemen."

Reece said soothingly, "Oh, but I was hoping to get your take on the Jarnagan decision. You're known for it, I believe. It helped change the course of environmental laws in the state." Clayburgh relaxed and nodded as Reece turned on the recorder again.

They continued the interview for half an hour before Clayburgh said he had another appointment. As he saw them to the door, he added, "I could compile a list of friends of Duffy's. Maybe you can talk to them, too, if any are still around. I have to admit I've lost touch. But I know they'll vouch for him."

After Drayco and Reece exited the house, Reece said, "That should set your mind at ease about Genna Ransford's grandfather."

"We'll see. But if Clayburgh follows through on that list—"

"I'll let you know. Natch."

Drayco looked up an address on his cellphone. "Funny how much better the cell service is down here. Money talks?"

"We'll get service that reliable in Cape Unity. In a century or so."

Drayco found the address he sought in seconds. "Looks like that construction company, Prophett Properties, has offices not too far away. Up to another side trip?"

"Lead the way, oh capable assistant."

10

On the drive out of the golf course and country club, Drayco took note of the homes in various stages of construction that snaked across the sandy soil, through the scrub pines and along the inlets. A few marshlands were filled in through the years, but dozens of ponds remained. They weren't all that far from Kiptopeke State Park, but he saw no signs of the migratory birds it was known for. Too early in the season?

The houses were cookie-cutter. The recipe was pretty basic—take one pinch of Colonial, add a few dollops of contemporary, and toss in a two-car garage. A couple of the projects were mostly complete and landscaped, including small trees wearing their winter-bare look.

A few blackish-red leaves still clung to the limbs of trees in one yard, and he pointed them out to Reece. "Goth trees?"

"Japanese maples. I think that's the Bloodgood variety. Perfect for your line of work."

Drayco continued to catch glimpses of the new houses as they drove by, which prompted Reece to say, "Nice homes, huh?"

Drayco just shook his head.

"You want one, but don't think you can afford it?"

"It's not that. It's all about the façades."

"Oh, so it's the architecture that isn't to your liking?"

"Figurative façades. In my experience, the nicer the homes are, the deeper the secrets they hide from the world. Grief, anger, sadness, violence, white-collar crime."

Reece wagged his finger. "You really are in a mood. You should binge-watch a bunch of horror movies. Get it out of your system."

Following Drayco's GPS directions, they pulled up beside a building that housed Prophett Properties, which was oddly vintage considering the company was in the business of creating new projects. The three-story brick structure resembled an old bank, with tall columns, expansive windows, and lofty dreams of becoming a palace when it grew up.

A secretary greeted them and looked puzzled when they explained the reason for their visit. She disappeared briefly and returned to usher them into the office of the CEO, Pamela Kye. With a heart-shaped face and a pixie cut, any casual observer might assume Kye was the secretary, not the older woman wearing a pinstriped jacket who'd ushered them in. But Kye's take-no-prisoners air hinted she often had to do battle against such stereotypes. Her dangling silver shark earrings sealed the deal.

Kye took a seat behind her massive L-shaped desk, which matched the other solid golden oak furniture in her office. All the pieces looked equally burly and ready for a furniture fight club. Kye asked, "Now, what is this all about?"

Drayco replied, "Has the Prince of Wales County Sheriff's Office been in touch with you?"

"Not that I'm aware. And my staff keeps me informed. So I ask again, what is this all about?" She spoke in honeyed tones, but her body language was like a bee ready to sting.

"Two days ago, a movie company filming scenes at a house up in Cape Unity discovered a skeleton entombed behind a wall. The house was built by Prophett Properties in 1930."

It almost felt like watching a computer program running through a list of non-incriminating replies, before she reacted with, "You say 1930? Not long after Prophett Properties was founded by my great uncle George Prophett, Sr., and his partner. Owned by the family ever since. We've always had an excellent reputation from day one."

"You specialize in subdivisions and new neighborhood development?"

"Primarily. Also commercial projects. We built the Gombert-Schlesser Convention Center." She had a proud gleam in her eye, but Drayco caught a blink-and-you'd-miss-it grimace from Reece.

"I don't suppose any other skeletons were found inside the walls of your houses?"

"Most assuredly not, this is a first. We're a reputable company. And if you're wondering if we cater to fetish requests like slave dungeons or anything along those lines, think no further. We don't. We have specific blueprints our clients can modify, but the basic scheme is mostly the same."

"Would you still have information regarding this specific Cape Unity house in your records? From its construction or later renovations?"

"I'm not sure." She hesitated. "I can't do a back-of-the-envelope calculation right here and now. And I'd rather not give out private details about financing and such willy-nilly."

"I'm sure I can make such a request official from the sheriff's office. Via a subpoena."

"If you return with a subpoena, we'll circle back on that, but I'm unclear how it would help. We do have blueprints, but from a project a century old? Maybe not." She hastened to add, "If you think anyone in our company had anything to do with this skeleton find, you're boiling the ocean."

"Any legal request would likely include personnel records from that era." Drayco fought the urge to parrot business-speak back at her. *Brain dump triage stat.*

She leaned forward, splaying her fingers out on the desktop. "We hire good people. Most of our problems come from outside threats."

"Such as?"

"People squatting in houses and trashing them, for one."

That wasn't a shock. Sheriff Sailor once mentioned a similar problem in his county, but Pamela Kye was a bit too hasty to absolve her entire company of secrets. Drayco asked, "How can you be so certain about previous employees, even ones who predated your tenure?"

"Despite family connections, I started out as a secretary and had to claw my way to the top as I would at any agency. I've seen it all and heard it all. But no reports of anything in the past."

"And nothing present?"

"The usual weirdo job applicants. Unqualified or with criminal records, like this guy right here." She grabbed a paper on the desk and waved it in the air. "This jackass did time for animal abuse. I can assure you we'd never hire someone that awful. And this other fellow kept harassing us for a job. Wouldn't take no for an answer."

"Did you call the police on the harassing wannabe employee?"

"No, but I swear I would have if he'd come by again." She wrinkled her nose. "Look, I know the job market can be tough. Especially around here. Maybe this insistent guy even had a sob story. I'm not entirely heartless."

She pressed a button on an intercom and called for her secretary, then said to Drayco and Reece, "I don't think I can help you gentleman any further. I'll look for that subpoena. If you manage to get one."

Before they left, Drayco pointed to Kye's earrings. "Fan of sharks?"

"I like to fish on my off days."

"Including sharks?"

"I prefer being the predator instead of the prey. Shows everyone who's boss." Kye gave Drayco a brief mocking smile.

After the secretary ushered Drayco and Reece outside, Reece said, "Hoo, that was a prickly pear. Hiding something much?"

"Or considering the legal side of things. Company reputations can live or die by scandals. Can't blame her for that."

Reece reached the Starfire first and leaned against it. "I'll bet she knows that an ancestral familial somebody or other was a miscreant. Even involved in your skeleton girl's demise?"

"But it's unlikely such a killer would casually announce his crime at a family Christmas party."

With a tilt of his head, Reece said, "Why, Scott Drayco. Are you turning into a contrarian?"

"I'm a card-carrying member."

Reece whipped out a microfiber cloth from his pocket to clean his monocle and squinted at Drayco with his good eye. "Yep. I see it. It's in those wrinkles on your forehead."

"What wrinkles?"

"You're thirty-eight. You won't know about wrinkles for decades. But I had you going for a minute, didn't I?"

Drayco ignored him. "So what was up with your reaction when Kye mentioned the Gombert-Schlesser Convention Center?"

"That monstrosity? We're lucky it's down in Virginia Beach and not around here. Locals refer to it as 'Gombert's…well, think of a certain male anatomical reference.'"

"Oh?"

"The design comprises a tall, thin tower in the middle and two shorter, rounder buildings on either side."

"I see. Architecture can be unintentionally, um, whimsical."

"Farcical is more like it."

Drayco winced. "Don't tell your parrot about this. But I sure hope the city got their money's worth. And that there are no skeletons buried within its walls."

Reece grinned. "I could make more sophomoric jokes. But I'll keep it clean and say, 'amen.'"

11

After dropping Reece off at the Historical Society in Cape Unity, Drayco made a quick stop by the Opera House to inspect acoustic panels delivered earlier. Troy Mehaffey, back from his not-too-serious family emergency, had signed for them but didn't have a chance to check the cartons. Drayco cut open the nearest one and held up a panel. Looked like what they'd ordered—after a delay of months.

Those panels were critical. The auditorium was a rectangular box, and the geometry could be problematic if proportions weren't just right. Poorly managed reflections could lead to a dead sonic space with little reverb. The slight slope of the floor and walls helped, as did the small balconies, but the acoustician recommended adding panels and clouds. Would it work? The renovation funds would only stretch so far.

Having zero experience running an arts venue—let alone overseeing its restoration while still holding down his crime consulting job—Drayco relied on picking good people to do the tasks and trusting them. He wasn't accustomed to that. Trust was something he didn't give out freely; it had to be earned.

As far as his new maybe-client was concerned, he'd have to trust the process and let the Medical Examiner's office do their thing whenever they got around to it. But he had to admit that a ringing endorsement from a former state Supreme Court justice on behalf of Genna Ransford's grandfather matched her own faith in the man.

When he reflected on his visit with Pamela Kye, the behavior of the Prophett Properties CEO was puzzling. As he'd told Reece, it was likely more about reputation. But Kye's family could also have figurative skeletons in their own closet.

Again, it could all be academic, depending upon the medical examiner's results regarding the timing. Sailor may even be right about a lack of evidence that murder was involved. Perhaps consensual BDSM was to blame, and someone panicked when it went too far.

Drayco paced around the stage, with its new subfloor topped with rift sawn red oak. It brightened up the place more than he'd expected. The blood stains on the old floorboards from his first introduction to the building were now gone, also a plus.

He'd even asked Troy to add a small orchestra pit in front of the stage, which was removed at some point in the building's history. It meant losing a few seats, but an opera house would have problems staging operas or musicals without one. The new flooring, new lighting, new seats, new carpeting—it all added up to a rebirth for the aging venue.

He patted a nearby wall. "What am I going to call you, old girl? Everyone needs a name."

Looking out over the hall, he imagined what it would look like filled with real people instead of "ghosts." Ghosts like the unfortunate man murdered on stage, but also the souls of those who once played here, worked here, or visited here—anyone who'd come to laugh or cry or listen to music, to be transported to another reality where art tries to make sense out of the senseless.

Maybe it was all the rumination about ghosts, but a sudden creaking noise caught Drayco's attention. Couldn't be the new floorboards, could it? Did they need more time to cure? To be safe, he took a quick tour of the back rooms to see if there was anything—or anyone—that shouldn't be there, but the place seemed to be empty. Just him and his ghosts.

As if by an unseen force, Drayco was drawn toward the storage closet where the piano lay hidden away. He rolled the instrument out and checked every inch of it, as he always did. It still gleamed from its recent refurbishment, was still in tune, and still alluring. There was no better invitation to transport himself to an alternate reality—Bach instead of bloodstains.

He sat down at the keyboard, rubbed his right arm for five minutes, and launched into Bach's Great Fugue in G minor BWV 542, as transcribed by Franz Liszt. Bach's fugues might not be "fatal," but they certainly felt fateful. Bach allegedly improvised this fugue based on a Dutch popular tune in only a half hour. Drayco happily settled into the piece, working through two countersubjects in all their contrapuntal glory until he reached the jubilant conclusion.

But try as he might, he couldn't push thoughts of Madalena out of his head. Was she invited to the Eastern Shore by someone she knew? Or was she lured here to escape the unrest and violence in her home country she'd tried to leave behind? He'd once visited the region of Spain where she was from and enjoyed its laughter, camaraderie, food, and music. Especially the music.

Drayco rubbed his troublesome right arm some more before launching into the Spanish Dance #2 by Enrique Granados. He soon got lost in the plaintive melody and the arabesque accompaniment, a nod to the Moors and Romani who lived in the southern region of Andalucía. When Granados composed this, did he have a premonition of his own tragic end, drowned when a German submarine torpedoed his ship during the First World War?

Drayco eased from the haunting opening Andante into the middle Lento Assai section in six-eight time, bringing out the secondary melody of eighth notes hiding among the sixteenths in the left. And he once again marveled at how much the melody held echoes of distant castanets. As the last notes of the final pianissimo chord died away, he closed his eyes. *That one was for you, Madalena.*

When he opened his eyes again, he jumped into high alert thanks to an unexpected sight—someone pressing their face against a small window next to the rear exit. Thanks to the darkness and lack of exterior lighting, Drayco couldn't tell who it was, so he hopped up and dashed to the door. But when he flung it open, his "visitor" had vanished.

He hurried outside to look around the building using his cellphone's flashlight. Cape Unity didn't have as much gang graffiti or vandalism as in the District, but it did happen. He breathed a sigh of relief that the Opera House's brick walls were untouched and the windows unbroken. So far, so good.

A quick scan of the parking lot showed his Starfire, which was safely there and also intact, but no other cars. He didn't see anyone running away, but with a few other buildings close enough to hide behind, Drayco's visitor could be long gone. Or still out there, watching him.

The new alarm system wasn't wired up yet, which meant Drayco's presence at the Opera House was good timing, preventing a break-in. Unless the mystery visitor had followed Drayco? But for what purpose? He had no active investigations of interest to anyone here. And by now, word had got around he wasn't some kind of billionaire investor who'd make a primo robbery target.

As Drayco started to head inside the building, he spied an object on the ground and grabbed it. A pocket Spanish dictionary. More Spanish-speaking people were living or working on the Eastern Shore than ever before, so, perhaps whoever dropped this wanted to communicate better with a friend or colleague? Yet the timing—with Drayco's musings about Madalena and playing the Granados—was a little unnerving.

He shook off the feeling. As Sheriff Sailor said, "Sometimes a coincidence is just a coincidence." But as the chilly night air seeped through his clothing, he shivered and made a mental note to have Troy Mehaffey bump up the alarm system and exterior lighting to the top of the priority list.

12

Another day, another trip to a movie set, part of his new routine. At breakfast, Maida Jepson said that as often as Drayco was showing up at the set, they should put him on the payroll. A film credit wasn't high on his bucket list. But they should at least acknowledge him as a consultant, since so many of the cast were asking him technical questions.

Drayco turned to Reece, standing nearby with Lucy Harston in the corner of the drawing room. "Okay, you said you had a reason for wanting me present today. I'm afraid to ask, but exactly *why* am I here?"

"They need a piano player for a scene. I recommended you."

Drayco groaned, "Reece, you know my arm—"

"But that's the beauty of movie magic. You can do multiple takes if someone flubs their lines. Or if a pianist's arm cramps up."

Assistant Director Chrystina Valentine saw him and hurried over. "I didn't know you played the piano."

Drayco glared at Reece. "A bit. And I didn't know you had a piano. I haven't seen it before now."

"A rental. The other piano guy we hired got the flu. But don't worry. It's a background shot during the party where the actors are milling around. You won't have to say anything."

"What music should I play?"

"Oh, I don't know. Festive. But not too festive. It can't cover up any lines. And it can't break any copyright. Has to be something we won't get sued over."

"Isn't that sort of thing added in post-production?"

"Our esteemed director said she wants more 'authenticity.' To be honest, I think she wants to save money."

Drayco smiled. "Because I'm cheap?"

Chrystina waved her hand in the air. "You'll get scale. I'll have you sign something later."

Reece was going to owe him big time for this. Drayco headed toward the piano with little enthusiasm. It was a Yamaha upright, and when he played a few notes, he relaxed to hear it mostly in tune. He mulled over Chrystina's stipulations—festive, but quietly festive? He racked his brain, trying to think of a piece that would fill both requirements and also be "legal."

One benefit of having an eidetic memory was never having a slip while playing, but he didn't want to start now. So he opted for one of his own recent compositions, a still-untitled gavotte. He was pretty sure he knew who held the rights to that one.

To his relief, he got through it without having to do any retakes on his part. Frazier Prentiss forgot a line, so they had to do the scene twice, but Drayco was just glad it wasn't his fault.

They took a break after that, and the actress doubling as makeup artist, Jaxine Gordon, sidled over to Drayco while he was still seated on the piano bench. "That was lovely. Haven't seen many types like you in this podunk town. The director didn't say she'd hired a stud."

Drayco did a double-take. "Um, I'm the lowly piano player. No lines, even."

"Only a couple hundred dollars, then. I could change all of that for you. If you get one line, it's a step-up of a thousand dollars. We could talk about it tonight after the shoot wraps for the day."

"I'll, uh, keep that in mind. Do you play the piano?" *Change of subject, commencing now.*

"Too hard. But I play the guitar. Grew up listening to Segovia records."

"They should have you perform in the scene instead."

"Oh, lord no. I play when no one else is looking. But I could make an exception for you."

Lucy must have witnessed his plight and hurried over to tell the woman that Chrystina wanted to see her in the kitchen. Jaxine rolled her eyes and said to Drayco as she walked away, "I'm staying at the Fairmont. Room 212."

When she was out of earshot, Drayco asked Lucy. "Chrystina didn't really ask to see Jaxine, did she?"

"Not as far as I know."

Drayco grinned. "Thanks for rescuing me."

Lucy huffed. "That woman has hit up all the men in the cast and crew. She's shameless."

"Thank god."

When Lucy gave him a sideways glance, he added, "I'm glad it's not just me."

Drayco saw Ashleigh Salinger waving at him, and he waved back. Lucy looked from her to Drayco and said, "If I were you, I'd worry more about that one."

"She's being polite."

"Uh-huh." Lucy shot him a skeptical look.

"Anyway, I'm sure everyone isn't solely being polite when they rave about your catering."

"Flatterer. I'll have to press you into service with deliveries someday soon."

"Be happy to help. Although my car needs work, including bullet holes and a faulty trunk latch. But it could still function as a delivery wagon."

Drayco asked Lucy how Virginia was doing, but a sudden loud *bang* from the backyard got their attention instead. It apparently wasn't in the script because cast members rushed outside, with Drayco close behind. In all the confusion, he almost tripped over Jaxine, Isaac Batey, and Sachio Spafford on his way out the door.

Rada Bluestone was already there and yelled in the same commanding voice she used to direct scenes, "What the hell is going on?"

Wisps of smoke and tendrils of orange flames shot up from a steel barrel twenty feet away. Drayco rushed toward it while keeping what he hoped was a safe distance. But he had to step back when showers of sparks spewed out in all directions, accompanied by popping and sizzling noises.

Rada marched up to him, dodging the sparks. "So what is it? We've used that barrel before, and this never happened."

Drayco held out his hand to keep her from getting closer. "It wouldn't, unless you'd put an explosive device inside. On first impression, I'd guess fireworks."

"We didn't order any pyrotechnics. What the hell?"

"Might be a teenage prank. I should probably contact the Sheriff's office and have them take a look, regardless."

"If you must." Her bristling tone dialed down a few notches as she added, "Is it safe to go back in and resume work?"

"I can't say for sure."

She groaned. "We cannot afford more delays." Her eyes pleaded with him, much like Chrystina Valentine had recently, as she said, "Do something."

Mindful of safety but also the town council piling pressure on Sheriff Sailor, Drayco replied, "Why don't I do a quick sweep? If it's clear, you should be fine." Maybe he was going out on a limb, but this wasn't his first brush with explosives after a decade with the FBI.

She thought about it. "Our attorneys won't be happy, but do it. And hurry. We can't go into golden time."

Drayco went from room to room in the house, looking for anything that could be an explosive device or more fireworks, but he came up empty. When he gave the news to Rada, she yelled, "All right, everyone. Back on set. Now."

Cast and crew shuffled back inside as Reece said, "That was fun. We needed the fresh air, anyway."

One by one, the actors rearranged themselves in their places for the next scene. Chrystina had a production log she was consulting, but stopped, looked around, and frowned. After disappearing briefly, she re-entered the living room and headed for Drayco. "Have you seen Ellery Smith, the actor playing the butler? I don't see him, and he's got a scene coming up." She grumbled, "I'll bet he's taking a nap. He likes to do that."

"I doubt anyone could have slept through that explosion."

"You're probably right. But I guess I should check the honeywagon."

As she started to head off, he grabbed her arm. "Honeywagon?"

"A mobile trailer. We keep it outside, out of view of exterior shots. Dressing rooms, a production room, and a bathroom for the crew. On a tight budget, we can't afford a trailer for everybody. Even with what's essentially a two-hander like ours."

"Two-hander?" Drayco really needed to get a Hollywood terminology dictionary.

"A movie with two main leads."

Drayco said, "I'd like to go with you to check this trailer. I haven't cleared it yet."

She agreed, and the sheriff-actor, Frazier Prentiss, said he wanted to go, too, since he'd left his "badge" in there. Drayco held them at bay as he went inside the trailer to give it a quick once-over.

A man in a white sweater sat with his back to Drayco, his head lying on a table as if sleeping. Drayco went up to him and tapped him on his shoulder. No reaction, so he gently pulled the man upright. It was the missing Ellery Smith—and it was pretty obvious why he was unresponsive. The handle of a large knife protruded from his chest, blood seeping down his sweater, which had soaked up most of the bleeding. His eyes were wide open and unblinking.

Drayco took Ellery's pulse but didn't find one. The man was dead, but for how long? He was still warm with no pallor or rigor mortis. The blood was free of clots, and the wound site bright red with recent bleeding—meaning the stabbing likely happened minutes ago, possibly during the explosion.

Ellery's hands were blood-free. If this was suicide, it was a magically neat one.

Chrystina and Frazier hadn't obeyed his stay-outside request and followed him in. Chrystina stopped cold when she saw Ellery, the knife, and the blood. "He's not supposed to film any scenes as the corpse today. Is this some kind of joke?" She added in an annoyed voice, "Ellery, this isn't funny."

Drayco shook his head. "I wish, but no. Not a joke. He's very much dead."

Chrystina's eyes widened. And then she screamed.

Frazier just stood there, staring at the dead man. "Oh, great. I don't want to be the one to give Rada the news. We're behind schedule as it is, thanks to that skeleton." The sheriff-actor then added in all seriousness, "Maybe I should go in there and tell everyone to stay put and not leave the set?"

Once again, Sheriff Sailor and his team combed over the movie set, only this time they concentrated on the new crime scene, the trailer. A deputy herded the cast and crew into the main living area of the Victorian house, allowing them to come and go under the watchful eye of another deputy.

Drayco noted most of the crew looked subdued, but they also appeared to take the murder in stride. Did no one mourn the loss of this victim, either? Or did being immersed in make-believe all day cause an actual murder to feel like more of the same?

Chrystina Valentine approached Drayco, smiling a little too brightly as she pulled out the familiar orange-vanilla lip gloss. "If this movie ever does get made, we're definitely going to have to press you into service." As if punctuating her words, she pressed her body closer to his as she touched up her lips.

That teensy bit of flirting was not normal behavior from her, and it was certainly a big change from screaming only an hour ago. Adding to the odd exchange, she said, "Sheriff Sailor's deputies questioned me, and it was so exciting. I'm writing a screenplay too and picking up all kinds of ideas."

"A crime drama?"

"It is now. I was going for more of a psychological relationship concept at first. But I think my new idea will work better. So tell me. Does the town have violence like this often?"

He was getting whiplash from her changes of subject. "Nothing this dramatic. But Cape Unity doesn't host many movie productions."

She put the gloss away and pulled out her cellphone, which she checked as she continued to chat with him. "When Rada Bluestone chose this location, I was baffled. But the sunrises on the marshes are pretty. And Chincoteague is like out of a sound stage. So quaint."

"Yes, I've always found the Eastern Shore to be picturesque." Drayco glanced out a side window where he could just catch the rear of the trailer and the swarm of deputies buzzing around it. At least, *mostly* picturesque.

He asked Chrystina, "Did you know Ellery Smith well? Or have any reason to suspect he'd be targeted for murder?"

"Murder? But wasn't it suicide?" She gaped at him and stopped checking her phone. "And no, I didn't know Ellery well. Pretty ordinary guy. Boring, even. But it's gotta be suicide, right?" She noticed one of the sheriff's deputies strolling through the hallway and grimaced. "I've got to visit the powder room. But we must get together. To discuss my script."

"Ah—"

He barely had time to react before she was gone in a flash, and another woman took her place. Drayco stifled a groan when he saw the same flirtatious woman from earlier, Jaxine Gordon, the actress and makeup-hair "guru." He looked for Lucy Harston to save the day again, but she and Reece had headed outside a while ago and were still AWOL. Flirting must be a stress reliever…or something.

Jaxine said to him, "Hey, if it isn't the piano guy."

Her eyes were also a little too bright and glassy—as in "recreational pharmaceutical" glassy. From the corner of Drayco's eye, he saw Sheriff Sailor quietly approaching them, listening in.

Drayco replied, "And you're the guitar girl."

Jaxine giggled and then asked, "I hadn't seen you filming before the piano scene today. Are you an actor?"

"Not by trade."

"What a shame. Because you have the right look and height."

Sailor spoke up in his grunting baritone voice, "Don't forget that whole synesthesia and photographic memory bit."

Her jaw dropped. "What—you mean you could read a script and have it down pat, just like that? Oh my gawd, you are so wasted. And sinth seeja? I saw that on a T.V. chat show. What happened? Did you hit your head?"

Drayco gamely held back a grin at her pronunciation of the term. "No, I was born with it."

"What's it like? Kinda weird, huh?"

"Hard to say, since I've never known differently."

"Come on, you've gotta give me a hint." Jaxine poked him in the arm. "What's it like?"

He chafed at that. It wasn't a conversation he wanted to have right then. "When I hear music and sounds, it's like a cloud filled with textures, colors, and shapes." Drayco deflected the topic away from him. "How close were you to the deceased, Ellery Smith?"

She shrugged. "He was an extra. Not many lines. Too bad about his suicide. But I do wonder what will happen to his cat."

"His cat?"

"He made friends with a feral cat on the set. I think he took it to his temp rental room. I thought it was kinda sweet."

When Jaxine saw Rada Bluestone barging over, she beat a hasty retreat. Bluestone had been pacing in and out of the house with a cellphone glued to her ear, but now she made a beeline for Drayco and Sailor. "Tell me the bottom line, Sheriff. I've got too much money riding on this. I need to know if we have to shut it down. Again."

Sailor gritted his teeth and replied, "Having everyone stick around for a few days would be helpful. And since the death happened in the trailer, we can tow that to the impound lot. As soon as my team is finished here, I don't see why you couldn't continue. Minus the trailer."

"You mean you want to keep all the suspects in one place? Is that it?"

"Did I mention the word suspects? We don't know yet if this was a suicide or not."

Rada folded her arms across her chest. "If it *is* murder, I hope you won't try to pin it on one of my crew. It could have been a local. I heard about a murder not long ago in Assateague. Where that lighthouse museum is."

"I assure you, I will overlook no one in our investigation. And I mean anyone." Sailor looked pointedly at Rada.

Nelia Tyler popped her head through the front door and motioned to Sailor, who looked relieved for the excuse to take his leave. But he added, "Oh, and we're taking away that barrel with the explosive remnants. Don't be surprised when it's gone."

As she watched him go, Rada told Drayco, "I suppose that crack about not overlooking anyone includes me."

"He'll be thorough, but fair."

"I hope you're right."

Drayco asked, "I'm curious. Why did you pick this area for your project?"

"The production coordinator, Chrystina, does all that."

"She said it was largely your idea."

A brief look of annoyance passed across Rada's face. "I have the final say so. But I had family ties here, and I guess she thought it would be a good choice."

"Family ties? Anyone I might know?"

"Oh, I doubt it. My father, a war hero. Derrell Bluestone." She gritted her teeth. "This area has turned out to be a bad choice for a movie shoot. I didn't believe it when the crew said this production was cursed. They may make a believer out of me yet."

Drayco's ears perked up at the mention of her father. "War hero, as in the Second World War? Did your father know Duff Ransford, Genna's grandfather, by any chance?"

"Possibly. I mean, if he lived in the area, right?" Her cellphone rang, and she hastened outside the house to take the call, although he heard snippets of her half of the conversation as she disappeared. "Shut it down? I don't think so. Look, give me more time, Sid. We're over halfway through shooting."

Ellery Smith was a fading memory. And the body was barely cold.

Drayco surveyed the few personnel left in the living room after most had wandered outside with the deputy's blessing. One in particular caught his attention, the young man who was friendly with Ellery on the first day Drayco visited the set. Reece and Lucy had filled him in on the various crew, and he'd learned this fellow was none other than Trent Josiah Clayburgh, the grandson of retired Justice Talbott Clayburgh.

Drayco approached Trent and said, "I'm sorry about your colleague. This must be quite a blow."

Trent stuffed the rest of a half-eaten chocolate bar in his pocket. "Too much like a movie plot, isn't it? I expect Ellery to bound in at any moment. Rada will yell, 'Cut,' and we'll find out it was all part of the story. Otherwise, I can't make sense of this."

"Was Ellery depressed or anxious? Or did you hear anyone threaten him?"

"Nah, he was the life of the party. And threaten? Nobody other than Chrystina making sure he didn't forget his lines. He only had a couple, but she feared he'd blow it."

"So you have no idea why Ellery was targeted?"

"Targeted? Wasn't this a suicide?"

"That remains to be seen."

"I didn't know him that well. But I considered him as much of a friend as anyone else in this production. I think I heard rumors of drugs. Maybe it was that?"

Considering Jaxine's glassy eyes, Drayco thought it a good bet. "You mean the victim did drugs himself? Or dealt drugs?"

"I didn't see it. But it's a big thing in Hollywood. I'm not much interested, myself. Except for alcohol. As in, I could use a nice, stiff drink right now."

Drayco motioned for Trent to take a few steps back as a deputy sailed past, almost knocking them over. Drayco said, "By the way, I spoke with your grandfather the other day."

"You spoke with Dad-Dad? Why?"

"A colleague of mine is writing a history book on the Eastern Shore and wanted to interview him."

Trent's cheeks dimpled. "That makes perfect sense."

"He said you have political aspirations, yourself."

"I want to serve the public like he did. He's not only my grandfather, he's an inspiration."

The same deputy breezed past again, going in the other direction, making Drayco step back this time. "I would say it's a big leap from acting to politics, but as your grandfather pointed out, there's precedent for it."

"Reagan, right?" And Trent launched into a spot-on impression of the former president, "Politics is like show business. You have a hell of an opening, you coast for a while, you have a hell of a closing."

Drayco smiled. "Pretty good."

"Not that I'll follow his acting blueprint. But acting's a good stepping stone. Everything is video this and video that nowadays. If you want to be an influencer and make a name for yourself, it's all about the video. I've got channels on all the platforms."

"You'll have to become a governor if you want to emulate Reagan. And switch parties."

"Reagan did do that, didn't he? I'm an independent, but I'm thinking of bringing back the Whig party." Trent grinned.

"Did your friend have similar aspirations about politics or videos?" Drayco really needed to check out those video channels.

"Ellery?" Trent puckered his forehead. "I don't think so. We were two like minds, though. A couple of extras trying to have fun, make connections."

"If you think of anything else, I'm sure Sheriff Sailor would like to know."

"I've got my 'interview' coming up soon. They're working around to everybody." Trent looked toward the doorway, where Nelia Tyler waved him over. "And there it is. My number's been called. Wish it was for grilled hamburgers and not another kind of grilling."

Drayco prowled around the living room, examining the furniture, props, and every piece of technical gear to match them to his memory of their status before the explosion and Ellery's death. But it also made it easier for him to eavesdrop on conversations.

A couple of people discussed the murder, but surprisingly few. Mostly meet-ups, the best bars in the area, swapping war stories from other productions, comparing agents and directors. Apparently, Rada

Bluestone wasn't the most popular among the latter but generally respected.

The Nelia-deputy actress, Ashleigh Salinger, bumped into Drayco as he headed outside again to get fresh air. He apologized and added, "I expected to see you hanging around with Frazier Prentiss."

"Oh, so you thought it would be like other movies where the stars hook up both on camera and off?"

"More like strength in numbers."

"As I said, he's gone too much into character and acts like I'm really his deputy. It's driving me insane. Plus, Frazier's not the brightest bulb. Anyway, I think he's more interested in spending time with Nancy."

"Nancy?"

She pointed at a young woman chatting with Prentiss, who had his customary bottle of sparkling water in hand. He recognized the woman as the "Nancy" who'd befriended Virginia Harston. Ashleigh grabbed Drayco's arm and pulled him toward a yellow Porsche in the parking lot. He asked, "This yours?"

"A rental. Like it?"

"It's quite…yellow."

"Yellow like sunshine or yellow as in lemon?" She smiled. "I mean, it's better than other rentals I've seen. Like Frazier's ugly green model, or Trent's car that's red inside and out, or even Rada's black car that looks like a hearse."

She punched his arm lightly. "I'm sure you have this murder all figured out. The whodunit and whydunit and all that other stuff."

"These things don't wrap up as neatly as on television or in the movies. Certainly not in a couple of hours."

"Then it's like a mini-series."

That made him laugh despite the seriousness of the situation. "How did you find out about this job with the production?"

"My agent. Sounded like it would be fun."

He asked her the same question he'd put to Trent about knowing the victim, and she replied, "I never met him outside of the lot, other than group hangouts at a bar. He struck me as an odd duck."

"Odd? How so?"

"Out of place. Uncomfortable, even. Didn't naturally socialize with anyone."

"Trent Clayburgh said Ellery was the life of the party."

"When he was drunk. But who isn't in that state?"

"I understand. Something else may come to you later. And if it does—"

"I'll give you a call." She pulled out a business card from her pocket. "Got a pen?"

He handed one to her, and she wrote a number on the card. "You can phone me any time. I mean, in case you have any more questions. Or anything else."

She truly did remind him of Nelia, which made his pulse race more than it should. But according to Nelia, the likeness was by design—complete with the blonde dye and braided hairstyle.

As Ashleigh headed off in search of Rada, Drayco had a moment of sympathy for Sheriff Sailor's position. Any murder case was taxing enough without headaches from a Hollywood production. Add in the community with their hands out for Hollywood cash and the town council putting Sailor in a vise, and Drayco wouldn't be shocked if the lawman wasn't thinking about a career change.

If Trent Clayburgh was right and drugs were involved with Ellery's death, then it might be a straightforward case, quickly solved. But why would drug dealers go to all the trouble to stage an explosive distraction and kill Ellery in the trailer? Unless said dealers hoped to implicate the Hollywood crew. And why not? Everyone else in the area seemed drawn to the production in one way or another. It stood to reason criminals would, too.

With twilight an hour away, the sheriff's team would soon finish the exterior work and stay long after dark to search the rest of the building and trailer. Since they had their hands full, Drayco had promised to be at Sailor's office in the morning to give a more detailed report. Not that he'd have much to add.

Maybe the house wasn't cursed, but it had experienced two violent deaths on the property. It would be a stretch to think those deaths were related, yet Drayco couldn't shake off one oddity. Why was Ellery Smith so keenly interested in the skeletal find when everyone else appeared more bothered than anything?

Was it merely to entertain his law enforcement family? Or was he part of the "everything is video these days" that Trent mentioned? Perhaps Ellery even had his own channel, seeing as how he'd taken an assortment of cellphone photos and videos.

Trent and Drayco could agree on one thing, though. Drayco also had a sudden craving for a nice, stiff drink.

14

The following day, Drayco caught Sheriff Sailor between meetings with his staff, the mayor, and town council members. For once, Sailor looked happy to see him. To sweeten the deal, Drayco had brought two freshly made pies from Maida Jepson, which he handed over, adding, "To feed your addiction."

Sailor put the boxes on his desk and peered inside. "Pecan and apple?"

"Chocolate pecan and Dutch apple with oatmeal streusel."

Sailor opened one to take a sniff and said, "Haven't had a homemade Maida pie in months."

When Drayco dropped a folder on Sailor's desk, the sheriff asked, "Your report?"

"Thought you might appreciate one in Sarg Sargosian-style, complete with bullet points."

Sailor cracked a smile at that. "How's Sarg doing? I promised him a fishing trip."

"I had a feeling if the two of you ever met up, you'd hit it off. Makes a guy feel unwanted."

"Your former FBI partner only has eyes for you, I swear."

Drayco faked a scowl as he eased his tall frame into his favorite swivel chair, noting it could use a nice, fat cushion. "Were you up all night? You kinda look like it."

"Thanks a lot. But no. That is to say, I wasn't. The rest of my crew left the movie set around four this morning."

That's why Drayco hadn't seen Nelia Tyler yet. She was likely among the last to leave the scene and probably one of the sleep-deprived. "Have you been able to determine if it was suicide or not?"

"Tyler did a preliminary test of the weapon used. And let's just say if someone wanted it to look like suicide, they botched the job. No fingerprints on that knife whatsoever. And the victim wasn't wearing gloves."

"This 'someone' may have planned on putting Ellery's hand on the weapon but got spooked first."

"It's one possibility."

Drayco nodded. "Murder, it is. I don't suppose you found any gloves the killer was wearing lying around?"

"Nope. But we'll search nearby trash cans and dumpsters."

"Too bad. Might be able to lift prints off those gloves. Uncovered any motives?"

"Nobody in the crew knew him well. Zero complaints about him to our office, no rap sheet. He was described as boring, quiet, and ordinary."

"Did the victim have a large estate worth killing over?"

"Can't tell yet. Found a birth certificate in state records. His mother, Elleana Beatrice Smith, died thirty-five years ago. No father listed, just 'unknown.'"

"Unknown?"

"Yeah, I know. Lots of problems with that. But we're on it."

Drayco frowned. "That's odd. The guy told me he had family members in law enforcement."

"For real? We'll check on that, too. But a friend of his mother's and her husband raised him, and they weren't cops. Both are now deceased. Natural causes."

"What about his personal effects? Any clues there?"

"The victim, Mark William Smith—now there's a normal name for you, the only one among the movie set—was staying at a local motel. Paying by the week."

"A 'normal' name, says the man called Ernest Hemingway Sailor? Besides, the victim went by the moniker of Ellery."

"His legal name, according to movie payroll records, is definitely Mark William. Ellery must be a nickname."

"Or a stage name, as he indicated to me."

"We'll check for name changes in the records." Sailor pulled a smallish cardboard box from behind his chair and laid it on the desk. "This is everything that was in his room, except for his clothing."

Drayco got up briefly to open the lid and look inside. "Rather spartan."

"No signs of any large bank accounts. But you know the drill. It's all preliminary."

"I don't see a cat in this box."

"Cat? Oh, you mean the mongrel in his hotel room. One of my deputies took it home with her. At least the cat isn't giving me any grief."

Since Sailor didn't mention the deputy by name, Drayco assumed it wasn't Nelia Tyler. But he was happy to hear the cat's fate, making him wonder how his own half-feral "mongrel" at his D.C. townhome was doing.

He said, "I wasn't kidding about you looking exhausted, Sheriff. I should have brought you a quad espresso. Or Manhattan Special sodas."

Sailor shrugged. "Comes with the territory."

"What does, staying up all night or pissing people off?"

"In this job, I'm always pissing people off. I have to juggle all the various actors—pardon the pun—and manage to keep the peace. Guess that's why they used to call us peace officers."

Drayco made a note to buy Sailor a case of Manhattan Specials *and* a four-leaf clover and deliver them later. "Did you mean it when you told Rada Bluestone the production can resume?"

"The last of my crew are over there wrapping things up as we speak. Plus, we had the trailer towed to our impound lot. So, no, I don't see any reason the production can't continue, which is why I told the director as such. I think she's starting back up tomorrow."

"Good news for the town's coffers. Did you find anything in the trailer?"

"We've begun the analysis, but every person working on the show was in there at one point. And it's a mess. The only blood was on the victim."

Drayco added, "And no defensive wounds that I saw."

"Likely too shocked to act quickly, or it was someone he knew."

"What about that conveniently timed explosion?"

"Are we tracing the components and materials used, you mean? What do you think?"

Drayco leaned forward. "Naturally, you're on top of it. So why wasn't the victim at the explosion, too? Unless he was meeting someone in the trailer and that person took advantage of the confusion. Or triggered the explosion themselves as a distraction."

Sailor glanced at Drayco's bullet-pointed report. "You notice anybody missing from the crowd when that explosion went off and everybody rushed outside?"

Drayco gestured at the report. "It's in there. I was busy making sure the fire didn't spread, but I bumped into a few of the crew on their way out of the building. When most people saw it wasn't too big a deal, they drifted back inside."

Sailor scratched his chin. "Huh. Well, any of them could have an accomplice."

"That would take coordination." Drayco studied the small cardboard box. It contained a paltry amount of belongings. Was Ellery Smith broke or an anti-hoarder? If he was close to broke, he wouldn't get wealthy on the pittance the tiny movie role would bring. So why take the job at all?

Sailor's office wasn't its usual starched, pristine, obsessively neat sheriff-y sanctum, with large piles of paper making it harder for Drayco to spy an object he'd hoped to see. So he asked point-blank, "Have you had a look at the movie script? I've only observed bits and pieces of the action. As Reece summed it up, there's a party, a murder happens, and no one can leave the premises."

"About that..." Sailor pushed a pencil around on his desk.

"A script that came to life?"

"More than I'm comfortable with. The party in that plot is a wrap party following a play's run. And the movie victim—played by our real victim—was also stabbed."

"Sounds like you get to have a nice chat with the screenwriter, in addition to those Hollywood stars. Lucky you, Sheriff."

Sailor picked up a paper airplane and launched it at him. "Right. Lucky. On to a different subject, you'll be happy to know we got a break in the forensic angle with the skeleton."

Drayco sat up straighter. "I'm all ears."

"The M.E. handed off the examination to a staffer working on finishing her PhD. Specializes in older remains using the latest tech toys."

"So that's why it got expedited."

"Yeah, this staffer probably wants to include the case in her dissertation."

"What did this doctorate-wannabe find?"

"I'm getting to it. The remains date from the same timeframe as that paper and the clothing remnants found with the body." Sailor tapped a printout on his desk. "The staffer even got viable DNA. We can try to match it with any family members."

"Anything on cause of death?"

"The giant gaping hole in the skull was a giant clue. Likely bludgeoned to death. Or almost."

"Almost?"

"It's impossible to tell at this point if the victim was still alive when walled in. But if so, she wouldn't have lasted long."

Drayco sucked air through his teeth. The image of the young woman being walled up, while potentially still alive, made his blood boil. "This kinda rules out any might-be-an-accident theory."

"True, but it doesn't get us far. The owner of the house and pretty much anyone he would have known are all dead. This is one cold case that's positively Arctic."

"The place had renovations around the time the skeleton was put inside the wall. Could have been a member of the construction crew."

"Same problem. Most likely, they're deceased."

"Have you subpoenaed the employee records of the real estate company Prophett Properties?"

"You kidding? We have a contemporary murder to work on, which is more pressing. Plus all those other various cases I mentioned earlier." But with one look at Drayco's raised eyebrow, he added, "Okay, I'll put a deputy on it. But don't expect fast results. Or miracles." He pushed a pencil around on the desk. "There was one other thing about our skeletal victim."

Drayco raised the other eyebrow. "And that is?"

"There were signs she'd given birth."

"What signs?"

Sailor looked at the printout again. "Dorsal pitting, grooves, and scarring on the inside surface of the pubic bones. The M.E. acknowledges that's a controversial sign. Still, her office also discovered calcium, magnesium, and phosphorus concentrations were lower in the bones."

"But no fetal remains found?"

"None."

Drayco leaned back. "This is the point where I should tell you the current homeowner wants to hire me to exonerate her grandfather—if the timeframe of the victim's death matched the years he owned the house."

"Figured that was why you were so interested. Other than your criminal curiosity. Also figured your Bureau days could come in handy on something like this. One reason I'm cutting you some slack here."

"You said the M.E. staffer extracted viable DNA?"

Sailor poked the top paper in a stack on his desk. "We're working with the Spanish Embassy to find matches for any living family overseas. We found one dead relative on this side of the Pond."

Drayco stopped himself from snatching the paper, even though he desperately wanted to see it. "If you found a name that fast, it was in a criminal database. Let me guess, the missing baby?"

"The DNA sample from his CODIS file indicates it was *likely* the skeleton girl's son. He'd be the right age. Fellow by the name of Pauley Harrington."

"What was his crime?"

"Suspected arson. That's the charge he was arrested for in Capps County. Got off on a technicality. A break in the statutory timeline thanks to a paperwork error." Sailor's disgusted expression was enough to scare a honey badger.

"No other criminal relative matches?"

"Nope. Nor did this son have heirs. Or no *official* record of a partner or kids."

"Someone must have adopted him. Or else he grew up in an orphanage or with foster families."

"I had a deputy look into that this morning. No records so far there, either."

Drayco looked at the ceiling. It had a new fan with wooden blades in a scimitar curve that looked like they flew off a 1920s Fokker airplane. "Two murder cases on the same property decades apart. A little unusual."

"Those cases aren't linked."

"How can you be so sure?"

"Because I don't want them to be linked."

Drayco scowled at him for real. "Seriously?"

"Okay, that part is true, if I'm honest. But the actual reason is the time gap. This is one of those coincidences we talked about. Where it really is just that."

"Still, my research may stray into your investigative waters. I promise not to get in your way. Too much."

"And if you do—"

"I'll share what I find."

"Good luck with that. I suspect my original suspicions about a drug-crime connection to Smith's case will be borne out. The Eastern Shore Task Force is working the local drug cases. Heroin or fake heroin that's fentanyl or something else." Sailor grabbed an evidence bag. "We found these in the victim's coat pocket."

"Looks like pills."

"An analysis will tell us what kind. But they sure don't look like aspirin."

"Don't you think it's odd for drug dealers to create a distraction and kill their victim in such a public place?"

Sailor grumbled, "Semantics." Then he peered at Drayco and added, "Still, if you overhear anything along those lines, I want to know."

"And you will."

The sheriff sprawled in his chair, causing an extra-loud squeak. "You'd better. The damned movie cast and crew are being evasive."

"Evasive? How so?"

"The grunts are easy to talk to. The lead actors and the director are much harder. I wrangled interviews with the actors as long as the production attorney was on hand. The guy playing the movie sheriff actually tried to give me pointers."

Drayco stifled a grin. "And the director?"

"Rada Bluestone is playing hard to get. Production attorney notwithstanding."

"Wonder why?"

"Her husband is a legal beagle in La-La Land. Bluestone is making us contact her through her agent, Zenon Graddick." Sailor scoffed, "Such a preposterous name. Like out of a bad script."

This time, Drayco couldn't hold back a laugh. "Anything of interest from the grunts?"

"They didn't hear or suspect a thing. It was all rainbows and sunshine."

"No unicorns?"

Sailor launched another paper airplane at him. "Stick to your promise and don't add too much else to my plate if you can manage it, Drayco. It's already slopping over."

When the sheriff got a quick phone call, Drayco picked up his cellphone and snapped Sailor's picture.

Sailor ended his conversation and said, "What was that for?"

"I've always wanted to say I shot the sheriff."

A female voice added through the open doorway, "But you didn't shoot the deputy," and a familiar blonde head poked into the room.

As usual, Drayco's pulse raced at the sight of Nelia. But also as usual, he put a lid on unprofessional feelings. Not that he had the chance to talk to her about anything, when she gave them a little wave and popped out again.

After Drayco left Sailor's office, he started to head outside the building but stopped, backtracked, and sought out Nelia in her lab. Her expression was neutral-professional. Every bit as neutral-professional as he hoped his own expression looked to her.

He asked, "Would you be able to do a forensic reconstruction of the skeleton girl as she'd have looked while alive?"

"How would that help with such a cold case?"

"It might not. But I want to bring her back to life. Give her more of a voice in obtaining justice."

Nelia's expression softened. "My job-share, Regina Reymann, is an artist and studying up on such techniques. She'll welcome the excuse to work on a real project."

Drayco thanked her, Nelia gave him a small smile, and that was that. *See? They could do professional.* He didn't ask her about her divorce, or any new beaux, or even her upcoming law school term. That one night of passion they'd shared felt like a lifetime ago. In some ways, it was.

When Drayco was back outside in his Starfire, he made a quick call to Genna Ransford to fill her in on the findings from the medical examiner's office. Genna replied, "Then you have me as a new client. And just in case, I dug up those personal files of my grandfather's."

He said he'd drop by, but she suggested he meet her at a place called the Archery Annex. He was curious about the choice of venue but agreed.

Poor Sheriff Sailor. Dealing with Hollywood "celebrities" through agents and attorneys would be as fun as wrestling a boa constrictor. Maybe the director was simply using cover-your-ass tactics to protect herself. Understandable that, given her power-attorney husband.

He'd looked up Rada Bluestone. She was born in the '60s, allegedly on the Eastern Shore, according to her bio. Yet, she got the details wrong about the murder news story she'd referred to and other basic info she should have known. Assateague wasn't a town per se but a national seashore park. And the Assateague Lighthouse wasn't a museum. They allow tourists to climb up the winding stairs inside to the deck supporting the former light, but that was it.

She was also hesitant when he asked whether her World War II hero-father knew Genna Ransford's grandfather. If he did, and if it coincided with the timing of Madalena Zamora's death, then that was very interesting.

Rada was never without that odd necklace of hers. Drayco had looked it up out of curiosity. It was a Celtic Wheel of Being symbol, a "five-fold symbol," with four circles forming a diamond and the fifth circle in the center. The outer circles symbolized the seasons, and the fifth represented their unity. Druids believed striking the perfect balance between all opposing things was the true mark of power.

There were all kinds of balance. A physical balance, a work-life balance, a balanced diet. If riding a bike counted, Drayco had managed the first, and he was working on the second. The third, he'd just as soon avoid at all costs. Besides, "balance" seemed like a myth. Was there ever any true balance? None long-lasting, anyway.

Lives, truths, and universes smashed together, tore apart, and danced around each other in what was ultimately a fatal fugue of the cosmos. But if Drayco could somehow bring balance to one brief moment in time and space by finding justice for one lost soul, he'd still take that chance. And if doing so meant keeping his own life off-balance, so be it.

15

Haffey's Auto Body Repair Shop looked the same as when Drayco was last there two years ago. Car parts lay in piles alongside battered vehicles in various stages of transformation. He found Barry Farland in a large maintenance bay bent over the hood of a Chevy.

Barry looked up as Drayco approached, and with a broad smile, he asked, "Didja bring it?"

"She's sitting outside," Drayco pointed toward the gravel lot.

"Ever since I saw that car, I've wanted to get my hands on it. I didn't think it would be on account of bullet holes."

"Just a few."

"If the gunfire cut through the frame, or damaged wiring, or hydraulic lines, or suspension components, we'd need to fix that first."

"I took it to a mechanic afterward. He said it was mild damage to sheet metal in the doors and not structural."

"Let's go take a look." Barry hurried out the door, not waiting to see if Drayco followed behind.

When Drayco pointed out the damage, Barry ran his fingers along the holes. "This is one sturdy land yacht. But we need to fix these before rust sets in. Could make it much worse."

Observing all the various other cars in the lot, Drayco said, "You look swamped. I hate to impose."

"Mr. Haffey lets me work on whatever I want. Guess he trusts my judgment."

"As well he should. So, how long do you think repairs will take?"

"Not too long. We have this new body filler reinforced with short fiberglass. Makes it easy." Barry laughed. "I don't let the customers know how easy, or they'd do the work themselves. Kinda like a paint-by-the-numbers kit."

"Will it need an all-over paint job to match things up?"

"These holes here are lower down. Not as visible. Plus, we have this new computer doohickey, a portable unit. Uses a laser to scan the paint and create an exact match. Works pretty well. Think I can blend it so you may not even notice. Unless you look real close."

"Then I shall leave it in your capable hands. I have another question for you, unrelated to the car. I'm told you and Virginia got the opportunity to be on the movie set thanks to a friend hired on the crew?"

"Zach. I've known him since high school. He's a gofer and helps with movie grunt work when needed. He owed me a favor, and Ginnie's interested in drama stuff. So it was a way to tie it all up in a neat bow."

"Did you or Zach get to know Ellery Smith at all?"

Barry rubbed his nose, which spread grease from his hand onto his face. It wasn't the first time Drayco witnessed the younger man doing that. When he handed the young man a handkerchief, Barry grinned. "Should change my name legally to Grease Monkey."

After wiping his nose and hand, he looked at the now-greasy handkerchief, unsure what to do. Drayco held out his palm. "Maida's got an industrial-strength washing machine."

"Oh, you're right," Barry replied, returning the handkerchief to Drayco. "And as far as Ellery was concerned, he kinda kept to himself. Didn't talk much."

"So you didn't hear him say anything odd?"

"Not that I recall." Barry started to rub his nose again, but stopped himself. "Okay, one thing, but it wasn't something I heard, it was something I saw. I stayed late to help Zach load in a prop sofa. Most folks had left for the day, but Ellery was still there."

"Doing what?"

"Walking around outside."

"That doesn't sound too strange."

"It's not just that he was walking. He was moving slow and looking at the ground. Like he was doing a square pattern. I mean, it's winter, so not many plants or wildlife to look at. I didn't get what was so fascinating."

"Was this before or after the skeleton was found in the wall?"

"Before. I think." Barry crammed his hands into his pockets as he thought about that. "It was definitely before, because they needed that sofa for the film."

"It's odd behavior, I'll grant you. And if you think of anything else you noticed about Ellery—"

"I know where to find you." Barry grinned.

Drayco said, "I'll need to rent a car."

"No, you won't. We've got a loaner right over there. If you don't mind driving a lowly pickup truck for a day or so."

"I used to drive my uncle's truck years ago. It'll be a blast from the past."

Barry nodded at the pickup and said, "Need to get you cowboy boots and a Stetson."

Drayco looked down at his chinos and brown loafers. "I'm more of a suburban cowboy. Call me whenever it's ready."

"You bet. And don't you worry one whit. There's no way I'd let anything happen to this baby."

Drayco got the keys to the truck, a mammoth Ford Raptor. After Drayco made sure he had the hang of driving his temporary wheels, he headed for the next stop on his agenda, an appointment with his now-official client.

§ § §

When Drayco pulled up at the address Genna gave him, he wondered if he got it wrong. Archery Annex sat beside BJ's Skeet and Shoot, an outdoor gun target range he knew well. But Archery Annex was a brand-spanking-new indoor facility. BJ's business must be booming if he'd already expanded.

Drayco found Genna inside and between sessions, sitting on a bench with a recurve bow at her feet. An instructor called out pointers to a group of kids off to Genna's left, but Genna had a lane all to herself. She wore a monochromatic outfit once more, all in red this time, matching one of the rings of the target.

Drayco told her, "Even though you are now officially a client, I feel I should stress again what cold cases are like. Some take months or years. Most are never solved. We'll need to set a limit on this."

"I understand. Who knows? Maybe I'll win the lottery. That would be tight, wouldn't it?"

"You won the lottery of becoming an unlikely criminal suspect. The one day you chose not to be on the movie set, a murder happens."

She wrinkled her nose. "Can you believe it? I had to run errands."

"Has the sheriff's office grilled you yet?"

"Yesterday, and it was pretty ratchet. Not that the deputies were evil or anything." She ran her hand along the empty seat beside her. "It's just…well, murder. It was one thing when it was all make-believe and Hollywood fake knives and blood."

"This is not something most people have to deal with. Fortunately."

"The deputies didn't say much about it."

"It's too early in the process."

She looked around the facility, populated by the two of them and the small instructor-led group. "I hope you don't mind meeting me here. I needed a stress reliever."

"It must be rough—not able to live on your own property, even temporarily. Then an entombed skeleton and a murder."

"Oh, it's rough, all right. A couple of the crew blame me for some kind of curse." She mumbled, "All I wanted was to make money for a retirement fund."

Genna hopped up, grabbed the bow and finger sling, and held the bow at arm's length as she positioned the sight. She dispatched a few carbon arrows in quick succession. She did fairly well, with a grouping in the red ring a few centimeters outside the center gold ring, and he complimented her.

She studied him, handed over the bow and finger sling, and pointed to the case on the floor filled with arrows. "It's a modern type. An Olympic recurve. Give it a try."

"I'm rusty." He picked out an arrow, gripped the bow in his right hand, and raised the weapon, drawing the arrow back under his chin as he tilted his head to the right. After adjusting his stance, he pointed toward the target, stilled his breathing, and sent off a shot. Not bad, but slightly off-center.

She wrinkled her nose again. "Ooh, my bad. I didn't know you were left-handed."

"I've used right-handed bows before. Enough to know how to make adjustments." He tried again, edging the bow more to the side, and released another arrow. Better.

They both headed to the target, where the arrow was dead center. She stared at it. "If you call that rusty, I'd hate to see how you do when you're at the top of your game. That's pretty lit. Where'd you learn to shoot like that?"

"I have a cousin who was into archery. Hoped she might make the Olympics, but it wasn't to be. She taught me a few pointers." Years at the Bureau shooting targets with a gun didn't hurt. Different gear, same philosophy.

He returned the bow, and she gave it another try, getting closer to his arrow. Seemingly satisfied, she said, "Nearly a bullseye. You inspired me. Or I need more coffee." She pronounced it caw-fee again.

"Your accent—and slang terms—are not entirely Eastern Shore."

"I grew up in Salisbury, then spent a decade in New York thinking I could pick up acting work. Too crazy for me. Makes the movie shoot kinda ironic, right?" She dropped the bow to her side.

After a squeal from one student caught her attention, Genna slid down onto the bench. "I haven't been in touch with Rada since the murder. But I suppose this spells the end. It'll be Disappointment City around here. For me, the cast, the locals...."

"Not necessarily. There are investigative reasons to keep the cast around. Sheriff Sailor even said production could likely resume tomorrow." Drayco didn't mention what that decision had cost to the sheriff's peace of mind.

"Really? That's deadass good news." A big smile bloomed across her face.

He asked, "Did you interact much with Ellery Smith?"

"To be honest, when they told me who died, I had to ask which part he played. I don't think he's from around here. Not the Shore."

Drayco relayed what Ellery had told him, "Unionville, Virginia, allegedly. He said he saw an ad in a trade publication about the movie needing extras."

"Then it makes less sense he was killed, doesn't it? With no local connection?" She hopped up to grab another arrow, shooting with a little too much force. The arrow went wide.

Drayco said, "There's a possible drug angle."

She placed the bow on a nearby table, took a quick look around, and lowered her voice. "You mean dealing?"

"Sheriff Sailor mentioned a recent increase in drug crimes."

"Oh, that's just great. If they don't shutter the production over the murder, the drugs angle will spell the end." Her cheeks turned bright pink. "That sounds insensitive. I mean, a man was killed."

"You hadn't heard rumors about anything unusual on the set? Not only drugs, but rivalries, arguments, fights?" Drayco reached to finger the carbon bow, lightweight for something so deadly.

She lowered her voice even further. "The sort of thing you'd expect. 'So and so's makeup is better.' Or 'I don't think my character would say that.' Or 'This outfit is all wrong.' Petty stuff."

"No scandalous affairs?"

That prompted a small smile. "They don't confide in me much. But I overhear things. Like the AD, Chrystina, talking about a guy she'd hooked up with."

"But not who?"

Her cheeks reddened again. "It's none of my business, is it?"

"You said you had to be reminded who the victim was. So you don't recall ever seeing him much, on set or off?"

"I saw him chatting with a couple of people. Like the actor playing a party-goer, Trent Clayburgh. But Trent's friendly with everybody. Oh, and one other crew member. Her name is Nancy Farmery. And then there's Chrystina. Everyone has to work with Chrystina. And her brother, Hoyt."

"I've spoken with Trent, but talking to Nancy and Hoyt could be helpful."

She looked pensive. "The murder can't be related to the skeleton find, right? Coming so soon afterward, it feels odd. But isn't that why you're asking questions about the murder victim?"

Drayco replied, "It's unlikely." But he could see Sheriff Sailor's scowling face as she voiced that thought. Drayco asked her, "Could you get me a copy of the script?"

"I'll bring it by later."

He turned toward the sudden sound of more squeals, where a child of roughly ten years hit a target dead center and put Drayco to shame. Another potential future Olympian? Hopefully, with a brighter outcome, unlike Drayco's cousin.

Drayco turned back to Genna. "I chatted with Trent's grandfather the other day. He said he was good friends with your grandfather, even playing golf and running marathons together. He didn't recall your granddad hiring a domestic worker from Spain. And he was as adamant as you that Duff Ransford would never have been involved with a violent crime."

She tilted her head. "Mr. Clayburgh? I was a tiny tot, so I don't recall much about him except how he was this big important person. But Gramps talked about him fondly. A real mensch."

Then she gaped wide-eyed at Drayco. "Wait, I just realized what you said. Trent Clayburgh is the grandson of Talbott Clayburgh? I hadn't put two and two together. Now I'm dying to talk with him. That could be fun."

"If you do, and he thinks of anything else helpful to your grandfather's case, please let me know."

"Of course." Her face grew pensive. "I'm so relieved to hear Mr. Clayburgh thinks my grandfather is innocent. But if Gramps didn't put the body in the wall, who did? And why?"

"That's what you hired me to find out."

She replied, "You'll want those notes, diaries, and photos, then. I hate to give them up. I don't have copies."

"I promise to return them to you soon."

"Just treat them like the treasures they are to me, okay?"

Drayco assured her he would. In addition to having an industrial strength washing machine, the Jepsons' B&B also had an office grade photocopier. He could make copies of all the materials to minimize handling—and potentially destroying—her grandfather's materials.

He said, "In the meantime, I have a favor to ask of you."

She furrowed her brow. "A favor from me? Other than the copy of the script?"

"If the movie production isn't going to resume until tomorrow, that means a whole evening with your Victorian house empty. If I get permission from Sheriff Sailor, would you like to accompany me there tonight before it bustles with activity again?"

She hesitated. "I wouldn't want to be alone there. Could look kinda sus after a murder, you know? But since you'd be my chaperone, it's okay."

They agreed to meet there in an hour, which allowed Drayco to unload the documents she'd given him at the Lazy Crab. He'd sort through them later. Not that he had a lot of hope of finding anything if Duff Ransford was the paragon of virtue everyone believed him to be.

When Drayco headed outside to the half-grass, half-sandstone-gravel lot, his heart skipped a beat when he didn't see the Starfire. Then he remembered it was at the automotive beauty salon. He was grateful for the loaner truck, but driving it was the difference between a lumbering red walrus and a nimble blue gazelle.

It was interesting Genna had voiced the very thing Sheriff Sailor didn't want to be true, when she wondered if Madalena's case and Ellery's were connected. But they did have one connection in common—neither victim had anyone who missed them. Plus, they both died away from home or family and likely alone, except for their killer. With luck, Ellery's suspicious death would be solved within months, not decades.

Drayco looked around at the eastern redcedar trees ringing the outer edges of the property housing the skeet and archery facilities. Those trees looked bucolic and peaceful enough. But if you flew above them, as he had, you could easily see all the forested areas and marshes beneath and realize how many good places existed to cover up crimes—and bodies. That was the trouble with his line of work. Even the trees were suspect.

He hopped into the truck, grateful for his long legs. Still, he had to practically launch himself into the cab. He cranked up the engine and flipped on the radio, trying vainly to find anything classical. So he settled on an "oldies" station playing a song from his teen years, "Deathtrap." *The heart's a lonely hunter in search of a name / It's a life-or-death game / And you burn, oh you burn / like a moth drawn to flame.*

Drayco pointed the truck down the isolated stretch of sandy road, heading again toward Route 13. What life-or-death game had Madalena, and later Ellery, gotten involved with? The games of real life were too much like poker. Play your cards wrong, and you wound up losing everything.

16

Genna's Victorian house-turned-movie-set looked much more like the site of a murderous scene at night, and it wasn't just the air of an actual murder permeating the grounds. The cheery red turrets were a darker blood color in the dim light from the gibbous moon, and the carved porch spindles cast long shadows on the ground, resembling the bars of a jail cell. Chilly wind gusts tossed around fallen leaves that smacked Drayco in the face.

Thankfully, Sheriff Sailor agreed to allow Drayco and Genna access to the house. Granted, the decision was easier with the trailer in the sheriff's impound lot. As Genna and Drayco headed inside, Genna asked, "What do you hope to find here?"

"I want a close-up look at the hole in the wall where the skeleton was found. Before the crew stomps all over the place again."

"But it's been days."

"True. But it will only get worse as each day passes."

Genna looked around the room as they entered and wrinkled her nose. "It's hella eerie in here." She peered into the parlor and listened. "What my great-aunt used to call quiet as a grave."

It wasn't "quiet" to Drayco, since even low-level sounds had colors and shapes in his synesthesia world. But he was paying more attention to the general state of the interior. He said, "Everything looks the same as yesterday. Not as messy as I'd feared. Just typical movie-messy."

She ran her finger along a bookshelf. "I'm thinking I'll sell the place when this is all over. The movie's bound to make the price go up, right?"

Drayco smiled briefly. "Probably so." He could imagine the realtor's headlines now: *Come see the infamous Movie & Murder House. Own this one-of-a-kind slice of historic Hollywood heaven.*

She moved closer to him, but unlike Chrystina's calculated move, he didn't think Genna was aware she was doing it. Her behavior made even more sense when she shuddered and said, "If it's all the same to you, I'd like to take a quick look around. Make sure they haven't destroyed anything. Give a shout-out if you need me."

She left him to his task, and he studied the hole in the wall, snapping photos with his cellphone camera. He also took measurements after removing the yellow crime scene tape. Not that he didn't trust the sheriff's staff to do a thorough job, especially Nelia Tyler. But he hated to keep bugging the busy sheriff about details from the official report.

The crawlspace behind the hole wasn't big, around three-by-four. But if you were putting a deceased young woman inside, you didn't need standing room. Curious, Drayco propped his flashlight on the floor and eased through the opening, barely wide enough for him to wedge himself in. He had to squat down to fit, and even then, it was tight. The familiar wave of claustrophobia welled up in his chest, and he ducked back outside into the main room to take some deep breaths.

After his blood pressure returned to normal, he studied the construction of the wall's edges and observed two types of plaster with different colors, one off-white, the other pinkish. The former was likely lime plaster, while the latter could be gypsum-based. Considering the renovations, that would make sense and might help verify the date of the skeleton's entombing.

When he rescued his flashlight from the floor to shine it into the space, he didn't see anything the forensic team left behind. Not that he'd expected it. But then the flashlight caught an object in its beam, reflecting the light back to him.

He reached into the hole with a handkerchief and picked up a small metal item, a lapel button shaped like a dolphin. As he shifted it around in his hand, he remembered seeing something similar. The murder victim, Ellery Smith, wore it the first day Drayco spoke with him on the set.

Nelia Tyler, or anyone on the sheriff's team, would have found this. So someone dropped it or placed it there after the team left, but before Ellery was murdered. If Ellery dropped it there, it meant he'd examined the space up close.

Why was he so intensely interested in this skeleton find? Amateur archaeologist or historian? Perhaps he was writing his own book on the history of the Eastern Shore. Or maybe it was merely morbid curiosity. That was the option Drayco *might* pick—if the guy wasn't found murdered himself three days later.

It was also possible someone stole the dolphin pin from the victim and placed it inside the crawlspace. But why? That made even less sense. Drayco examined the pin and held it up to the light. It certainly resembled a dolphin, but he'd check into it more tomorrow.

He pocketed the lapel pin wrapped up in the handkerchief, with plans to take it to the sheriff. Maybe it wasn't the same pin the victim wore after all. Were there similar pins worn by the cast and crew? He hadn't seen any others, but that didn't mean they weren't handed out like party favors at the start of production.

As he stood there surveying the scene, he tried to imagine the perpetrator killing the young woman, placing her in the wall, then adding the quicklime and methodically plastering over the hole. Whoever it was had an idea there'd be enough time that residual odors from a decaying corpse wouldn't be noticed. Or they explained it away as an animal that crawled under the house or died in the attic.

Still, it didn't bode well for his client. The only person with such a reasonable expectation of not being discovered would be the homeowner—Genna's grandfather.

Right as he had that thought, Genna appeared from around the corner, scowling. He asked, "Did you find something wrong?"

"Rada Bluestone promised me there'd be no painting or structural changes without my permission. Yet one bedroom was painted black. And there's a new light fixture I'm not sure is up to code. Good grief, the last thing I need is for this place to burn down. There goes my big, fat notorious-house profits."

"Can you speak to the director about this?"

She wrinkled her nose. "I'll try. Rada's hard to pin down. I could snag the ear of a tech guy. Sachio Spafford's a local. We get along pretty well."

"The director does seem...frazzled."

"Rada's had flops lately. Guess she's hoping this movie marks a comeback. Or so the rumor goes. Some crew members think this film may end up as one of those Alan Smithee things."

"You mean, when a director uses that fake name if they're not proud of their work?"

"Yep. Again, it's all rumors."

"Ouch. Then all this added drama can't be helping."

"I would say that's a big fat nope."

"If the production is on such shaky footing, why would the more experienced actors sign on to the project?"

"Frazier and Ashleigh have worked with Rada before. Her career may be on the skids, but Rada still has a reputation. And connections."

Something moving low to the ground caught Drayco's attention. He shined a light on the crawlspace as a medium-sized brown rat crawled inside. Had it been a few minutes earlier, Drayco would have had a roommate.

To his surprise, Genna didn't shriek but heaved a heavy sigh. "I need more traps."

"You've had a problem?"

"Not since the crew arrived. The commotion scares the vermin off."

"Are you sure you don't have a secret room or access point in the house?"

"I asked an exterminator guy, and he thinks they get in via the roof soffit vents." She put her hand on Drayco's arm. "Please don't tell Rada. She'll blow a gasket."

"It's a deal." That sort of thing would work itself out, one way or another. Not that he would mind chatting with Rada Bluestone if he could ever get her alone, away from an agent or attorney.

He'd looked up her war hero father after she said that's why she chose this area for a production shoot. The man was in his mid-twenties when living here at the same time as Madalena, like Rada said. That meant there was an outside chance he was involved in Madalena's murder. But it would be a stretch considering his injuries from the war, losing part of his left leg and hand. It would be hard for him to manage such a physical feat—unless he had help, a partner-in-crime like Duff Ransford.

A sudden movement coming from the front of the house got Drayco's attention. But Genna hadn't noticed, because when Frazier Prentiss strode inside with a cellphone glued to his hand, she yelped.

Frazier stopped cold. "Bloody hell. I'm sorry, Genna. I didn't know anyone would be here, or I would have called first."

Genna's shock turned to anger. "You mean you'd break in if you knew I wasn't here?"

Frazier held up a key. "Rada gave me this."

"Why?"

"Thought I left my cellphone here. I can't do without it."

Drayco pointed to the phone in Frazier's hand. "Looks like you have it there."

"I have another one. I was using this to call it and see if I heard the ring tone."

"Two phones? Why?"

"One is for personal calls. The other is strictly for business. And the one I left here is my business phone."

"Did you square this visit with the sheriff's office?"

"Rada told me it was okay. That we resume filming tomorrow."

Drayco studied his face. "Are you sure you left it here? The sheriff's team went all over the house and said nothing about finding a phone."

"Where else would I have left it?"

Genna said, "You can look for it tomorrow. When it's daylight."

Frazier rubbed his eyes. "Sure, okay. Who knows? With any luck, it'll make me look more important to my agent or potential gigs. Less desperate, like I'm too busy to take their calls."

He gave a half-hearted wave and disappeared out the front door. After he was out of sight, Genna said to Drayco, "You think he was telling the truth? About looking for his phone?"

"I don't know. But I'll keep an eye on him. And I'd recommend you do the same."

§ § §

True to his word, once Drayco returned to the Lazy Crab, he started on the documents Genna gave him from her grandfather's files. He read each one as he made copies with Maida's copier, scanning the text for anything of interest to the case.

He hadn't expected to find any direct mentions of hiring a Spanish worker, but he did come across an interesting tidbit. Duff Ransford kept financial records during the house renovations. One line item was for "domestic services," which could mean various things. Or it could refer to Madalena.

Drayco didn't see anything else relevant to the case, but the letters and other documents gave him better insight into the character of Genna's grandfather. The man was devoted to his wife, volunteered with the Methodist Committee for Overseas Relief following the war, and initially planned to specialize in civil rights litigation.

Such a straight arrow seemed unlikely to be the type to entomb a young girl inside a wall. Still, even if he wasn't the killer, perhaps he helped cover up the crime for whatever reason.

Drayco hadn't taken on many cold cases in his private consulting career, but this was among the oldest and the coldest. His by-the-book father would disapprove of his son taking on such a case. Even Drayco's former partner, Sarg, might question the practicality of it. They both knew the painfully long odds. Funny thing about odds, though—the long shot always paid off the most.

17

With apologies to the Jepsons, Drayco got an early start the following day, fortified with his favorite salted coffee in a travel mug and a couple of Maida Jepson's "power muffins." When he'd asked her what made them so powerful, she replied, "Protein powder. Or it could be the apples, raisins, carrots, flax, honey, and cinnamon." Despite that list of ingredients, they were quite edible.

He pointed his loaner pickup truck down Route 13, through the Chesapeake Bay Bridge-Tunnel, and into Newport News, heading toward Charlottesville. Since the drive would take a hair shy of four hours, he'd left just after five a.m.

Sheriff Sailor had told him Pauley Harrington, the man from the police database whose DNA was a close match to Madalena's had lived not too far from Charlottesville in the small town of Manahoack. From Drayco's research, he'd discovered Pauley once worked as a janitor at the local courthouse. However, when Drayco pulled up in front of it, the smallish, white Federal-style building was gleamingly new. A black oval plaque next to the front door sported a completion date after Pauley would have worked there.

Drayco had called ahead and found a records clerk on duty, Burl Merton, a former colleague of Pauley's. But Merton dashed Drayco's hopes right away, verifying the current courthouse was indeed new, built after the old one burned down—along with all of its non-digitized records. That left no way to track down anything official about Pauley Harrington's family.

Merton waved Drayco into a beige room with pungent whiffs of fresh paint, which explained the presence of a frog-shaped doorstop propping the door open. The room held bookshelves and a few file cabinets, but mostly computer kiosks. Drayco stopped himself from taking photos to show Reece a "modern" facility.

Merton adjusted his crooked red tie as he sat across from Drayco at the lone table in the room and started off with an apology. "My voice is a touch wheezy today. I'm still getting over a bad cold."

"I'll try not to make you talk too much, Mr. Merton."

"That's right fine of you, innit?"

It took Drayco a moment to translate the man's regional use of "innit" for "isn't it?"

Merton continued, "You wanted to chat about Pauley Harrington?"

Drayco took a page from Reece's excuse book and replied, "It's for a history project."

"Ah, well, Pauley's the reason this here building is newish, you see."

Drayco tilted his head. "I'm not sure I understand."

"When this place burned down, suspicion fell on Pauley. No one could prove he was behind it, but some of us believed it. Pauley was a bit odd." Merton picked up a paperclip and started bending it apart as he talked.

"Odd?"

"Oh, I hate to speak ill of the dead. But he was often aloof. And bug-eyed, kind of. Not a lot of social graces."

"What led you to believe he may be behind the original building burning down?"

Merton leaned back, his head scraping against one of the few file cabinets. "That arson charge. He got off, but the police must have felt he was guilty, or they wouldn't have arrested him in the first place."

"Did he have any family nearby or close friends? He may have been adopted."

"I vaguely recall a mention of that. Nothing concrete, you see. Other than I think his parents—adopted or otherwise—died when he was in his teens. Car crash. That's what you meant, innit? Sorry I don't have anything more for you. As I said, he was a loner, although there were those rumors." Merton stopped and cleared his throat.

"Rumors?" Drayco waited patiently, grateful for his eidetic memory. Whipping out a notepad made people more tense. Every single time.

"It's a delicate matter. But allegedly, he got a local woman pregnant. Elleana Beatrice Smith. I think she went by 'Ellery.' Pauley never owned up to it, and the woman moved to the next county. Died young. But not from a house fire or anything. Brain aneurysm. Not sure why she never pressed Pauley for child support."

Drayco made sure the man spelled the woman's name out for him. It matched the mother's name on Ellery Smith's birth certificate, according to Sheriff Sailor. Drayco asked, "What about Pauley Harrington's alleged child? Did you know him?"

"No, and I have no idea where he wound up. Don't even recall the child's name. I'm not much help for a records clerk, am I?"

Just then, an older woman poked her head in. "I didn't mean to eavesdrop, Burl, but you left the door open." She looked at Drayco and added, "A history project, eh? You've come to the right place for that. Anyways, I remember Pauley, too. How could you not? He was an odd fellow." She introduced herself as Ida, and Drayco tried not to stare at her short, spiky turquoise hair resembling a field of blue thistle.

Drayco asked her, "Did he discuss where he came from? Or talk about his family?"

Ida cocked her head. "Didn't say boo to me, no. But my mother knew his parents. There was some mystery there."

"What type of mystery?"

"They were a childless couple, Mr. And Mrs. Harrington. Then one day, they suddenly have a baby boy. Told my mother it was a distant cousin's child who could no longer care for him. Mom and everyone else suspected that wasn't the truth, but those were rough times. Too many kids were left without fathers and even mothers due to the war. Some adoptions took place under the table. No one questioned it."

"And the boy's adoptive parents, the Harrington's? What happened to them?"

"Burl here was right. They died in a car crash when Pauley was fifteen. I think he got jobs doing handyman work and kinda lived on his own after that."

§ § §

In a move that would make Reece proud, Drayco checked with the local historical archives housed at the small library in town. Having *not* burned down, the library was older, and it showed. The peeling external clapboard siding and the interior plaster walls could use some of the courthouse's fresh paint.

What mattered was their files were intact, unlike the courthouse. He dug up an article from the newspaper about the fire where Pauley Harrington died. And another about the courthouse fire.

His luck picked up when he found the same local newspaper had an obituary for the woman Burl Merton had named, Elleana Beatrice Smith, brain aneurysm and all. It mentioned an infant son in the "survived by" section and a name, Mark. A common first name, but take the full name Mark William Smith and add in the woman's nickname, "Ellery," and you had the same name as a certain murder victim.

Drayco used his cellphone to take snapshots of the various articles. He also found photos of Mrs. Maggie Harrington, who allegedly adopted Pauley, Madalena's son. She still had a surviving sister, Yasmin Park, who would be around eighty-six. He checked the phone records and located a landline number for Mrs. Park.

He retreated to his rental monster truck and tried the number. When the woman answered, she started coughing right away and apologized profusely. "Getting over the flu."

Something must be going around town. Drayco made a note to take a bunch of Vitamin C later if Maida's power muffins didn't do the trick. He mentioned the "history project" again and said, "I won't make you talk long, Mrs. Park, so you can rest your voice. But I did a little research into your sister's adopted son, Pauley."

"Oh, poor Pauley. Such a sad, tragic case. For all of us."

"You're referring to your sister's untimely death?"

"That, too. But Pauley…well. You see, my sister worked at a local church. And one day, someone deposited a baby in a basket on their doorstep. Maggie had been trying unsuccessfully to have a child, so she adopted him. Like he was a gift from God. You know, Moses in the bulrushes."

"No note? Or a way to track down the biological parents?"

"No note whatsoever. And the world was topsy-turvy then. Maggie made up a fake story about our cousin. I didn't fault her for it. Here was a child who needed a family."

"What did he do after his parents were killed?"

"That's where I have regrets. And that's why I say the poor thing never had a chance. When Maggie and her husband died in that crash, nobody wanted responsibility for Pauley, who was around fifteen, as I recall. The family pushed him out, and he had to do for himself. I lost track of him after that. Later, I heard he'd been charged with arson. And then I saw a death notice in the paper. It was all of two sentences long. After all he'd been through. Only two sentences."

"Do you recall any next of kin listed in that death notice?"

"No, but I've seen that happen before. That type of notice is usually from a funeral home. When no one claims a body, that is. Is there anything sadder than that?"

"Did Pauley himself ever mention tracking down his biological family?"

"Nothing like that. We all wondered if he was from South America. Tallish but had black wavy hair, brown eyes, and olive-ish skin."

That wouldn't be surprising, seeing as how his mother—if Madalena—was originally from Spain. Drayco asked, "One of Pauley's colleagues at the courthouse mentioned a son of his?"

Mrs. Park sounded confused. "A son? I never heard tell of anything like that. If you find him, please put him in touch with me, you hear? I'd like to try to make amends for Pauley."

Drayco didn't have the heart to explain the son was now dead, too, if that child was Ellery Smith. Drayco thanked her for her help and suggested she try hot tea with honey, which Maida always recommended. Well, with something more than honey, but Drayco wasn't sure if Mrs. Park was a teetotaler.

He'd parked in the gravel lot of the library, situated in the middle of the town's Main Street. It had similarities with Cape Unity, with the standard roll call of small-town Americana—courthouse, library, post office, and church. Maybe the recent infusion of Hollywood money lay behind it, but Cape Unity had more of a beating heart. Manahoack felt as frozen in place as the Civil War statues and cannons in the town square.

If Madalena died in Cape Unity, then how did her infant son get left on a church doorstep two hundred miles away? Madalena likely didn't have a car, and the train came nowhere near here. Did the baby's biological father drop him off? But why here, unless he had ties to the area? And just as importantly, was it before or after Madalena's murder?

Then there was the puzzle of Mark "Ellery" Smith. Was it really possible he was Madalena's grandson? Because it sure looked that way. If so, the odds of him coincidentally taking a movie job in the house where his grandmother was killed were astronomical. It was much more likely he suspected she died there or nearby. But how in the world did he find this out if his own father didn't even know who his biological parents were?

Drayco looked over at a Civil War statue of a Confederate soldier. He doubted any of those soldiers knew much about the Native American tribe for whom the town was named. But Drayco had researched them. They were a small band in this area of Virginia who lived close to the Rappahannock River, themselves descended from the prehistoric Eastern Woodland cultures. Explorer John Smith encountered them in 1608, but their numbers shrank after wars against enemy tribes—and diseases from contact with Europeans. By 1728, they'd disappeared from the historical record.

It seemed fitting for Pauley Harrington to have lived and died in this location. Another of the many lives—the Manahoack, Civil War soldiers, European explorers—that burned brightly in one cosmologically brief flare-up before fading into the embers of time. For a moment, Drayco imagined he heard the statue laughing.

18

After grabbing a lunch of Choo Choo Chicken at a diner built from old railcars, Drayco considered his options. He wanted to make one other stop while he was in the area. While researching Pauley Harrington in the local archives, he'd come across a photo of a woman, Earleen Eskin, who'd worked as a riveter in an aircraft factory for the war effort.

In that same photo, a younger woman had her back turned to the camera as she held a baby. The caption identified that woman as Eskin's nanny, "Maddy." Not able to see the younger woman's features, he couldn't be sure of her ethnicity, but her hair was dark and wavy— like Madalena's son, Pauley Harrington.

Earleen Eskin passed away years ago, but that baby, Wilma Eskin, now in her seventies, lived in a small town on the return route to Cape Unity. He found her at her log cabin-style home, but she was more reluctant to talk to him than Pauley's aunt. Once again, Drayco mentioned Reece's book on Virginia history. Reece *had* referred to Drayco as his "assistant," had he not?

Wilma finally let him into her living room, saying, "I have a few minutes for a chat. A brief chat. I got church choir practice in a half hour."

Unlike the courthouse clerk with her spiky turquoise hairdo, this woman's dyed hair was the color of mango. Had Drayco missed a rainbow hair trend? He opted to sit in a chair near the door—less threatening that way.

A tall multi-level cage sat in one corner, filled with blankets, mini-hammocks, and colorful accordion-ridged tubes snaking along the sides and emptying into the cage. Drayco pointed it out. "Ferrets?"

A little smile brightened her face. "They're under a blanket, sleeping. Bandit and Stinkbag."

That would explain the musky smell that greeted him when he walked in. He said, "I appreciate your assistance. I'm mainly interested in your nanny, a Spanish girl, who would have cared for you while your mother worked in an airplane parts factory."

"Maddy? I got a vague recollection. Just the name, mostly. She was Spanish, eh? I reckon I recall her having an accent. But I was so young."

So, his stab in the dark about Madalena was correct. "How long was she your nanny?"

"Not long. One day, she up and vanished. Mama was fit to be tied. Thought she'd run off with a young man and left Mama in a lurch. Especially after my mother allowed Maddy to work during her pregnancy. That was a scandal then, you understand, eh?"

"I'm aware of the historical stigma."

"It was hard to find nannies. So many women were working in the factories during the war." Wilma tended toward noisy breathing through her nose, and Drayco sympathized with her choir director. She also liked to stick out her tongue while thinking.

"You said your mother thought Maddy had run off with a young man. Do you recall a name?"

"Sorry, but no. Mama said Maddy was pretty in an exotic way, you understand, eh? Any of the young fellows not yet drafted would have drooled over her."

Drayco had no doubt about that. But without a name or description, this bit of information didn't help.

Wilma must have noted his disappointment, quickly adding, "I have a pile of old letters Mama wrote to my father. He was fighting in the war overseas. I'll see if I can dig those up."

"So your mother didn't know the identity of the father of Maddy's baby or what happened to the child?"

And out went the tongue. "I have no recollection of any such thing."

"Did Maddy vanish before or after she gave birth?"

"I have no idea. I was so young, you understand, eh?"

Drayco thanked her and gave her his card. Hopefully, she'd follow through on her promise to find those letters.

Ellery Smith had said he was from Unionville, which wasn't far from Drayco's current location. If he had more time, he'd like to check it out. But he'd also promised Sheriff Sailor not to step too deep into Sailor's briar patch.

Since Drayco had stayed in this area for four hours, and it would take him four more back to the Lazy Crab, he'd likely found all he could for now. Unionville would have to wait for another day.

Before he left town, he made a call to the Capps County sheriff's office in Manahoack. He verified from their records that Pauley Harrington was found dead of natural causes in his apartment after a landlord went to check on unpaid rent. Just as Pauley's adopted aunt, Yasmin Park, had surmised, the body wasn't claimed and sent to a funeral home to be cremated, with the ashes added to the communal grave kept for such occasions.

When Drayco asked how many unclaimed bodies the area had each year, he was told dozens and sometimes more. *Ashes to unclaimed ashes? Meet dust to unmarked dust.*

His return trip took him back through the Chesapeake Bay Bridge-Tunnel, which couldn't be helped. His claustrophobia wasn't a fan of tunnels. But he also drove through Cape Charles and made a brief detour through the new Prophett Properties construction.

The half-built houses didn't have electricity wired up yet, nor were there streetlights, so the area was dark and quiet. Drayco didn't mind the dark because he could see the twilight sky much better that way. He stopped the car and looked up to spy a meteor streaking overhead.

When his attention flipped back down to earth, he thought he saw another flash of light, but this came from inside one of the empty houses. An intruder? A fire? He waited a few moments, but the light didn't repeat, and he didn't see any smoke. Must be his meteor-fueled imagination. With a shrug, he returned to the main road and headed north toward Cape Unity.

19

Drayco made it into town five minutes before Haffey's Auto Body closed. He was just in time to pick up his Starfire from Barry Farland and was amazed Barry had done the work so fast. Drayco examined the car from all angles while Barry hovered nearby with a worry-wreath face, chewing on his cuticles. Drayco knelt to inspect the area where the most noticeable bullet hole once was, but no signs of it now.

He stood up and turned to Barry. "You, my friend, are a magician. This is amazing."

Barry grinned. "Not so much me, but that fiberglass body filler I told you about. Pretty cool stuff."

"Still, even the best props need a magician to know how to use them. How much do I owe you?"

The figure Barry gave him sounded reasonable—a little too reasonable. Fearing the young man was short-changing himself, Drayco handed over a couple of extra Ben Franklins and called it a "tip."

Barry thanked him profusely and added, "Oh, and I noticed your trunk latch isn't working right. But I don't have the parts to fix it. I've got it on order and will do the work when it arrives. On the house."

Drayco made a slight bow toward the massive pickup truck, thanking it for its service, but he was eager to get back into his Starfire. The truck turned out to be a decent set of wheels, but he and the Starfire had been through a lot together. They deserved each other.

Before Drayco drove off, his cellphone chirped, alerting him that he'd missed a call—not unusual in light of the area's spotty cellphone coverage. He listened to the message. It was his potential power-player client in D.C., wanting to know his status. He almost pressed "delete" but didn't. Crafting excuses was never his strong suit, but he'd think of something to hold them off. For now.

§ § §

When Drayco returned to the Lazy Crab, he apologized to Maida again for having left at the crack of dawn. She smiled at that. "We're crack o'dawn people ourselves." Then she studied him with a frank appraisal. "I've been meaning to tell you how spiffy you look. Not that you ordinarily dress badly."

He fingered his blue cable knit sweater. "Brock's—my father's—new girlfriend loves to shop. Since I'd rather spend a day at the DMV than in a store, that's fine with me. Fortunately, she has good taste."

"Rare is the man who inherits the shopping gene. Unless it's for gardening gear. Just ask Major."

She waved Drayco into the kitchen, where Major pored through seed catalogs. Drayco peered over his shoulder. "Holy Ghost Root and Lovage? Don't think I've heard of those."

Major pointed at a photo. "Holy Ghost Root is also called Angelica. Celery-like stems but tastes more licorice-y."

Maida chimed in, "You can cook the stems or add raw leaves and stalks to salads. And use roots to make herbal tea."

Major added, "Lovage tastes like fresh celery, and rabbits hate it. A big plus." He grabbed sticky notes to slap onto those pages. "It's that season of the year when my better half looks through all her recipe books and finds new things she wants to try. I call it the annual Seed Catalog Bacchanal."

Drayco grinned. "Bacchanal?"

"Because I feel a little drunk by the time I slog through all of these." Major reached under the table and grabbed a dozen catalogs he plopped on the tabletop.

Maida rolled her eyes and asked Drayco, "How was your trip? Find out anything useful?"

"Yes, but if I'm right, I opened up a whole new can of worms. Or make that a can of heirloom spinach."

"What do you mean?"

Drayco knew the Jepsons received tons of gossip, but they weren't ones to dish it out. He trusted them. "It's possible the recent murder victim at the movie set was the skeleton girl's grandson."

Major looked up from his seeds. "That sounds kinda woo-woo, right there."

"I'd agree with you, if Ellery hadn't been unnaturally interested in the skeleton find."

Maida asked, "You think he knew it was there?"

"Or nearby. It's possible."

"Surely his murder wasn't connected to that. Only a coincidence?"

"Sheriff Sailor thinks so."

"But *you* don't." Maida tapped her foot on the floor. "An awful lot of tragedy followed that family."

Drayco nodded his agreement and poured himself a freshly brewed espresso from the machine on the counter. He eyed a tiny tub of hazelnut creamer and decided to give it a try. Man could not live by salt alone.

Maida ceased her foot tapping and leaned against the sage green-painted cabinets. "I can't stop thinking about Madalena. The poor young thing. Giving birth to a baby that was either taken from her or she had to give up. Just a girl herself. Far from home. Having her brief life end in such a sad way."

"Happens all too often. Not a great commentary on the ethical state of the human race."

"If anybody can find justice for her, you will. It's too bad there aren't family or contemporaries left to help."

"A few people are still living. Talbott Clayburgh, a friend of my client's grandfather, for one. And I got an email list from him today, by way of Reece, of other friends he thinks are also with us. Unfortunately, Clayburgh doesn't recall Duff Ransford hiring a young woman from Spain."

Major piped up, "You said Clayburgh is ninety-two? I don't care how well you keep your body in shape, memory is like Swiss cheese even by your sixties. Too much info swirling around in there. Stuff gets pushed out."

Drayco smiled. "Yours seems pretty sharp to me, Major. But even if our retired judge doesn't remember, he may have mentioned it to his son."

Major asked, "What's the son's name?"

"Terrell Clayburgh. Or I think he goes by Terry."

"I remember that name. Bit of a scandal." Major stroked his beard. "Talk about memory problems, I don't recall details. But it would have been years now. A drug bust or some such thing?"

Drayco's research hadn't dug up anything like that, but it didn't mean Major's memory was faulty. With a state Supreme Court justice as a father, family dirt often got swept under the carpet.

After promising Maida a recital of excerpts from her favorite Bach music, including the second English Suite, Drayco topped off his espresso and carried the cup upstairs to his room. The aroma blended nicely with the caramel-chocolate scented candles Maida kept on the nightstand. Smelled like a coffee shop.

He opened his laptop and conducted more research into Terry Clayburgh's background. The man had no social media presence—he obviously didn't belong to the video generation. If anything, he came across as an ordinary, law-abiding small business owner who'd even got a commendation from the Chamber of Commerce.

Drayco also conducted a quick search on movie terminology. The combo of finding the pocket Spanish dictionary and having to ask the movie crew to define terms made him realize he needed a Hollywood lexicon, too. If he was going to work with these people, it would help to speak their language. He found various websites, scanned them, and bookmarked the best ones.

Drayco shut the laptop, settled into the toffee-colored down comforter and Mount Everest of pillows, and grabbed his book. Finally, he could finish the biography of Lili Boulanger.

He started to open it, but then it struck him that the young French composer was nineteen when she won the prestigious Prix de Rome for composition in 1913 for her cantata, *Faust et Hélène*, the first female composer to do so. She died from pneumonia five years later.

The Prix de Rome at nineteen, the same age as Madalena. What was there about youthful talent the universe hated so much? How else could you explain the long list of such untimely deaths? Or career-killing injuries?

He put down the book and grabbed the copy of the *Fatal Fugue* script Genna Ransford had dropped off earlier for him, which he'd learned was a "for hire" work on the part of the screenwriter. Flat fee, no residuals. The script format made for a pretty quick read, and an hour later, he'd finished it.

The story was a standard crime drama that hit all the right tropes but was hardly Oscar-worthy. The plot contained no hidden skeletons buried in the walls. Like Sailor said, it involved a wrap party for a theatrical group that comprised the list of suspects when one actor is stabbed to death. But the culprit turns out to be the deputy Ashleigh was playing. He'd have to ask her about that.

Ellery Smith, playing the butler, did only have a few lines. However, he made a silent appearance in other scenes, in addition to portraying the corpse in the script. Drayco learned from Genna they wouldn't bother recasting his roles, hoping they had enough in the can.

Why was Ellery so eager to get such a gig? Knowing his grandmother may have died on the movie site property made as much sense as anything.

Drayco tossed the script aside to grab the Boulanger biography again. From the ridiculous to the sublime. Too bad all of life's transitions weren't as simple as that.

20

After having dreams of shadowy figures launching projectiles out of an abandoned warehouse, Drayco awoke to bullet-thwacks from cold rain mixed with sleet against the window in his room. Not that he minded rain—better than day after leaden day of gray skies that threatened but didn't follow through. He had a few chapters left in his book, so he finished that and let Maida and Major Jepson sleep longer.

He was rewarded with a home-cooked, king-sized Maida breakfast instead of a power muffin. And that was why, when he called Sheriff Sailor to arrange a quick meet-up, he wasn't too excited about Sailor's choice of a coffee bar. More so since his room at the Lazy Crab was already like living inside a coffee shop. But it was a Saturday, so the sheriff naturally preferred to escape from the office.

The meeting place turned out to be brand new, one that Sailor said, "Is a license to print money."

Drayco asked, "Why is that?"

Sailor grabbed a table for them and pointed to the menu board. "They sell CBD coffee."

"I get that it's trendy, sure. But it's not addictive."

"I'm making certain everything is legal and aboveboard." Sailor watched as a group of four twenty-somethings scurried inside and said, "It's giving Grounds for Glory a run for its money."

"I was once poisoned at Grounds for Glory."

Sailor grunted. "From one kind of poison to another."

"But CBD isn't toxic."

"Gotta keep an eye on any potential drug outlets. A few of these CBD and vape shops sell the harder stuff. Under the table, naturally. We've made more drug arrests at CBD outlets than in the usual dingy places. Looks more legit to buyers."

Drayco had grabbed a regular black coffee from the counter on his way in and reached for the salt shaker, making Sailor shake his head. "Blecch. What do you see in that?"

"Makes it sweeter."

"No, it most certainly does not. It makes it salty."

"To each his own taste...bud." Drayco regarded Sailor's mocha drink, heavy on the sugar, and at the pecan tartlet he'd bought to go with it. It resembled a mini-pie. Of course.

Drayco asked, "Any luck tracing the fireworks used at the movie set?"

"Not yet. And nobody in the film crew saw anybody put them in there. From analysis of the residue and type of manufacture, they're garden-variety fireworks. The kind they sell everywhere. Except for one little thing."

"And that is?"

"That form of fireworks is illegal in Virginia. But surrounding states can sell them. Though it'd be a federal crime to carry them across state lines."

"Out of state, harder to trace."

"Everything on this damned case is hard to trace. This Ellery Smith fellow had no living family, no friends that we can find. None recent. Not much of an employment record before this movie. Odd jobs here and there."

"Did you question the screenwriter about the similarities in the script and your real-life murder?"

"The guy was shitting bricks. He's what they call a 'Tyro' or 'Baby Writer.' One who's new to the industry, ergo cheap. But I don't think he's involved. Has an alibi, no motive. In fact, all the cast and crew claim to have alibis. As in, they were all outside looking at the explosion."

"The script's similar storyline can't rule out a copycat motive for Ellery's murder."

"Or a way to cast more doubts on the movie production, the director, or the crew. Definitely not an ordinary, straightforward case."

Drayco added more salt to his coffee and took a sip, allowing the liquid to trickle down his throat. Not too hot, not too cold. Goldilocks coffee. "Here's something else not quite as ordinary."

"The salt? Yeah, I know."

"No, this."

Sailor squinted as Drayco pulled an item from his pocket with his free hand. "What's that?"

"A lapel pin I found when Genna accompanied me to the house the other night. This was inside the hole in the wall."

With a frown, Sailor picked up the baggie with the pin. "We missed this?"

"I doubt it. I think it ended up there afterward."

A tinkling bell at the front entrance signaled the arrival of an individual who wasn't a twenty-something CBD groupie. Wearing a brown deputy uniform, the woman headed into the cafe, holding an umbrella in one hand and papers in another. Sailor said to her as she approached, "Thanks for stopping by on your way to the station, Regina. Sorry you have to work on the weekend."

Drayco recognized her as the other half of Nelia's part-time job share. Regina smiled and handed a printout to Drayco. "Sheriff Sailor told me you'd be here and I could give you this in person."

Drayco took the printout, but at his questioning look, Regina explained, "I don't have access to the skull to make a 3D reconstruction. But I got the M.E.'s office to send me a digital photograph with measurements. I uploaded it into my new software. And then I tweaked it by hand."

"This is what Madalena Zamora looked like?"

"I think it's a good approximation."

Drayco studied the computer drawing. The face was of an attractive young woman with prominent cheekbones and full lips in a

Mona Lisa half-smile. "This is outstanding, Regina. You even got the wavy hair right."

Sailor shot him a pointed look, but didn't say anything.

Regina beamed at Drayco's praise. "I considered getting a job as a forensic artist after I had a cousin who went missing and was never found. That's why I understood the reason you wanted this. If my cousin's body is ever unearthed—assuming she died—then I want someone to do this for her, too."

Drayco offered to buy her coffee, but she declined. He thanked her again, and on her way out, she said, "When I have the 3D model, I'll let you know."

After she'd left, Sailor took a swig of his mocha and blinked at Drayco. "Wavy hair? How'd you know that? Are you psychic now, too?"

"Have you compared Madalena's DNA with that of the latest murder victim, Ellery Smith?"

"We had no reason."

"You might want to." Drayco filled him in on his trip to south-central Virginia, and Sailor gritted his teeth. "I wish you'd run it by me before talking to those people. You really do like to make things hard on me, don't you?"

"Not my intention to make things harder for you. Just trying to serve my client's interests. But it does bring up the all-important question—if Ellery Smith *is* Madalena's grandson, did he know the remains would be found on that property? Barry Farland told me his friend Zach once saw Ellery examine the grounds in a methodical grid pattern. That would make sense if he suspected his grandmother could be buried there."

Sailor puffed out his cheeks. "Doesn't explain how he knew, does it? Unless *he's* psychic. Let's not jump to conclusions. We'll go by the book, as always."

"Funny you should mention by the book," Drayco handed over a baggie with a pocket Spanish dictionary inside.

Sailor studied it. "Thanks, but I've got one. That is, my wife does."

"I had an uninvited guest at the Opera House the other evening. Caught a glimpse through a window of a figure but no features, but whoever it was dropped this on the ground."

Sailor picked up the baggie. "You think this could be related to Ellery Smith's case?"

"I don't know. But fingerprint analysis could answer that."

"And since my tech team doesn't have nearly enough to do…" Sailor tossed the baggie on the table and attacked his poor, hapless pastry.

A chirpy feminine voice made both men look up, and Drayco thought Regina had returned. But it was Jaxine Gordon who bounced up to them. "Lookee, who we have here. The piano player and the lawman. In your natural habitat, no less. Donuts?" She peered at the table.

Drayco bit back a grin, and the muscles around Sailor's eyes were doing a mambo. Drayco asked, "Is the set not providing enough food for the crew?"

"Their coffee is sinfully bad. So bad, you should arrest it for impersonating coffee. This is much better. Plus, this shop has everything-bagels to die for. With smoked salmon, chive cream cheese, and peppercorns." She batted her eyelashes at Drayco. He didn't know women still did that.

Drayco said, "I'll, uh, have to try that bagel."

"You'll love it. It'll put hair on your chest." Before he could even think of a reply, she turned to Sheriff Sailor. "Got Ellery Smith's murder solved yet? It's been three days."

Her comment made Sailor's eye muscles switch from mambo to jitterbug. Drayco was impressed when the sheriff didn't miss a beat. "It usually takes at least five."

"Surely you know who's guilty. It was Rada, wasn't it?"

Sailor leaned back. "The director? Why her?"

"If looks could kill. Besides, I think she was exasperated with Ellery. Always blowing his lines. And he didn't even have that many."

"Right. We'll keep that under advisement."

When the clerk at the counter called Jaxine's number, she waved her ticket in the air and said, "My number's up." And she winked at Drayco as she sashayed to pick up her order.

Sailor watched her leave and shook his head. "Maybe flirty girty there had an affair with Ellery, too. A lot of that going around."

"Yes, but if she killed him, it was with an accomplice. She was one of the crew I tripped over heading out to the explosion that day."

"Perhaps she set up that explosion as a distraction. That ditzy broad act isn't working for me."

"You mean, she's not that great an actress?"

Sailor snorted. "What do you think?"

Drayco let Sailor finish eating his mini-pie before he asked, "Were you able to get a subpoena for the construction company?"

"A waste of effort."

"Why?"

"The company CEO, Pamela Kye, said when she dug around, those old personnel records no longer exist. Burned in a fire twenty years ago."

"A fire?" Drayco pushed his coffee cup away. "A little too convenient, don't you think?"

"You tell me. And yes, I looked it up. The fire marshal's report was inconclusive."

Drayco was accustomed to grumpy Sailor, so he let it slide. "Madalena's son was arrested for arson. And may or may not have set fire to the courthouse. Since he was still alive twenty years ago, he could also be behind the Prophett Properties fire."

"For what reason?"

"Burning down a records trail, possibly. But he's deceased, so we may never know."

Sailor puffed out his cheeks. "Sounds like your cold-case killer. Unknowable, that is."

Drayco shouldn't take offense at that, but he did. He'd had those same thoughts about his case, but it didn't mean he approved of it voiced by someone else. And not a man he respected, like Sailor. Was Genna Ransford right in her assessment that the sheriff wasn't all that interested in pursuing Madalena's case? Drayco allowed himself a moment to stew before he turned down the heat. He needed to cut the frazzled lawman a break.

A whiff of something burning reached Drayco's nose, and Sailor's head whipped toward the source. They both watched as a barista wearing a Kiss My Assateague T-shirt rescued a charred black tart from the oven. Another poor pastry bit the dust.

So, was the Prophett Properties fire arson? Or another charred tart, or faulty wiring, or even lightning, for that matter? Drayco traced the paper of the computer reconstruction of Madalena's image with his finger. The only one who might know was her son, the arsonist. Psychologists could argue whether arsonists arose from abandonment issues, sexual abuse, or another trauma. But maybe it all came down to faulty genetic wiring.

Sailor studied Drayco over his coffee cup. "So where you off to next? And please don't say you've found another skeleton."

"Close. I've got an appointment with a skeleton whisperer. And I don't mean a medical examiner."

21

When Reece Wable learned Drayco planned on a chat with the former supreme justice's estranged son, Terry Clayburgh, he wanted to tag along. Reece added, "If I'm going to write a section about the Great One himself, then I need to get the other side of the story from his progeny."

As he cranked up the Starfire, Drayco asked, "Who looks after the Historical Society while you're gone? Surely not your parrot?"

"Mrs. Hammontree. Does a fine job. Though Andrew Jackson knows a few touristy phrases. Maybe he'd do a decent job at that."

"What kind of touristy phrases?" Drayco was familiar with what Reece's parrot usually said, and it wasn't often family-friendly.

"Things like 'how ya doin' and 'come back and see us sometime.'"

"That doesn't sound too bad."

"Now that I think of it, he does like to say, 'The weather's a bitch.'"

"And who taught him that?"

"Mrs. Hammontree."

Drayco grinned. "Of course."

Reece held up a book he'd brought with him. "Guess what I found?"

"Looks like an old yearbook."

"A law school yearbook."

"From the Duff Ransford era?"

"And Talbott Clayburgh. And other men who later became rich and powerful. Thought it might come in handy."

"Thanks, Reece. I can't wait to look through it. When I'm not driving, that is."

"Don't thank me yet. Most of the souls have since departed this earthly vale of tears."

"That's what I'm finding, too. I tracked a couple to nursing homes, and they were in the memory care ward."

The rain continued to fall as Drayco drove through the more deserted areas of the peninsula along bumpier roads. This was the "old" Eastern Shore—acres of farmland playing an endless tug-of-war with the marshlands and seasonal floods. A land and an era on borrowed time since tidal erosion would continue its relentless assault, while the Wallops facility transformed the economy from rockfish to rocket launches.

When Drayco found the address he was after and pulled in front, Reece said, "Yeesh. This is where Terry Clayburgh lives? What a comedown from his father's country club mansion. Looks even worse in the rain."

"Actually, this is related to his job. He said he was so busy, this was the only way we could pin him down for a Q&A."

"What sort of job? Construction?"

"He has a crime scene cleanup business."

Reece stared at Drayco. "Come again?"

"He also deals with other nasty jobs."

"As in, for instance…?"

"On this gig, he's working to clean up a house where an elderly woman died in her chair and wasn't found for two weeks."

Reece groaned. "Wish you'd told me that sooner."

Drayco grinned as he climbed out of the car. "You'll be fine. And don't forget I'm still your 'assistant,' right?"

The man who welcomed them inside the front living room bore a passing resemblance to his father, Talbott Clayburgh, in shared facial features like a prominent brow ridge and slightly crooked nose—a combination reminiscent of a Picasso painting. In every other way, he was the direct opposite of his father. Terry Clayburgh sported a full, bushy gray beard, twirled mustache, and colorful tattoos below his jawline. Drayco couldn't tell what the tats were, since Terry wore coveralls and a filter mask hanging around his neck.

Reece was closer to Terry and apparently had a better view of the tattoos and commented on them. "That's unique. A griffon?"

Terry chuckled. "I got these when I was trying to stick it to my father. And the griffon? I hoped it would bring me luck. The guardian of treasures." His voice was on the gravelly side, and he stopped to cough loudly, followed by an apology. "Sorry. Years of smoking. But I finally quit."

Drayco also noted pads in front of Terry's ears that attached to a thin wire around the back of his head, which prompted Drayco to ask, "Bone conduction headphones?"

"I can answer my cellphone hands-free. Plus, it helps to listen to tunes or that ASMR stuff while I work."

Reece scrunched up his face. "ASMR?"

Drayco explained, "Autonomous sensory meridian response. It's a big deal on YouTube. People create audio-visual triggers like whispering, tapping, or hand movements. For those sensitive to it, it can cause a tingling sensation and relaxation."

Terry nodded. "I'm partial to gentle whispering in Korean. Or the one where they pop bubble wrap over and over. It's very Zen."

"Yes, well, that sounds...interesting." Reece glanced around the room, and the color drained from his face. Drayco had the feeling some ASMR might be helpful to his friend right about then. Terry had finished most of the hard work, judging by the mostly empty space. He'd assured Drayco that he followed all OHSA regulations, and Drayco and Reece would safe from any pathogens. Still, faint hints of leftover brownish stains seemed to make the often-squeamish Reece queasy.

Reece asked if they could hold the interview in another room. Terry agreed with an "Okee doke" and a look at Drayco, who was studying the scene with interest. Terry told him, "You don't look bothered in the slightest."

"I've seen worse."

"A historian who's seen this before? What kind of historian are you?"

"You could say I'm an historian of crime."

They moved into the kitchen area, where Drayco observed tendrils of mold from dampness that crept in while the house sat idle. Smelled like it, too. The gurgling radiator heater shot feathered indigo thorns at Drayco, which were much sharper in here. But color was returning to Reece's cheeks, so the kitchen it was.

Reece once again started off the conversation with the excuse of getting fodder for his book. But Terry was even less enthused than his father about the tape recorder, so Reece said he'd take good notes and whipped out a pad and pen.

Reece started off, "It must be glamorous being the son of a state Supreme Court justice. And hobnobbing with powerful people."

"Glamorous?" Terry's laugh was bleak. "It was so glamorous, my father and I have been estranged for years. I saw what politics is like. The whole learning how the sausage is made. And I saw how it turned good people into monsters."

"Your father included?"

"Dad's a contradiction. Done charity work. He's revered by many. But, at the end of the day, he's still a lot like a politician."

Reece asked, "I gather you never wanted to follow in his footsteps, then?"

"You could say I've taken on crime in my own small way with this business of mine. Other people create criminal messes, and I clean them up."

Drayco almost said, *That makes two of us*, but decided to stick with Reece's cover story for him instead.

Reece scribbled more notes on the pad. "So your estrangement came about because of politics?"

"Mostly." Terry gave a bleak smile. "But my father and I both had our sons later in life. Late-bloomer fathers. Guess that's another reason we don't get along that well with our offspring—the age gap—him and me, me and my son."

Reece replied, "Politics has split apart the best of families."

"It didn't help that my father ruled on that Campfield vs. The State of Virginia case. You've probably read all about it if you're researching that book of yours. Not that I have anything to hide. I just don't care anymore. About my father, politics, even women. Especially my ex."

Reece said, "You mean the case that redefined obscenity laws?"

"That's the one. I had a successful adult entertainment retail store. But that law made it so ambiguous about anything that 'affronts contemporary community standards,' it drove me out of business. And nearly put me in prison. Even drove a wedge between me and my son since he idolizes my father so much. Sometimes, I think my son wishes his grandfather was really his father. Calls him Dad-Dad, which is a clue."

Drayco said, "Your son, Trent, is an extra on a movie being shot in Cape Unity."

"I'd heard that, and yay for him. He's got political aspirations of his own. Since I'm leery of him going into politics, I was happy to hear he was pursuing acting. Hollywood can be tough. But politics is much uglier."

Drayco added, "You may have heard a skeleton was found in the wall of the house where the movie is filming."

"Huh. No, I hadn't. Old skeleton or new skeleton?"

"Decades old."

"Interesting. There's precedent for that, believe it or not."

"There should be a pretty noticeable odor coming from a decomposing body in a wall. Have you ever had to deal with anything like that?"

"Not yet. If that movie skeleton had been new, I'd likely have gotten the call."

Thanks to Drayco's earlier instructions on the way over, Reece asked Terry, "That house was once owned by a man who was a friend of your father's. Duff Ransford."

Terry leaned against a cabinet. "I remember Duff. He was okee doke, a good man as far as I knew. One of the few ethical politicians. Can't say the same about his son. Guess we sons have a problem being heirs to legends."

Drayco spoke up again. "Do you recall Ransford discussing hiring a young woman from Spain? Right after World War II."

"Duff didn't like to discuss the past. Don't know why. With most older folk, that's all they want to talk about. Hell, I'm fifty-one, and my friends are already doing it."

Reece tapped a pen on his notepad. "Since that's why we're here, to discuss the past, I've got a few more questions. If you'll indulge me."

Terry patiently answered Reece's queries for the next half hour. When he finally looked at his wristwatch, he said, "Geez, look at how late it's getting. If you think you've got all you need, I gotta get back to the blood and guts."

Reece paled again. "Thanks for giving us some of your valuable time away from those…blood and guts."

"Okee doke. Let me know when the book comes out."

When Reece and Drayco were safely outside, Reece took deep gulps of the cold air. "And that is why I'm a boring, paper-and-book historian. Dealing with blood on the page. Not blood on the walls."

Drayco promised to pay for milk and something in the carb family to help ease Reece's upset stomach. Drayco added, "Another vote for my client's grandfather being a paragon of virtue."

"Too bad. It's titillating tidbits that sell books. If I want mine to sell more than two copies—one I buy and one you buy," Reece looked expectantly at Drayco, "Then I'll have to get some dirt."

"As long as it's not on my client's grandfather."

"I do think I'm getting good fodder for mysterious skeleton finds on the Eastern Shore. Thanks to you."

Drayco groaned. "For the last time, those skeleton finds are Not. My. Fault."

Reece grinned, "Mrs. Hammontree calls you the skeleton magnet."

Of all the things Drayco thought he'd be known for, that wasn't one. World-famous concert pianist, maybe. Respected FBI agent, yep, for a while. Successful private crime consultant, perhaps, depending upon how you measured "success." But skeleton magnet?

Reece squinted at Drayco. "How do you know so much about— what was it?—ASMR?"

"I've been doing YouTube research. Some psychologists think there may be a link between ASMR and synesthesia."

"So you're in that group affected by this ASMR?"

"Actually, no. I find it rather boring." Drayco studied Reece's face to see if the color had returned. Drayco asked, "Were you able to verify the rumor I found online from an old industry magazine article?"

"I assume we're not talking skeletons anymore. You mean about the Prophett Properties construction company?"

"That's the one."

Reece held up his hand. "Your trusty historian here had a bit of luck. I contacted an acquaintance of mine who loves arcana. Keeps old journals in his basement."

"And he found it?"

"He found it. Said he'd email me a copy. You want me to send it to your phone?"

Drayco nodded. "Thanks, Reece."

"Prophett Properties was more a de-struction, not a con-struction company for part of its history."

"And possibly still is. Not so much actual skeletons as financial ones."

"If Prophett did the renovations on Duff Ransford's house—"

"Then they had the best opportunity to put Madalena's body in the wall. Other than Duff himself."

Drayco still couldn't rule out Duff covering up for the actual murderer. But another angle could be even more impossible to prove. Did Duff accidentally kill Madalena and panic? Even a "good" man might snap under those circumstances if he saw his aspirations in danger of flying out the window. That would be an unsatisfying end to the case.

But that was tomorrow's problem. Right now, he still had a client and a burning desire to find a semblance of justice for Madalena. And with any luck, he could get those titillating tidbits that sell books to give to Reece. If it ever became a bestseller, Reece would owe his "assistant" a five-course gourmet dinner. With Cabernet Sauvignon. Or was that too blood-colored for Reece? Might have to make that a good Sauvignon Blanc instead.

22

After Drayco soothed Reece's nerves and stomach with skim milk and crackers from a convenience store, he dropped the historian off into the comforting hands of Mrs. Hammontree and Reece's swearing parrot. It remained to be seen how "comforted" Reece became, judging by the phrases Drayco heard Andrew Jackson squawking through the open front door.

The movie set, humming back to life, wasn't Drayco's next target—instead, he headed to a warehouse a quarter mile north of the set. He'd nailed down the names of cast and crew who were friendliest with Ellery Smith, and one was Production Designer Hoyt Valentine, Chrystina's brother. The warehouse served as a makeshift prop studio, and Hoyt spent much of his time there.

When Drayco arrived, one other car sat in the parking lot, and he pulled next to it, dodging new puddles from a sudden rain deluge. As he entered the building, its purpose was hard to miss. Various backdrops and set pieces occupied every square inch, with all manner of furniture, area rugs, lights, and paints. Drayco found the man bent over a small bird statue, chewing on an unlighted cigar.

Drayco walked up to take a closer look and said, "The Maltese Falcon?"

Hoyt paused in mid-brush-stroke. "Kinda. It's supposed to be one of the 'Easter eggs' the director wants planted around the set. But it's the wrong color. So…" Hoyt tapped a nearby paint can.

"More of a Maltese pigeon."

"Best I could find on short notice."

Drayco pointed to the unlit cigar. "Trying to kick the habit?"

"Used to be sexy, but nobody smokes in Hollyweird anymore. Except vaping. It's all tanning beds, green smoothies, and the latest de-aging pill fad. Where I'm from, people would call that puttin' on airs."

"You don't live in La-la land?"

"Now, I do. I'm originally from Texas. Chrystina gets embarrassed whenever she lets any twang slip in. I'll bet you've heard it. 'Nahht' instead of night."

"Isn't that putting on airs?"

"Touché." Hoyt put his brush down and wiped his hands on his smock. "You're the piano player. And my sister tells me you're also some kind of private cop."

"In a manner of speaking. What do production designers do exactly?"

"Collaborate with the director, lighting techs, prop masters, and carpenters, among others. And what do private cops do exactly?"

"Collaborate with various law enforcement agencies and clients, among others."

Hoyt smirked. "A wannabe FBI agent?"

"Former."

Hoyt's eyes widened. "Hey, that's cool. I'm a wannabe artist who graduated from art school and had minor success with my paintings. A few hanging in galleries and homes. But no patrons, no advocates, no rich friends."

Drayco looked at a canvas not too far away. "Is that one of yours, or is it for the movie?"

"Both. Rada needed art to hang in the bedroom for an upcoming scene. Who knows? Maybe someone'll see it on the silver screen, and that'll be my big break. At any rate, I can add it to another gallery exhibit."

Drayco studied the painting. "Reminds me of Salvador Dalí. Or Joan Miró. But I think this is better. Sort of surrealist impressionism, which I suppose isn't technically a thing."

"Not in the art books. But that's a pretty cool description. I've always been attracted to Spanish surrealism." Hoyt hopped up on a nearby stool. "But I doubt you dropped by to talk art."

"I don't know, I like talking art. But, in this case, it's more the fine art of justice. Namely, the unfortunate demise of Ellery Smith."

Hoyt grimaced. "That was…I don't even know how to describe how awful that was."

"Sheriff Sailor's team has interviewed you?"

"Interview? What a nice word. More like interrogation. Makes me wonder why you're here right now. Told them everything I could."

"I'm investigating that skeleton found in the wall of the house."

"I know nothing about that." Hoyt grabbed his brush to dab more on the Maltese "falcon," then studied it and shook his head. "I'd have to be a time traveler. My next movie gig, by the way."

"Really? When does it come out?"

"Hasn't left the pre-production stage yet. These things'll take a few years from planning to finish."

Drayco examined a couple of realistic-looking guns. He asked, "Props?"

Hoyt twirled the paintbrush in his hand. "Usually kept under lock and key. But the sheriff's people wanted to see 'em."

After a quick look around, Drayco said, "I don't see any knives."

Hoyt's expression darkened. "The cops took all of 'em away. They said Ellery was killed with one, hence my interrogation. But just because it looks like one of ours doesn't prove it is. It could even be a kitchen knife. I mean, would I use my own prop knife if I wanted to avoid getting caught?"

That was news to Drayco. Sheriff Sailor had neglected to mention that little angle about the knife, which seemed rather important. Was he *that* worried about Drayco stomping in his sandbox?

Drayco asked Hoyt, "How well did you know Ellery?"

"Look, I'll tell you what I told the sheriff. We had some beers together. But he didn't talk about himself much. Mostly sports, the weather, the movie shoot."

"He didn't mention any family?"

"No, and that's odd, now that I think about it. Chrystina and I kept sharing our family stories, yet he never jumped in with his own."

Drayco shifted his feet, which made him off-balance, knocking into a suit of armor he had to steady to keep from falling over. With so many props crammed into the space, he'd have to watch it. But seriously—a suit of armor? He said, "Was Ellery acting strangely before his death? Or seem to be afraid?"

"Those deputies asked me that, too. But no."

"And did they ask if Ellery did any drugs? Or anyone else on set?"

"Yeah." Hoyt stared at his painting. "Suppose that's what everybody thinks. Drugs." He barked out a short laugh. "Hollywood types are at the center of this, right? So, of course, there's drugs, right? As if there were no drugs in town before we arrived."

"Statistically, there's been an increase in drug crimes since the production began. It might be related. Or not. But the sheriff took note."

"Look, most of the cast and crew are hardworking folk. Sure, nobody'll confuse 'em with saints. Flawed with the same demons other people have."

Voices echoed from the entrance, and Drayco turned around as two men sauntered inside and headed toward Drayco and Hoyt. Hoyt called out, "Hey, if you're here to load in more gear and props, we've got a loading dock in the back."

The men looked at each other and back at Hoyt. One of them said, "Sure thing. Thanks for letting us know."

They weren't acting like delivery men, but they and Hoyt appeared to know each other. The taller of the duo looked especially out of place, with tattoos of a dripping knife on his neck, an upside-down cross under his left eye, and a chain of numbers above one eyebrow. Ex-con? Or a gangsta-rapper "wannabe."

Mindful of Hoyt's accusation that Drayco and the sheriff's office were guilty of stereotypes, Drayco merely made note of the man's facial characteristics. Even if he were an ex-con, ex-cons needed jobs, too.

Hoyt told Drayco, "Look, I've got scads of work to catch up on. What with all the interruptions that keep happening. You mind?"

Drayco took the hint, but he didn't see the two men when he exited the building. He noted the addition of an ordinary black pickup truck with red-colored spikes on the wheel rims. This wasn't a van or a typical delivery-style truck. And even the bed of the pickup looked empty.

He peered through the windows into the rear passenger area but couldn't make out anything due to the dark-tinted windows. Was it worth checking in on Hoyt to ensure everything was okay? Drayco let it alone for now, but he memorized the pickup's license plate.

Dodging a few cold raindrops as he headed to the Starfire, Drayco contrasted the Hollywood crew with Hoyt's visitors—possibly shore locals. Aside from the temporary Hollywood invasion, the Eastern Shore was a place in transition. Fishermen, crabbers, and farmers mingled with the newly arrived engineers and scientists at the Wallops Space Launch Center.

Hoyt was right about stereotypes. A small percentage of the hard-working locals wound up in the sheriff's jail cells, but one or two flight engineers had, too. It wasn't just about not judging a book by its cover; it was to never judge a book without putting it in context. Still, it wouldn't hurt to have Sailor's office run the truck's plate, since Drayco didn't have a legitimate legal reason to access any databases himself. Yet.

Drayco climbed into the Starfire and headed onto the access road toward the main highway. He liked this stretch of land, which flanked the marshes dotting the Eastern Shore landscape. But he'd barely driven a quarter mile down the scenic road when he caught a whiff of smoke.

Couldn't be a wildfire in the wet conditions, could it? He didn't see any smoke—until a quick look in the rearview mirror showed grayish-black plumes leaking from the Starfire's trunk.

As he fought a wave of coughing, he yanked the Starfire onto the shoulder and scrambled out. He popped open the trunk and immediately saw the source of those plumes, a smoke bomb. But what lay next to the smoke bomb almost made his heart stop—fireworks and firecrackers of various shapes and sizes.

He grabbed a pair of work gloves he kept in the car, picked up the smoke bomb, and hurled it into the marsh. Then he snatched the fireworks and firecrackers and started to toss them into the brackish saltwater...when one went off.

No time for niceties. He lobbed the entire lot of them onto the road instead, and one by one, they started to ignite, sending sparks flying in all directions.

When some of those sparks got too close, he jumped back and checked to make sure *he* wasn't on fire. But then he had an even worse thought—if any sparks hit the Starfire's gas tank, it could create a fireball. He'd actually worked a case at the FBI with that very scenario.

He couldn't take the chance of a passing car getting caught in a fireball blast if the tank ignited, so he jumped back in the Starfire and drove the car fifty feet down the road. He parked and hopped out again to open all the doors and ventilate the smoke.

The fireworks kept on popping, sounding a lot like gunfire, and it was almost hard to tell the difference. But an even louder barrage of machine-gun style pops made him duck down behind the car to make himself less of a target. He hadn't seen anyone following him from the warehouse, yet he couldn't be certain. Fireworks would make a perfect cover if he had an attacker taking potshots.

Maybe the weather gods were trying to help, because the light misting rain turned into a downpour. His clothes were getting drenched, but so were the fireworks.

The explosions petered out bit by bit and faded away, but Drayco gave it another five minutes as he listened for any new threats. Hearing none, he called the local fire department and Sheriff Sailor's office to report the incident.

While he waited for firefighters to arrive, he monitored the sites where he'd dumped the smoke bomb and fireworks. He didn't have warning cones to divert traffic, but the fire crew got there in record time with their own orange markers. They even managed to retrieve the soggy remains of the smoke bomb.

One firefighter held up some of the fireworks and asked Drayco, "You found these in your trunk?"

Drayco answered in the affirmative, and the firefighter added, "Then you got lucky. These right here are Roman candle mortar shells.

If that smoke bomb had ignited them in your car and set off all those other fireworks, you might not be standing here now."

"The smoke bomb looked damp when I grabbed it. That must have kept the fuse from igniting fully. Just enough to set off a firework chain reaction."

"Then you definitely got lucky. You should buy lottery tickets."

Drayco felt more angry than lucky, furious somebody had tried such a prank. But with that much potential deadly firepower involved, it was likely no simple prank.

The culprit must have put the materials in the Starfire's trunk when Drayco was inside the warehouse with Hoyt. Drayco was angry with himself for not fixing the car's faulty trunk latch sooner, even before his chat with Barry. But the perpetrator wouldn't have known about that latch unless...Drayco had mentioned it to Lucy at the movie set, hadn't he? When most of the cast and crew were around, as a matter of fact.

The warehouse wasn't all that far from the movie-set house. That would make it easy for a crew member to pull into the lot, toss the smoke bomb and fireworks into Drayco's car, and head off. Since Hoyt was inside the building with Drayco at the time, it might knock him off the suspect list unless he'd arranged with an accomplice, or even the two men at the warehouse, to do the job for him.

But what was the motive? Why would Drayco's investigation of a decades-old murder be a reason for such a dangerous stunt?

Sheriff Sailor wouldn't be happy to have more work dumped on him, but it couldn't be helped. And it would be instructive if Sailor tied these fireworks to the ones from the movie-set explosion. Those fireworks could be written off as disgruntled townspeople or trickster teens—unless they really were a distraction from what was happening in the trailer when Ellery was killed.

This time, the trickster-teen or distraction motive didn't hold up. There was no other reason for the smoke bomb and fireworks to be in his trunk except to cause a deadly explosion. Presumably, with Drayco himself squarely in the middle of it.

23

After Drayco finished up with the fire crew and Deputy Monroe, who were sent by the sheriff's office to oversee the evidence collection, Drayco longed for a nice, strong Maida toddy. He was well on his way to becoming a toddy addict, it seemed. But having spoken with the son of the legendary state Supreme Court justice, Drayco thought it might be worthwhile to chat with the youngest of the Clayburgh line, Trent. More so, since the young man had seemed friendly with Ellery Smith.

When Drayco checked with Lucy Harston, she suggested he try Fiddler Green Tavern, as she'd overheard Trent and other crew members say they liked to spend time there. Okay, so not one of Maida's toddies, but still potent.

Drayco asked Reece if he wanted to tag along again, since it could be vital to Reece's book to interview the entire Clayburgh clan. Reece almost said no, as he'd only been at the Historical Society a half day, but Mrs. Hammontree practically pushed him out the door.

Mindful of Reece's asthma, Drayco sprayed down the interior of the Starfire with a can of hypoallergenic air freshener and secured half a dozen open, laundry-sized boxes of baking soda in the trunk. It must have worked, since Reece appeared unaffected.

When Drayco and Reece arrived at the tavern during the tail end of Happy Hour, Drayco was relieved to see it still looked like the same "Ole Trunk and Drunk," as Maida called it. The interior hadn't changed—same hints of wood, dust, and whiskey, the wide-plank flooring, and ship figureheads carved in mermaid shapes rescued from local shore wrecks.

The one new addition was the young man with a preppy green shirt and blow-dried blond hair sitting at a table to himself, looking out of place among flannel and cable-knit regulars. Drayco approached Trent, introduced Reece, and reminded him about Reece's history book.

Trent beamed. "Yeah, you did mention that. Documenting Dad-Dad. A great project."

They sat down as Reece ordered green chili beer and Drayco, his standard Cacao Espresso Stout. Trent had to push aside books to make room, and Drayco studied the titles. "Law books?"

"I want to go to law school. The movie gigs can help my profile, but judges like my grandfather all went to law school. So I'm going to try for it. I'm not too old, and it'll only take three years."

For him, maybe. For part-time Nelia, it would be four or five. Drayco looked around the bar. "Why study here?"

"The guys leave you alone. And I get tired of that damned hotel room night after night."

Drayco surveyed the items on the table. "But no chocolate candy?"

"Dark chocolate's good for the heart. And libido." Trent grinned. "I want to live as long as Dad-Dad, but in case I didn't get the super-ager gene, gotta give it some help."

Once again, Drayco let Reece take the lead with questioning about Trent's grandfather, colleagues, and stories he'd heard through the years. Unlike his father, Trent was happy to have the conversation recorded. He was a native of the media generation, after all. As he'd said, if it wasn't on video or audio, it "didn't happen."

After an hour filled with one humorous anecdote after another about "Dad-Dad," Drayco steered the chat from Talbot Clayburgh to Ellery Smith. "You two socialized on and off the set. I'm curious—did Ellery mention ulterior motives for poking around?"

Trent took a sip of his ale. "What do you mean?"

"Was he surprised by the skeletal find?"

"Weren't we all? That was trippy."

"When I spoke with Ellery, he seemed interested in every detail."

"I think he mentioned being a history major. Or archaeology. Or something like that."

"Aside from you, who were the people on set he spent the most time with?"

"Let's see. There's Chrystina. And her brother, Hoyt. And Nancy. Who's sitting right over there, by the way."

Drayco turned to the table Trent pointed out and spied a head with long, curly brown hair. Since she had her back to them, he hadn't noticed her before. Trent added, "I should be more sociable. But this is kinda my one chance to be alone." He quickly added, "But I'll make an exception for you. I'm always happy to talk about Dad-Dad."

Drayco let Reece stay behind to continue his interview with Trent while Drayco headed over to Nancy. When he asked if he could sit for a minute, she agreed, but at the same time resembled Drayco's half-feral feline, "Cat," who arched her back and danced sideways if feeling threatened.

He tried to put Nancy at ease. "Have you tried the chocolate stout? Though my friend over there prefers the green chili beer."

That elicited a slight relaxing of her tense shoulders. "Don't think my stomach's up for chili anything. But thanks for the tip about the stout." Her eyes darted over to the table with Reece and Trent, then over to the door, then back to Drayco.

Whatever was bothering her, bringing up the topic of Virginia might help. Nancy's face brightened at that, and she gave him a brief grin. "Virginia is such a sweetie. And an inspiration. I don't make friends easy, but with Virginia, I feel like I've known her forever. She's so mature for thirteen."

"She's had to be."

"I guess so." Nancy fiddled with her hoop earrings.

"Virginia told me you grew up on the Eastern Shore, yet you don't have an accent."

"My mother forced me to go to charm school." Nancy used her fingers to put an imaginary gun to her head. "Mom also encouraged me to attend UVA, hoping I'd snag a rich doctor husband. And I did major in Kinesiology. But I've bounced around from one physical therapy job to another, much to Mom's disapproval."

"Charm school, eh? I didn't know they still have those."

She shuddered. "Had to learn to talk properly, walk properly, sit properly, laugh properly, what to wear, what not to wear, ad nauseam."

He smiled. "Then it's a shame you don't have lines in the movie."

That made her laugh. "Tell that to the director, okay?"

"I may do that. But I don't think she'll listen to me."

Nancy sighed. "Don't think she'd listen to much of anybody. She's very, well, direct. And forceful. And doesn't suffer fools gladly."

"To be fair, she didn't count on a skeleton and a murder."

"No, but I get the impression Rada's often like this."

"So I've heard." Since Nancy was still doing a little of the human equivalent of feline back arching, he added, "I'm curious—what does your charm-school-loving mother think of your movie career?"

"I'll ask her tonight. Mom's staying with me after her house got flooded." Nancy played with her earrings again. "I need to find her a new place. Sooner rather than later."

"The empty nest syndrome in reverse?"

"She needs her own nest for sure. I love her, but she still thinks I'm three." Nancy had a pained smile.

"They're building a new housing development outside Cape Charles. I was down there the other day. Something to check out."

"Will do. Thanks for the tip."

Drayco glanced at Reece and Trent, who were still in deep conversation, punctuated by loud laughter. Drayco asked Nancy, "Trent Clayburgh said you were friends with Ellery Smith. How did he strike you? Normal, odd?"

"If by normal you mean a typical male with a typical libido, then yes. *Very* normal." She gulped down the rest of her beer. "I hope you don't mind, but I've got to run, okay? Make sure Mom doesn't forget to turn off the tap and flood my own house."

"Perhaps we can chat more some other time."

She waved at him and hurried out of the tavern. That was the first he'd heard anything about Ellery and romantic interests. Judging by Nancy's body language, not so much romance as sexual harassment. Were there other women he'd pressured? If so, did those women or a boyfriend take offense—enough to put a permanent end to it? Sheriff

Sailor hadn't mentioned revelations along those lines, but neither did he mention the source of the murder weapon.

Drayco rejoined Reece and Trent, who were getting along quite well. So well, Drayco had a feeling he'd have to drive both of them home for the night. He counted seven beer glasses on the table, and only one was Drayco's. Good thing Reece was recording their chat because otherwise, his handwritten notes would need a translator. If Reece didn't get anything helpful on that recording, their trip was a bust unless Nancy's hint paid off.

Drayco got a whiff of something rancid and turned to see a patron whose stomach had declared a revolt and launched a gastric assault onto the floor. Quite appropriate since Drayco's case was stinking from its rotten leads. Maybe he just needed to sprinkle a little quicklime all over it.

The front door banged shut again, heralding two more *Fatal Fugue* escapees, Sachio Spafford and Isaac Batey. After they'd snagged a seat, he left Reece and Trent to their cheery drunken gabfest and approached the new arrivals. "Mind if I join you?" he asked.

Sachio and Isaac looked at each other and nodded in unison. "Sure, man. Join us for the martini after the martini shot."

Having scanned websites on Hollywood slang, Drayco learned film crews called the last movie shot of the day the "martini shot," since the next shot would be out of a glass. He slid into a seat. "Popular place for movie personnel."

Isaac replied, sans his customary chewing tobacco, "We tried other joints around, and this one's got the best beer. Martinis, too."

Drayco said, "I'm surprised to see you both here since you commute every day."

Sachio pushed up the rim of his fedora. "Rada's got a red-eye call for tomorrow. We decided to bunk at Zach's place."

Drayco guessed they meant Barry Farland's friend and set gofer. Drayco smiled as he said, "Sachio's an unusual name. Another case of a Hollywood stage moniker to avoid being mistaken for someone else?"

"Nope, it's my real name. My grandfather was a big jazz fan. Wanted to name me after Louis Armstrong's famous nickname,

Sachmo. But the hospital put the wrong name on the birth certificate. Turns out, Sachio means 'good fortune' in Japanese. Funny, huh?"

Drayco signaled a passing server for a soda, as it seemed Drayco was turning into the designated driver. "Do you often have double duty as gaffer and grip?"

"First ever. It's a bitch, and I hope to never do it again. There's overlap, sure. I'm the head electrician as gaffer, and I handle all the non-electrical rigging as grip. They'd never combine the two in big-budget blockbusters. And both jobs would have best boys."

"Assistants."

Sachio nodded. "We had to get a waiver from IATSE for me to do both jobs. It's all making me real nervous, which is why I keep making mistakes. But I need the money. This film may not have a blockbuster budget, but Rada's well-known and respected in the industry. Despite her recent flops, it'll be a good credit."

Isaac agreed. "It's good for me, too. Better than doing sound for commercials."

At Drayco's questioning look, Isaac explained, "That's what I do between movie and TV gigs. But talk about pressure—I'm the sole production sound credit on this movie. Oh, there'll be sweetening and editing in post, but Rada'll hire a company on the West Coast for that."

Drayco asked, "Have either of you considered moving to LA to find better gigs?"

Isaac replied, "Been checking it out. It could mean working my way into my dream job of audio engineering for movie scores. But even if that doesn't pan out, I'll have more opportunities. Foley, doing mixing for pop stars, fun stuff."

Drayco prompted Sachio, "Are you heading out west, too?"

Sachio hesitated. "I, uh, I can't right now. My baby brother lives with me. But who knows? Maybe someday."

He excused himself to go to "the head," and Isaac waited until he was out of earshot to explain. "Sachio's brother has problems."

"What kind?"

"Running with the wrong crowd. Sachio took him in after their parents kicked him out of the house." Even sloshed, Isaac spoke in his usual monotone style, which was incongruous for an audio guy.

Drayco said, "Sounds noble of him."

"Yeah. Noble." Isaac grabbed the mug of ale the server delivered to the table and took a couple of swigs. "Man, I wouldn't do it."

He clammed up when Sachio rejoined them, and Drayco changed the subject to their late colleague. "Did you two hang out with Ellery Smith?"

Sachio snuffled and wiped his nose on his sleeve. "Nah, we have to get up at god a.m. to make it to the set on time. Then we race at the end of a long day to do it in reverse. The commute's insane."

"And it sounds like you were too busy once on set for socializing?"

Sachio joined Isaac in taking a sip of beer as they drank in unison. "Busy? Try slammed."

Isaac huffed. "I mean, we shoot the breeze during breaks. But Ellery wasn't like the others. Kind of a fish out of water. Always went around with this eye-blinking of his. Like this." Isaac did a pretty good impression of what Drayco had witnessed with Ellery.

Sachio applauded his performance and added, "Isn't that part of the whole third eyelid thing? You know, the kind fish have?"

Isaac grinned, "So he was a real fish, you mean? A mermaid or merman or whatever?"

Sachio pounded the table as the two men laughed. They'd obviously already imbibed a round of alcohol before hitting up Fiddler's Green. Round-robin booze. At this rate, Drayco would have to drive the whole lot of the bar home.

Perhaps he was in masochist-sleuth mode, but he tried again. "Ellery didn't appear worried about anything?"

Sachio let out a string of burps almost in pitch. "Nah, but sure was interested in that hole in the wall. After the cops left, it was all he talked about. Kept going up to it and staring inside. A little creepy. But they say you can't judge a book by its cover."

Isaac poked him in the shoulder. "Man, what did I tell you about clichés?"

A loud peal of laughter behind Drayco made him turn. Reece was getting pretty shit-faced, and Drayco figured he should step in to save his friend from the mother of all historian hangovers. Since his "witnesses" were all getting drunker by the minute, it was unlikely he'd find out much more here.

He rubbed his eyes and headed to join Trent and Reece. As the equally clichéd saying went, "Tomorrow is another day." And with any luck, a far more sober one.

24

Another four guests of the Lazy Crab had checked in and out before Drayco had much of a chance to spend any time at the B&B. With the Jepsons down to themselves and Drayco, they opted to have a late dinner at the kitchen table, which he preferred.

As Maida served him oyster stew and sweet potato biscuits, she said, "Not that I ever want to speak ill of customers, but one couple who just left had me going for a while."

"Did they try to stiff you?"

"Nothing like that, thank heavens. The husband works for a funeral home and enjoyed telling the rest of us all the gory details of the embalming process. That was bad enough since it's not dinner-friendly conversation. But when I put fresh towels in their room, I saw a couple of glass jars in the bathroom with cloudy brown liquid and objects floating in them. Almost had palpitations thinking the guy carries specimens around."

"And were they?"

"I got him to reveal he has two sets of dentures. The liquid is a special antibacterial solution."

Drayco laughed. "Can't be worse than the guest who kept taking raw fish to his room, and you found out he had a baby alligator in the tub."

Maida stuck out her tongue. "I have other bizarre tales to share. But I think I'll save those. Wouldn't want to spoil your appetite."

"Since we're on the topic of strange stories, what have you heard about Prophett Properties, the construction company based in Cape Charles since the early 1900s? I'm mainly interested in the period from around the 1940s or so. It was founded by George Prophett, Sr."

Major was the one to answer as he stroked his braided beard. "See their signs every now and then. A company of that vintage would have struggled during WWII. With the menfolk overseas and all."

Maida added, "Many women took over jobs to help. Probably there, too. I imagine construction supplies were scarce."

Drayco said, "As I understand it, they cobbled together scrap wood not needed for wartime purposes."

Drayco's now-empty plate disappeared as Maida whisked it away to shovel on seconds before he even asked. Everyone was still trying to fatten him up. He'd need to go for a run in the morning. A nice, long run.

Maida said, "You said strange stories, Scott. Those don't sound all that odd."

"The company is the outfit behind renovations of Duff Ransford's house around the time the body was sealed in the wall."

"Oh, I see. Very strange, indeed."

"The current CEO, Pamela Kye, told me Prophett Properties is a 'reputable company,' and they don't have skeletons popping up in their projects. But it took a subpoena to get old employee records. And then we discovered they were conveniently destroyed in a fire."

"You think she's trying to cover up company involvement with that skeleton of yours?"

"It's a family-run business. Despite the lack of personnel files, I was able to check up on Prophett family members who were still alive back then. The founder, his wife, and their two sons are deceased. No record of arrests, but maybe that means they just didn't get caught."

Drayco polished off the waiting stew. He figured he'd gained three pounds right then and there. "In my research, aided by Reece, I found a shady incident in the company's past. A female employee was rumored to have embezzled funds, which the company kept quiet. And also hints of possible drug dealing, even by the founder's son, George Prophett, Jr., but again, no arrests."

"Oh, my. Hardly reputable. But surely they've changed over the years?"

"With rumors of illegal business dealings by Kye's brother, Rait Prophett, perhaps not. I'll have to see about digging into FinCEN records."

"FinCEN?"

"Financial Crimes Enforcement Network."

"Oh, my. Positively Mafioso."

"Or local small-time organized crime."

Maida excused herself to get up to answer the front doorbell, and soon, voices streaming from the hallway revealed the arrival of Barry Farland and Virginia Harston. Virginia headed straight to Maida and handed her a framed painting of Chincoteague ponies by the seashore.

Maida held it up to take it all in. "Virginia, this is absolutely beautiful."

"You really like it?"

"I not only like it, I love it. It's perfect for the den."

Drayco asked Virginia, "Your first commission?"

The teenager nodded. "Not the last. I hope."

Maida added, "Of course, you'll stay for a piece of S'Mores Cheesecake to celebrate."

Drayco pushed his plate and tableware aside, pointing to a couple of empty chairs. He was soon reminded of the healthy appetites of young people when they wolfed down their slices of cake in about a minute. Put him to shame.

He waited until Virginia finished before asking, "Are you still friendly with Nancy Farmery at the movie set?"

"You bet. Why?"

"She knew Ellery Smith, to an extent."

Virginia put down her fork and glared at him. "Sounds to me like you're fishing for rotten tuna. I really like Nancy."

"Not fishing. Just curious if she and Ellery were close."

"You know what I think? I think she tried to avoid him. And there's no way Nancy could be involved in any murder or anything else bad. I would know."

"Does Nancy have any other friends on the set?"

"Nancy and that actor playing the sheriff, Frazier Prentiss, get along pretty well. I saw them holding hands."

"Did Frazier also try to avoid Ellery?"

"I saw him give Ellery the stink-eye once. Thought he'd forgot his lines."

What was it Nancy said earlier at Fiddler's Green Tavern regarding Ellery? Maybe Drayco's suspicions about a love triangle, or make that a potentially deadly love triangle, might not be too far off.

Virginia picked up her fork and drew random patterns in the traces of chocolate frosting still on her plate. "Have you found out anything about that skeleton girl? What's her name again?"

"Madalena. Madalena Delfin Zamora."

Virginia sounded it out, "Mad-ah-lay-nah. Dell-feen. Zam-or-ah. She was young, wasn't she?"

"About nineteen."

Virginia chewed on her lip. "Only six years older than me."

Barry chimed in, "But she didn't have family and friends around her like you do, Ginnie."

"Yes, but don't you think that makes it even sadder?"

Maida cut two more slices of cake and placed them in front of Virginia and Barry. "This will cheer you up while Scott helps me hang this painting. It'll only take a minute."

Drayco gave Maida a questioning look, but didn't say anything until they were alone in the den. After he'd "helped" by merely placing the painting on the fireplace mantel in its temporary spot, Maida asked, "Should we be worried about Virginia on that set? And should we also worry about Nancy being Virginia's friend? I couldn't tell by your line of questioning."

"Lucy, Barry, or Reece are always on the set with her, so I think she's fine. And I don't have any reason to believe Nancy is anything other than harmless. In fact, I'm more concerned Ellery may not have been harmless, at least where Nancy was concerned."

"Oh. I see where you're headed with this. I'll stop worrying. For now."

They returned to the kitchen, where Major regaled Virginia with stories of his pranks from his school days in Britain that made her giggle. As Maida cleared away dishes, Drayco waved to Barry to join him in the hall, where Drayco asked, "You got a minute to look at the Starfire?"

"Uh oh. You find a problem with my work?"

Drayco hastened to reassure him. "No, I'm still amazed at how good a job you did. I have something else to show you." And he led the younger man out to the car, opened the trunk, and shined his pocket flashlight inside.

Barry peered inside and whistled. "Oh, man. It sure didn't look like that when it left the shop."

"A little unwelcome present—a smoke bomb and fireworks. Lucky for me, they didn't have a chance to fully ignite inside the trunk."

"Whoever would do that to this classic beauty deserves to be strung up." Then Barry's face looked a little stricken. "It's partly my fault since I couldn't fix the trunk the other day."

"This is in no way your fault. Don't worry."

Barry scrunched up his face. "Bullet holes and now this. You should drive your other car more often. You still got that—what do you call it? The Generic Silver Camry?"

"It ended up in the bottom of a marsh."

"A marsh? Are you serious? I wasn't kidding when I said you lead an interesting life."

Drayco grinned. "My cars do."

Barry patted the car. "Why don't you bring her by in a day or two, and I'll check her out in the daylight. And I promise I'll fix that trunk latch and anything else I find."

They rejoined the others inside, but Barry decided he needed to get Virginia home. After they'd left, Drayco took the chance to give Major and Maida downtime without having to entertain anyone for a change and headed to his room.

He grabbed the recording device Reece gave him under penalty of death if not returned in pristine condition. As Drayco listened to

Reece's increasingly tipsy conversation with Trent, he didn't get much from it, other than Trent made for an amusing drunk.

The youngest Clayburgh told one funny tale after another about his grandfather. Then Trent and Reece launched into myths about the founding fathers, like George Washington's wooden teeth and the infamous cherry tree. If nothing else, Reece had entertaining fodder for his book.

Drayco turned to his laptop with a sigh. Time for another trip into social media hell. As he'd told Nelia, he'd done preliminary checking on various popular social media networks for the cast and crew. Even Ashleigh Salinger. The vast majority of them were active on several sites.

The actors were among the worst offenders. Ashleigh's posts were about the quirky things that happened to her daily, and she was entertaining with a sharp sense of humor.

Frazier Prentiss mainly posted about football. That was unsurprising, seeing as he started out as a football player in Missouri until he was discovered by an agent. He also posted he was working on finishing his degree online—in psychology, of all things.

Trent Clayburgh and Chrystina Valentine were more into videos, with hundreds of thousands of subscribers. Trent's were primarily political, again not surprising considering his career aspirations. He had dozens focusing on his grandfather and the man's cases, with mini-history lessons involved. They were well thought out. Did he write them himself? His law school research must be paying off.

In stark contrast, Chrystina's videos on her Hollywood Hoedown channel were gossipy. She liked to tease about various scandals in the entertainment world, past and present. She was careful not to name names or include detailed personal info. Still, it would only be a matter of time until someone's attorney got involved, waving the defamation flag.

She had a winning strategy because her subscribers far outnumbered Trent's. But when Drayco read the details about step-up payouts tied to video views and subscriber numbers, he understood Chrystina's scheme. Sex sells.

So did kickbacks and money laundering, albeit in a much different way. Was Prophett Properties involved in illegal activities? And had Ellery Smith been aware of it? Drayco was kicking himself now that he hadn't coaxed Ellery into meeting with him after Madalena's remains were found. But Ellery's interest had seemed more quirky than quixotic.

More tired than he'd realized, Drayco leaned against the headboard with his eyes closed. Then he grabbed the laptop again and called up a video of Van Cliburn playing the first of Liszt's piano concertos. He hadn't awakened from nightmares much lately, but using music as a nightmare talisman often did the trick…as long as he didn't listen to another Liszt piano work, the *Totentanz*. Dance of Death.

A sudden coughing spell made him hop up to grab a glass of water, hoping he hadn't disturbed the Jepsons. A leftover from the smoke bomb? The more he considered that little stunt, the more he was convinced it was no prank but a warning, or worse. And since fireworks had preceded Ellery's murder, Drayco wasn't about to let his guard down.

While he was still up, he shed his clothes. When he tossed his slacks over a chair, a folded-up copy he'd made of Regina's forensic sketch of Madalena fell out of a pocket. He rescued it and sat on the side of the bed, studying the portrait.

The paper felt cool and slick as he smoothed out the crinkled edges. The depiction was good, even if the eyes were still lifeless. But as he stared at Madalena's likeness, for a moment he thought he saw a spark of life in those eyes. Just his imagination? Or another reminder it was always the poorest, most helpless, most invisible victims who ate away at his psyche the most.

25

Sunday, January 16

Drayco pulled up to the Prophett Properties headquarters on the dot of ten. He hoped he'd timed it right, after his morning trail run took longer than he planned. It was earlyish, but he had a tip that CEO Pamela Kye was working in the office over the weekend. With luck, he'd have her undivided attention without other staff around. But as he surveyed the lot, he saw no cars. So maybe his tip wasn't accurate?

Finding the front door to the building unlocked, he headed on in. No receptionist, so Drayco went to Kye's office door and knocked. When Kye opened the door and saw who it was, her expression morphed instantly from surprise to annoyance. She hesitated for a split second, then ushered him in. Kye again wore the silver shark earrings, quite on brand.

He said, "When I didn't see your car, I was afraid I'd missed you."

Judging by her still-annoyed expression, she clearly wished he had. "I don't like to drive. My husband drops me off. And what the hell are you doing here on a Sunday?"

"A mutual acquaintance told me you often work on Sundays. I have a couple of questions."

"You could have called."

"I wasn't sure you'd take my call."

Drayco snagged a chair, but she opted to perch on the edge of her desk. "If you're here about that subpoena, you're wasting your breath. Sheriff Sailor's office delivered one. And we told him the records were destroyed."

"In a fire, yes, I know. I checked the fire department reports. No sign of arson."

"Absolutely not. Faulty wiring. It happens."

"Why weren't the records stored here? From what I've read, this building has served as your company HQ since its founding."

"We didn't see a need to keep them here. They take up too much room. And we hired a firm to digitize them, anyway."

"But the fire made that point moot."

"Unfortunately. I'm just glad no one was hurt."

Drayco surveyed her office walls. No older photos of employees, except for George Prophett, Sr., the founder, and one of his sons, George Jr. Come to think of it, no historic photos in the lobby, either. He said, "Last we spoke, you mentioned a prospective employee insistent on getting a job to the point of hounding you. Was his name Ellery Smith?"

She furrowed her brow. "That's the one. How did you know? He wasn't qualified. Kept calling every day. Also showing up at our office. We were close to filing a restraining order."

"What job was he after?"

"A low-level file clerk."

"Meaning he would have had access to all your records in such a job?"

"Yes, why? Does it matter?"

"It may have, to him. Doubly so if he didn't know they'd burned in that fire."

"Why this obsession with our records? First him, now you?"

"And I could ask why you're so hesitant to discuss staff from decades ago? Prophett can't be sued for an action an employee undertook on their own. More so, if the statute of limitations applies."

"So you'd think. Society is very litigious."

"Still, unless the company engaged in illegal activities—a murder, for instance—it seems unlikely."

"Murder? That's preposterous." She gave him the same mocking smile she'd used on him last time and added, "Only an idiot or a madman would think that."

"Every business has scandals, large or small."

"Any hint of scandal, even embezzlement long ago, could hurt our business."

"I didn't mention embezzlement."

Her eyes narrowed. "What?"

"I uncovered an old report about a case of possible embezzlement by a company employee. But I didn't mention it to you until just now."

"Ancient history. And as you said, every company has scandals."

"That same report hinted at drug dealing—cocaine, barbiturates, amphetamines."

She folded her arms across her chest. "Now, look. Those are old crimes and have zero to do with us today. If all that is even true. You said 'hints,' which smacks of rumors and innuendo. A disgruntled employee fired for being lazy. Nothing more."

"A few newer lines of investigation are more interesting. I didn't find any FinCEN complaints about Prophett. But since you're a family-owned business, you'd know of any less-than-legal transactions. Or so I would imagine."

A deep voice from a new arrival startled Drayco, as a broad-shouldered man, with hair that matched his gray suit, entered the office. "Pammy, what's this? Who's this guy, and what does he want?"

As Kye looked up at the man, her eyes flashed danger signs. From her to her visitor or the other way around, Drayco wasn't sure.

The man added, "Look, I don't know who you are, but I got snippets of your words. Sounds like something you don't have any right suggesting. And if this is blackmail, I don't take too kindly to that."

When he stomped over to Drayco and towered above him, Kye jumped off her perch on the edge of her desk and hastened to put a hand on the man's shoulder. "Now, Rait, no reason to get excited. This gentleman is helping the Cape Unity sheriff's office about that skeleton they found."

Rait pointed his finger toward Drayco. "Didn't sound like that to me."

From the name Kye used, Drayco gathered this was her brother, Rait Prophett. She said in a soothing voice, "It's nothing. I know you're on edge because of the strike."

Drayco spoke up, "Strike?"

She replied, "A workers' union is threatening to call a strike. Would set all our projects back by weeks. Or even months."

Rait growled, "Damn union. Trying to nickel and dime us out of business." He glowered at Drayco. "And we don't need more trouble on top of that."

When Rait moved even closer to Drayco, Kye said to her brother, "We got in a delivery of those new computers Friday afternoon, Rait. Haven't even opened the boxes. Why don't you check them out? Make sure we weren't sent the wrong items like the last shipment."

Rait looked like he'd rather punch Drayco in the face, but with another look at his sister, he relented. "Sure, Pammy. But you," he pointed at Drayco again. "You got any more questions or accusations, you go through our lawyer. And I want you off our property. Right now. Or else."

After he'd left, Kye half-apologized. "We're all upset about the possible work stoppage, as you can imagine. Now's not a good time for this. And Rait is on the money about one thing." She darted over to her desk and pulled out a business card. "Here's the name and number for our company attorney. If you have any other questions, go through him."

Drayco took the hint and headed outside, keeping an eye out for Rait. If the man hadn't been a football lineman, he'd missed an opportunity to put all that muscle and girth to good use. But Drayco had noticed something else—Rait had hearing aids in both ears. That could explain his overly loud tone of voice, but more likely it was his habit. Wonder who else was the object of the man's verbal abuse?

Rait also wore a suit. No jeans? And his sister's jacketed dress and heels were likewise too formal for a weekend stint at the office. Perhaps they were planning on attending a church service later. Or they were expecting company—the type of company best received on a day with no other employees as witnesses.

So much for new information. But Drayco had verification of his hunch about Ellery Smith pestering Prophett Properties for a job. So, Ellery wanted to get his hands on historical records about the movie-set house, and then he took a job at said house. Even with possible familial ties, it was an odd obsession.

Pamela Kye and her brother might want to cover up any wrongdoing from company employees regarding Duff Ransford's house, but was the company's reputation all she was trying to protect? Those company employees from years ago included family members—parents, grandparents, uncles, aunts. But with most of the staff and records long gone, proof would be unlikely. Very convenient.

It also made it harder to determine if someone other than Genna Ransford's grandfather had the opportunity to entomb Madalena in that wall. Drayco would have to go at it another way.

He had a near-perfect record as an FBI agent and private consultant. He knew when he took on this case that his chances of clearing Duff Ransford of involvement in Madalena's death would be difficult, if not impossible. But he wasn't only doing this for his client and her grandfather. He was doing it for Madalena and all the other forgotten girls. And for all those mothers still waiting for their missing daughters to come home.

Drayco squinted at the sky, which seemed even brighter than usual after the recent rains. He needed to throw more sunlight on the case, but where to find an opening in those investigative clouds? Maybe he should try consulting a death expert again.

26

Drayco squinted up at the *Live Crawdads* banner on the side of Limping Mike's Bait Shop. When he stepped inside, it was clearly not a "bait and switch," as there was indeed a tank next to the counter filled with what resembled mini-lobsters. A few clustered in clumps on the bottom, while others appeared to be duking it out in a territorial dispute. Very human-like behavior, that. He'd always felt sorry for live lobsters in seafood restaurant tanks huddled in the corners, resigned to their fate. He'd have to add crawdads to that pity-list.

Otherwise, the shop looked the same as when he was last there. And it would look exactly the same if he didn't return for another year. Or ten. Rib lizards, salty rat tails, crappie rigs, casting rods, and even live leeches—just in case the crawdads got lonely.

Drayco waved at owner Mike Dickens. "Long time no see, Mike. Hope business is still good."

"You kidding? When times get tough, people go fishing. Plus, you can't beat fresh flounder from Wachapreague stuffed with crab meat."

"Now you've got me craving a seafood dinner."

Mike grinned. "And to wash it all down, I restocked your favorite Manhattan Special sodas."

Drayco grabbed several sodas from a refrigerated case, which was the secondary reason he was there. The main reason was a tip from Maida Jepson. As Drayco put the sodas on the counter, he asked owner Mike Dickens if he knew Terry Clayburgh, estranged son of the ex-justice.

As Mike rang up Drayco's drinks and a can of Skipjack nuts, he replied, "I knew him, oh, about a decade ago. Decent man. Had his demons like most of us."

"He wasn't a former Navy Seal like yourself, though."

"Demons come in many forms. Stress is a big part of that. Whether it's trying to guess *where* your enemy is out in the field or trying to guess *who* your enemy is—like in politics."

"I spoke with Terry. I gathered he wasn't a fan of the political scene."

"Who is? Except politicians."

"What form did Terry's demons take?"

Mike squinted at a pyramidal stack of soap bricks to the right of the register and lined them up until they weren't threatening to topple. "Pharmaceuticals."

"The not-so-legal kind?"

"I didn't see him dealing or dosing, myself. Just knew he had a problem. Could be that Lady Macbeth of his who drove him to it, I don't know."

"His ex-wife, you mean?"

"Not sure she's so 'ex' unless they made it official. Separated and went their different ways. And she got into local politics afterward. As if to stick it to Terry even more."

"So, he was getting a political beating on all sides—father, son, wife."

"You've heard of the term political football? That was him. The well-used, beat-up kind, with the laces come undone from all that kicking."

"I didn't find an arrest record for him."

"Doubt you will. Having a powerful father can do that for you. Record expunged. Oddly enough, I think Terry resented that."

"That his father was more interested in keeping his own reputation clean than his son's welfare?"

Mike tapped his nose.

"Have you spoken with Terry recently? Or been around him enough to know whether those demons still haunt him?"

"The wife keeps me on a tight leash. I only get to hobnob with saints."

Drayco looked at him skeptically, and Mike added, "Of course, leashes come in handy with all that BDSM stuff."

Drayco groaned and said, "Too much information, Mike," to which the other man waggled his eyebrows and laughed.

With his new purchases juggled in his hands, Drayco managed to open the door of his Starfire and stow the bottles without breaking any. He rolled down the windows, ignoring the cold air. Hints of the smoky smell still lingered in the car's interior, and he didn't want it clinging to his clothes.

He arranged himself in the driver's seat, shaking his head at the intrusion of drugs again into the investigation. It might turn out Sailor was right about the motive for Ellery's murder. But could someone like Terry be involved?

Ellery's death wasn't *technically* Drayco's case, but…maybe Reece hadn't got all he needed from Terry for Reece's upcoming book. And Drayco could go on playing Reece's "assistant" to see if he could uncover additional fodder. What harm could it do?

But first, he had a phone call to make. When he got a brief look at the paper on Sheriff Sailor's desk a few days ago with information on the Spanish embassy, Drayco caught a number for a potential descendant of Madalena's. He'd memorized it and looked it up—the number belonged to a distant cousin, Josefina Ruiz, on Madalena's father's side. With the six-hour time difference, he should be able to catch her at home if he was lucky.

Josefina was surprised to hear from him, but yes, she'd received a call from a representative of the Spanish government about the skeletal remains. As she explained, the story of Madalena's immigration was passed down through the years among the family. Madalena left Spain during the troubled era of the Franco regime, hoping to make a new life for herself. But no one heard from her again.

Since her English seemed a bit of a struggle, Drayco asked in Spanish, "Why did they not look for her when she didn't return or even send letters?"

"It was after the war, things were crazy. And it's America, yes? A world away. A universe away. As the years passed, we all preferred to believe she'd decided to avoid any memory of her former life. Rather than accept the fact she was dead."

"Did that government representative mention arrangements for the remains to be returned to the family plot?"

The voice on the other end was filled with a touch of bitterness. "No one wants to pay for that. She was not an important person, you see."

Alas, Drayco couldn't give her any reassurances that he could make it happen, either. He did promise to find out if he could do anything to help. Or at least arrange a decent burial on this side of the Atlantic.

Josefina replied, "There was a toy, a small stuffed animal. A giraffe. Passed down through the years. It was said to belong to her, her favorite. She should be buried with it."

"You can mail it to the embassy over here or the office of Sheriff Ernest Sailor."

She was silent for a few seconds and then asked, "Could I send it to you instead? You have a nice voice. I think I trust you more."

Drayco decided to give her Maida Jepson's address. Maida would understand. She'd also be a faithful guardian of the toy until it could be reunited with its original owner, in whatever humble burial Madalena ultimately received.

Drayco shook his head at that thought. In the Varna Necropolis in Bulgaria six thousand years ago, wealthy people were buried with gold pendants, bracelets, and headpieces. Ancient tombs found at Saqqara in Egypt held mummies of noblemen entombed with hundreds of bronze statues covered in precious gems. A warrior's tomb from ancient Greece had an ivory-and-gold sword, beads of amethyst and jasper, and engraved seal stones.

Grand statements, those other tombs. But Drayco doubted the privileged people buried there cared much about the items they were buried with. Perhaps the real treasure was a much-loved stuffed giraffe that once gave a child much happiness and joy?

He made another phone call, this one to a familiar number. The man's voice that answered had the same gold-and-green timbre, shaped like a sine wave, that made Drayco think of Debussy. It was the same synesthesia reaction. Mark "Sarg" Sargosian asked, "You still over on the shore?"

"Turns out I had a case come my way."

"Figures. What is it now? Another buried manuscript? Or another buried skeleton?"

Drayco winced. "Funny you should say that second one."

"You're kidding me. For real?"

"The Medical Examiner verified it's human, so yes, real. Buried in a wall since shortly after World War II."

"Got an ID?"

"A nineteen-year-old immigrant from Spain who'd recently given birth. Worked as a nanny."

Drayco heard Sarg's teeth grinding on the other end. As the father of a daughter himself, Sarg had never liked these types of cases. Sarg said, "You need something, you got it."

"I've conducted preliminary research on serial killers in the area and the U.S. at the time, but nada."

"I'll double-check the databases."

"I'm also wondering if the Bureau has any active investigations that include a construction company based in Cape Charles, one Prophett Properties. That's with a 'PH' and two 'T's.' The current CEO is Pamela Kye, who runs the outfit along with her brother, Rait Prophett."

"What, you think they're into money laundering?"

"Or trafficking. Or mob ties. Both during and after the war and up to the present."

"I got a current case helping out the SEC and Treasury. So those pipelines are open and primed."

"Seems like fate, then. And for your trouble, I'll get you tickets to a polka concert."

Sarg laughed. "Make it 'Polkamotion by the Ocean' in Rehoboth, and we're square." Then his voice grew more serious. "A seventy-year-old cold case. I'm surprised you'd take it on, knowing how you feel after that Jane Doe years ago."

"Maybe there's nothing I can do about that case, but I'd like to close this one."

Several seconds elapsed on the other end until Sarg said, "Then I hope you do, Junior. I hope you do."

Drayco sighed. "Dad would tell me I'm insane. Taking a pittance for a cold case when I have a potential power-player client in D.C. hounding me."

"Power-player client?"

"Langstrom and Ailes. Insurance fraud."

"Your oh-so-favorite type of case."

"Still, it would be good money."

Sarg exhaled with a loud *oof*. "You said the company was hounding you?"

"They called me six days ago. And again two days ago. And again today. They're wondering why I haven't started yet."

More silence on the other end for a few moments, prompting Drayco to ask, "You still there?"

"I was thinking. Last year, the Bureau worked with someone who works with these guys. I could make a few calls. Do a little additional stalling for you."

Drayco took his time replying, prompting Sarg to ask, "Are *you* still there?"

"I can't ask you to do that, Sarg. But it sure beats asking Brock to cover for me."

"I was wondering about that. But I understand not wanting to bug your dear ol' Dad for this. Besides, you're not asking me. I'm volunteering. Let me see what I can do, and I'll get back to you."

Drayco was grateful on many levels, not the least of which was knowing Sarg was one of the few people on the planet who'd understand why Drayco would pursue a potentially hopeless cold case—jeopardizing a more lucrative, newer one. Sure, he could try to do both cases simultaneously, as he'd told Maida, and that's what he might wind up doing. But the murder investigation of Ellery Smith, likely Madalena's grandson, was still warm. And if any connection whatsoever to Madalena's cold case existed, that lead could cool off fast.

Damned if you do, damned if you don't. If Drayco ever wound up creating a private investigator video game, that would be the perfect name for it.

27

Drayco found Terry Clayburgh at a small shoe repair business in Accomack County, once again following the man's directions over the phone. Terry didn't greet him, but when Drayco reached the front door, it was propped open.

Drayco had a pretty good idea why, as he made his way toward noises from the rear, which led him to a one-bedroom apartment attached to the shop. Even with the back door and all the windows wide open, the space still reeked. He noted an ozone machine on the floor. It didn't seem to be helping.

This wasn't Drayco's only rodeo with a messy crime scene aftermath. But it was years since he had such a pungent experience, and it stirred up some not-so-lovely memories. Since this was a newer project than the last one, Terry wore a hard hat, gloves, goggles, shoe covers, and a respirator in addition to coveralls.

He motioned for Drayco to follow him back to the shop area, but the pungent odor lingered there, as well. Terry grabbed a mask from his kit box and handed it over, along with a small tub of Vicks, which Drayco dabbed under his nose before putting on the mask. Then Terry swapped his respirator for a regular mask to make it slightly easier to talk.

Terry said, "You told me you were experienced with this kind of thing. But I work in the business, and even I need it," and he pointed to his own mask.

As Drayco examined the shop, Terry explained in his muffled voice, "The owner was in here when a guy broke in and tried to rob the place. The owner grabbed a gun, but the robber had a bigger gun and shot the owner dead. The body was here for days before anyone started asking questions when the shop didn't open."

"Did they catch the shooter?"

"He got as far as Baltimore, but they nabbed him."

Most of the bedding, carpeting, curtains, and anything made of fabric was already tagged and tossed. But the decomposition of a body could progress rapidly within days—especially in a small space like this with the heat cranked up on high. Bodily fluids and tissue found their way into floorboards and walls, and once the maggots and bacteria got going, it became a forensic dirty bomb.

This room had served as a de facto tomb, not all that far off from Madalena stuffed in the crawlspace. Drayco had a moment of intense depression for the deceased shoe-repair owner. And yet, who knew what otherwise would have felled him—heart disease, stroke, cancer? Was it better to suffer a long, drawn-out death or be surprised into it? Still, just like Ashleigh said about Madalena, this victim should have had the chance to live and die on his own terms.

Terry had yet to throw out all of the dead man's projects, and six pairs of shoes sat on a table in various degrees of repair. Their owners wouldn't get those back, if they wanted them at all.

Terry said, "I'm confused to see you so soon since we spoke yesterday. And where's the other guy? The one who kept turning green."

Drayco grinned. "I thought it wise to let him take a breather today. So to speak."

"Okee doke. So what else can I tell you? I've not done anything interesting that warrants a mention in that book of yours. Certainly not in twenty-four hours."

"Interesting can be a matter of semantics. As in, say, an expunged drug record."

Even with the mask, it was easy to see Terry's expression harden. "How do you know that?"

"That's what historians do. But is it ancient history? And not recent history?"

"Look, okay, so I had a drug addiction years ago. I'm clean now. I can give you the name and number of the counselor I see every week."

Drayco nodded. He might take him up on that offer. "They've had an increase in drug crimes in the Cape Unity area since the movie crew moved in."

"It's not my son, if that's what you're implying. And if it was, it's not like I would tell you, would I? Besides, Trent would have nothing to do with that. He wouldn't want to poison any future chances in politics."

"Like your own father didn't want his son having a drug record, for fear it would make a state Supreme Court justice look bad?"

Terry gave a bitter laugh. "Exactly."

A large bottle perched against a wall looked unfamiliar, so Drayco moseyed over for a closer scrutiny. An industrial-strength enzyme solvent. Of course. One had to kill viruses and bacteria and to liquefy dried blood somehow. He asked, "So you finished up the other house yesterday?"

"Yep, but this one's gonna be harder."

"How long did the other take?"

"Several exhausting twelve-hour days."

"So you weren't working on that four days ago?"

"Four days ago? Nah, I was getting over a cold. Stayed home, sleeping it off with my dog. Who makes a great nurse, by the way."

Drayco spied red biohazard bags outside, marked with the iconic symbol of four black interlocked rings. "Do the police hire you for their projects, or is it mostly families?"

"Both. Fifty-fifty. Okay, more like forty-forty. Realtors hire me, too."

"At least you won't have to work the case up at the Cape Unity movie set."

"That's the one you mentioned yesterday, right?" The muscles on Terry's forehead contracted into a frown. "You know what's funny?"

"I'm not sure what you mean."

"I looked up that story on the news after you told me about it. They had a photo of the guy who was killed, and I've seen him before."

That got Drayco's interest. "Where and when?"

"If it's the same guy, he called me up. To check out my business, he said. So we met for a beer. I didn't put two and two together until I saw that photo. He started off by asking a few questions about what I do and my rates. But he also wanted to know how bodies decompose. Kind of an odd thing to ask. He told me he was interested in the topic and was thinking of going into forensics. Like at a university."

"What did you tell him?"

"Oh, the basics. And he asked about using quicklime on a body. To cover up any odors."

"You should call Sheriff Sailor's office to inform him of this. It may not matter, but you never know."

Terry groaned loudly enough to be heard through the mask. "I should. Guess I will."

Drayco thanked Terry for his time and handed the extra mask to him, happy to leave the man to his unpleasant job. Drayco headed outside, gulping in the cool air. Even in winter, you could catch whiffs of brine from the marshes that snaked a path toward the coast. The smell could be a little on the malodorous side, with a rotting-egg component from the sulfuric algae. But today, it had a cleansing aroma in stark contrast to the scene he'd just left.

So, Terry swore he was no longer doing drugs. And that his son was clean, too. But if Terry was home alone with his dog on the day of Ellery's murder, it meant he didn't have an alibi unless the dog had learned to talk. That was an interesting facet to the kind of job Terry had—without a partner or staff to confirm he was working where or when he said he was, he wouldn't have an iron-clad alibi.

Maybe it was a mere coincidence the fireworks and smoke bomb turned up in Drayco's car after he and Reece talked to Terry yesterday. And yet, it would be ironic if a crime scene cleanup job made the perfect cover for a brand-new crime.

28

Fiddler's Green was quite the popular hangout with the movie crew. When Drayco asked to meet up with Chrystina Valentine, she suggested the tavern. Well, one could never get enough of Cacao Espresso Stout. Coffee, dark chocolate, and beer—a glass of thrice-vice goodness.

Unlike the other night, Chrystina was the lone crew member in evidence when he arrived. *Oh well. Give it time.*

He'd visited there countless times, but late in the evening, with the reduced lighting and more raucous patrons, the place seemed not just darker but grungier. When he pointed it out, Chrystina replied, "I love it. Sure beats the sanitized Hollywood world I inhabit. I get so sick of Botox and breast implants. This is real people, real problems, real life."

As always, Chrystina had her cellphone in hand, scrolling through it as she spoke with him. So, that "real life" wasn't quite enough entertainment, apparently.

He said, "About that Hollywood world. I looked you up in the internet movie database."

"And you didn't see a long list of credits. I know. This is my first big gig. I've had a bunch of television jobs with shows on those off-brand cable networks, so I was thrilled to get the job. But with all the sordid drama on the set, I'm not so sure anymore."

Drayco took a sip of the stout. It tasted more tangy than usual. Maybe instead, he should have ordered a Creamsicle soda in honor of Chrystina and her orange-vanilla lip balm. "In your interactions with Ellery, did you hear him mention any personal dramas? Like ex-wives or girlfriends? Or boyfriends?"

"What, you mean a love affair gone wrong? Isn't that clichéd?"

"It's clichéd for a reason. Twenty-five percent of people are assaulted by a partner. And one-fifth of homicide victims are killed by an intimate partner."

Chrystina put her phone down to clutch her whisky sour. "Ellery said it had been years since his last serious relationship."

"Let's chat about his less-serious relationships, then. A crew member overheard you discussing a guy you'd hooked up with. That guy was Ellery, wasn't it?"

Chrystina chewed on her lip. "That bitchy Jaxine gave me up, didn't she? Look, it wasn't anything. Not much more than a one-night stand. And it was consensual. We didn't argue, nothing like that." She pronounced it one-nahht stand, so her brother's comment about the Texas twang was on the mark.

Drayco asked, "Were there drugs involved?"

"I didn't see any signs of drug abuse while I was with him."

Drayco noted her careful, nondescript phrasing. He'd have to pursue that angle elsewhere later. "What did you two talk about?"

"The usual sorts of things. But he asked bunches of questions. About the area, the house, the owners, its history, etc."

She took a long sip of her whiskey before adding, "You should talk with Nancy Farmery."

"Why is that?"

"Ellery hit on her more than once. Came on a bit much, more so after drinking. I don't think our big-shot star, Frazier Prentiss, was happy about that. He's taken a shine to Nancy."

"Were you jealous of Ellery's interest in Nancy?"

"Are you serious? He's not my type. Awkward. A real gomer, you know?"

"And yet you hooked up with him."

"When you have an itch to scratch, you find a back scratcher. The tabloids get one thing right. Sex is everywhere in Hollywood. The young, the beautiful, the rich, the powerful. Everybody wants to get ahead. Everybody wants to get a score of whatever. And everybody wants to get laid."

"If Ellery wanted the latter with you and Nancy, it begs the question of who else he set his sights on."

"Too bad you can't ask him."

Drayco signaled the server to order a roast beef sandwich. The extra protein would offset the alcohol, since he was driving. Chrystina ordered a vegetarian cheese and tomato sandwich for herself, then looked around at the other patrons while they waited. Was it out of curiosity or to avoid looking at him?

He asked, "How's your screenplay coming along?"

"Still doing research. I'm getting a shitload of ideas."

"Will you consult with your brother? About the artistic design?"

"I can't guarantee Hoyt would get the job *if* anyone wants to produce my project. That wouldn't be up to me. But I'd put in a good word for him."

"He was in the IMDB records, too. Several impressive credits."

"Hoyt is an incredible production designer. You should have seen that house we're shooting in before he got his hands on it."

"I doubt he planned on adding a skeleton into the mix."

"Not even close. But it's given him ideas for future productions. Heh, that's one silver lining. The gig's good for our creativity."

Drayco tried not to get annoyed by that. The cavalier attitude everyone had over the decades-old murder still rankled. "Madalena wasn't a cheap Hollywood prop."

Chrystina grabbed her orange-vanilla gloss to apply to her lips. "Madalena. That was the skeleton's name?"

"Madalena Zamora." Drayco reached into his pocket to rescue the photocopy of the sketch Deputy Regina Reymann gave him. He unfolded it to show Chrystina. "That's a forensic sketch of what she could have looked like."

"Very pretty. And so young."

Drayco looked from the paper to Chrystina. "You resemble her a little. Do you have any Spanish ancestry? Hoyt looks like he might."

"Our family isn't big on that genealogy stuff. I can't even tell you much about my grandparents. Let alone farther than that."

"Your Texas twang gives you away."

She grimaced. "Funny, I didn't think I had an accent. I've worked hard to get rid of it."

"It's not strong. You have to know how to listen for it." Drayco didn't want to bring up the whole synesthesia bit. Far too complicated to explain. But in addition to each voice having its own unique color, shape, and texture, different accents shared similar chromesthesia traits to his brain. Just another part of the odd soundscape he lived in.

As Chrystina attacked her newly arrived sandwich, Drayco mused on her fling with Ellery Smith—who also had a thing for Nancy Farmery. And who knows who else? Chrystina may have danced around the issue, but drugs were likely among that mix. Would all those salacious details wind up on Chrystina's gossipy YouTube channel? With an inward sigh, he resigned himself to being forced to watch more of her content later.

With Ellery having to concentrate on his job and his romantic pursuits, it was a wonder he had time to be obsessed with his ancestry and a skeleton found in a wall. Drayco took another sip of the beer. He didn't believe in clairvoyance. Ellery *knew* the skeletal remains were on that property. But how? If Drayco solved that one puzzle, he had a hunch he'd be closer to finding answers for his client. But how do you get answers from a dead man? Hopefully, Sheriff Sailor was having better luck than Drayco was.

§ § §

Drayco might have to rethink that whole clairvoyant bit because when he left Fiddler's Green for his car, his cellphone rang. Sheriff Sailor's gruff voice sounded even more tired than usual. "Thought you'd like to know we analyzed that smoke bomb and fireworks someone gifted you. Homemade bomb with a small dark glass jar, cap, and cotton fuse soaked in sugar and potassium nitrate. You were lucky the rain dampened the fuse, or it could have been much worse. Thanks for not tossing the fireworks into the water, by the way. Saved me tedious EPA paperwork. Perchlorate compounds in certain fireworks are toxic to wildlife and water."

"Glad that worked out for all involved."

"We're still trying to track down the source of the materials from the bomb and the fireworks that caused the barrel explosion. But that's not the main reason I called. You were right all along. Damn you. We got the official lab results from comparing Ellery Smith's DNA against Madalena's."

"And it's a close enough match for Ellery to be Madalena's grandson."

"I told you not to make the two cases related, didn't I?"

Sailor sounded like he was only *half*-kidding. Drayco said, "Seems unlikely he's killed in the same location where his grandmother was murdered decades ago."

"I'll grant you that. But then there's the timeline difference. Just ask your friend, Reece 'Mr. Kismet' Wable. Fate is fate, and Ellery Smith was destined to die in the same place she did. If you believe in those sorts of things."

"I prefer not to."

"Yeah, I'm still putting my money on drugs."

"I've never known you to be so single-minded about a motive."

"Not so single. I'm working all angles—drugs, jealousy, money. Due diligence and all. But since the two cases have that one link in common, you know the drill. Don't hold out on me. Whatever you find out, I want to hear about it. Last I checked, obstructing a police investigation is still worth a year in the hoosegow. Our jail food is decent, but I doubt you'd like it."

After Drayco ended the call with Sailor, he drummed his fingers on the Starfire's steering wheel, dissatisfied. His hypothesis was correct. But he was no closer to knowing how Ellery knew where his grandmother was possibly buried. So what now? The records at the library archives in Manahoack only hinted at Madalena's work as a nanny, with no mentions of Cape Unity or Duff Ransford, the grandfather of Drayco's client.

Even if Ellery had tracked down where his grandmother spent her last moments on Earth, what did he have to gain from it? Was he seeking closure? And did he ever try to connect with his father, Madalena's son, Pauley Harrington? If so, had he told his father about his research into Madalena's death, or did all of that happen after his father's demise? Too many questions, too few answers.

Perhaps Ellery sought a connection to any semblance of a family left after everyone around him died—his mother, his father, and the couple who raised him, some of whom expired through violent means. If those were his aims, then he'd failed spectacularly. And, if in the process Ellery discovered who'd killed Madalena, he'd taken that secret with him to the grave.

29

Monday, January 17

The following day dawned without rain or sleet and enough sunshine to make Drayco don a short-sleeved shirt. But that was apparently too much sun for the movie set, because the first thing Drayco noticed when he entered the house was a blackout drape newly added behind a window curtain. Meanwhile, poor Sachio Spafford was suffering another tongue-lashing by the director about yet another light setting she didn't like.

Harangue completed, Rada Bluestone headed in Drayco's general direction, and he expected her to sweep on by and ignore him as she'd done with Sheriff Sailor. Instead, she stopped a foot away and glared at him. "Your sheriff is falling down on his job again. We had a shoot scheduled on Hook Head Beach. Got the permits, and hired extra security to protect the crew, only to find an enormous fish kill. Stank to high heaven."

"He's not 'my' sheriff since I live up in the District. And I doubt Sheriff Sailor has control over the weather. Or if he does, he's been hiding it from me all these years."

Rada fiddled with her Celtic necklace. "The crew is grumbling about that curse again."

"Murder isn't a curse, it's a crime. And you can't blame people for being unsettled. Two bodies found on a set is an unusual situation."

"Damn straight, it's unusual. Virtually unprecedented. I was already having trouble keeping the exec producers happy."

"The moneybags?"

"The fussy moneybags who don't want their good names tainted or their funds sucked down a black hole." She glared at the new lighting setup and scurried away to talk to Sachio Spafford again. And that was that. So much for a chance to question Rada in-depth.

Mere moments after Rada left, Ashleigh Salinger clicked her way over in the same high heels Nelia Tyler had made so much fun of. Ashleigh lowered her voice to say, "Don't listen to Rada, Scott. The exec prods were upset, sure. Until they realized all this notoriety was making the trade mags and bringing our little project plenty of attention. Now they're gloating about how it will increase box office sales."

"You think that's likely to happen?"

"Notoriety equals bankability. But since my contract doesn't include a percentage take, sales don't matter that much to me. Our pretend-sheriff," she glanced to where Frazier Prentiss stood fidgeting with his hair, "got a cut of gross. I need a better agent."

"Sorry to hear that."

Ashleigh looked up at Drayco with a smile to rival the sunshine. "I'm glad you're here today."

"Oh?"

"I still want to pick your brain about detective work. I can't get anything from Sheriff Sailor's office."

"They've got their hands full."

"Exactly why I need you." She linked her arm with his. "My room at the Fairmont Hotel is pretty 'roomy' since I snagged a suite."

"For an interview, you mean."

"I'm sure you give good interviews." She added, "I gave you my business card. Now it's your turn."

He extricated his arm and pulled out a card. She grabbed it and stuffed it into her bra with a grin. "Got another joke for you. What did the cop say to the musician?"

Before he could think about it, she said, "Stop, you're under a rest. Since you're a pianist, I thought you might like that one better."

He groaned and then laughed. "Please tell me you don't have more of those."

She started to reply, but when Chrystina Valentine called her name, she clenched her jaw, gave Drayco a wave, and headed off. Drayco craned his neck, looking around for the real reason he'd shown up today. He saw the same familiar faces, including Nancy Farmery, who stood next to Frazier Prentiss in animated conversation. Did Frazier know of Ellery Smith's interest in Nancy? Would he be he jealous enough to wish Ellery harm?

It was also interesting that Frazier got a cut of the gross box office. Seeing how lousy the film's prospects had appeared initially, that would equal a minor amount of cash for Frazier—until the convenient trade magazine "notoriety" boost Ashleigh mentioned. Murder was apparently good for business.

After several additional minutes of fruitless searching, Drayco caught sight of his target, Genna Ransford, and hurried over before he got snagged by anyone else. He asked, "Is there a place we could talk in private?"

She hesitated, but dutifully herded him toward an alcove under a stairwell, just big enough for the two of them. After she'd checked to see no one was around, she asked, "What's wrong?"

"Sorry to bother you here, but I couldn't reach you by phone."

Genna's cheeks reddened. "I let my cellphone battery charge get down to zero. And I don't always think to check missed calls."

"The Medical Examiner's office conducted a DNA test on the cold-case victim and compared it with our latest murder victim. The results show Ellery Smith was likely Madalena's grandson."

"You're kidding, right? What are the chances?"

"Pretty good if the grandson was intentionally looking for his missing relative."

"How would he know where to look? That happened so long ago. Before he was even born."

"We're not sure yet."

She frowned. "And how does it prove my grandfather's innocence?"

"It doesn't. But it opens up new lines of investigation."

Sudden yelling from the front of the house got their attention, and they headed toward it. When Genna saw that a crew member, whom Drayco suspected was Barry's gopher-friend Zach, had ripped open an heirloom settee of hers, she muttered under her breath and raced over to check on it. As entertaining as it might be to watch Genna in full-outrage mode, Drayco stayed out of it and made his way to the den, where filming would resume later.

Sachio had disappeared, probably to get away from Rada for a breather. Drayco looked up at the banks of lighting anchored overhead on booms and then at the noisy fans temporarily blowing air around to offset the heat from those lights between scenes. A bright, sunny day, and they relied on manufactured lighting. With drapes across the windows. Filmmaking was a strange art.

He spied a yellow "X" taped to the rug and headed for it. Was that part of the blocking? He parked himself on it for fun, but the moment he did, he caught a faint creaking noise not coming from the fans. With hairs on the back of his neck standing up, he turned around to see a dark blur disappearing toward the rear of the house as the creaking noise became more of a loud groaning.

He looked up just in time to jump back as part of a bank of lights crashed onto the "X" where he'd stood moments before, shattering into dozens of sharp, jagged pieces of glass. Then he caught a burning smell. He looked down to where sparks from the hot light had set fire to the carpet, and he stomped it out with his shoe—then realized the sparks had caught the bottom of his pants leg on fire. Spying a nearby pillow, he grabbed it and snuffed out the flames.

Cursing, he limped in the direction of where the "dark blur" vanished, but he saw no sign of anyone, inside or out. The delay in putting out the fire must have given whoever it was a chance to vanish, but where? He'd have to ask Genna later about possible hidden doors.

With a shake of his head, he returned to the "X," where Genna and Zach stood staring at the debris. Zach said, "Ah, shit. The director's going to spit bullets."

Ashleigh soon joined them and skirted around the others to head straight for Drayco. "What happened? Are you okay?"

Drayco pointed up at the section of the light panel that was now empty. "That fell with little warning. Lucky for me, I got out of the way."

"Dear lord, that's hot metal and sharp glass. Are you sure you're all right? No shards in your hair?" She sifted her fingers through his hair and rubbed her hands over his clothing.

He said, "I'm fine, I'm fine. Can't say the same about my slacks."

When he pointed to the charred spot near his ankle, Ashleigh bent down and lifted the hem of his pants. "You've got a slight burn here. I'll go get cream from the first aid kit." She smirked at him. "Maybe you should take your pants off so I make sure it's not worse."

Rada Bluestone stomped into the room, took one look at the mess, and barked at Drayco, "One of our rented Baby Fresnels. We didn't get insurance for those. It'll cost a couple grand to replace it. What the hell did you do?"

"It fell without much warning. Inches away from me."

Rada's eyes widened as she realized the even more expensive human liability barely avoided. "Sachio!!" she yelled. Whether Sachio was more likely to be fired or quit at this point was fifty-fifty at best.

Genna said something about grabbing a camera to take pictures of the damage and vanished toward the kitchen. Zach shook his head and followed her, perhaps to plead for forgiveness for the couch incident.

Ashleigh dashed out to grab the cream and returned in less than a minute to rub some on Drayco's ankle, which had started to throb. She made a pretty decent nurse. She might be taking a *little* more time than she needed to as she rubbed her hands along the skin on his leg, and *maybe* he didn't mind all that much.

Frazier Prentiss rushed in to join Ashleigh and Drayco, saying, "I heard a loud crash," as he gawked at the pieces of lighting gear on the floor. "Not again. More of that curse nonsense?"

Drayco hadn't seen Frazier before the light fell. Truth be told, he hadn't seen Ashleigh either. Or most of the other personnel, who were supposedly in other parts of the building, except for the mysterious "dark blur." The only people he could account for were Genna and Zach.

Drayco said, "Unless ghosts hate lighting gear, this wasn't a curse."

Ashleigh shot Frazier a look that would make a barking dog cower. Ever since Frazier had joined them, she'd inched away from him in increments as if he had mange. She did barking of her own as she told him, "Stop the curse talk. You'll make things worse."

She turned to Drayco and added, "Thanks for the business card, Scott. I'll call you," and also scurried toward the kitchen.

Drayco asked Frazier, "You didn't see anything that could have caused this?"

"Me? I don't do lighting. Though I'm beginning to think I should. Might do a better job than Sachio."

"A second career?"

"You kidding? Pays squat."

Drayco had researched how much lighting directors, gaffers, and grips made. Not "squat" by most people's definition. He replied, "Psychology could be more lucrative. I understand you're working on a degree."

"Not sure how useful it'll be. But who knows? Could help me figure out how directors think. So I can deal with them better."

"And help with characterizations?"

"That, too. Maybe."

"An actor and a scholar. That should impress the ladies."

"In Hollywood? Not so much."

"What about Nancy Farmery?"

A genuine smile spread across the other man's face. "Nancy is real. Not Hollywood-fakey, the type who gives you air kisses in front while stabbing you in the back."

Before Drayco could ask him if he knew of Ellery Smith's interest in Nancy, Rada poked her head into the room and called out for Frazier. The actor-sheriff scurried in her direction and vanished faster than a mouse chased by a cat. Drayco was once again alone, though he made sure to stand well back from any lighting.

He'd meant what he said with his earlier crack about ghosts, but he'd never heard of lighting being such a dangerous business before.

Maybe the beleaguered Sachio Spafford wasn't up to the job or else Rada's demands were too difficult to accommodate.

The lighting mishap with the skeleton's discovery was definitely an accident. But this latest drama? Possibly another accident, but what was the dark, blurry shape right before the light fell? A crew member pushing the boom over on purpose?

If so, that crew member could also be Drayco's "stalker" at the Opera House and be behind the fireworks in his car. Plus, there was the matter of the knife used on Ellery. Sheriff Sailor wouldn't have confiscated all the production crew's prop knives if he hadn't suspected one must have served as the murder weapon—another potential crew link to violence.

And yet, despite Sailor's observation that a couple of plot devices in the movie's script had come to life, it contained no bombs, no fireworks, nor any lighting disasters. Whoever was behind these attacks seemed to be writing a revised version where Drayco had a starring role, minus a happy ending. Funny thing about crime dramas—they often had a twist. He just had to make sure this one twisted his way.

30

Still fighting traces of adrenaline rush from the near-miss disaster with the lighting, Drayco was almost relieved to see Reece Wable was in a dark mood when he picked him up from the Historical Society. Misery, or at least rumination, loved company.

Drayco asked, "Did Mrs. Hammontree lower the boom on you this morning?"

He'd already filled Reece in on the lighting incident, and Reece just snorted at the bad pun, then said, "Oh, I have no doubt Mrs. Hammontree could successfully wrestle an alligator. And have the alligator thank her for such a spirited match before he slunk back into the swamp. But no, I spent the entire morning fighting with creditors."

"I thought you received new grant funding."

"And we're grateful for it. But it turned out to be less than we hoped."

"You should try murder. Apparently, it's good for box office sales."

Reece stroked his chin. "Hmm. Or we could sell tickets to alligator-wrestling with Mrs. Hammontree."

Drayco steered his Starfire through the flat-as-a-postcard landscape of Route 13 toward Cape Charles. "You sure Talbott Clayburgh said to meet him at the country club instead of his mansion?"

"He plays golf every day at this time."

"Reece, I'll grant you it's been a mild winter, but hardly Palm Beach."

"You'd be surprised at the kind of weather avid golfers will put up with. My uncle liked to play on his favorite course in the snow."

"How did he find the holes?"

"Flags."

"And the fairways?"

"They marked the outlines with red balloons."

Drayco laughed. "Now you're just making it up."

"A minor exaggeration. Or two. Mostly, Uncle Marshall tipped the groundskeeper to plow the course for him."

"Sounds like your Uncle Marshall isn't hurting for money. I don't suppose you could tap him for funding?"

"Alas, he's in a group home in Rhode Island. Made bad investment decisions."

When they eventually pulled up in front of the country club, Drayco said, "These people did not make bad investment decisions."

"Old money. Most rich people nowadays are rich because their ancestors got rich."

Drayco and Reece made their way inside the club, which was decked out in a decor-outfit of pricey Aniline leather, golden prints on the carpet and drapes, and dark oak panels. It even smelled expensive.

Upon seeing no sign of Clayburgh, a staffer pointed toward a green not too far away. "Looks like they're on hole six."

The walk to the hole wasn't far, and as they approached, Drayco saw why the staffer said "they" were on the green. Clayburgh's grandson, Trent, served as his caddy. Drayco said to the younger man, "You're not on the set?"

"The crew finished one of my scenes earlier."

Since the wind had picked up, Drayco was glad he'd brought along a jacket, but the elder Clayburgh didn't appear to suffer any ill effects from the cool weather. To say he was inspiring was an understatement. It was one thing to read about super-agers, but it was another to watch them in action.

Clayburgh, senior, turned to Reece and said, "How's that book on the history of the Delmarva coming along?"

"The research is the hardest part of it all."

"Yes, understandably. I don't suppose you tackle biographies?"

Reece blinked his non-glass eye at Clayburgh. "I haven't yet. But it's a topic of interest to me, as you might expect."

"The fellow who was working on my as-told-to biography wrote a bestselling potboiler. Got out of the nonfiction business altogether. I'm looking for a new writer."

"I'd be happy to discuss it with you. Writing a biography is like marriage. Writer and subject have to be a good fit."

That made Clayburgh chuckle. "I like you already."

Trent bent down to gauge the lie of his grandfather's golf ball, nine feet from the hole. "This one breaks left-to-right, so if you adjust for that, you should have an easy tap-in."

Clayburgh did a little wiggle with his feet to change his stance, looked from the ball to the pin, and tapped the ball toward the hole. It reached the edge, teetered, and dropped in.

Trent exulted, "I knew you'd do it! You're amazing, Dad-Dad." Trent turned to Drayco. "I told you he's good at whatever he does. Could have been president if he chose to run."

Drayco smiled. "He's a much better golfer than I am."

Clayburgh asked, "You play golf?"

"Years ago. Best I can do is shoot hoops with my father."

"So you have a good relationship with your father. That's rare, in my experience."

Drayco latched onto that opportunity for a segue. "Did you know the father of Rada Bluestone, who's directing Trent's movie? Name of Derrell Bluestone, who lived not too far away in this area of Virginia. A World War II hero. Medal of Honor."

Clayburgh leaned on his putter. "Bluestone. Can't say it rings a bell, though we came of age at the same time. Sounds like the type of fellow I'd be happy to have known." He then said something that made it clear his mind was as sharp as ever. "That young man who was killed on Trent's movie set. You think it involved PTSD? Is that behind your question about a military angle?"

"You'd have to check with Sheriff Sailor. However, the victim didn't serve in the military."

Clayburgh glanced at a couple of figures in the distance moving closer, hole by hole. "Should let those fellows play through. Unless whatever you wanted to ask me won't take long?" He looked expectantly at Reece.

Taking the hint, Reece whipped out his recorder and started quizzing the former justice about more of his cases. With Drayco and Talbott Clayburgh standing off to the side, Drayco lowered his voice to ask Trent, "Your grandfather teach you how to play?"

"Starting when I was a toddler. I'm not nearly as good." Trent spoke in a near-whisper, too. "Truth be told, it's not my favorite pastime. But all the power people are into it. If you want to make big connections, you have to play golf."

"So I've heard."

Trent cocked an eyebrow. "You hobnob with powerful folks, yourself. I looked you up. Pretty impressive record."

"I'm a lowly servant of justice, and that's the extent of my connection to greatness."

"I'll keep you in mind if I ever need dirt dug up on somebody. And you gotta dig up dirt on your opponents to stay ahead."

"Did your grandfather do that, too?"

Trent jutted out his chin. "Dad-Dad didn't have to. He can charm anybody. And everybody saw right away how brilliant he was."

"If you're a chip off the old block, you should turn out the same."

"Times have changed. Politics is global, and it's not that simple. I wish it was."

"Are you sure you won't get bitten by the acting bug instead?" A cold breeze picked up, seeping through Drayco's jacket, but Trent didn't seem to notice.

The younger man replied, "Like golf, I'm not great at that, either."

"But you don't have to be. Zillions of channels and streaming services mean zillions of shows. And producers must fill the zillions of roles needed for all those shows."

"Lucky breaks rarely ever happen to most wannabes."

Drayco smiled briefly. "Spoken like a true jaded Hollywood insider. And you haven't even been at it that long."

"That's why I prefer politics. Less competition. Easier to work your way to the top."

"Like your grandfather."

"You should see the photo and write-up on him in the State Capitol. There's even a statue at his alma mater. He's a legend."

"It'll be Hollywood's loss when you run for office. But there's less murder. I think."

Trent grimaced. "I'm not convinced the sheriff will find out who killed Ellery. I heard most drug crimes go unsolved."

"You believe it's a drug crime?"

"With all the snorting, injecting, and pill-popping I've seen since I started the gig, it's a sure bet."

Drayco looked over at the two golfers Clayburgh had gestured at to play through. They all knew each other because they waved and shouted, "See you at happy hour, Talbott!"

Was Drayco the only person who thought the concept of "happy hour" a bit puzzling? Happy hour meant alcohol, everyone's favorite legal drug, but attitudes toward drugs changed with time and place. The ancient Sumerians used opium, and the original Coca-Cola had cocaine. The main thing that changed was the law.

Drayco asked Trent, "If Ellery's death comes down to drugs, have you seen anyone shady hanging around much? Such as a fellow with tattoos on his neck and face?"

Trent frowned. "I think I saw a guy like that at the prop warehouse. Talking to Hoyt. Thought he was one of those artiste types, but I guess not. Is he a drug dealer?"

"As you say, he may be an 'artiste' type. Or a delivery man."

"I'll keep an eye out for him. And let you know if I see him again."

Drayco nodded his thanks. "So you've avoided the siren call of easily available drugs?"

"You kidding?" Trent held up two fingers in a cross. "Blasphemy. I can't afford to have that on my record."

Isn't that exactly what Trent's father, Terry, had said about his son? Drayco added, "Politicians from various parties have been charged with worse and still got elected."

"Sure, but if you go head-to-head with Mr. Clean Marine, the Clean Marine will beat the druggie. It still works."

Talbott Clayburgh's laughter caught Drayco's attention, as the man pointed at Reece's recording device. He said something to Reece that Drayco couldn't hear, and the historian shook Clayburgh's hand and headed in Drayco's direction.

Drayco asked, "Got what you need?"

"For now. We may schedule another session if I wind up doing his biography."

The wind whipped the flag around even harder, but Talbott and his grandson just headed toward the next hole. Reece was right about avid golfers and the weather.

As the historian and his "assistant" climbed into the welcoming shelter of the Starfire, Drayco asked, "Don't suppose he added anything helpful about Duff Ransford?"

"Not much. I tried to steer our chat in that direction. But Clayburgh wrote the textbook definition of going off on a tangent."

"Nothing on the Prophett Properties clan?" Another topic Drayco had suggested Reece try.

"Tangent. So, nope."

That was disappointing, but the trip wasn't a total waste. What to make of Trent seeing the mystery tattooed man with Hoyt Valentine? Hoyt led Drayco to believe that Mystery Man and his companion were part of a delivery crew. Maybe they were. But delivering what? Drayco had asked Nelia if she could run the plate off their truck but hadn't received a reply. Well, it wasn't as if she didn't have other things to worry about.

Drayco's "quick trip" to the Eastern Shore was spilling into its third week. His potential deep-pocketed client in D.C. grew more impatient by the day. They wanted Drayco and were willing to wait, but only up to a point. He hadn't heard from Sarg, who likely wasn't able to swing any stalling on his end. Not that Drayco had expected it.

Genna Ransford knew cold cases could take a long time, and as he'd already suggested to her, he could work on her case off and on. Plus, Sheriff Sailor's team was more than capable of handling Ellery Smith's murder. So why was Drayco still here?

Some might say it was Reece's "kismet," since the Eastern Shore had a way of luring him here and not wanting to let him go. Quicksand, quagmires, and quandaries—they literally and metaphorically sucked him down. His fate seemed tied to this peninsula and its people, for better or worse.

31

After Drayco dropped Reece off at the Historical Society, Drayco got a call from Ashleigh Salinger letting him know her scenes were finished for the day, and now was a good time to "pick his brain," as she'd phrased it. She suggested the Fairmont Hotel, and he was a little relieved when she chose the hotel's restaurant to meet instead of her room.

Before heading in, Drayco took a moment to appreciate the historic building, a centerpiece of Atlantic Avenue, which had withstood hurricanes, a fire, and the collapse of the mid-twentieth-century tourist trade. However, he didn't know what to expect from the restaurant since he'd never been inside.

As he strolled in, he noted it would make an artistic backdrop for shooting a movie scene or two, with its Ionic columns, empire chandeliers, and inset paintings of Virginia scenery on the walls. The "wood smoke bonfire" scented candles on the tables reminded him of the carpet fire from the lighting incident. But he tried to push it—and the memory of Ashleigh's handsy first aid touch—out of mind.

He sat at the table Ashleigh had snagged for them and looked up to see Jaxine Gordon sending a frown in their direction from the lobby. He waved, which made Ashleigh turn around briefly. After she turned back toward Drayco, Jaxine pulled out her cellphone camera to take photos of them.

He told Ashleigh about it, but that just made her laugh. "Jaxine is jealous. I'll have a bad hair day on set tomorrow with clown makeup, but I don't care."

"I'm told she flirts with every male in proximity."

"True. But she watches you closely whenever you come on the set."

"Why? Am I that scary?"

Ashleigh tilted her head. "You definitely aren't Hollywood. Most actors would preen and say, 'Of course she does.' But you have no idea how appealing you are, do you? I mean, mysterious. Kind of exotic."

Drayco crossed his arms. "Feels more like she's fishing for information from me. Plus, taste is subjective. And anyway, I'm only a humble piano player."

"A piano player who finds killers for a living."

"Oh, I'll grant you that."

She smiled. "You play so well. Did you ever consider that for a career?"

"A long time ago."

"What happened to change your mind?"

"An accident." A violent carjacking wasn't exactly an accident, but it was just easier to tell people that. He looked around the room and asked about any filming there.

She replied, "Not yet. But I think it's a grand idea. I'll have to mention it to Rada." Ashleigh studied the interior details. "Has a Spanish flavor to it. Like Park Güell in Barcelona. One of Gaudí's more fantastical projects. And before you ask, I minored in architecture."

"I've been to Barcelona but couldn't do much sightseeing."

"That's too bad. The Güell gardens have this sculpture Gaudí created with Joseph Maria Jujol, a younger architect. It's this multicolored mosaic lizard known as 'El Drac.'"

Drayco smiled, "The dragon."

She slapped her forehead. "Dragon, Drayco. Or Draco, but I take it your family spelled it differently."

"Yes, but we're not Spanish. That I know of."

"I wondered, with that dark hair of yours. But those blue eyes— where do those come from?"

"I'm a typical American mutt."

"Mutts are the smartest. And the friendliest."

He grabbed his water glass to take a swig. Ashleigh looked far too much like Nelia for him to be comfortable, especially with the flirting, real or otherwise. It didn't help that she wore a red dress which was low cut, almost down to her navel. He said, "Dinner with a killer. You make an attractive one."

"Killer?" Her eyes widened with astonishment until she picked up on what he meant. "You mean in the script. I don't have the chance to play the villain too often. I think I could get used to it."

He smiled. "You wanted to 'pick my brain,' but that goes both ways."

"What could I possibly teach you?"

"Not so much teach as report. I've heard about drug use on the set."

"Show me one Hollywood set that doesn't have drugs, and I'll show you a Martian who eats imported green moon cheese." She stopped momentarily and then made a check mark in the air. "A fun idea for a movie. Don't steal that one."

"Are you writing a screenplay, too?"

"Isn't everyone?"

"Guess I'm a late bloomer." He picked up his water glass to take a sip, wishing it were something stronger. He'd need it if she kept looking at him like that. Forcing the topic back to work, he said, "There's been a rash of drug-related crimes in the area. Dealing, thefts, and raids."

"Since we arrived, you mean? I doubt most of the cast and crew need to steal drugs. Not here. Hollywood insiders prefer the designer kind."

"Did you ever see Ellery Smith do drugs? Or any of the people he hung out with, say, Nancy Farmery or Trent Clayburgh?"

"He seemed pretty ordinary. Not the druggie type. Same with Nancy and Trent."

"If Hollywood is filled with drugs, as you say, then that's why you would know 'the type'?"

She picked up the menu but put it down after barely glancing at it. "I was that type once. I had a problem, got help, and got clean. Believe it or not, I never did drugs during a shoot. I wasn't a true addict, just a regular user. But I saw what drugs were doing to others, and I didn't want any part of that. My way of nipping it in the bud."

"Kudos to you. That takes guts."

"Thanks. Look, if it helps, I think I heard someone in the crew arranging a score with a person named Corwin." She grabbed the menu again as the server approached them and pointed at it. "I'll have the Creamy Peppercorn Pasta."

Drayco hadn't checked the offerings yet, so he tossed his menu on the table and said, "Make it two."

After the server left, Drayco asked, "Any hookups on set?"

"Hookups? Oooh, that's more like it. If you're talking sex, that is."

"Has there been much of that going on? Particularly with Ellery Smith?"

She pursed her lips. "Ellery was cute, in a puckish sort of way. But quirky."

"Did you two hook up?"

"No, but I suspected he and Chrystina had a fling."

"I've also heard Ellery was interested in Nancy Farmery. But the feelings weren't mutual."

"She's fallen hard for Frazier." Ashleigh fingered her wine glass. "And to my utter amazement, I think Frazier's fallen for her, too."

"Was he aware of Ellery's interest in Nancy?"

"A jealousy triangle? I see where you're going with that. But I can't imagine Frazier having the balls to kill anyone. Not over a girl. A plum role, now that's another story."

The server brought their pasta, and Ashleigh dug in with gusto. She wolfed down her food in record time, and his amazement must have been obvious because it made her laugh. "I know what you're thinking. Actresses have to starve themselves to stay skinny for roles. Not me. I got the lucky gene. I can eat what I want and not gain an ounce."

"You must be an exercise demon."

"Oh, sure, I do gym work. But not bodybuilder-level."

Drayco tried hard not to look at that body of hers right then, but she was making it difficult by leaning over the table. "What do you do when you're not working?"

"I like to read superhero graphic novels. And don't sneer. There are cultural, philosophical, and sociological underpinnings in those. Plus, I want to be in a Marvel or D.C. movie. Research." She grinned.

"There are certainly a lot of them."

"Guaranteed butts in seats. And rentals and streaming. Studios don't like to take risks, thus the tried and true."

"*Fatal Fugue* seems, well…"

"Not risky?"

"Not very original."

"Oh, I'll grant you that. Rada Bluestone hopes this will be a huge success that'll pump new life into her career. She's had a couple of bombs. They weren't all that bad. Just not what moviegoers expected."

"She should try her hand at a superhero movie."

Ashleigh grinned. "Ray guns, lasers, shoot-'em-up and all. Would get a bigger budget than *Fatal Fugue*, which is an in-betweener."

"An in-betweener?" Drayco didn't recall that term from any Hollywood slang website.

"A genre film a studio makes on a small budget to fill their release schedule. If it breaks out like *Texas Chainsaw Massacre* or *Blair Witch Project*, great. If not, it might make its budget back on DVD or streaming."

Drayco lifted his glass. "Here's to breakouts. The good kind."

She crossed her fingers. "So, when are we going to a firing range so you can show me those expert marksman skills of yours?"

"Anytime you have a hole in your schedule, if you'll pardon the pun."

"I'll make time."

"I hear Rada has all of you on a pretty tight leash."

Ashleigh ran a finger around the rim of her wine glass. "Rada has my sympathy for being a woman in a traditional man's realm. But I don't know. There's something a little off with her."

"I haven't read about any scandals in her background."

"You've been doing research on the cast and crew."

"Part of my job. Nothing personal."

"Anything you want to know about me, feel free to ask. I'm an open book. And I love to talk, especially when I'm gazing into those eyes of yours. You'd make a great hypnotist."

"I'll have to remember that if my present job doesn't work out." He smiled at her smile, then forced himself to focus on his task. "You said Rada Bluestone feels 'off' to you. Because of those recent flops or *Fatal Fugue*'s miniscule budget?"

"Miniscule makes it sound bigger than it is. Try microscopic. Don't know where they plan on getting the money for promotion."

Frazier Prentiss might not be the only one thinking how the notoriety from an on-set murder could boost the box office. Rada had an even stronger motivation for that.

When Drayco caught movement out of the corner of his eye, he looked toward the entrance. Nelia Tyler picked up a takeout order, without glancing in his direction, then left. What were the odds of her appearing at that exact place and time while he was with Ashleigh again?

There's no way she was following him, right? No, that wasn't like her. Must be a roll of the dice. Drayco, Ashleigh, and Nelia were all "single" and therefore takeout veterans. But Nelia had her own place with a kitchen. Maybe it wasn't Drayco who Nelia was following, but Ashleigh? Or Jaxine?

He wolfed down his own entrée, but it tasted a little bitter. The dinner company, however, was far more pleasant. Due to his schedule, he didn't date much. So why not relax and enjoy the evening for a change?

Yeah, he could do that. He took more sips of his Pinot Noir, a wine close to the color of Ashleigh's dress, as the scenery across the table looked more and more attractive by the minute. No one ever said investigative work had to be all drudgery and bullet holes.

32

Tuesday, January 18

Having made a late night of it, Drayco slept in longer at the Crab than planned. As always, Maida Jepson was understanding and whipped up another special "power" breakfast just for him. A guy could get used to being spoiled that way.

He also hadn't planned on dropping by the movie set, but once again, he couldn't contact his client on her cellphone, which meant actual face-time. He really needed to buy her a new phone charger.

Genna was indeed at the house, but few crew members lingered inside—save for Virginia Harston and Nancy Farmery, over in a corner munching on brownies from a food table. No sign of Virginia's mother, Lucy, which was odd. Who brought the brownies?

He waved at the duo and headed to Genna. "Where is everyone?"

"Doing a shoot outside. And I mean a real shoot. With guns. Well, prop guns." She scowled. "When I found out there were going to be weapons, I made the production sign all sorts of legal waivers."

"Sounds prudent." He added, "Before I forget, I wanted to ask if you knew of any hidden doors in the house."

"Hidden doors?" She bit her lip. "None that I'm aware of. Please don't tell me you think there are more bodies buried in the house."

He smiled. "Fret not. Nothing like that."

She peered up at him. "You can't stay away from all the fun, huh?"

"Actually, in looking through your grandfather's papers, I discovered he'd kept meticulous financial records during the house renovations. One line item was for domestic services, but no description. Did he ever mention this to you?"

"You mean a maid?"

"Possibly."

She scrunched up her nose. "You're thinking that young woman, the skeleton victim?"

"It could as easily be a cleaning crew, a laundry service, maintenance, a cook, etc."

"Oh. Because I thought you were supposed to *clear* my grandfather's name, not implicate him."

"I haven't found evidence your grandfather was involved in anything criminal. But as I said, I follow an investigation wherever it leads me."

Her headband slid forward, and she pushed it back up. "If it helps, I don't remember anybody like that when I visited Gramps. My grandmother was a strict housekeeper. Since Gramps was often away, if someone got hired, Granny did it."

"This would be before he was married."

She started to reply when a loud *crack* from the rear of the house got their attention. Drayco hurried out the back door and looked around. No blood, no bodies, no explosions, no panic. No one even appeared injured, but Hoyt Valentine and Frazier Prentiss both had red faces and dagger eyes as they gestured wildly at each other.

Drayco trotted up to them and asked Frazier, "What happened?"

"Fuck it all. Hoyt used blanks. We were told there wouldn't be any blanks. That audio would be added in post." Frazier cupped his hand over his ear. "I was closest to it. I'm going to sue if I lose my hearing."

Drayco held his tongue to keep from pointing out that if Frazier's hearing *were* affected, he wouldn't be talking in a normal voice. As Hoyt beat a hasty retreat, Chrystina Valentine called out to Frazier from a shed twenty meters away, and Frazier stomped over to her. And that was another sign—Drayco doubted Frazier could have heard Chrystina from that distance with impaired hearing. Regardless, Drayco had a feeling Rada Bluestone already had her lawyers on it, from her red, splotchy face as she yelled on her cellphone.

When Drayco was satisfied no one was hurt, he headed back inside the house. He didn't need to get in the middle of a pissing match. But upon entering the main living room, the scene there wasn't much better. Virginia looked pale, with her arms crossed over her stomach, and Nancy Farmery was nowhere to be seen, though he heard a sound like someone throwing up in the kitchen.

He rushed to Virginia and touched her shoulder. "Are you all right?"

"I feel awful."

"When did this start?"

Virginia pointed at the brownies. "When we began eating those."

"Where's your Mom?"

"She has a catering event later tonight. I told her I'd be okay with Nancy nearby."

This time, Drayco was most definitely going to get involved. He called Sailor's office, which promptly dispatched EMTs. While Drayco kept an eye on Virginia and waited for the medical techs, he asked around to see if anybody would own up to bringing the brownies. But no one admitted to it or saw who did. The EMTs arrived within ten minutes and tended to the affected brownie-eaters while Nelia Tyler hurried in to survey the scene.

After Drayco explained the situation, Nelia pulled gloves out of her pocket, picked up the plate of brownies, and gave them a sniff. "No strong odor. But I'll have these analyzed. Where did they come from?"

"They were in an unlabeled cardboard box on the kitchen counter. A crew member assumed they were for everybody and piled them on a plate."

"From the symptoms, it doesn't match fentanyl or a drug equally bad. Might be THC. Not toxic, but it can cause problems if too much is added."

Rada Bluestone spotted Nelia and strode over. "Are you here about the shooting or the poisoning?"

Nelia tilted her head. "Shooting?"

"A miscommunication. Our crew used a gun with blanks after I asked for unloaded weapons."

"Was anyone hurt?"

"Frazier's grumbling about hearing damage. But no injuries."

Nelia nodded. "I'll notify Sheriff Sailor. It might not require an investigation. But we may still have to file a report."

"I figured as much." Rada stood with her hands on her hips. "I've put Hoyt on notice. He's out if there's another incident. And if I discover who's responsible for the brownie fiasco, their head will roll, too." With more of a growl, she added, "I'm surrounded by incompetents."

One EMT joined them to relay an update to Nelia. "Everyone is no worse for wear. Once they threw up and got rid of whatever substance was involved, they all felt better."

Nelia asked, "Should they go to the hospital?"

The EMT shook his head. "I didn't see anything that would indicate the need for it. No dizziness, numbness, or confusion. Their vitals are all good. I asked if anyone felt they wanted to go. They all refused."

Rada blurted out, "Oh, thank god." Perhaps realizing how cold that sounded, she added, "I'm glad no one was hurt. And it seems we can continue work here today. We're way behind, and we have a tight schedule."

The medical tech gave her a funny look and headed outside. Rada scowled at Nelia, who said, "I'll have the brownies analyzed and dust that cardboard box for prints. But if there are any ill effects from the blanks or brownies, call us."

Nelia's tone was firm enough that even the ordinarily gruff Rada got the message. She replied, "Of course," and then she scurried off.

Drayco waited as Nelia bagged the brownies and secured the box, then asked, "The town council still putting pressure on your office not to interfere with the cash cow?"

Nelia frowned. "Doesn't matter. We'll be thorough."

"I would expect nothing less. I'm only sorry you're caught in the middle." She'd taken offense at his words as if they were an accusation. Didn't she know him any better than that?

As if appreciating how she'd overreacted, her expression softened. "It's why sheriffs in other towns get in bed with local politicians. Then the corrupt law officers can look the other way when the corrupt politicians do their illegal whatever."

"And vice versa."

Nelia winced. "Sheriff Sailor would quit before allowing that to happen."

"Damn straight."

Switching to professional mode once again, Nelia changed the subject. "Did you witness the gun incident?"

"No, I heard the commotion." Drayco looked around for Hoyt, but he hadn't made a reappearance. "It's odd Hoyt would be so careless with the prop gun."

"What, you think someone else did it intentionally?"

"I know the town council is one hundred percent behind this project. But have you heard rumors of locals wanting to shut down the production? We still haven't uncovered the source or motive for the fireworks, and then there's this gun episode. Plus, the small matter of a murder."

Nelia shook her head. "Not at all. Quite the opposite."

"I figured as much. Just considering all possibilities."

As Nelia sealed up the bag with the brownies, she said, "I don't see Ashleigh Salinger. Did you enjoy your dinner with her at the Fairmont?"

"Decent food. And decent company. But it was mostly questioning her about Ellery Smith and the other crew."

"Mostly?"

During his Bureau days, Drayco had learned the technique of keeping your expression blank when you need it to be. And right then, he really needed it. He didn't want Nelia to suspect Drayco's dinner with Ashleigh led to a visit to her suite later and to a close-up inspection of the bed…and of Ashleigh. He also didn't want to explain how he'd wished it was Nelia instead, and kept thinking of her the entire time. Or even why he'd let himself be tempted since he wasn't a one-night-stand kind of guy.

He replied, "It was enlightening."

"Uh-huh."

Drayco rushed to add, "Let me know when you get the results from your analysis. I'm going to drive Virginia home. I promised Lucy when I called her earlier."

Nelia left with the evidence, and Drayco went in search of Virginia. He was glad she was okay but almost ready to agree with cast members about the curse.

Yet, whenever he was in the house, he felt like the spirit of Madalena was there, too. Watching, waiting. But for what? Closure? To finally rest in peace? If so, he didn't want to disappoint her or Genna, but as he'd told Maida, most cold cases stayed cold. And even among the small percentage of old murders solved, there seemed to be no rhyme or reason as to the why of it all.

Always the why. The "how" and "who" were often the easiest parts of the equation. Everyone suffered disappointment, frustration, and anger, but most people didn't kill over it, so why only a few? Possibly a mysterious defect of brain chemistry or genetics, which he'd have to leave to the psychologists and neurologists. Medical science still had no cure for cancer—so was it too much to hope there'd one day be a cure for psychopathy and murder?

33

Lucy Harston wasn't hysterical when Drayco brought Virginia home, but she was seething. Drayco couldn't blame her. He was pretty angry, too, at whoever laced the brownies with the drugs. Accidental or intentional, it was a lousy thing to do. Despite the all-clear from the EMTs, Lucy said she'd take Virginia to the doctor to be safe.

After he made sure Virginia was in good hands, Drayco initiated some phone calls. Ashleigh had mentioned a man named Corwin who dealt drugs to members of the movie crew. Drayco struck out three times in a row, with sources not knowing or unwilling to admit knowing anyone by that moniker.

But another source might be able to help. He stopped by Limping Mike's Bait Shop to snag Manhattan Special sodas for Sheriff Sailor and to ask Mike about Corwin.

Mike scratched his chin. "I remember that one from a credit card. Unusual first name. And kinda scruffy. I get folks in here who aren't Rockefellers or supermodels. But I can tell you one thing—this Corwin guy wasn't a fisherman. When you've been at this as long as I have, you know."

"I'm not a fisherman, either."

"But you don't give off sketchy vibes like these two."

"Two?"

"He was with another fellow. Don't like to profile my customers, but once in the military, always in the military. I've seen his kind before."

"Can you describe him?"

"Had these weird tattoos on his face. Upside-down cross under his left eye. Some numbers above his eyebrow. Corwin called him Cyrus."

Drayco knew exactly the guy Mike described. It was the same man who'd headed into the warehouse where Hoyt Valentine worked on sets and props. That guy had a companion then, too.

Drayco asked, "Did the other man, this Corwin guy, have a reddish, close-shaved head and a shaggy red beard?"

"That's him. All swagger and attitude. Thinks he's hot shit, but I guarantee if he was facing an enemy with a grenade in a foreign swamp, he'd run like hell."

"Do you have a contact for either of them?"

"Nope. Maybe it's better I don't. Had enough of facing down those enemies when I was younger. Nowadays, I tend not to poke into other people's business."

"I understand. And thanks for the tip."

Mike added one parting shot as Drayco left. "If *you're* thinking of poking into their business, be careful. I don't think they're selling gummy bears and lollipops if you get my drift. One of them mentioned great bear and kush."

Well, now, Drayco could be closer to justice for Virginia Harston. He'd heard from Nelia when he parked at Mike's that a preliminary test showed the drug in the brownies was a specific type of marijuana, kush, from a premium cannabis flower. Although this batch was laced with a little detergent, which led to the vomiting. But how to pin down Corwin and Cyrus without tipping them off? Then he had an idea.

Ignoring the little voice in his head that he was very much swimming in the sheriff's waters now, Drayco called Ashleigh, who sounded disappointed when he told her why he was calling. Nonetheless, she gamely offered up that it was Sachio Spafford she'd overheard talking about Corwin. When Drayco then phoned Spafford, he half-expected to get stonewalled. But after explaining he wasn't interested in ratting out Spafford but preventing more poisonings on the set, Drayco got a cellphone number for a Corwin Callon.

Corwin, himself, answered and didn't sound fazed when Drayco told him he worked on the movie and heard Corwin had kush to offer. Corwin said he could help and offered a meeting time and place for the "bake sale." That got Drayco's hackles up since he guessed Corwin knew about the brownie incident and thought it was funny.

The address Corwin gave him turned out to be an abandoned warehouse an eighth of a mile from the newer warehouse that served as Hoyt's props workshop. If this was where movie crew members came to score drugs, it was awfully convenient.

As Drayco parked, he saw the building looked more like a crime drama setting than the Victorian house did. Weeds half as tall as Drayco poked through cracks in the parking lot. Graffiti blanketed the concrete-block exterior, and someone had used sections for target practice.

The only windows were on the old loading bay doors. That lack of light wouldn't help Drayco's recon of the interior. Dusk was less than an hour away, and he doubted a place like this had working electricity.

Drayco headed inside, despite not seeing the same black truck with red-spiky wheel rims outside the prop warehouse from the day he spoke with Hoyt Valentine. If Corwin and Cyrus showed, they showed, and if they didn't, they didn't. Still, he patted the shoulder holster under his jacket to ensure the Glock he carried for such dicey situations was at the ready.

Drayco barely had a moment to adapt his eyes to the low light levels when the door banged open and two men entered. From their now-familiar appearance and Mike's description, this was Corwin and Cyrus. Mike was correct about the swagger and attitude. Drayco just hoped he was also right about their cowardice.

Corwin stopped short when he saw Drayco, giving him the once-over. "You were with Hoyt the other day."

Drayco nodded. "I was."

"And Hoyt didn't want you around. For some reason."

"He was busy. I was busy."

"Uh huh. I'm gonna want to see the money before anything else. An ounce of kush'll cost you five hundred."

Drayco gave a low whistle. "Prices have gone up." Last he'd heard, the cost of current street drugs wasn't this steep.

"Everybody's making bank off the movie shit. And you types can afford it. It's called capitalism. You should look it up."

"Chrystina Valentine didn't say anything about prices. Neither did Hoyt."

"Why should they? As I said, you Hollywood types can afford it."

"I thought they bought crank. But perhaps I got it wrong."

"They bought crank. And blow. But you want anything else, we can get it."

Drayco reached into his pocket to pull out his wallet and flashed a wad of cash. "You'll miss us when we're gone. Though one actor, Ellery Smith, is already gone, am I right?"

"That guy who was whacked? Heard about him. That was too bad and all, but he wasn't one of our better customers."

"I've shown you the money. Now you get to show me you have the goods."

Corwin narrowed his eyes. "Most people aren't that cagey."

Drayco shrugged. "Just being careful."

"And you don't act like a guy obsessing over his next hit. You don't have that look in your eye."

"Not all users are addicts."

"But you aren't even nervous. The others all seemed afraid the cops would show up at any minute."

Corwin crooked his finger at Cyrus, motioning toward Drayco, and the two men approached him, flanking him on both sides. As they got closer, Drayco gauged how long it would take to pull out his gun if they attacked. But before any of them could make a move, the door banged open again, and Hoyt Valentine trotted in, minus the customary cigar dangling from his mouth.

He stopped dead in his tracks, gaped at the trio, and called out, "What the hell?" Hoyt and the two drug dealers stood there frozen into statues of confusion. Seconds dilated into minutes.

That agonizing pause shattered when flashing blue lights pierced the darkened space. Cyrus ran for the door and yelled at Corwin, "Come on. We can make it to the truck."

The drug dealers sprinted from the building, with Drayco close behind. The two men hopped into their truck right as Deputy Monroe stepped out of a patrol car. Monroe ordered Corwin and Cyrus to stop, but they gunned the engine to peel off the lot. Knowing he couldn't catch them, Drayco stopped running. The truck roared onto the main road, with Monroe back in his car and now in pursuit.

Moments later, another patrol car pulled up, and Nelia Tyler hopped out to head for Drayco, who stood next to the dazed Hoyt. Drayco explained what happened, prompting Nelia to say, "They won't get far. I heard Monroe on the radio talking to Wylie, who will cut them off near the turnoff to Parksley."

Drayco had met Deputy Wylie. No way would that mountain-of-a-man let the drug dealers get past him.

When Nelia turned her attention to Hoyt, the man's expression was resigned. "I can explain everything, deputy."

Nelia stared at him. "You mean, why you happened to be at an abandoned warehouse where a couple of drug dealers were making a deal?"

Hoyt thrust his hands in his pockets. "Should I get a lawyer?"

"That depends. Right now, I think you need to come to the office with me for a little friendly chat." Nelia looked at Drayco. "You okay?"

"No worse for wear. Thanks to you and Monroe getting here so soon after I called earlier. And thanks also for running that plate."

"You mean fake plate, don't you?"

"Bit of a red flag, there."

She put her hands on her hips. "You should have waited for us. Sheriff Sailor is going to have kittens. Not the cute kind, the hissing spawn-of-Satan kind."

"I'll deal with him." Drayco added, "Hopefully, he'll give Hoyt here credit for saving my ass. His arrival was perfect timing."

After Nelia ushered Hoyt into her squad car to make the trip to the station, Drayco followed them in the Starfire. Might as well get those pesky reports out of the way. And with any luck, Sailor wouldn't banish him from his office, not that Drayco could blame him.

34

Sheriff Sailor and Deputy Tyler sat with Hoyt at the table inside the police interview room. Drayco stood in a corner, wondering why Sailor let him stay. But he understood when Hoyt said, "So, I ask again—I should have a lawyer, right?" and Sailor replied, "I'm not as interested in the users as the dealers."

"You're not charging me with a crime?"

"You didn't have any drugs on you, so we didn't catch you with possession. As far as any attorney would say, you were passing by, saw Drayco's car, and went inside that building out of curiosity. Besides, any helpful information you give us will only help your chances of avoiding charges."

"You want me to rat on other crew members?"

"The Eastern Shore Task Force is handling the drug angle. Though they're more interested in Corwin Callon and Cyrus Winborne. I want to know about Ellery Smith."

"I've told Deputy Tyler everything."

"Including Ellery's drug use?"

Hoyt licked his lips. "Not in so many words. It was casual use with him. Nothing serious."

"So you witnessed him using drugs?"

"Once or twice."

"By himself?"

"My memory's fuzzy on that."

"Did he say anything about owing drug dealers money? Or mention stealing drugs?"

"Not while I was around him. Nobody else mentioned it, either. You think Corwin and Cyrus killed him over drugs?" Hoyt's face paled even further.

"We were hoping you could help us determine that."

Hoyt bit his lip. "I wish I could. I didn't know Ellery well, but he was a decent guy. His death kinda shook me up. Shook us all up."

Drayco didn't chime in that he hadn't observed much of that "grieving," but instead said, "Last we spoke, you told me Ellery never talked about his family, which you thought was odd. But by any chance, did he mention a grandmother?"

Hoyt peered at Drayco. "What? Now that you mention it, he said one odd thing. I think it was that his grandmother was likely killed in a place like the movie-set house."

"You didn't press him on that?"

"I thought he was joking. A newbie wanting to break the ice. Plus, it was at a bar, and he was stinking drunk."

"Who else was around when he said that?"

"Most of the cast. Chrystina and me, Frazier and Ashleigh, Trent, Nancy. I think even Rada was nearby. Why?"

"Perhaps nothing. Perhaps everything." Drayco studied Hoyt, which made the other man squirm in his seat.

Sailor pressed Hoyt, "Does your sister Chrystina know about the drugs? Was she involved?"

"She didn't know anything. Chrystina's addicted to shopping, not drugs."

Drayco had one another question on a topic he hadn't heard Sailor mention. "Hoyt, why did you switch out the gun, adding blanks?"

Hoyt rubbed his eyes. "As I told Rada, though she didn't believe me, I don't know who did it. It certainly wasn't me. This isn't my first gig, and I damn well know how to do my job."

When Sailor seemed satisfied he'd extracted anything helpful from Hoyt, Nelia offered to drive him to pick up his car at the abandoned warehouse. After they left, Drayco held out his wrists.

Sailor looked at them. "If you want me to give you a high five—"

"Are you going to arrest me now for obstructing a police investigation?"

"I could. I probably should. So don't tempt me." Sailor scowled at Drayco. "You're keeping me from my wife's excellent lasagna. And you said you wouldn't play cop."

"I didn't. I called your office, did I not?"

"But you poked the wasp's nest without asking in advance. You're lucky you didn't get stung. Badly."

Drayco folded his arms across his chest. "They hurt Virginia Harston. Even if indirectly."

Sailor sighed. "I know she's your friend. And my blood boils when kids are put in harm's way, too. But your little stunt could have compromised an ongoing investigation by the drug task force."

"Did it?"

"I don't know. Guess I'll find out. Or maybe they'll give you a medal. Anyway, since we're on the subject of drugs, the pills found in Ellery's pocket were oxycodone. But the post-mortem tox screen didn't show any drugs in his system."

"Planted, then?"

"Could be." Sailor tapped his thumb on the table. "Anyway, the Bobbsey Twins are cooling their heels in a cell. We've got them on felony eluding and possession with intent to distribute a Schedule I or II drug."

"Bobbsey Twins?"

"That's what Corwin Callon and Cyrus Winborne call themselves." Sailor chuckled. "Because they're the opposite of the saccharine kids in that children's book series."

"They were on your radar before?"

"Ours and the Task Force's. The 'twins' kept their heads down, and we had no prints on file to match with recent drug thefts. But now we do."

"I don't suppose they 'fessed up to killing Ellery?"

"They're singing a sour tune on that. Swear they had nothing to do with it."

Drayco pulled a small foam juggling ball out of his pocket and squeezed it. His right hand was cramping up, and he needed the therapy. "And there's no physical evidence or DNA from Ellery Smith's body to match to Corwin and Cyrus?"

"We don't have the full medical examiner's report. But the killer didn't leave behind much apart from a few hairs and fibers on the victim. The M.E. is still working on those."

"It's as if someone involved with crime-scene stories would know how to avoid leaving evidence."

"Like people in a crime drama, you mean?" Sailor squinted at Drayco. "Why did you want to know about Ellery's crack about his grandmother? And anybody who heard him say it?"

"That may have alerted our killer to Ellery's true motives for working on the set. A killer who didn't want him to be successful in finding his grandmother's final resting place."

"Nobody on this project was alive when that murder happened."

"They weren't, no."

"You're not withholding info from me—again—are you?"

"Not this time."

Sailor studied him and nodded, adding, "Speaking of DNA. You'll be happy to know we got official results from a woman in Spain related to the name on the immigration papers for our skeleton girl."

"It matches?"

"Yep. So the cold case victim was without a doubt Madalena Zamora."

"Madalena *Delfín* Zamora."

"Is the middle name important?"

"There's that dolphin pin I gave you from the hole in the wall at the movie set. The one found after your team left, meaning a curious person must have dropped it there."

"You said you saw Ellery Smith wearing that pin."

"Exactly. And *delfín* is Spanish for dolphin."

Sailor glanced over at the stuffed piranha on his wall, which always seemed to be mocking them. "You said he wore the pin before the skeleton was found."

"Which indicates even more he suspected she was buried on the property. I still don't know how. But I aim to find out."

"Don't forget our agreement about you working with us and not against us. Because we've been checking that angle, too." Before Drayco could reply, Sailor hastened to add, "Out of an abundance of caution."

Sailor shifted in his chair, which now made musical squeaks a perfect fifth apart. "Oh, and the fingerprints on that dictionary you found from your Opera House stalker? Belonged to Ellery."

"He was trying to learn the language. To connect with his grandmother in a sense."

"Pure speculation. But what I want to know is why was he following you?"

"He must have known I was working on his grandmother's case."

"Who told him?"

Drayco did a quick mental recounting of his contacts with Ellery. "He may have overheard Genna Ransford discussing it."

"Or someone else." Sailor frowned. "And if that person doesn't like what you're doing…"

"I'll be careful."

"You'd better be. I haven't yet tracked the smoke bomb or fireworks an asshole so thoughtfully dumped in your car. I also heard about that lighting rig that almost fell on you. Which you 'forgot' to mention."

"And you didn't tell me the knife that killed Ellery came from the movie's prop department, so we're even."

Sailor started tapping his thumb again. "So we both forgot. What's more important is that I recall over the past few years, you've been shot, poisoned, and nearly drowned on our fair peninsula."

Feeling guilty for adding to Sailor's plate of worry-salad, Drayco doffed an imaginary hat. "But I'm still here."

"Keep it that way." Sailor stood up and stretched. "Not that I'm getting all sentimental. I don't want another murder to solve."

"Sure thing, Sheriff."

Drayco left Sailor's office, musing on timing and luck. Hoyt came along at exactly the right time. Tyler and Monroe might have saved the day, anyway, but maybe not. Sarg used to say if you don't have a dozen close calls in a case, you're not doing it right. He was half-joking, but only half.

Sarg was definitely tuned into Drayco's wavelength. More of those psychic connections? First Sailor and now Sarg. Because when Drayco's cellphone rang, it was his former partner, relaying the news he hadn't found any info on serial killers to match Madalena's case. Nor had he uncovered anything criminal charged to Prophett Properties during the war. He explained, "But wartime, you know. Records fell through the cracks."

"I'm finding that, too. Most people were trying to piece their lives together again."

"Bingo. The current status of Prophett Properties is more interesting. But I'm not at liberty to discuss that bit of dirty laundry right now."

Drayco's ear perked up. "Oh, ho. That sounds intriguing."

"Let's just say I may be the one who owes *you* tickets. To a piano gig at the Kennedy Center. You still go to piano concerts, right?"

"Do honky-tonk bar brawls count?"

"What?" Drayco grinned at the confusion in Sarg's voice.

"Kidding. Although I had a walk-on as a piano player in a movie. I'm soon to be famous."

"Don't get too cocky. They'll probably leave your scene on the editing room floor."

"You wound me, Sarg. But I'll get my hundred dollars either way. Who says Hollywood can't make you rich?"

Sarg chuckled. "Hurry back to the Drama District soon. I need your cucumber-y cool to counteract all the hot air up here."

"There's the Langstrom and Ailes case—"

"Oh, didn't I tell you? Seems their trial date got rescheduled by a coupla months. Fancy that."

"You conjured a little hocus pocus and bought me time. I owe you one, Sarg."

"Yes, you do, so I guess we're back to tickets for me. And don't think I'm not keeping track."

Drayco hung up, wondering about Sarg's hint. Dirty laundry was code for money laundering, so Drayco's intel appeared correct. The question remained whether Ellery Smith got in the middle of it all. Or if Rada Bluestone or any other members of the crew were involved.

He looked at his watch. Getting late. Maida always waited up for him as long as she could stay awake, and he hated making her worry. Besides, he could really use one of her hot toddies, heavy on the toddy.

Was he becoming an addict? Maybe she'd make the kind with whiskey, bitters, lemon juice, Earl Grey tea, and pepper honey. A sip of that cleared your sinuses and senses simultaneously. No wonder Major called her the Miracle Maven of Magic Medicaments.

35

Wednesday, January 19

Sunrise on the Eastern Shore could be the Eighth Wonder of the World or a muted gray mess. Today, it landed somewhere in the middle. It made a nice day for stalking.

Fortified with salted coffee, Drayco headed to his still slightly smoky car. The Starfire wasn't his tailing vehicle of choice, but this was hardly a ploy to follow a criminal. He needed to find his target alone. And he did, when she pulled up to the Art of Arts Gallery.

Drayco let her have a head start, then strolled inside, which was stocked with its customary eclectic assortment. A painting of an opera-singing frog in an evening gown hung above a small clay figure of a gray alien wearing a pope's hat, which sat perched next to a macramé skeleton. He caught Nancy Farmery studying two side-by-side prosaic paintings of seashells.

He approached her and pointed to the painting on the right. "Shark's eye shells. One of my favorites."

Startled, she froze. When she finally turned to see who it was, she relaxed. "Mine, too. And yet, I don't have anything like this in my collection."

"You collect seashells?"

"Sort of. I collect paintings of seashells."

"Less sand."

She grinned. "And you won't accidentally step on one."

"Nice to see you're not feeling any side effects from those tainted brownies."

"Temporary trauma. But I detest throwing up."

That made him grin, too. "I checked on Virginia this morning, and she's also doing fine."

"What a relief. I was going to call her if I didn't see her on the set today."

Drayco studied the seashell paintings. Stunningly photorealistic. "Have you ever bought a Virginia Harston original?"

"That's how I met her, here at the gallery, even before production started. We struck up a conversation, and I purchased one of her paintings on the spot. She's very good. Especially for someone that young."

"We're trying to encourage her without piling on too much pressure."

"She told me all about her mother hens. But Virginia's pretty shrewd. I think she'll do fine."

Drayco stepped aside as another gallery visitor elbowed her way up to study the two paintings. After the person didn't grab them off the wall to take to the register, Drayco almost laughed when Nancy heaved a sigh of relief.

He said, "I'm surprised Virginia's mother allows her on the set as much as she does."

"I think the home-school project is a marvelous idea. I doubt Lucy anticipated a murder, though."

"Someone did."

Nancy stood between the two paintings, comparing them. "Which do you like better?"

One had a rainbow-colored shark's eye shell against a smudge of beige hinting at sand. The other had an intact shell, with another broken shell in shadow against a plain white backdrop. Drayco pointed at that one. "This is more like real life—objects both whole and broken. Plus, the white makes them stand out more."

She frowned. "I'm glad Virginia didn't get to know Ellery. Would have made his death harder."

"Harder on her or on you?"

"On her, like I said."

"But *you* knew him."

She took a step closer to scrutinize the two paintings, not looking at him as she replied, "A little."

"You met on the set?"

"When we had our initial cast and crew pre-shoot blocking sessions."

"But you got to know him better later?"

She twirled a strand of her hair. "A bunch of us were at a bar. He took a shine to me, I think."

"Did he say anything odd?"

"After too many beers, he hinted around about his past."

When she didn't add more, Drayco asked, "Any details?"

Nancy scrunched up her nose. "His mother died young, and his father was a deadbeat. But maybe he came by it honest. The father was adopted and once told Ellery's mother there was something not on the up-and-up about the adoption."

She stopped talking when another customer sidled over to look at the shell paintings. But when the customer moved on after a minute, Nancy continued, "The weirdest thing was him saying his father's biological mother—I guess that would be Ellery's grandmother—might have been murdered."

"Did he give any names?"

"About a murderer, you mean? Nothing like that."

"Then how did he know she was murdered?"

"A parent told him, I think. I got the impression they didn't have any evidence. Just a hunch. One of those family folktales."

Drayco waited as Nancy took the painting off the wall to examine it closer before re-hanging it. He asked, "Was there anything else he discovered about his heritage?"

"Ellery paid for an online DNA ancestry search. It said he had Spanish blood, so he did a little digging. From hints his mother told him about his father's adoption, Ellery checked local archives. Found a photo of a young woman from Spain who worked as a nanny at the same time and in the same area his father was adopted. Magda-something? Ellery even looked like her, he said."

"Did he find out what happened to her after that?"

"I don't know. But he spent hours in those archives and uncovered a photo of our house."

"You mean the one serving as the movie set?"

She nodded. "It didn't look much different on the outside then. Anyway, that same nanny was in the background. At a party where she was working as a maid."

"Was this the last known mention of her he found?"

"I got the impression it's why he went to work on the movie. To find out more about what happened to her. As if that was his last hope."

Drayco felt like doing a tap dance because she'd answered the riddle about how Ellery wound up on the gig. Ellery wasn't psychic at all, but a dogged researcher working on tips from his mother to track down his grandmother.

Drayco asked, "Why didn't you mention all this to the sheriff?"

Nancy shrugged. "It's a movie, in case you haven't noticed, okay? Drama on-screen and off. But I absolutely didn't believe it had to do with Ellery's death." Her expression morphed from dismissive to curious. "I mean, it doesn't, does it?"

When he didn't answer, she bit her lip and added, "Look, when he told me, it was just the two of us knocking back brewskis. And before you ask, yeah, he was a little tipsy. But he kinda reminded me of my brother, who died five years ago. I felt protective."

The other customer interested in Nancy's painting grabbed a conch shell decorated with a lighthouse and carted it to the register. Guess she liked shells, too. Drayco said, "Someone on the set hinted Ellery came onto you a bit too strong."

She took a moment before replying, "At first, yeah. But he backed off when I told him I was seeing another guy."

"That other guy you're seeing—Frazier Prentiss?"

"I don't want to jinx anything." She bit her lip again as her face turned a mottled crimson. "This is Hollywood. Plus tabloids and all."

"Was Frazier jealous of Ellery's interest in you?"

She jutted her chin. "Why should he be? Ellery and I were platonic colleagues, as I said."

"Fair enough. Did you ever see Ellery doing drugs? By himself or with another person?"

Again, she hedged. "Tabloids, remember?"

Drayco was getting more than a little irritated by how everyone he talked to clammed up at the mention of drugs. But he let it go for now. "What about other hookups Ellery had on the set?"

"He was pretty chummy with Chrystina. I saw them chatting quietly a few times, like they didn't want to be overheard. But that could be anything, you know? Even work-related."

"Maybe they were discussing local stores. I hear Chrystina is a shopaholic."

"I'm not an expert on money management, okay? I mean, I'm no millionaire. But Chrystina? I heard her say she's in debt up to her eyeballs."

Drayco pointed to Nancy's face. "Since you mentioned eyeballs, no eyeglasses today?"

She gave him a half-smile. "I don't need them, they're just glass. I wear them so people will take me more seriously." Nancy grabbed her cellphone to check the time. "Gotta be on the set in a half hour. If you don't mind…"

She snagged the rainbow-colored shark's eye shell painting to take to the register, the one Drayco hadn't preferred. He retraced his steps outside the building and saw a Virginia Harston painting in the front display window of the gallery. She truly was talented, but he wasn't kidding when he told Nancy he didn't want to pressure Virginia about her artistic future. Probably best for her to diversify. Look at what happened to Drayco's piano career—here one day, gone the next.

Nancy had verified most of what Drayco already knew or suspected about Ellery Smith. But Ellery found one thing Drayco hadn't, namely the photo with Madalena in Genna's grandfather's house—the house where she was entombed, if not killed.

If Drayco left right away, he could make a half-day round trip to the Manahoack library, find that same photo Ellery uncovered, and print a copy. Or there might be an easier way if he could convince Sheriff Sailor to cut him a break.

Drayco paused, deciding whether to head into the gallery to buy the other painting with the shark's eye shell. A man from another case, another budding young artist who met a tragic end, had collected those shells, sand and all. But buying the painting might feel too much like collecting case "trophies," which he'd once known an agent to do, much to Drayco's disgust.

Then again, what defined a "trophy?" Drayco pulled out the facial reconstruction sketch of the cold-case Jane Doe from his wallet. After studying it, he put it away and strolled back into the Art of Arts gallery to snag the seashell painting. Nothing wrong with supporting local artists, was there?

It must be a big shooting day for the movie crew, since Drayco had difficulty getting in touch with anyone except for his brief encounter with Nancy. At least he got through to his client on her cellphone for a change. Genna sounded exhausted and ready for a break from filming, so he asked about a quiet place they could meet. When she nixed all the eateries he listed, he suggested she drop by the Opera House.

He needed to check in on it again, anyway. But after being separated from his beloved Steinway at his townhome, he was going through withdrawal. A session with the Opera House's refurbished instrument would give him a welcome "hit."

He put the law school yearbook Reece gave him on top of the piano, pushed the instrument onto the stage, and eased onto the bench. But mere moments later, a series of knocks on the rear door tapped out, "Shave and a Haircut. Two bits." He checked the time. Genna was twenty minutes early. So much for his piano-therapy.

After Drayco let her inside, she made a beeline for the apron of the stage and turned around in a circle, taking it all in. "Wow. I've never been here before."

"It was all but abandoned for years."

"A murder took place inside, didn't it?"

"That was my introduction to the place, sad to say."

She gave him a half-smile. "Does murder follow you around?"

"Only because that's my job."

He looked for a chair, but she lowered herself off the stage and snagged a new audience seat in the front row. She rubbed her hand along the velvety maroon fabric that contrasted with her all-yellow attire. "About that job of yours. I realize you don't live here. And cold cases can take a hella long time. And I'm not going to get dumb rich off the house or movie. That's the cold, hard facts, you know?"

"Would you like me to stop investigating?"

"I want to see this through. Just don't know if I can afford it."

He smiled. "I've had a couple of high-paying cases lately. Consider this one quasi-pro bono. You've already made a down payment."

Her expression brightened for a moment, but then she frowned. "I can't ask you to do that."

"You didn't ask. I offered."

She slumped down in her seat. "I'm not sure my case would interest most people. Trying to clear my grandfather's name when he was never charged with anything. Over something that happened decades ago, at that."

"I don't like injustice in any form. Whether it's the reputation of a respected man being tainted or the murder of a young immigrant girl."

"And her killer going free, is that it?"

"Not that closing any cold case is easy, but yes."

"Wish I could help more."

"You've given me information and access I wouldn't have otherwise." Drayco peered down at Genna and wondered what it would look like when all the seats were filled with people. He'd have to add her to the list of invited guests for the opening concert.

He asked, "I have another question for you. What are your impressions of the director, Rada Bluestone?"

"Rada? A taskmaster, but not unreasonable."

"Does anything seem off with her?"

"Why do you ask?"

"I've done research on her connections to the area. For instance, regarding her father, the World War II hero, I only found a reference to one daughter who died young. News accounts could be spotty after the war. But why no mention of another surviving child?"

"Born after he returned from the war? Or she's illegitimate? People don't like to own up to that."

"Was it possible your grandfather knew her father, Derrell Bluestone?"

"Sure, since he's a war hero and all. But I was so young." She shifted in her seat. "You're not thinking Rada's a killer, are you? I can't see it. She's an extraordinary woman. A trailblazer." Genna's eyes lit up. "A true role model."

Drayco hadn't seen Genna's hero worship of Rada before. But the enraptured expression on her face made Drayco think there was more going on there. A crush? He replied, "She's too young to be involved with Madalena's death."

"See? It's impossible."

Drayco got up to stand in the crook of the piano, where he could look at her more directly. "I have another unpleasant topic to bring up. We now have official proof some of the recent increase in drug activity in the area is coming from the *Fatal Fugue* crew."

"You mean they've done drugs in my house?" She clenched her jaw. "The police'll blame me. Or I could get sued."

"What does your written contract with the production say?"

"My cousin-attorney looked at it before I signed it. He said I wouldn't be liable for anything. But who knows? Guess I should ask him." Genna gave him a calculating look and added, "You're friendly with the local law enforcement. So do you think you could—"

"I'll check into it." Drayco cut her off before she could lead the conversation in a direction she shouldn't. Instead, he steered the topic back to the cast and crew. "I almost forgot to ask if you ever chatted with Trent Clayburgh since your grandfathers were good friends?"

"We had a nice lunch at the Island View Restaurant. Charged it to the production budget. Since we were sorta talking shop."

"He's learning the political ropes pretty fast."

"That's because he's in awe of his grandfather. Thinks he hung the moon and wants to be exactly like him. He also said his grandfather thought my Gramps would have made a terrific justice." Genna's hunched shoulders relaxed, and she managed a little smile.

"No doubt. But it's all in the timing and who you know."

"Hollywood and politics are a lot alike that, right? Timing and who you know."

"So they say. I don't suppose Trent had any new insights into Ellery Smith?"

"We didn't discuss Ellery much." She bit her lip. "Not that we didn't care. We all want to put that behind us." Genna hopped up to stretch her legs. "He said he once caught Ellery breaking into the house one evening. After shooting ended. He thought I should know."

"Did you tell Sheriff Sailor this?"

"I thought I had. If I didn't, I will."

"Trent didn't report it?"

"He asked Ellery point blank. Trent didn't want to get anybody in trouble and thought Ellery just forgot something. Like Frazier and his cellphone the other night."

"Had he?"

"Ellery was kinda vague. But he didn't appear to have stolen anything. So Trent let it drop."

Genna noticed the law school yearbook he'd laid on top of the piano and pointed to it. "That looks vintage."

"It's from your grandfather's class. I've been going through the list of his law school colleagues. I'd hoped to find an alum still alive."

"Please say you did."

"A couple of men, but with dementia in care homes."

She used the stairs to make her way to the stage and grabbed the book, flipping through it until she found her grandfather's photo. "He was such a handsome fellow. It says here he was an editor of the *Law Review*. I didn't know that." With a wistful look at the book, she added, "Do you have another copy?"

"No, but I'll make sure you get this one."

"Thanks." Genna looked toward the rear of the stage, visible through the open curtain drapes. "While I'm asking for favors, would it be possible to have a tour of the place?"

He gave her a thorough tour, pointing out all the historic aspects of the building, including the scenery storage, old prompter's box, and lighting booth. He also regaled her with stories of the famous performers in its heyday—from vaudeville to touring opera companies and icons like Harry Houdini, John Philip Sousa, and Mark Twain. An hour later, she thanked him and said she had to run errands, but she was very much looking forward to the grand re-opening concert.

As he shut the door behind her, he grabbed the yearbook she'd left on the bench to place on top of a nearby box. But first, he thumbed through it again. Nicknames, hobbies, affiliations. Yearbooks were dated snapshots of lofty hopes—for life to be lived and dreams fulfilled. But were they? If those smiling faces could have seen their futures, what would they have changed? Anything? Everything? Drayco knew his own answer to that if he'd possessed a crystal ball.

He copied Genna's three-sixty-degree circle from the front of the stage, taking in the renovations. It looked more like an actual performance hall. That was the "easy" part.

The re-opening concert meant harder decisions in many ways— what to put on the program, whether he'd risk performing himself. Everybody wanted him to. But most of them had never heard him play live or had only listened to his old recordings from another lifetime ago.

Would he still be touring in houses like this one if that carjacking hadn't ruined his career? Probably. Would he still be enjoying it? Maybe. Maybe not. He could argue himself blue in the face about how he'd helped people he never would otherwise. Or, like he'd told Genna, how finding justice was at the center of why he did what he did and life as a concert pianist would have prevented that.

It took one night decades ago to end his dreams, but he'd survived his ordeal. Decades before that, Madalena wasn't so lucky. The little daily decisions everyone made didn't usually amount to much. All it took to ruin your day, your future, or your life was one fateful decision undertaken blithely—like crossing the road in the wrong place, getting fuel at a particular station at a particular time, or choosing to meet with someone you trusted but shouldn't.

Drayco sat at the piano and ran his finger along the fallboard before he lifted it. Samuel Barber was an underappreciated composer in Drayco's book, although his Adagio for Strings and the choral arrangement, *Agnus Dei*, were crowd favorites. A few years ago, Drayco made a piano transcription of the piece.

He played the opening b-flat minor chords and soon got lost in the elegiac dirge. Perhaps Barber intended the choral version as a musical salve to treat his depression and alcoholism, but it served as a plea for the entire world. *Miserere nobis*, have mercy on us. *Dona nobis pacem*, grant us peace.

Certain spiritual figures, such as Buddhist monks, could state they'd achieved a level of peace, but Drayco could not. The best he could do was find peace for other people. For the survivors, for those searching, for the wounded…maybe even for the dead.

37

Thursday, January 20

The polar vortex meteorologists were forecasting turned out not to be as deep as feared. Nonetheless, Drayco had to scrape ice off the Starfire's windows as the morning sun peeked from behind the clouds. If he'd timed it better, he could have stopped by Hooks Head Beach to see crystals on the sea oats, a rare sight around these parts.

His destination was a short distance from the southern tip of the Chesapeake Bay Bridge-Tunnel, and he hoped to make it there and back within a few hours, barring any major traffic tie-ups. It made another early morning for him, before six, but he headed out just before Maida was up.

He parked at a diner outside Virginia Beach that reminded him of the Lazy Crab—but only because the sign had missing letters and spelled out "The Hung y Di er." Shaking his head, he ducked inside where Sachio Spafford, with his purple scarf tossed over his shoulder, sat in a red booth digging into a Western omelet and grits.

Drayco slid into the seat across from him. "Glad you could meet me here, Sachio."

"Sure thing. I'm kinda surprised you didn't want Isaac along."

"You can get him grub-to-go, right?"

"I told him I would. So what's up with this mystery meeting?"

Drayco ordered coffee before replying, "I want to thank you again for giving me Corwin's number."

"Oh, that. I heard he got arrested."

"He and his partner-in-crime. But I have more questions for you concerning the drugs."

Sachio forked another big bite of omelet and chewed it slowly. After a swig of grape juice, he replied, "You said you wouldn't tell the sheriff about me. Since I wasn't arrested after we spoke, I guess I can trust you."

Drayco nodded, but didn't add that he *would* have told the sheriff, if he thought it relevant to Ellery's murder.

Sachio continued, "Those drugs I bought weren't for me. I never touch the stuff. They were for my baby brother. He started hanging out with these lowlifes when he was fifteen. Got hooked. Got into trouble. After my parents kicked him out, he had nowhere to go. Except me."

"And you're his drug dealer now?"

"It's nothing like that. Not at all. You see, I'm the one thing standing between him and prison. I want him to get into rehab. *He* wants to get into rehab. But it's pricey."

"You don't have insurance?"

"I made him my dependent for taxes and all, but I don't want to go through the union's health plan. Might raise red flags. And I need to keep working if I'm going to be able to afford to take care of him."

More reason not to rat Sachio out to Sheriff Sailor, but Drayco just hoped he was making the right call. He said, "I also want to ask you about the light that almost fell on me on the set."

"Gawd, that was one helluva day. I mean, I'm glad you're okay. But Rada tore me a new one. Threatened to take the replacement light out of my pay."

"You don't know how it happened?"

Sachio grimaced. "Wasn't my doing. Hell, I don't need more fodder for Rada to fire me. The one thing I have going is nobody else wants to do double the work without double the pay."

"Was anyone acting suspiciously before the light fell?"

"I don't think so."

"Who was on set at the time?"

Sachio took another large bite of the omelet as Drayco waited for him to finish. "Can't recall, to be honest. The days are all blending together. And I was so intent on fixing the problem and appeasing

Rada, I didn't notice anybody else. Sorry, man. You win some, you lose some, right?"

With Isaac not there, Drayco had to fight the urge to punch Sachio in the arm in his stead for spouting yet another cliché.

§ § §

With one of his reasons for traveling to Virginia Beach proving unfruitful, Drayco wasn't sure what he hoped to gain from his other motive for the trip. As he reached the Chesapeake Memorial Gardens Cemetery, it looked ordinary, with standard headstones marking the temporary blips in time passed by souls who'd gone before.

After he found out Derrell Bluestone was buried here and not in Arlington National Cemetery where most war heroes end up, he was surprised. But it made a scenic site for a final resting place, ringed with knotted older persimmon trees and younger cherries that still had a graceful form despite their leafless branches.

Drayco didn't see a map of gravesites, but as he scoured the first few rows, he saw headstones dating to the 1700s. It took him a few minutes of searching before he found the marker for Derrell Bluestone. Next to that was another for Bluestone's wife, who'd passed away before her husband, which might explain the choice of this location. And next to her grave was one with a smaller headstone labeled "Rada Bluestone." The dates on that stone showed she was nine years old when she died.

He saw one other person visiting the cemetery, a woman with short, gray hair and her arms full of flowers. When she took sight of Drayco, she hurried over. "Are you part of the Bluestone family?"

"A curious citizen paying my respects."

"Oh. I always wondered why I never saw any family visiting. Nor any flowers or wreaths. I volunteer here often, helping look after the graves and the grounds. I'm Lana, by the way. If you need any assistance, feel free to ask."

"You've never seen any family here whatsoever? Not even the Bluestones' daughter?"

"That's the sole Bluestone daughter right there." Lana pointed at the smaller headstone. "I went to school with her, in fact."

"Rada?"

"That's her. Poor little thing. Died when she was young. She was shy and quiet, and not many people noticed her. Or noted her passing."

"There's a movie director who goes by the name of Rada Bluestone. I thought she could be related to this family." Drayco's breath made billowing steam clouds in the cold air like filaments of ghostly forgotten girls—the real little Rada, Madalena, his FBI Jane Doe.

"I saw her photo in the news once, and I was puzzled by that. But then I recognized her. She attended school with me and Rada." Lana pointed at the small gravestone. "That Rada."

"I take it she had a different name then?"

"I knew her as Lynnette Wanless. Didn't put two-and-two together until I saw that photo. Ya know, I also saw another thing that disturbed me."

"From the same article?"

"Yes, her biography. It said she had a WWII hero-father. I mean, I know it's been fifty-plus years, so I may be misremembering. But I don't recall her father as any hero. I recall him being a real bastard." Her cheeks reddened. "If you'll pardon my French."

"What was Lynette Wanless like?"

"Now that I think on it, she was quiet, kind of mousy. Think her family moved away not too long after Rada's passing. Again, all those years…"

Drayco smiled. "This may be too much to ask, but do you recall if Derrell Bluestone had any connections to Duff Ransford, a former attorney in the area?"

"Nothing comes to mind. He's not buried here, I know that."

"How about Talbott Clayburgh, the former Virginia Supreme Court Justice?"

"I wouldn't be taken aback if Mr. Bluestone had such powerful connections. But you know how young people are, whether they're tots, teens, or even college age. Never paying much attention to adults or what they're up to. It's like the different generations live on different planets. And I was the same."

"Are there any Prophetts buried here?"

"Prophet? Biblical prophet?"

He spelled it out for her, and she shook her head. "Don't know anyone by that name."

Drayco hid his disappointment over her lack of memories connecting Bluestone, Clayburgh, the Prophetts, and Ransford. But it appeared that Rada Bluestone, the director, was guilty of identity theft. He asked Lana, "Why do you think the movie director took the name of a deceased classmate?"

She cocked her head. "Hollywood's a funny place. Almost real, but not quite. Maybe she got caught up in the whole fantasy bit and made a fiction out of her own life. Wouldn't be the first, I reckon."

"You never reported it to anyone?"

"Oh, I tend to let bygones be bygones. Her reasons may be good. Or they aren't. But me making waves for a woman who's likely been through the ringer felt kinda unnecessary. I mean, I've heard about women in Hollywood. No respect...and worse."

Drayco rubbed the top of the war hero's grave marker, which was fittingly made of a bluish stone. Lana pointed at it. "Blue pearl granite." She hastened to add, "I would have spoken up, you know, if I thought a crime was committed."

"Of course."

Drayco looked at the flowers Lana held in her arms. "Are those for a loved one of yours?"

"A local florist donates them. And I put them on graves that don't have any."

"Since your hands are full, do you mind if I—"

"Help yourself."

He picked out three long-stemmed roses, pink, white, and red, and placed one on each of the Bluestones' graves. For the Fourth of July, he'd have Maida arrange something fancier for Derrell's gravesite. And a flag, like at Arlington Cemetery. With more roses for the Bluestone female family members.

He thanked Lana for her help and watched her as she crept through the grounds, placing a flower here and there, dusting leaves off some tombstones, and removing small twigs and branches from others. Despite her protestations about her fading memories, she was a guardian of memory, keeping company with the spirits of history.

But what should he make of "Rada," the director? And what to do about it? Was her entire career based on a lie, or was it more of a career misdemeanor? Drayco hadn't found connections between war hero Bluestone and Madalena…yet. And Rada's choice of location for the movie could have more significance than met the eye.

What was it Keats said? Truth is beauty. But truth could also be ugly and a mirror reflection of ourselves we didn't want to embrace. That was one reason lies could be such a comfort. That, and a great way to stay out of jail. Like Lana said, maybe Rada's reasons for her lies were good, but maybe they weren't.

As Drayco made his way to the Starfire, a bird flew overhead with a call that hit Drayco with golden comb's teeth that split off into spirals. The bird was the size of an egret, grayish-blue with a contrasting deep purplish head and neck, a bicolor bill, and greenish legs. A Little Blue Heron? He'd heard Major Jepson mention a sighting of one once. Major had said that in Native American lore, herons were symbols of wisdom and patience. Weren't those the traits his former Academy instructor had mocked?

Drayco whistled to the bird. If it had a connection to the Great Spirits of Wisdom, maybe it would take pity on him. As long as it didn't use him for target practice.

38

As Drayco drove into Cape Unity, he navigated down Main Street, a sight he never tired of thanks to its old-fashioned feel. The suburbs surrounding Washington had been taken over by urban canyons and soulless towering steel and glass fortresses. Just more cookie-cutter architecture. Maybe he'd have to get Ashleigh's take on that. Or not.

He passed by the Art of Arts gallery, but no signs of Virginia Harston or Nancy Farmery. He slowed down when he neared the Island Trader store and spied a familiar figure inside. With an open space in the lot, front and center, it must be fate. He parked and headed on in.

Chrystina Valentine was in an animated discussion with the clerk behind the counter, and Drayco caught snippets of their conversation. Chrystina glared at the card in the clerk's hand. "That can't be maxed out. I made a payment last month."

The clerk explained patiently, "Perhaps there's a computer glitch. But I've tried the card twice and got the same result."

Chrystina tapped her foot and pulled out her cellphone. She flipped through a few screens and held up the phone. "Try this app. You do take this one, don't you?"

"I'm afraid we're not set up for that one yet. Soon, I hope."

"Aargh. I keep forgetting I'm in Nowheresville."

When the clerk's expression turned dark with annoyance, Drayco stepped up to the counter. "Maybe I can help. How much is the tab?"

The clerk showed him, and Drayco pulled out his wallet. He forked over the amount in cash, and the clerk bagged Chrystina's purchase, a jar of sea salts, with a grateful look at Drayco.

Chrystina said, "Not sure when I can repay you."

Drayco pointed at a small sitting area with two chairs. "Then a little information instead?"

Her expression flashed through a collage of conflicted options—stay or flee? But she slunk toward the chair. "I'm on a rare lunch break, so I've got a few minutes before I have to get back to the set." She grimaced and added, "Although Rada's not in a good mood today. It was kinda nice to escape."

"More 'curses'?"

"She was cursing a blue streak, if that's what you mean."

"What happened?"

"It might be that rumor."

"What rumor?"

Chrystina clutched her shopping bag against her chest. "Oh, it's just a silly rumor. That Rada isn't who she says she is. A fake background or whatever."

Drayco sat up straighter at that. The one person he'd discussed that bit of info with was his client, and Genna appeared to worship Rada. So why would she do anything that could endanger the director's reputation? If Genna had loose lips, what other information he'd thought was confidential between them had she let slip to others?

On the other hand…a light bulb went off thanks to something he encountered last night when doing a little online sleuthing. He asked Chrystina, "How's your video channel doing?"

"My video channel?" Chrystina chewed on her lip.

"I came across it on YouTube. You've posted an impressive number of videos. Your Hollywood Hoedown channel has close to a million subscribers."

"It does okay."

"Do you research all those Hollywood scandal segments yourself, or do you have an assistant?"

"It's all me. As if I could afford an assistant."

"A recent video referenced a 'certain director' with a skeleton in her closet."

With a nervous laugh, Chrystina replied, "That could be anybody. Which is why people keep tuning in. I report but don't name names. Won't get sued that way."

She gave Drayco a taunting smile as she added, "The sex stories get the most shares. Kind of like when a certain lead actress on a movie hooks up with, oh, say, a private detective."

Drayco had a good idea of the source behind that tidbit. Ashleigh didn't seem the kiss-and-tell type, but Jaxine had apparently shared the cellphone photos she took in the Fairmont Hotel restaurant. He ignored the jibe and asked, "Have you ever done any reporting on your brother?"

"Hoyt? Whatever for?"

"His drug problem, for one."

"Everybody does drugs. I don't bother putting up videos about drugs in Hollywood. It's old hat. Boring. No scandal."

"It would be scandalous if someone is murdered over it."

Her eyes widened. "Look, I'm not trying to ding anyone's reputation. I mean, your reputation is like gold in Hollywood. Nowhere more so, except politics. And I'm not even sure of that nowadays." She hopped up. "Thanks for bailing me out. But I do have to go. As I said, I only have a rare half-hour break."

With her exit a blur, she vanished through the front door. Drayco shook his head, bemused. Chrystina must be the type of person who could dish it out, but it became a different story when the lens was turned on her.

She was obviously in financial straits, and lack of money often leads people to do desperate things. The "Bobbsey Twins" hadn't confessed to any co-dealing with her, but that didn't mean she wasn't involved in a side gig like that to help pay for her expensive habits. The sex stories might get the most likes and shares, but absent a steady stream of those, maybe she'd had to come up with something different.

As he'd scrolled through her videos, the one she'd posted about Ellery's murder had by far the largest number of reactions, hands down. By his calculations, she'd earned ten to twenty grand from the extra engagement and the new subscriptions in one day. Yet she couldn't pay for bath salts?

Before he exited the store, he grabbed a couple boxes of Maida's favorite butterscotch salt water taffy and a bottle of Chincoteague Island Seafood Sauce for himself. He might be a lousy cook, but that elixir made even fast food takeout taste better.

As he headed toward his car, purchases in hand, he had to wonder. Were all Hollywood shoots as much of a mini-drama in and of themselves? He'd have to check out books on the industry's history, with a focus on the more notorious tidbits.

Maybe a turmoil-free production was the exception, and *Fatal Fugue* was even tame by comparison. Still, it was hard to imagine a situation more tumultuous—finding a skeleton in a wall, the murder of a cast member, a drug investigation, fake names and stolen identities, a still-unexplained explosion, a potential deadly prop gun incident, and a light that missed Drayco's head by inches. And the production hadn't even wrapped yet.

Like Chrystina, Drayco was on a deadline, too, and he'd be late for an appointment if he wasn't careful. He wasn't sure how welcome he'd be, but he had to give it a shot. He dropped off his current purchases in his car and ducked back into Island Trader to grab handcrafted chocolate truffles. With any luck, it would sweeten the deal.

39

Nelia Tyler started to put on gloves, but stopped when Drayco handed her the box of chocolate truffles. Her eyes lit up, but then she looked at him with a skeptical twitch of her brow. "Is this a bribe?"

"Yes. Yes, it is."

She put the truffle box on the ground long enough to don two pairs of gloves. Then, using her gloved hands, she inserted the key into the padlock and opened the door for Drayco. He headed inside the trailer, with her following close behind, watching his every move.

He said, "I'm well aware of the chain of custody legalities. I won't touch anything without your permission."

She pointed up at a camera installed in one corner of the trailer. "That's watching everything we do in here."

"And you've been over this trailer with a fine-toothed comb."

"If by a fine-toothed comb, you mean x-ray fluorescence, Leica 3D scans, and ALS tech, then yes. We're still waiting on results from trace evidence found on Ellery's body. But it might not pan out."

Drayco conducted a quick scan of the interior. It didn't look much different from the day when he, Chrystina, and Frazier found Ellery slumped over a table. Drawers lay ajar as if searched, but Sailor's forensic team was careful to disturb the scene as little as possible. The sheriff's decision to move the trailer to the impound lot was prudent—much easier to control any evidence.

Drayco copied Nelia, putting on two pairs of nitrile gloves to be safe. He filled Nelia in on his discovery regarding Rada Bluestone and Chrystina Valentine's dire financial situation.

Nelia placed the box of truffles on a chair. "That's interesting about Rada. Why were you investigating her? She's too young to be involved in Madalena's death. And we don't have her on our radar for Ellery's. But if you have any developments you'd like to share…"

"I've not uncovered anything that would point to Rada as a killer, no. But she's another odd coincidence. We have Ellery Smith taking a job where his grandmother was murdered. And then we have someone directing a movie in that same house not all that far away from where her alleged war hero father lived—at the same time Madalena was killed."

"So you wondered if her pretend-father was involved, and she found out?"

"I've heard of stranger motives."

"But if she lied about her past, then that war hero couldn't have done it, could he?"

"When I learned he was wounded in the war, I already had doubts."

Nelia pursed her lips. "What about her real father, then? You said the woman you encountered at the cemetery called him a 'bastard.' So maybe *he* was involved?"

"I did a little checking after the woman told me Rada's real name. Her biological father was in prison for part of the war and in the years following—including when Madalena was likely killed."

"Don't feel too bad. It helps to check suspects off the list, too."

Drayco peered under a nearby desk. "You said you were storing Ellery's personal effects in here?"

Nelia pointed to a box on a table and said, "Go ahead. We've photographed and cataloged everything."

He studied the smallish box, which looked like the same one Sheriff Sailor showed him days before. "This is all he had?"

"In his rental apartment in town, yes. I gather he hadn't planned on staying here past the movie shoot. He had a storage unit in Virginia Beach we checked out, but not much of interest there. Clothing, a few pieces of furniture, and the like."

"Any drugs?"

"None."

"And yet he had some in his pocket."

Drayco put the baggies with personal grooming products and utensils aside and focused on the papers. Not many of them, either, and except for a few receipts, most were photocopies of old news articles. As he scanned them, his pulse quickened.

These must be the articles Nancy Farmery mentioned to Drayco. One was identical to the copy Drayco made of an article about Earleen Eskin that included her nanny, Madalena, visibly pregnant and holding Wilma Eskin as a baby.

But he found another news article copy Ellery made, one Drayco hadn't uncovered in his research. It was the article Nancy mentioned of Duff Ransford and the construction on his house after the war, with the unnamed Madalena in the background. Madalena was no longer pregnant. So she'd delivered her baby, Ellery Smith's father, between the two jobs.

Drayco handed it to Nelia and pointed at the photo. "Madalena."

She squinted at it. "Are you sure? It's kinda blurry. Copy of a copy."

"Fairly certain. The photo matches the digital facial reconstruction Regina made for me from the skull and the nanny from this article." He handed that one over, too.

Nelia glared at it. "We went over these after Ellery's murder. But no one's looked at them since."

"To be fair, your office only recently found the DNA link between Madalena and Ellery."

"Which is why I should have gone through these again. I must be slipping."

"You don't look like you're standing on a banana peel."

She faux-glared at him, but his retort had the intended effect of lightening her mood. He added, "That article was the last mention of Madalena that Ellery could find, as if her trail ended there."

"And that's why he got a job on the set?"

"Quite possibly."

She tilted her head. "You really think Ellery was murdered over digging into the mystery surrounding his grandmother's death?"

"It makes more sense than the drug angle. A romantic falling out would be likelier than the drug motive, with apologies to Sheriff Sailor."

"Between what you've told us and what we've gathered during interviews, Frazier Prentiss would be a good candidate for the latter. He didn't like Ellery's interest in Nancy Farmery. Or maybe Nancy herself tried to fend off his advances, but it went too far, hence the knife. Oh, and Chrystina Valentine had a fling with Ellery, too."

She wasn't telling him anything he didn't know, but Drayco felt relief he and the sheriff's office were on the same page. He said, "If there's gold to be found in them thar hills, I'm sure you and Sailor's team will find it." Drayco returned all the items to the box in the exact order he'd removed them.

Nelia waited until he'd finished to ask, "Since you're spending a lot of time with Ashleigh Salinger, have you discovered whether she also had a fling with Ellery?"

"I can't say I've spent *a lot* of time with her. But when I asked her that question directly, she said no."

"And you took her denial at face value?"

Drayco gritted his teeth. If this truly was jealous Nelia, he didn't like it. "I've asked around. No one ever saw them together. As I'm sure you've discovered."

"Believe me, I checked. But just because no one saw them doesn't mean it wasn't going on in secret."

Drayco thought of his own secret rendezvous with Ashleigh and had to concede Nelia had a point, but he wasn't about to tell her why. He replied, "I have the utmost faith in you and Sailor's entire department to uncover the truth. Wherever it leads. As I plan to do."

Nelia's expression had a whiff of an apology, something she'd done often as of late. She said, "You haven't asked about the cat."

Drayco blinked at her. "My cat-not-my-cat? Dad's keeping an eye on her for me."

"No, Ellery's rescue cat."

"Oh, you're right. I was going to check on what happened to the critter."

"Regina adopted it. Named it Queenie. The cat and Regina's baby get along great. Even sleep together."

"That's good. Very good." He shifted his stance from one foot to another, wondering again how he should act around Nelia, especially when her idea of keeping things professional constantly veered off the rails.

She looked as awkward as he felt, adding a little too quickly, "Have you seen all you want to here?"

"I believe so. Thanks for making it possible."

She gave a quick smile and said, "Thanks for the chocolates," and they made their way outside into the larger world of possibilities and impossibilities—though Drayco wasn't sure which of those categories their relationship fell into.

Before they parted ways, he asked her if she'd watched Chrystina Valentine's video channel, the "Hollywood Hoedown."

Nelia looked confused. "Video channel?"

"It's full of Hollywood scandals of all stripes. She has close to a million subscribers last I checked."

"I hope you're not suggesting she killed Ellery Smith to have more fodder for her channel."

"I'm not suggesting anything. But your department may want to check her material to see if she's let anything slip that she shouldn't."

Nelia made a face. "Oh, that's delightful. Defense attorneys love that sort of thing. Much easier to declare a mistrial."

Even so, Drayco knew as well as Nelia did that trying to get Chrystina to stop her online activity would be tiptoeing around free-speech laws. Decades ago, a famous saying noted that everyone had their fifteen minutes of fame. Nowadays, everyone had twenty-four hours of microfame nonstop. Eat raw slugs, get subscribers. Video yourself sleeping, get subscribers. Show yourself "breaking wind" in public places, get subscribers.

As Trent said, if you want to make a name for yourself, it's all about the videos. Who needs to learn math or history or literature? All you need is a computer, a video camera, and a narcissistic streak. But there must be something to it—successful YouTubers made more money in a year than doctors and lawyers.

Drayco looked over as Nelia re-entered the main office. And then, you had women like Nelia Tyler. Dedicated, spending long days trying to find justice for crime victims without much financial reward or acclaim. He didn't know of a single YouTube celebrity-wannabe who could ever hold a candle to that.

40

Friday, January 21

Drayco skipped breakfast at the Lazy Crab, thinking he'd grab a bite from the Fairmont Hotel restaurant. He'd learned that Chrystina, in her role as 1st AD, was leading an off-set shoot today, and Rada might be available. She was given—or had taken—the top-floor penthouse suite. When she reluctantly let Drayco in after he knocked, it looked even nicer than Ashleigh's, complete with a sitting room and fireplace, dining area, and separate bedroom. *Fatal Fugue* might be a low-budget film, but you couldn't tell it from this place.

She was civil, but not in a good mood. "I don't have time for you. I have to get up to Baltimore for the day for an important meeting. It'll take four hours to drive since my regular pilot is down with the flu."

Drayco replied, "Does he fly out of Accomack or Salisbury?"

"Accomack. Why?"

"They have an FBO there and a couple of rental planes. If you don't mind flying in a lowly Cessna 172, I could ferry you to Baltimore. I've been needing to make a trip there soon to rescue a case of papers from a former client. You'd have to pay part of the expenses to keep the FAA happy, but it should only take a little over an hour."

"But I thought you were some kind of detective."

He didn't know whether to laugh or wince at the "some kind of" part. "I'm also a private pilot."

Rada tapped her foot on the floor. "I don't know." And then she rubbed a hand across her forehead, adding, "But I'm not sure I have a choice. I can't miss this meeting. I have to sign papers. The in-person kind."

"We'd have to land at Martin State Airport, not BWI. Would that be a problem? It's ten minutes from downtown Baltimore."

"I'll ring up my contact. If it's okay, they can send around a limo there."

They hurried down to his Starfire, which she gave an appreciative scan. "Nice. I'd love to use this in a movie. A classic."

"Looks better without the bullet holes."

"What?" She frowned at him.

He just smiled and opened the passenger door for her, grateful that Barry's tips for removing the remaining smoke smell seemed to have worked. After the short trip to the airport, the rental rigmarole and airplane preflight didn't take all that long. Drayco had flown out of there before and was in their system, which helped.

When they got their IFR clearance and lifted off, he climbed up to six thousand feet, and Rada stared outside the plane, fascinated. "I never pay attention to the scenery when we're in the jet. This is gorgeous."

"Sometimes low and slow is the best." He'd specified with ATC an inland route over the peninsula to minimize time over water and pointed out the Wallops Launch Facility and Assateague Island as they flew nearby, which looked like tiny models from this altitude.

Then he said, "I'm still not sure why you picked this area for the movie when you only lived here a few years. But you were Lynnette Wanless back then."

She turned her stare toward him, and her look of wonder from gazing down at the scenery morphed into red-faced rage. He could almost see tiny volcanic vents shooting out her ears. "You're the leak, aren't you? That rumor making the rounds on the set."

"I can't take credit or blame for that. Not directly."

"As if my reputation matters now. The executive producers are threatening to hire a new director mid-production after all the problems we've been having. They're blaming it all on me, even though it's not my fault."

"They'll come to their senses. Probably when they see how much an added delay would add to the budget. But I have to ask why you assumed the identity of a dead classmate from decades ago?"

She looked out the window again, and he expected her rage to cool into a frosty silence for the rest of the flight. But after a few minutes, she replied, "Hindsight is twenty-twenty. I've worried it would come back to bite me."

"Then why do it?"

"I was trying to escape my abusive childhood. I dreamed of having a father like Derrell Bluestone, a genuine war hero, a man you could admire. Plus, I needed a leg up in Hollywood. I figured having that in my bio would help my career."

"You never guessed anyone would look into it?"

"I suppose that was hubris on my part."

"Did Ellery Smith know about this?"

She hesitated. "He asked an annoying number of questions. About me, about the house, about its history." She heaved a big sigh. "I brushed him off, I'm sorry to say. Maybe if I'd listened to him more or suspected he was in trouble, I could have prevented the tragedy."

"As you said, hindsight is twenty-twenty. And I understand the playing field in Hollywood isn't level for women, directors more so than most."

"As a man, you can't possibly know what it's like to be judged by impossibly high standards. Then taken advantage of at every turn."

Drayco took a radio call from ATC as they gave him his requested cruising altitude. Once settled, he told Rada, "Things have changed little in decades, it seems. Take our skeleton girl, Madalena Zamora, for instance. She was a young woman who was also likely taken advantage of. Only she paid the ultimate price."

Rada fiddled with her seatbelt harness. "Sheriff Sailor said this Madalena emigrated from Spain and was barely nineteen."

"That's right."

She took in a deep breath before adding, "Something else not in my bio is more of my real heritage, not just the abusive father part. I've got American Indian genes on my mother's side. I was afraid that would be another strike against me in my field where white males still rule. That makes me a coward all around, doesn't it?"

"I'm a quarter Native American from my father's side. Navajo."

"And your mother?"

"Irish."

"So that explains the dark hair and light eyes. You should have tried your hand at acting. Blue eyes are favored in Hollywood."

"So I've been told. By your crew."

"That's a prejudice all its own, of course. Things are changing, gradually. There's more diversity among actors these days."

He nodded. "Is your fake bio the reason you didn't want to talk with the sheriff's department?"

"The production delays and this whole 'curse' rubbish have been tough. I've had a string of less-than-successful movies, as you may have heard. I hoped this one would restore that tarnished halo."

"And with the producers also putting the squeeze on you—"

"The police could drag me down further. And shut down the entire project."

Drayco made a heading change after instructions from Air Traffic Control before he continued the conversation. "Why did you agree to fly with me, then? Is it because you're in a bind?"

"This meeting is crucial. It's about funding."

"Ah."

"But hearing you play the piano didn't hurt. My mother used to play, and I think she once fancied a music career. My father would never have allowed it."

"Sorry to hear that. But shouldn't you still be careful since I'm part of that whole 'enemy' law enforcement camp?"

"Never met any law types who play the piano like that. I hope I can trust you."

Drayco took a call from ATC regarding traffic, noting how busy it seemed, more than the last time he flew. Then he asked Rada, "How much does your husband know about your real background?"

With a grimace big enough that Drayco saw it with his peripheral vision, Rada replied, "Not much. Only that I use a stage name."

"And your mother? What did she think about your name change?"

"She didn't know where I got it from. Plus, she understood why I didn't want to take my father's surname."

"She must be proud of you, regardless."

"I think she's saved every article about me. Even the bad ones."

"And framed them?"

Rada laughed. "Some, yes." She glanced at Drayco. "By the way, I meant to ask you earlier—what was that piano piece you played? I'm unfamiliar with it."

"You wouldn't be. It's one of mine."

"You're a composer, too?"

"Of a sort."

"I'm doubly impressed. I may have underestimated law enforcement types."

He chuckled. "I don't think Sheriff Sailor plays the piano. Or any instrument. But he's a good man."

They flew over Kent Island, and Rada watched the boats far below in the Chesapeake. "You must think I'm a horrible person. Few people remembered the real Rada Bluestone when she died. Even as a child, I found that appalling. But everyone should be remembered by someone, shouldn't they?"

"I like to think so."

"In a way, I gave her a longer life."

Drayco couldn't argue with that, even if the method was shady. They flew along the coast for a while as Rada marveled at the Thomas Point Shoal Lighthouse and the various marinas.

During a break between ATC call-outs, he said, "You have the relative of a locally famous man in your cast."

"Who do you mean?"

"Trent Clayburgh. His grandfather was a former Virginia Supreme Court Justice."

"That's the young man playing Rory. Makes more sense, then. He's always going on and on about politics. And here I thought he's just a nice, civics-minded fellow."

"He has political aspirations."

"Then we'll be seeing him in the news one day. Running for Congress. Another Reagan."

"Undoubtedly."

"Funny how it's easier to be a power woman in politics than in Hollywood."

"Change comes slowly. But you're a trailblazer, and the name 'Rada Bluestone' will be in the history books."

"As long as they focus on my successes and not the flops. I don't want 'Bluestone Blunder' to become synonymous with a failed movie project."

Drayco shook his head. "History books romanticize the past and gloss over the bad."

"I may hold you to that."

After chatting with ATC again and descending to a lower altitude, Drayco asked Rada, "You frequently wear that necklace. Any significance?"

"My mother gave it to me. She knew what it was like to be powerless. When she read about druid symbols in a book and found this, she couldn't resist."

"You mean striking the perfect balance between all opposing elements is the true mark of power?"

"I knew you were way smarter than an average law type. You're a secret druid, aren't you?"

He laughed. "A truth seeker. Not that I'd turn down a little mystical intervention if it helped Lady Justice."

They neared the Martin State Airport, and Drayco trimmed up the plane to enter the traffic pattern. He hadn't flown into this airport in a long while. Still, he'd not forgotten the approach above Frog Mortar Creek and the iconic Bowley's on the Bay restaurant. A friend used to pilot angel flights and animal rescues from this airport.

What should he make of Rada's story and explanation? It wasn't much of a stretch from lying about your background to lying about involvement in a murder. Rada had as large of a financial stake as Frazier Prentiss, if not more so, to want to see this movie succeed.

If she really was a killer but *not* suicidal, then he was likely safe flying her back to Accomack. Still, perhaps he should have rented a Cirrus equipped with a parachute. Just in case.

41

Drayco spent the day in Baltimore at Martin State Airport, not wanting to stray too far, on the off chance Rada returned from her meeting earlier than she'd said. He craved Bowley's jerk tuna cakes, but that would have to wait for another time.

After Drayco's former client delivered the case of papers to Drayco at the airport FBO, Drayco sat in the pilot's lounge and chatted with private commercial jet jockeys. It was clear how much they loved their jobs. Maybe a career for him to fall back on? No death, no murder, no violence, no drama—for the most part. Pilots were part of the human drama, too.

Between chatting and plane watching, he made a few phone calls, including one to Sheriff Sailor to fill him in on Rada's confession. Nelia had likely notified Sailor after Drayco's brief chat with her, but the man needed an official report from him.

He also responded to a voicemail from Wilma Eskin. She'd found the letters between her mother and her father stationed overseas during the war. She hinted about wanting to visit an actual movie set, so he said he'd see what he could arrange.

When Rada returned from her meetings, her expression was somber but also hinted at something else. Relief? He asked, "Did you accomplish everything you'd hoped?"

"I believe so. We shall see."

She didn't seem to want to parcel out details. So Drayco concentrated on giving her an even more scenic tour as they made the return trip to Accomack, and the sun began its artistic dance toward twilight and eventual sunset. It was his favorite time of day to fly, thanks to the bird's-eye view of the kaleidoscopic sky-canvas.

Once on Eastern Shore terra firma again, he dropped Rada off at the Fairmont Hotel and stopped by the Lazy Crab long enough to rescue an item he'd put off dealing with. But deal with it, he must.

He pulled up to a duplex with seafoam-colored shake siding and mailboxes carved into dolphins. This was not the brightest idea. He counted to ten, headed up the exterior stairs that led to the front door of the upper unit, and knocked.

When Nelia opened the door, he handed over a box wrapped in red and green paper. "Sorry I forgot to give this to you sooner." Okay, so *forgot* might be a stretch. Delayed, check. Agonized, check. Dreaded, fretted, and worried, check, check, and checkmate.

She peered inside the bag. "It's so lovely of Joelle to buy me a Christmas present."

"New Year's present. Well, it is now."

"I like your father's new lady friend."

Drayco grinned at that. Nelia knew how Drayco hated using the term "girlfriend," in regards to his father's love life. "She loves holidays. You should have seen Brock's house. Before she came along, Brock's nod to Christmas was to put a bow on top of the mug tree."

Nelia turned toward the kitchen. "Would you…would you like to come inside?"

"I don't know—"

"Coffee's hot. I just made a fresh pot."

Should he be rude and run away as fast as possible? Or should he try to maintain a modicum of professional distance like she said she preferred? His curiosity got the better of him because he was dying to see if she still had the Pepto-pink walls. Besides, they were grown adults. They could handle this.

As they headed toward the dining area, he realized the last time he was here, so were Nelia's mother and a couple of other people. And they'd sat on the outside deck at the picnic table, all nice and public and "safe."

But his curiosity was satisfied. Three living room walls were now a seafoam green that matched the duplex's exterior. But one was still pink.

He pointed it out, "Can't sink the pink entirely?"

"Paint's expensive. Have you priced it lately? I bought what I thought was enough and no more."

"It's um, beachy. But more of a Florida beachy vibe."

She grinned. "I'll get a potted palm tree for that corner."

They each grabbed mugs of coffee and sat in the living area, Drayco carefully choosing an opposite chair from the sofa where she'd plonked down. He looked at the present. "You going to open it?"

"Ooh, yes. Let's do it."

He was bemused to see she was the type who peeled back the taped seams and kept the wrapping mostly intact. Of course, she would be. She eased the gift out of its little box and held it up. "This must be one of Joelle's own creations. This is incredible. I didn't know she made small sculptures."

"Looks like a replica of the garden-sized metallic fish sculpture she created for a client."

Nelia turned the item around in her hands. "I loved that one. I'm touched she remembered."

"That case she was involved with did not end well."

"No, it didn't. But I have confidence you'll find closure for Genna and Madalena, one way or the other."

"Wish I shared your confidence."

"Cold cases are understandably hard."

Drayco looked around the room at everything but Nelia. Awkward didn't begin to describe it. "Has the M.E.'s office come up with more info on Madalena's remains?"

"That gung-ho apprentice tech was thorough, although she couldn't tell the exact type of weapon used to bludgeon the victim. She didn't see signs of damage to the larynx, hyoid, or other neck bones. And we found no ropes or ties in the wall section."

"So not strangled or restrained. A crime of passion, then? Or even an accident, but someone got scared and thought they'd be charged." Drayco added gloomily, "Everything I find makes a stronger case for Genna's grandfather to be the culprit."

"I hope Genna knows she can't be held accountable for a crime her ancestor did. Intentionally or not."

"She does. But she idolizes her grandfather. Like Trent Clayburgh does his, and Rada Bluestone idolizes her pretend-father. A lot of ancestral idolatry, there."

Nelia got up to put the metallic fish sculpture on her mantel and grab more coffee, so Drayco followed her into the kitchen. So far, so good. Purely professional. Why didn't that make him feel any better?

Nelia had a teasing smile on her face. "What did Darcie give you for Christmas while you were still dating?"

"Um, well…"

"Come on, it can't be that bad."

He cleared his throat. "It was a tiny, and I emphasize *tiny* little red-and-white fuzzy brief. With a matching Santa hat."

Nelia's cheeks turned pink, but she also had a puckish gleam in her eyes. She rummaged around in a drawer and pulled out plastic mistletoe that she held above his head. "A peck on the cheek for old time's sake?"

Should he? Just a small peck. For old-time's sake. Why not? He reached over, aiming for her cheek, but she grabbed him for a full-on kiss.

He gaped at her. "What was that all about?"

"It's my Christmas present to you. And payback for that image of you dressed only in a teensy Santa brief."

The words tumbled out of his mouth before he realized what he was saying. "I've still got it."

She replied, "You should have brought it," and kissed him again. He leaned into her embrace, knowing he was lost. This really *had* been an incredibly bad idea. An incredibly, wonderfully bad idea.

42

Saturday, January 22

When he awoke the next morning, it took Drayco a few moments to get his bearings in the unfamiliar bedroom and determine where he was. He looked over at the other side of the bed and saw no Nelia, only a handwritten note. It read, "Had to leave. Work. Sorry." When he checked the time, it said six a.m.

What was it she'd said to him last night when they were making love—that she *needed* this? And yet, here she was leaving him again like the last time. Was he just her emotional support animal now?

Drayco had a quick shower, grabbed his clothes, and headed to the Lazy Crab, where he tiptoed inside, hoping he wouldn't wake Maida or Major Jepson. He should have known better.

He'd no sooner set one foot on the stairs leading up to his room when compulsive-early-riser Maida appeared by his side. "Want some coffee?" She scanned his face. "Or something stronger?"

He joined her in the kitchen, where she asked, "Driving anytime soon?" And when he said no, she made him a mimosa, heavy on the champagne. He thanked her and was eternally grateful Maida wasn't one to pry into his personal affairs. She also started on a western omelet with chorizo. The spicy aroma from that was enough to lure Major downstairs as he inhaled the kitchen bouquet with a cry of "Hooray!"

Drayco grinned. "Major, I've never seen anyone as upbeat as you are every morning. Most people would rather go back to bed."

Major nodded at his wife. "If you had her cooking to look forward to, you'd be pretty chipper, yourself."

Since Drayco's customary breakfast comprised something microwaved or out of a cereal box, he agreed it was a pleasant change. Maybe he should take a cooking class. Not that it would help, but it might be entertaining for all the other students to watch him burn toast.

Major dug into his omelet with gusto, saying between bites, "Solved that skeleton mystery yet?"

"Certain aspects of it, potentially. The identity of her killer, maybe. Or maybe not."

"You'll get there. Down a mountain path, around a winding trail, over a few creeks, and down a few canyons. But you'll get there."

Drayco started on his second mimosa. "If Madalena had lived, she'd be in her nineties today."

Major stroked his beard. "I reckon that's so. You said she ended up working as a nanny?"

"In domestic services of various kinds."

"Not surprising she found her way down here, then. The area was a playground for the rich from up north. And the trains still came then. All the summer homes, golf most of the year…"

"And one opera house."

Major grabbed a new seed catalog and started riffling through it. "She didn't work there, did she?"

Drayco shook his head, but he had to admit he wasn't sure. The previous owners and managers didn't keep detailed personnel records.

Maida left the room upon a knock at the front door and returned with Reece Wable in tow. Reece promptly said, "Oh, goody, I'm in time for breakfast," as he placed a folder on the table and sat down, grabbing a knife and fork.

Maida laughed and piled food on a plate, which she put in front of him. Drayco looked at the crab-shaped clock on the wall and saw it was barely seven. "A little early for you, isn't it, Reece?"

"Au contraire. Andrew Jackson faithfully wakes me every morning at six, rain or shine. I don't know how he knows, but he does."

"What does His Birdly Highness say by way of an alarm clock greeting?"

Reece squirmed. "It's not repeatable in polite company. But it rhymes with 'wake up, sucker.'"

Major said, "Could have used him in my RAF days. Better than that damned bugle."

Feeling less out of sorts thanks to the mimosas, Drayco asked Reece, "So, you only dropped by for a free breakfast?"

"I did not. You tasked me with searching Historical Society records for anything about Duff Ransford's life in the 1940s."

"Since you're here in person, I'm guessing you had success."

"Duff's education wasn't continuous. Breaks in the war and all. But he completed law school prior to the date you said Madalena was killed."

Drayco groaned. "Then he could be guilty."

"Not so fast, my P.I. pal. I found an article from an old law journal." Reece fumbled with the folder and handed Drayco an article. Reece continued, "Duff Ransford clerked with a federal judge in Richmond after graduating in 1946."

Drayco did a quick scan of the article to verify the details. Reece tapped on the paper. "See the dates? That's him speaking at a colloquium, and it mentions how he's been there ten months. Would be hard to get back to Cape Unity since the Chesapeake Bay Bridge-Tunnel wasn't built until 1964. That's why he didn't notice the smelly corpse. He wasn't there."

"He wouldn't have to be there for the house renovations. Prophett Properties could have kicked him out while work was underway."

"About that. You also wanted records of Prophett Properties from that era. A work stoppage from supply problems happened after the war. That would have halted the Ransford house renovations, wouldn't it? I suppose that rules out the company being involved."

"Or it might make it more likely. Someone could have taken advantage of the absence of witnesses. Plenty of time to hide a body."

"But wouldn't construction workers have wondered about a freshly walled-up section when they returned?"

"Not if a company insider was the killer. Or helped cover it up."

Reece grabbed the mimosa Maida handed him and happily took a swig before replying, "Oh, FYI, if you were wondering where Talbott Clayburgh became best buds with Duff Ransford, it wasn't at law school. They both worked at that same Richmond firm. But years later."

After Maida placed an omelet in front of Reece, he cut it into symmetrical squares before forking one in his mouth. Reece was as methodical in the history realm as Drayco was in the sleuthing realm, but even Drayco didn't resort to that level of precise culinary subjugation.

Drayco looked at Maida, who laughed silently. No matter how you cut it up, it wound up heading down the same alimentary spiral of doom. Kind of like life. Sinners, saints, and sages cut their own little paths through life, but in the end, there was no escaping the Grim Reaper.

43

After Reece had consumed an amazing quantity of food for a man so rail-thin—except for the little pot belly he was getting from Lucy Harston's cooking—he went on his merry, sated way. Drayco left close on his heels when he got a call from Terry Clayburgh, who asked if Drayco could drop by. Fortunately, he asked to meet at the man's actual house, and what a house it was. Not like the Jepsons' Tudor-style B&B, the movie-set Victorian, the prolific beach cottages, or even the mini-mansions on "Snob Hill," as the locals called it.

Drayco studied the sleek, contemporary home, which looked custom built and not cheap. Large windows with slate-gray crossbeams dotted the exterior, and the upper floor cantilevered at an angle. The garage opened into the base of the small man-made hill on which the house stood, with stairs leading to the front door flanked by blue and gray stone bricks.

It seemed Talbott Clayburgh was wrong when he said his son was a ne'er-do-well. Perhaps the man hadn't kept up with his son's success following their estrangement? Drayco was a little annoyed with the former justice's behavior. Maybe his son was partly at fault, but family should be family, right? Even when a member strays.

Terry welcomed Drayco into the main room, where high ceilings let in natural light that illuminated various contemporary furniture pieces. One of those pieces was a green sofa shaped like a capsule, on which a fluffy white Samoyed sprawled fast asleep until the sound of voices made him lift his head and thump his tail.

As Drayco walked over to give the pup a little head scratching, he looked around and said, "This architecture is a relief from the boring houses going up in a new Cape Charles subdivision."

"You mean the one being built by Prophett Properties? Believe it or not, they built this house, too."

"Shows they have artistic range. Even if they don't exercise it much."

Terry smiled. "Quite true. And thanks for stopping by."

"To be honest, if you hadn't called me first, I was going to call you."

"Is that so? What I found might not be worth your time. But when I was cleaning out old storage containers, I uncovered this." He picked up a music box from a table and handed it to Drayco. "Duff Ransford gave it to my mother years ago. I have no idea if it's relevant to your investigation. Or not."

Drayco held up the rectangular music box with flowery inlay to examine the underside. Made in China. Not an heirloom, then.

He glanced up from his scrutiny of the box to see Terry grinning at him. "I looked you up. You're not a historian's assistant at all. I understand now why you weren't fazed by the crime scene muck like your friend, Mr. Wable. You should have told me, though."

"People are more likely to speak freely with academics or authors than detectives."

"I have nothing to hide. So it wouldn't have mattered."

Drayco turned the box around in his hands and opened the lid. It immediately started playing the Bach-Gounod "Ave Maria."

"Her favorite song." Terry got a faraway look in his eye. "Mom was a saint. Not that Dad was abusive, far from it. He sowed all his wild oats as a younger man. I don't know if you've noticed, but attorneys are players. Their wives get addicted to the money, which is why they don't leave their straying husbands."

"But your mother had no reason to worry?"

"After they got married, Dad was devoted to her. Kinda smothering. Didn't want to let her out of his sight. Maybe it was because she was twenty years younger."

"Apparently, your mother was friends with Duff Ransford, too."

"Duff and his wife and my parents socialized a lot. I think they even went on a few trips together. Plus, golf. Lots of golf."

Drayco noted a collage of photos in a frame on the same table and moved closer to get a better look. "Family photos?"

"I keep a few around. It's a chronology of all things Dad. Memories of better times."

One picture showed Talbott Clayburgh in his judicial robes shaking hands with President Eisenhower. Another captured Talbott as a boy in a private school uniform. The most interesting of all was Talbott as a young man dressed in coveralls with a hard hat standing in front of a building Drayco visited not all that long ago—one that had changed little since its founding. On the side of the building, Drayco could just make out a cut-off portion of a sign that read, *Prophett Prop.*

Drayco said, "This is why I wanted to talk to you. To see if your father had any odd jobs before or during law school."

"That photo is something else I found in storage. I'd forgotten all about it, but Dad worked for that company during the summers on break from college. The ole 'I had to work hard to get where I am today, you can too' rigamarole. He made good friends there. One guy in particular. A son of one of the founders, George Prophett, Jr. I think that's him in the photo with his arm around my father. But he's dead now."

"I've seen Junior's photo before." Hanging on the wall of Pamela Kye's office.

When the music box's song wound down, Drayco examined the box closer under a table lamp. Spying a tiny seam that didn't look normal, he felt along it until a small door slid open.

Terry said, "Wow, I never knew that was there."

Inside lay a small, folded piece of paper. When Drayco opened it, the headline showed it came from an old newspaper in Capps County. But the subject wasn't anything Drayco expected.

Terry asked, "So, what is it?"

"An obituary. Such as it is."

"A relative?"

"Pauley Harrington. Died over a decade ago."

"I don't know any Pauley Harrington."

Drayco replied, "The skeleton of the young woman found in the movie-set house up in Cape Unity. This is her son."

"I don't understand. Why would Mom have saved a copy of that and hidden it there? Or did Duff Ransford do it before he gave the box to her? What does it all mean?"

What, indeed? Drayco had entertained suspicions about this, but where was the ironclad proof? All he had were tantalizing clues, hints, and misdirection, the equivalent of investigative ethereal air. Madalena deserved more than that.

He returned the music box and asked, "Can I keep this news article?"

"I have no need for it."

Drayco put the paper in his pocket and extended his arm to the nearby table to run his fingers along a silvery-blue dolphin sculpture. "Are you a fan of the animal dolphins or football Dolphins?"

"Animal. Dad took me on one of those swim-with-the-dolphin excursions. I think I was three. I've been fascinated ever since."

Drayco thanked Terry for seeing him and headed outside. He almost stepped on a couple of frogs in his path, which hopped away in the nick of time. Frogs? He glimpsed a pond with a miniature waterfall in the rear of the house that was actually turned on. Well, it was above freezing today, right? And when your day job was cleaning up crime scenes, it made sense to have a peaceful oasis to come home to.

Drayco's grandfather told him frogs were those rare creatures in mythology that could stand for good luck and prosperity or plague and misfortune. In some cultures, they even symbolized balance, much like Rada Bluestone's Celtic necklace. He was glad his half-feral Cat wasn't around, or that was one froggy omen that might wind up as dinner.

Symbolic frogs and blue herons. Not a plague of locusts—yet. Either Drayco was in a fanciful mood, or the universe really was trying to tell him something. 44

Drayco swung by the movie set to meet up with Wilma Eskin. He'd arranged with Chrystina Valentine to allow Wilma on the set as long as she stayed with Drayco and out of the way. Wilma timed her visit well, able to watch part of a dramatic scene outdoors. No explosions or gun incidents, though.

She was wide-eyed the whole time. After Rada deemed the scene successful for a print, Wilma said to Drayco, "Oh, I'd love to have Frazier Prentiss's autograph. I saw him in that horror movie, *The Terror From Beyond*. And Ashleigh Salinger's autograph, too? She made a perfect Jane Austen. I can't recall the name of that one, but she was so good."

Drayco explained the situation to Nancy Farmery, who graciously introduced Wilma to Frazier and got the coveted autograph. While Wilma had Sachio take her photo with Frazier, Nancy told Drayco, "Thanks for the tip about those new homes in Cape Charles. Sounds perfect for my mom."

"Hope it works out for you both." Drayco wondered how much Frazier was contributing to the cause. It seemed unlikely Nancy or her mother could afford one of those homes on Nancy's paltry salary.

Nancy and Frazier walked off arm-in-arm, and Drayco looked around for Ashleigh. When he didn't see her, he told Wilma she might have to wait on that one.

Wilma grinned, "Aw, boo hoo, I'll have to stay here longer, eh? Not a problem. I'm having the best experience of my life."

"While we're waiting for Ashleigh, did you bring those letters you found between your parents during the war?"

"Oops, I almost forgot. And here you are, being all nice to me." Wilma led Drayco to her car, where she produced a box filled with yellowing papers.

Drayco peered into the box. "I'm not sure I'll need to look at all of them. Was there anything that relates to your nanny, Madalena?"

She grabbed a letter on top. "In this one, Mom tells Dad she's happy she found Madalena. And what a lovely young woman she is."

Wilma picked up another letter under that one. "And in this one, Mom talks about how a young man, Tally, visited Maddy several times. He was good-looking, too, and Mom could see how they'd be attracted to each other. Maddy and Tally. She thought it was sweet."

Drayco looked at the letter in her hand. It definitely read, "Tally." And that was very interesting. "You said when we first spoke, your mother was angry with Madalena, thinking she'd run off with some young man and left her in a lurch. Especially after your mom allowed her to continue working during her pregnancy. Did your mother write to your father about that?"

Wilma rescued another letter. "Right here, eh? Pretty much those words."

"And did she speculate on the father of the baby?"

"Naturally, she suspected Tally."

"No other mentions after that? And she never saw Madalena again?"

"That was the end of it. Sorry I couldn't be of more help."

"Oh, I think you were plenty helpful. In fact, if you don't mind, I'd like to take a photo of those three letters."

"Of course."

Drayco took out his cellphone and snapped the pictures. Right as he finished up, Wilma said, "Ooh, I think I see Ashleigh."

He followed her gaze, and sure enough, Ashleigh had popped out of the house and headed in their direction. Wilma squealed with delight. "Oh, my gracious goodness. She's coming over here."

Drayco handled the introductions, and Ashleigh smilingly signed the same book Wilma had brought along for that purpose. Ashleigh said to Drayco, "I've been meaning to call you. Do you mind if we talk in private?"

She looked toward Wilma, who said, "I've got to get back, anyway. It's a bit of a drive, eh? Thank you so much, Mr. Drayco, for making my day. Or year, for that matter."

Just like Frazier and Nancy before, Ashleigh linked arms with Drayco and walked with him to a tree on the fringes of the property. She grinned up at him. "I enjoyed your visit the other night. I've thought about you a lot ever since."

"Oh?"

"Um, hmm."

"As someone involved with this production told me not long ago, when you have an itch to scratch, you find a back scratcher. Am I that back scratcher?"

"You do make a nice one."

As he recalled it, the evening was a pleasant way to pass the time. But when he made love to Nelia again, it became even more apparent to him Ashleigh was a substitute. He truly wasn't a one-night-stand kind of guy, yet that's what his love life was turning out to be. And that was so not how he'd pictured it. Certainly not with Nelia. And as for Ashleigh...

He asked her, "How much longer do you think the production will last?"

"You mean, how much longer will I be in town? A week. More, if I stay around to do sightseeing." The way she was eyeing him, she was doing some of that already. "And Rada gave us tomorrow off for a change."

"Well, then."

"I'll be at my hotel tonight around nine. See you then?" She didn't wait for an answer, but smiled at him over her shoulder as she headed toward the house.

Would he see her then? At least she seemed to want to be with him, something he couldn't exactly say for Nelia. But that wasn't fair, was it? Nelia was still dealing with her parents' divorce, her own divorce, and in the middle of a grueling work-school schedule that few people would be able to handle. He had tremendous sympathy for her situation and wished he could help more. Obviously, a romantic relationship wasn't the right kind of help. Not now, anyway.

He sighed. Relationship purgatory was a tough place to be. Many people would likely tell him to cut his losses and that sometimes the next-best-thing turned out to be good enough. But then again, he'd probably be seeing Nelia again soon in the District, wouldn't he?

As watched Wilma's car driving away, he considered the importance of the letters she'd shown him. They might not be the smoking gun he was seeking, but they verified a theory of his that would be hard to prove. It wasn't true that dead men tell no tales. The main problem was in how those tales were told. And to a court of law, that made all the difference.

45

Sunday, January 23

Drayco had slept little after he returned to the Lazy Crab late last night. So he was allowing himself a rare sunrise stroll along the beach this morning to clear his head. Because of the cool weather and time of day, he'd gambled on having the place to himself, and he did.

Hook Head Beach, or "Crooked Beach," as someone on one of his previous cases called it, wasn't a big tourist destination. Out of the way and hard to find, just as he liked it. No leftover signs remained of the movie crew who'd shot a scene there, nor of the massive fish kill. It was as if none of it ever happened.

Last night at the Fairmont Hotel, after he'd hooked up with Ashleigh again in a moment of weakness with all sorts of apologies in his head to Nelia, he'd run into Rada Bluestone, who wondered why he was there. She seemed satisfied with his mumbled reply about "meeting someone" and proceeded to tell him that his flying her to Baltimore paid off.

She now had funding to set up her own production company, Phoenix Rose—so named because she hoped it would help her career rise from the ashes. She'd be better able to pick and choose her own projects that way, too. It turned out to be a deal she'd been working on for months, and the Baltimore trip sealed it, with contracts signed.

But it wasn't Rada, Nelia, or even Ashleigh who Drayco had on his mind. It was Madalena. Before her untimely end, had she walked along this very beach? He doubted it changed much in seven-plus decades and would have looked the same then as now.

Last evening, he also got a call from Wilma Eskin, who was so thrilled by her movie experience, she went straight home to fax him copies of additional wartime letters between her parents she'd found that mentioned Madalena. He'd read them this morning, and it filled in details on the young woman's life as an immigrant, alone, in a strange new world. But it left out a lot, too.

In a cruel twist of irony, one reason Madalena chose America was her dream of being an actress. But like other impressionable young women, she took her first steps toward disaster when she ran across a producer who promised to put her in a movie. She rode the train down to Cape Unity, a trip the man paid for. The "producer" had other ideas for her talents, and she'd run away from him as fast as she could.

Then she'd taken the only job she could find as a nanny. And that innocent-seeming choice led to her downfall. The depressing thing was, Drayco had a good idea about who had a hand in hurting Madalena. Even if he could prove it, it might not matter in the end.

Drayco reached down to rescue a bluish-gray-tan seashell with a dark eye pattern at the tip of the spire, a shark's eye. It resembled the one on the painting Nancy Farmery bought at the Art of Arts Gallery the other day.

Real sharks came in many forms, though in his experience, the human kind were far worse than great whites or hammerheads. The animals were doing naturally what they'd done for millions of years. People, on the other hand, had a choice of whether to help or hurt, develop, or destroy. Pamela Kye's shark earrings were as good a metaphor for that as any.

Just then, a surprise wave splashed on shore and got perilously close to soaking his boots and pant legs, making him jump. Too cold for that.

Maybe it was the sneak attack from the ocean or because he was lost in his thoughts, but he almost didn't notice a vibration coming from his cellphone. He called up a phone message that had gone straight to voicemail. Service was still spotty around here, even more so on an isolated beach like this one.

He listened to the message from Prophett CEO Pamela Kye. She had something important she wanted to give him and to meet him in an hour if he could make it. If not, she said she'd be happy to reschedule but was heading outside the country for an overseas trip in a few days.

Drayco checked the address. Part of that new housing development Prophett was building near Cape Charles. He had a few minutes to grab a coffee in Cape Unity before the trip down Route 13. Perhaps Kye found the missing documents that allegedly burned in a fire? With luck, it could even give him the elusive proof he needed.

46

Drayco made it down to the Prophett housing development in Cape Charles with a few minutes to spare. He didn't see a company car nearby, but an assistant had likely dropped Pamela Kye off since she hated driving.

This house looked closer to a finished state than others, but it was clear from the bits and pieces of neighboring homes they would all look the same. Prophett should re-brand as the Cookie Cutter Construction Company. Too bad they didn't build more houses like Terry Clayburgh's contemporary design.

Drayco edged along the still unpaved gravel-and-dirt driveway and found the front door unlocked. The interior wasn't as finished as the exterior. The flooring consisted of plain wooden plank boards, and the unpainted walls had penciled measurement marks. Packages of OSB wall materials lay in one corner next to cans of putty. One worker even left behind a box of tools.

He didn't see anyone and called out Pamela's name. When no one appeared, he called her name again and finally heard footsteps approaching. But it wasn't Pamela Kye who walked into the front room from a side hallway.

Drayco stared at the new arrival. "Trent Clayburgh. Fancy meeting you here. Are you in the home market, too?"

Trent nodded toward an open space under the stairs. "I'm here because of that."

Curiosity getting the better of him, Drayco took a few steps closer to get a closer look. Empty. He turned around to say, "I don't see anything," but then he most definitely saw something—something he'd much rather not.

Trent was holding a gun. "Like the rest of the movie cast, I've been to the shooting range. This isn't a prop, and it's not filled with blanks."

Drayco weighed his options. Play along and pretend it's all part of drama training? That he didn't know what was really going on?

But Trent took all other options off the table when he said, "You shouldn't have looked into that skeleton. Neither should Ellery."

"I'm guessing Pamela Kye isn't in the back."

"That was a deep-fake phone voice. Pretty good one, too, don't you think? I overheard you say to Genna you were looking into that Kye woman. So I called up a video of a conference where she gave a presentation. Downloaded the audio into AI software. Those things are incredible. Take anybody's voice and create a file of them saying whatever you want. Then I sent it to your voicemail."

"This is all about your grandfather, isn't it?"

Trent scowled. "Dad-Dad is one of the most awesome people who ever walked this earth. He is an important man, an honorable man. Nobody's going to sully his reputation. Nobody."

"It's not honorable to kill a young woman, is it?"

"It could have been an accident, nothing more."

"But it wasn't, was it? An accident? He valued his reputation and had big political aspirations like you do. Back then, having a child out of wedlock with a young Spanish immigrant would be a scandal hard to overcome."

"He had to do it. The bitch got pregnant, so what was he going to do?"

"Marry her. Bring up the child like he did your father."

"Marry a non-white woman? Rear a half-breed son? In the 1940s? Are you nuts? Your reputation, your moral code, was everything."

"Your grandfather admitted all this to you?"

"Why would he?"

Drayco mentally flipped through all the conversations he'd had with Trent. Then he remembered. "When you were cleaning up and organizing your grandfather's library and his papers, you found something you weren't supposed to see, didn't you?"

"You remember that? Wow, you're good. But yeah. I came across a secret compartment. Ironic, right? His journal was hidden inside."

"And of course, you read it."

"I don't know why he felt compelled to write it all down. But he's Catholic, so maybe it was a private confessional between him and his Maker. Or he meant to destroy it later and forgot."

"Did your grandmother find that journal, too?"

"What? I have no idea what you're talking about."

Drayco didn't want to get into the music box and newspaper article angle—he was too busy keeping Trent occupied and trying to think of a plan to wrest that gun away. And he doubted Trent would listen patiently. But he needed to keep him talking, so he asked, "Why didn't you burn the journal?"

"Came close. But it also has cool stuff about Dad-Dad and his cases. I couldn't bring myself to do it. Not that it'll matter. You won't live long enough to tell anybody. And no one else knows."

"Your grandfather worked for the construction company doing the Ransford house renovations when Madalena was killed. He had an employee of the company help him entomb her body in the wall, didn't he? George Prophett, Jr.?"

Trent's eyes widened. "You really are good. I see now I almost waited too long to do this. Especially when you didn't get blown up with those fireworks. You even dodged that lighting boom crash."

"Were you behind the prop gun and the blanks?"

"To keep that whole curse nonsense going. And throw any suspicion on Hoyt or some other cast member and away from me."

"What about Ellery Smith's murder? Why kill him?"

"We were at a bar, and he'd had too much to drink. He said his grandmother's skeleton was found in a place just like the movie house. What are the chances of more than one? I knew they were the same, and that he'd keep poking around."

Drayco looked toward the stairs. "What did you mean with that crack about being here because of the crawlspace?"

"Because that's where somebody will find your skeleton decades from now."

"Like grandfather, like grandson?"

"Fitting, don't you think?"

Drayco counted the steps between him and Trent. Eight or so. Enough time for Trent to get off a shot before Drayco could tackle him. "You got the idea to stab Ellery from the *Fatal Fugue* script? And then set up the explosion to create a distraction?" *Talk some more, Trent, talk some more.*

"An award-winning performance on my part. I figured unhappy townspeople or drug dealers would take the blame. It's why I planted the drugs on Ellery."

Trent pointed toward the crawlspace with the gun. "Get in. Now. After I shoot you, you'll be dead weight that's hard to move. And I can't roll you in. It'll leave blood everywhere."

Drayco had to fight off a sudden wave of panic as he thought of getting walled up in the small space. If Madalena was still alive when placed inside her tomb, did she feel it, too? He pushed his claustrophobia aside and focused on Trent. "Your plan won't work. The smell of a decaying corpse is intense. Plus, there are the maggots."

"I brought quicklime like Dad-Dad used. And if you think anybody'll find you soon, the Prophett Property construction workers went on strike. It was all over the news. The reporter said the two sides aren't anywhere near an agreement. May take months. And isn't it handy I got so many construction tips on the set?"

Drayco gave a quick closer study of the gun Trent was holding. A semi-automatic with a magazine of at least ten rounds. Trent might not be a member of the Quarter Inch Club, and target practice might not make Trent an accurate shot, but a cluster of bullets targeted at the body could do a world of hurt.

Still desperate to keep Trent talking, Drayco asked, "Was your grandfather's nickname Tally?"

Trent's eyes widened. "How the fuck did you know that? Nobody gets away with calling him that. It's a term from college he told me he hates."

Drayco readied himself to take advantage of Trent's surprise and make a run at him. It was now or never. But he didn't have a chance, because at that very moment, the front door flung wide open.

When Trent's eyes flickered toward the door, that was all the opportunity Drayco needed. He lunged at Trent, grabbed his arm, and twisted it behind his back. The gun fell from his hand, and Trent, off-balance, tumbled to the floor. Drayco slid the gun out of the way, hoping he wouldn't have to use it, but Trent lay there breathing hard with the wind knocked out of him.

Frazier Prentiss and Nancy Farmery looked from Drayco to Trent in shock. Frazier asked Drayco, "Are you okay? And what the hell is going on?"

"Pretty much what it looks like. An attempted murder—of me. Thanks for your help in thwarting it, by the way."

Frazier swayed a little on his feet, his voice shaky. "We were taking advantage of your tip. About the new homes here for Nancy's mother. We saw your Starfire, figured you were inside, and decided it would be a good excuse to take a look."

Drayco smiled in relief. First Hoyt, now Frazier and Nancy. He must have a guardian angel. "Your timing could not be better."

Frazier paused and then uttered words that made Drayco laugh despite the tense situation. "Should I make a citizen's arrest or something?"

47

Drayco was red-eyed after staying up late at the Cape Charles city police department, filing his report and returning to Cape Unity to brief Sheriff Sailor. It all seemed one big smeary time-blur. Seeing how late— or perhaps early?— it was, Drayco should have slept on a couch in the lobby of Sailor's offices. But the Lazy Crab's blissfully welcoming bed gave him a few hours of decent slumber.

As he half-stumbled into the lobby again the next morning, he waved at Sailor's secretary before heading down the familiar hallway, where he bumped into Deputy Nelia Tyler. She looked from his face to the fast-food cup of coffee in his hand and said, "Need a top off, since I'm your coffee supplier?"

They trekked to her office, where she had a pot filled to the brim. She gave him a sideways glance. "Some of us didn't get any sleep last night."

"Sorry about that. I think I got two hours."

"Comes with the territory when solving two murder cases." She yawned and added, "Thanks to you."

"I just got lucky because I was working a cold case that happened to tie it all together."

She grabbed his cup to refill it, opened a drawer where she rescued a salt packet, and poured it in for him. "Puts Sailor and the DOJ in a bind."

"I figured. I'll bet Sailor is even more his syrupy, happy-go-lucky self this morning."

"I'm sure he'll kill you gently, like he usually does."

"Just remember I'd like to be buried at sea."

She grinned. "I'd have thought you wanted to be buried with your Steinway. Be kinda hard to fit a piano on a boat."

"Piano cremation. I think it's a thing now."

Her grin broadened, but then just as suddenly faded. "I want to apologize for the other night."

"Apologize that it happened? Or that you left again?"

She perched on the edge of her desk. "A little of both. Not that it wasn't amazing." Her cheeks flushed a bright pink. "But I was the one who initiated the sex both times. Mea culpa."

"Ah, Nelia." Drayco shook his head. "You think I don't understand the situation. But I do. Truly. Not that I like it."

Sliding off her desk, she grabbed herself a cup of coffee with normal-people cream and sugar. "We could simply be friends with benefits."

"Or stay professional instead?"

She blew on her coffee before taking a sip. She asked, "Is that what you want?"

"To be honest, I'm not sure I know the answer to that anymore."

Her face fell. "I don't want to lose this," she gestured between them.

"You won't. One way or another."

She looked mollified by that and happy not to have to discuss it further. But Drayco certainly didn't feel any better, more the opposite. There would be no escape from his relationship purgatory...for now. Deciding it best to literally move on for the moment, he headed to Sailor's office, fortified with the extra caffeine.

A glum sheriff was getting off the phone when Drayco gave a token knock before heading on in. Sailor explained, "That was my counterpart in Northampton County. We're working on the extradition to bring Trent Clayburgh here. But between the red tape and the Clayburgh family attorneys, it's not a walk in the park."

"Has Trent confessed to anything?"

"He's as silent as the Sphinx. And since those two movie people, Prentiss and Farmery, came in *after* his little confessional to you, prosecutors would only have your word as to what he said. The only prints on that gun were his, so there's that. We've got him on gun and kidnapping charges for now. Those same family attorneys are fighting even that. It was all a joke, a prank, and so on."

"You think he'll beat the murder charge?"

"I wouldn't go that far. The M.E. found red fibers on our murder victim. Trent has red carpeting in his car, which they can now try to match. Plus, they've analyzed strands of short, blond human hair on Ellery Smith's bloody shirt. They weren't Smith's. And if they're a close match to Trent's, we'll have a stronger case."

"Was the follicle attached to that hair sample?"

Sailor nodded, and Drayco relaxed a few degrees. "A DNA match will be a much surer bet."

"Yep."

"That same DNA analysis could potentially show Trent is related to Ellery Smith." Drayco leaned against the wall. "Assuming all those felony charges stick—"

"They will. We'll nail him. You can count on that."

"Unless, in a twist of irony, his attorneys pull a 'Fatal Fugue' defense."

Sailor frowned at Drayco. "What?"

"As in the psychiatric use of the term. They could argue Trent wasn't in his right mind when he killed Ellery Smith.

With a grim smile, Sailor replied, "Not if I have anything to say about it."

"I suspect Trent Clayburgh will have to consider changing his career plans. I don't know of any justices who are convicted felons."

That elicited a deep frown from Sailor. "That brings me to another tricky problem."

"A tricky problem that has jurisdictional issues attached?"

"Yes and no. The cold case murder did happen in my county." Sailor grabbed a pencil and tapped it on his desk.

"Are you bringing Talbott 'Tally' Clayburgh in?"

"His attorneys say they'll only allow us to see him at his home, in light of his health and age. Tomorrow. But they'll be present."

"Which means he's guaranteed not to say anything."

"But we got a sympathetic judge for a warrant. Already searched the apartment where Trent's been staying."

"Did you find the prize?"

Sailor grabbed a box behind his desk and tipped it so Drayco could see the weathered leather journal inside. "Any way I could join you tomorrow for this little outing?"

"I may be able to arrange that." Sailor grinned. "Hell, if worse comes to worst, I could temporarily deputize you. Something I've secretly wanted to do."

"Why, Sheriff Sailor, I'm honored."

"Don't be. It's so I can keep you under my thumb."

Drayco was pretty sure the man was joking. Pretty sure. "I don't suppose Reece could be there, too?"

"Wable? Why?"

"He's been involved with this from the start. That history book he's writing."

"I'll have to clear it with the DA. And Clayburgh's attorneys."

"You know where I'm staying."

"The pie capital of the world, yes. If attorneys could be bribed with pie, it might help." Sailor leaned on his desk. "And since we're talking food, Jaxine Gordon was behind those laced brownies. Finally 'fessed up. Not that we're going to arrest her since she didn't know the CBD she bought from The Bobbsey Twins was tainted with detergent."

Drayco's cellphone rang, and when he saw the caller ID, he excused himself to head into the lobby and take the call. "You must truly miss me, Sarg."

"Like a cold sore. But I digress. You may be happy to know Rait Prophett is shadier than an elm tree. He's been operating under the federal radar. But it turns out he was the missing link to a case the Money Laundering Unit's working on. He's likely to be arrested."

"How soon?"

"Oh, as we speak."

"Nice job, Sarg. And his sister, Pamela Kye?"

"May have known about it, but we couldn't pin anything on her. Or anybody involved with the movie production. But Prophett Properties as a whole is in a lot of hot water."

"No more cookie-cutter houses. What a darn shame."

"You architectural snob, you."

"Hey, I almost became part of one of those delightful designs." And Drayco filled him in on the case and where it currently stood. Or didn't.

Sarg had him repeat the details so he could write it all down. "A former state Supreme Court justice. Wow. Guess DOJ is involved."

"That's all beyond my pay grade now. But it's looking even worse for his grandson. In this case, hero worship was a false idol too far."

Sarg grunted. "That's showbiz for you."

48

Tuesday, January 26

Drayco was certain all the various legal beagles would say "no" when Sailor asked about Drayco and Reece joining in on the trek down to Cape Charles. But to his amazement, they agreed. He thought Sailor had waved his magic sheriff's wand until Drayco and Reece pulled up to Clayburgh's mansion and saw a couple of suits arguing with Sailor, the Northampton Sheriff, and the Cape Charles police chief. The attorneys were red-faced and gesticulating wildly, but Sailor stood his ground.

When Drayco and Reece joined the group, Sailor half-smiled. "No one thinks it's a good idea you two have any part of this. Except one."

Sailor's bemused expression wasn't giving any hints, so Drayco asked, "And that one would be?"

"Talbott Clayburgh. He says he'll only talk to you and Reece. No attorneys. No police."

One of the suits said, "We advised him against this."

Sailor chuckled. "I'll bet you did."

As if to put any doubts to rest, the elderly man in question came to the door and waved directly at Drayco and Reece. Before the two men headed inside, Drayco held out his hand, and Reece seemed to know what he was after. He handed over his recorder, which Drayco, in turn, handed to Sailor along with Drayco's own cellphone. The attorneys didn't need any other reason to question the whole process.

When Clayburgh led them inside, he looked more like his ninety-two years. Gone was the healthy tan, replaced by a grayish pallor, and his step was no longer spry but halting. He ushered his guests to the same room as before and indicated they should join him in taking a seat.

Clayburgh started by saying, "They arrested my grandson. Weapons and kidnapping charges that have to do with you," he looked at Drayco.

"Those are the initial charges, yes."

"There are going to be more?"

"Possibly murder."

"You mean that person who died on the movie set, don't you?"

"The victim's name was Mark William 'Ellery' Smith. His father was Pauley Harrington. Which makes him Madalena Delfin Zamora's grandson. And also yours."

Clayburgh's hand shook as he picked up a glass of water from a nearby end table to take a sip. "That's quite a story you have there."

"Oh, it gets even more interesting. You worked for the construction company, Prophett Properties, which did renovations on Duff Ransford's house. The same house where the skeletal remains of Madalena were found decades later. The medical examiner pinpointed a time of death to the period you were employed with Prophett."

"Sounds like you have some interesting, but very circumstantial, details in your little fiction."

"DNA can show a family connection between you and Ellery."

"I admit to being a typical red-blooded young man in my day. And I had a few flings. But I didn't go around killing my love interests."

"But Madalena made the mistake of getting pregnant. And that wouldn't do for a man with lofty ambitions. Not in the 1940s."

"Again, I don't think I have to remind you that getting a woman pregnant isn't the same as murder."

"No, and after all these years, it would be difficult to prove, even so."

"There you go."

Reece gave Drayco a sharp, sideways look, but Drayco replied to Clayburgh, "There is this, however."

Clayburgh watched intently when Drayco pulled a folded piece of paper from his pocket.

Drayco said, "This is a photocopy. But I'll read you an excerpt. It's from a personal journal found in your study and is in your handwriting. It details meeting a young immigrant Spanish girl named Madalena and mentions the pregnancy. And how you gave the baby up for adoption, leaving it at a church. The journal goes on to say, 'I didn't expect the hammer to cause so much damage to her skull. All that blood. It took George and me forever to clean up the mess. And then there was what to do with the body. Then George got this crazy idea to avoid being seen dragging a body out of the house'—"

"Stop," Clayburgh said, wiping his brow with his still-shaking hand. "That's enough."

"George was George Prophett, Jr., heir to the Prophett Properties construction company, a friend of yours, isn't that right?"

Clayburgh asked, "Who found that journal, that piece of claptrap?"

"I think you've guessed by now. The person you tasked with cleaning and organizing your library and papers."

"Trent." Clayburgh closed his eyes.

After minutes ticked by, Reece looked at Drayco as if to say, "Should we check on him?" but Drayco shook his head. If the man were to pass away from a stroke or heart attack right then, it could actually be for the best.

But Clayburgh opened his eyes again and said, "I don't have many years left. Knowing my grandson could spend the rest of his life in prison for something he believes I did to protect my reputation…that's going to haunt me every single second I'm alive on this earth."

Once an attorney, always an attorney. Clayburgh was still hedging his bets about any involvement in murder. To be truthful, a journal entry could be explained away as an imaginative piece of fiction, like the man said. A man who wouldn't last long in prison. And would spending a few months or a year or two incarcerated be justice enough? That was more of a question for theologians and philosophers at this point.

But Drayco had a client he needed to help, so he asked, "Was Duff Ransford involved with the skeleton found in his house?"

"Absolutely not. And I will not see my friend, a good man, dragged down into the mud. He did complain about an odd odor in the house. But he chalked it up to the home renovation and rats dying in cupboards."

Satisfied he had some closure for Genna Ransford, Drayco motioned to Reece that they should leave. Clayburgh wasn't looking all that healthy, and it wouldn't be surprising if the shock didn't lead to a rapid decline. Drayco hadn't noticed a doctor or EMT standing by outside, but it might have been a good idea under the circumstances.

Drayco had one more parting shot he needed to say. "Mr. Clayburgh, you should know that Madalena's son, Pauley Harrington, had a miserable life. His adoptive parents died young, he had nowhere to go, and he went from one odd job to another. He was arrested for arson and ended up dying alone, his cremated remains dumped into a communal unmarked grave. One has to wonder how differently things would have turned out if he received the resources he needed early in his life."

Drayco turned to leave, with Reece trailing behind as they retraced their steps to the front door. Reece finally asked, "That's it?"

"Maybe."

"But when you asked him if Duff Ransford was involved—"

"He denied it, as only one who had inside knowledge could say for sure. He's guilty, all right. Oh, there will be back-and-forthing about charges, and challenges to charges, and warrants and subpoenas and appeals, and on and on. When you're dealing with the rich and powerful, these things can take years."

"And he'll be gone by then."

Drayco paused before they headed outside. "So, what will you put in your book on the history of the Shore?"

"I'll stick to the facts. His career, his accomplishments. Unless things are wrapped up before the book's publication date. Or I'll write another book entirely about him. True crime books are pretty popular, right?"

At Drayco's feigned scowl, Reece said, "I know, I know. Honestly, though? I've decided I'm more interested in writing Madalena's story."

Drayco patted Reece on the shoulder. "You've got my full support."

Madalena may never have achieved her dream of becoming an actress, but a book like that would grant her a level of fame and immortality. Rada could even adapt it into a movie with her new production company.

Sometimes, the next best thing had to be good enough.

49

Thursday, January 28

A couple of days later, Drayco stopped by the movie house. For once, it seemed relatively quiet, with only Sachio and Barry's gopher-friend, Zach, bustling around as they dismantled set pieces and cleared away lighting and props. The actors had all left, although Frazier Prentiss stayed longer in the area to spend time with Nancy Farmery.

Ashleigh had a new gig starting in a week and had to fly to Los Angeles, but she and Drayco managed to get in a nice dinner at a restaurant in Salisbury before she departed. She'd promised to call him, something Nelia had not. She'd also told him, when he asked point blank, why she hadn't ratted out Sachio and the drug angle to Sheriff Sailor. She'd said simply, "I knew about his brother. It was just between them."

Drayco went inside the open front door of Genna's Victorian house and found Genna with her feet propped up on a coffee table watching a video device. For once, she was wearing all black. In mourning? She waved him over and patted the sofa. He sat and peered at the video, which included rushes from the production.

She said, "I wanted to see what the credits would look like. You know, the house and all. I decided I didn't need the lookie-loos stopping by at all hours, so I asked to have my name listed as a 'location consultant.'"

"But they don't add credits until the movie wraps, right?"

"This is a mock-up."

They watched as the temporary credits scrolled past, and Genna stopped on one. "There it is. Looks good. Exactly as I asked." She resumed the credit roll for a few more moments and then stopped the video again. "Will you look at that?"

Drayco followed her pointing finger as she read out, "Piano player, Scott Draco."

"They misspelled it, but I'll take that credit. Piano player. I kind of like the sound of that." He ignored the little tendrils of grief that popped up when reminded of the fact that's not how his life turned out.

He asked her, "Has this reignited the acting bug in you?" She shuddered, and he smiled. "I'll take that as a 'no.'"

Sachio Spafford knocked over a lighting pole—again—that made a loud *thwack*. He looked in their direction with an apologetic shrug and an expression that indicated he was glad this job was almost finished. With luck, his next one wouldn't be as "cursed" with gaffes. A gaffer making gaffes. Drayco doubted he was the only person to think of that bad joke.

Genna's nose twitched. "Hollywood is not for me. I'm thinking about going back to school. Phys Ed, maybe ODU. I'd like to start an archery program in the schools around here."

"An admirable goal. Once everyone is gone, are you putting the house on the market like you hinted you might?"

"I don't know. Eventually? I've got to decide what to do about that hole in the wall. I mean, do I patch it up like nothing happened? Besides, the sheriff will want me to keep it available a while longer, right?"

"I'd say as long as you don't need the money from the house sale, there's no rush."

"That's my thinking, too. But I've never seen anybody want to rush out of here as fast as Rada Bluestone."

"She'll land on her feet. Even if this movie's a flop, she's got a new production company in the works. And who knows? *Fatal Fugue* could be a massive hit, thanks to the notoriety. One actor dies during filming, and another is arrested for his murder."

Genna winced. "Know what's funny? I don't think I have any interest whatsoever in seeing it when it finally opens."

Drayco wasn't enthused about it, either. A few years from now? Possibly. Since Drayco's father had missed so many of his son's piano performances, Drayco should force Brock to watch it in his stead and report back. Fair was fair.

And speaking of reporting back, Drayco had promised someone he'd do just that. It wouldn't be a pleasant conversation, but it must be done. As he left Genna to monitor the remaining crew, he headed outside toward his car.

He doubted there'd be any closure, more like a trip into the nebulous world of "Death and Transfiguration" that Richard Strauss composed in his musical opus, *Tod und Verklärung*. Sometimes, the answers were the easy part. Knowing which questions to ask was much harder.

§ § §

Drayco pulled up to the contemporary home, the gray slate exterior colors blending in with the gray skies above. Terry Clayburgh was even dressed in a gray turtleneck when he escorted Drayco into his den. Drayco took a seat on an Art Deco leather lounge chair, but Terry chose to stay standing and parked himself next to the tall glass windows.

Drayco looked around the house. "No dog?"

"Out back. Samoyeds love cool weather. He's in doggy bliss." Terry cleared his throat and said, "But I feel like I'm in a bad movie."

"How much have you been told?"

"Only the few details you've given me. When Trent's mother called me, I didn't even know what to tell her."

"You mean his attorneys—"

"Dad's attorneys." Terry turned around with a scowl on his face. "That says it all, don't you think? I can't get anything out of them."

"Trent's facing pretty serious charges. Weapons, assault, kidnapping, murder."

"And you say Dad's involved somehow?"

Drayco nodded. "How much information do you want to know?"

"You mean, would it be easier on me to stay ignorant? Don't forget, I clean up messes left behind by violence and death. I live in that world every day."

"It can be different when it's your own kin."

"But I'm estranged from my father and not on the greatest terms with my son."

"All right, then." Drayco filled him in on everything he knew, not sugar-coating it. When he finished his recounting, Terry sank into a chair across from Drayco and gazed at the floor.

Drayco studied him and asked, "Are you okay?"

"I just found out my father and son are both killers. How do you think I feel?"

"Angry, confused, shocked."

Terry continued his blank stare at the floor. "This is where most people would say, 'it's partly my fault.' "

"But you weren't even alive when Madalena was murdered."

"And I'm not going to take any blame for Trent's behavior, either. Don't get me wrong, I love my son," Terry's voice had a slight hitch, and he paused a moment before continuing, "But between the political fervor from his mother and grandfather, he got sucked into some bad mojo."

Drayco grimaced. "He's made it abundantly clear how much he idolizes your father. Even made videos about him."

Terry put his head in his hands and stayed silent while Drayco waited patiently. Then Terry sat up taller and said, "This Ellery Smith who was killed. That makes him Dad's grandson."

"That's right."

"Which means he was kin to me, too. What happened to his other family?"

"He didn't have much in the way of family. They're mostly gone."

"Then where will he be buried?"

"I'm not sure. There's a mass grave in Prince of Wales County for unclaimed bodies where he might end up."

"And Madalena? Will her remains be shipped back to Spain?"

"Unlikely. No one wants to pay for it."

"That doesn't seem right."

"No, it doesn't." Drayco thought of the toy stuffed giraffe that now lay in a box in his room at the Lazy Crab, waiting to be reunited with its childhood owner.

Terry looked at Drayco with eyes that were clearer and more composed. "Ellery and Madalena are family. They should have a proper burial. My business is doing pretty well, and I can afford it. Though I don't think Dad would approve of me putting them next to Mom in our family plot."

Drayco replied, "I know a scenic cemetery not long after you exit the Chesapeake Bay Bridge-Tunnel. It even has a WWII hero buried there. And since Madalena immigrated in part due to the horrors following that same war—"

"Sounds perfect." A small smile spread across Terry's face.

Drayco added, "If you do arrange it, let me know. I have an item that should be buried with Madalena. And one to be buried with Ellery, too." Sheriff Sailor would likely be willing to return the little dolphin pin.

When Terry nodded, Drayco asked, "You told me you loved dolphins, didn't you? There must be a cosmic link there. Madalena's middle name means dolphin in Spanish."

Terry's smile grew even broader, his eyes shining with something akin to wonder. He replied, "Maybe you're right."

Drayco left him with assurances to keep him informed of all case developments, even if no one else did. As he headed to his Starfire, a bird with a grayish-blue body and deep purplish neck flew overhead. The same Small Blue Heron from the cemetery? If so, the call was slightly different, less like the golden comb's teeth from before and more like green-and-purple sparklers.

This would mark his second sighting of the rare bird lately, a symbol of wisdom and patience. Drayco didn't feel wiser or more patient, and his cold case had ended in only a partial resolution since Talbott Clayburgh might never see the inside of a prison cell. So, after all of this, *had* Drayco found some semblance of justice for Madalena? Perhaps he'd leave that to Reece and his book to sort it all out.

When Drayco reached the Starfire, he pulled the paper out of his wallet with the facial reconstruction sketch of his FBI Jane Doe. Forensic techniques had improved dramatically in the past twenty years—as Madalena's case proved—not to mention the type of forensic genetic genealogy Ellery had used and the NamUs database. Jane Doe's case documents, which Drayco copied before he left the Bureau, occupied a space in his office file cabinet. That case file still waited for someone to care. And for someone to try again.

The blue heron flapped off, heading north, and Drayco followed it in his car as it flew parallel to Route 13, leading the way. Drayco popped in a recording of the Granados Spanish dances and let the music lift his soul upward toward the bird and beyond. And for a brief moment, he imagined a young woman with wavy dark hair sitting next to him and smiling as they listened together.